D0173231

A REVEALING RIDE

Their eyes met and held for a moment, measuring each other. Then she said, "Last night was rash . . . reckless."

"Yet you accepted my invitation to ride in the country and brought no chaperone," he countered as his fingertips lightly caressed her cheek.

He wore no gloves and she was surprised to feel slight calluses on his hands. She'd expect that of her father or brothers, but not of a self-confessed English dandy. Her thoughts spun crazily at his touch. His intense gaze mesmerized her until all she could think of was melting into him like wax in the Italian sun.

Rather than make a reply to his teasing retort, she raised her lips to his, initiating the kiss with a boldness that surprised her more than him.

She was a witch, an enchantress, knowing just what to do to drive him wild. He pressed her backward against the soft velvet of the curricle's seat, knowing full well they could not satisfy their desire in the small vehicle. He cursed the desperate impatience that led him to murmur against her mouth, "I want to touch every inch of you . . . caress . . . lick, taste . . . I can't get enough of you, Beth."

Beth moaned her assent as his knee moved between her legs and rubbed intimately against her thighs. The ache that throbbed wickedly in her blood now centered low in her belly and moved to that most secret place, which was untried but eager . . . so eager.

OTHER *LEISURE* BOOKS BY SHIRL HENKE:
WICKED ANGEL
WHITE APACHE'S WOMAN
RETURN TO PARADISE
LOVE A REBEL ... LOVE A ROGUE
BROKEN VOWS
PARADISE & MORE
TERMS OF LOVE
McCRORY'S LADY
A FIRE IN THE BLOOD
TERMS OF SURRENDER
NIGHT WIND'S WOMAN

SHIRL HENKE

WANTON ANGEL

LEISURE BOOKS   NEW YORK CITY

For Rita Oakes, who is always "on call"

A LEISURE BOOK®

March 2002

Published by

Dorchester Publishing Co., Inc.
276 Fifth Avenue
New York, NY 10001

If you purchased this book without a cover you should be aware that this book is stolen property. It was reported as "unsold and destroyed" to the publisher and neither the author nor the publisher has received any payment for this "stripped book."

Copyright © 2002 by Shirl Henke

All rights reserved. No part of this book may be reproduced or transmitted in any form or by any electronic or mechanical means, including photocopying, recording or by any information storage and retrieval system, without the written permission of the publisher, except where permitted by law.

ISBN 0-8439-4973-2

The name "Leisure Books" and the stylized "L" with design are trademarks of Dorchester Publishing Co., Inc.

Printed in the United States of America.

Visit us on the web at www.dorchesterpub.com.

WANTON
ANGEL

Chapter One

Washington, D.C., Spring 1811

The Honorable Derrick Lance Jamison was a spy.

Of course, Beth Blackthorne had no idea of this as she watched him stride back and forth on the springy moss, admiring the way his tall, whipcord-lean body filled out snug doeskins and a beautifully cut jacket of fine buff-colored kerseymere. Why was she, an artist and a free spirit, even noticing his lithe and pantherish movements? Or his perfectly chiseled features? Absurd. The distance was far too great to be certain anyway. His beauty was probably a trick of the light.

As if to distract her, Barney took off at a ground-eating lope, headed for Mistress Smollett's chicken coop behind the inn. "Come back here, you rascal," she hissed. Luckily, the handsome stranger paid her no heed. Barney returned to her, tail dragging disconsolately. Barnsmell, or Barney, was her brother Benjamin's huge brown sheepdog, whom she had taken along as protection. Being the youngest of five siblings and the only female in the lot, Elizabeth Isolde

Blackthorne had always felt smothered and misunderstood.

Take this afternoon's painting excursion for example. The only way she dared slip from the house was to promise Ben that Barney would "protect her." Otherwise her brother would have tattled to their father, and that would have put a finish to her day of freedom. As if she required protection! Beth had grown up surrounded by male relatives, all of whom were crack shots. She had always been a tom-hellion, riding, shooting, engaging in unladylike pursuits to the despair of her mother and father. Over the past few years her brothers, formerly co-conspirators, had become patronizingly and most irritatingly concerned because she'd had the misfortune to be born female.

Putting aside all thoughts about her "inferior" status, Beth strolled over the hill in search of a scene suitable for a spring landscape. A tall stand of sugar pines surrounded by a rolling field of deer grass and trout lily beckoned her. Soon even thoughts of the beautiful young stranger who had so taken her seventeen-year-old fancy faded as she set to work.

Her new palette of colors was almost perfect to capture the delicate shades of green, the rich purples and soft buttery yellows of wildflowers. But the sienna for the muddy earth tones was a bit off. She began mixing and blending from several vials of color. "There. Perfect," she sighed and resumed painting.

His Excellency Luis de Onís y Gonzales, the Spanish ambassador to the United States, was a royal pain in the arse, Derrick Jamison decided as he paced in front of the inn. The brash young Englishman had waited for nearly an hour in the execrable heat of this glorified swamp the Americans called a capital. What a drab little town it was. Derrick would not dignify the motley collection of buildings with the appellation of city.

Brushing a lock of sweat-dampened dark hair from his forehead, he scanned the miasmic marsh surrounding the rude post inn where his assignation was to take place. He paced beneath the shade of an ancient willow tree, watching what passed for a road, fervently hoping Onís would arrive soon. "I won't complain if I'm sent to Gibraltar or even Tunis after this assignment," he muttered, combing long slim fingers through his hair.

Even the worst pestholes of North Africa had dry climates. The wet heat of the Virginia coast was intolerable to one born and bred on the Scots borderlands. Of course, this being his first posting abroad, he had no real knowledge of Tunis or Gibraltar. But surely they could be no worse than this. "One does what one must for king and country," he sighed as the ambassador's coach at last pulled up.

Onís y Gonzales had just handed Derrick a sheaf of documents detailing American incursions into Spanish Florida when the thunderous roar of a weapon rent the air. "*Madre de Dios,* we are found out!" he croaked in terror, crouching down so his spindly knees nearly gave way. "The Americans are upon us!"

"The shot came from behind the inn. It was not intended for us," Derrick reassured the old Spaniard. The blast was followed by furious barking and the squawking of chickens. Derrick could well envision what was going on but felt compelled to make certain.

He turned to say so to his companion, but Onís was scrabbling off toward his coach. "I shall report to you regarding the filibusters into Florida next week," he flung over his shoulder.

There was another deafening roar, followed by more barks, squawks and a string of rather startling oaths from the innkeep. Derrick had made Mistress Smollett's acquaintance earlier in the morning when he broke his fast. Perhaps it might be best to let her deal with the chicken thief and be on his way. He carefully inserted the papers inside the lining of his jacket, then smoothed the expensively tailored garment.

He had been enjoined by his superiors in the Foreign Office to play the role of fop. No one, especially uncouth Americans, took fops seriously. Such concern with sartorial splendor had been alien to him back on his family estates, but that was a world and a lifetime ago, he thought sadly. The uproar out behind the inn continued as he strode toward the stable to retrieve his mount. Hoping to avoid the fracas, he quickly turned the corner of the building. "Oomph!" The sound of air escaping from his lungs was the only noise he could make as he was knocked to the ground hugger-mugger by a harlequin.

Derrick realized his harlequin was a flame-haired female, or at least he believed it to be a female. As they struggled to disentangle arms and legs, she scooted away from him on her hands and knees. The wench was dressed in utter rags, brightly smeared with splotches of paint in every color of the rainbow.

As she shook her head to clear it from the force of their collision, a great mane of dark russet hair flew about her face in riotous fuzzy curls. The gesture reminded him of the large shaggy herd dog that worked sheep on his father's estates. Upon closer inspection, he saw that part of her raggedy garb consisted of a greatcoat of some sort, with large pockets bulging with more rags and paintbrushes. A look of utter consternation covered her paint-smeared face.

"My sienna!" she shrieked.

"I beg pardon?" he replied, certain now that he was dealing with either an escapee from the American equivalent of Bedlam or a Gypsy caught stealing the innkeep's chickens.

"Oh, I spent ever so long mixing it and used all the raw umber and gold ochre Cousin Alex sent me from London," she babbled on, eyeing his chest with decided apprehension.

He followed her gaze and saw with shocked horror the multicolored swirl of thick paint that covered the front of his shirt and jacket. A small wooden artist's palette with the remnants of color smeared across it lay incriminatingly at his side. "You're an artist?" he asked in an incredulous voice, alarmed that the documents from Onís might be irreparably damaged. His first impulse was to pull them out to check, but just as he reached inside his jacket, he realized that would not do in front of a witness.

"Oh, your jacket—and that lovely white lawn shirt! I am ever so sorry," she said. Climbing over his legs on all fours, the demented creature extracted a rag reeking of turpentine from one of her multitudinous pockets. "Here, let me—"

He seized her wrist as she tried to daub at his jacket. "That is quite all right. No sense in making matters worse," he remonstrated. Damnation! All he needed was for the foolish twit to dissolve what was left of the papers with spirits. The delicacy of her bones surprised him. Her hands, although paint-smeared, were soft and well manicured, not at all the hands of a scrub woman or a Gypsy.

The mysterious Englishman, for with that accent he could be nothing else, studied Beth's face as she returned the favor. Good Lord above, it had been no trick of the light. He was the most beautiful male she'd ever seen in her life. Beth suddenly found her tongue, which was normally so glib, sticking to the roof of her mouth. Breathing had inexplicably become difficult and her heart was pounding so furiously she felt positively muzzy-headed.

He got lithely to his feet and extended a lean elegant hand down to her. She reached out to him just as another report of the blunderbuss erupted from the other side of the stable. "Barnsmell! I completely forgot!"

Before he could pull her to her feet, a second creature moving at an alarmingly swift speed collided with him, this time making painful contact with his posterior.

Derrick tried to maintain his balance while holding on to the flailing girl, but it was hopeless. He was propelled into her and they fell in a compromising sprawl with him on top. A dead, bloody chicken bounced off the side of his head as a huge shaggy brown cur leaped over them with a loud, "Arf!"

"Barnsmell!" came a muffled cry from beneath him.

The beast paused only a moment before rounding the opposite side of the building, racing toward the road.

Head ringing, he struggled into a sitting position. Some of the feathers from the ill-fated chicken had fallen and stuck in the gooey multicolored mess of drying paints on his chest. He shuddered with distaste but found that recovering his breath was a bit less difficult than it had been the first time.

Perhaps he was getting used to being knocked insensate, he thought wryly before the dull throbbing of his nether parts began in earnest. Gingerly, he rolled up to his knees and rubbed his buttocks before realizing he was in the presence of a female, albeit certainly not a lady. What the devil was she babbling about as she tried unsuccessfully to climb to her feet—something about a barn smell? Her wild gesticulations toward the chicken, then the road stretching toward town, made no more sense than her choked raving as another boom of the blunderbuss shook the ground.

Americans! They were all deranged.

"There ye be, missy!" Mistress Smollett said as she rounded the side of the stable. "I sent yer accursed hound back toward the city, tail tucked 'twixt his legs right and proper, I did." As if to prove her point, the squat, raw-boned woman tightened her grip on the blunderbuss.

Beth had scrambled away from the Englishman and once more attempted to rise, but the hem of her paint smock caught on the heel of her shoe and she would have fallen on him again if not for the proximity of the stable wall. Reaching out frantically for a splintery board, she righted herself, panting and humiliated. For once in her life, she was speechless.

By then Mistress Smollett noticed for the first time the gentleman kneeling in the dirt. "Mr. Jenkins, sir, I'm that sorry, I am! Ooh, look at yer fine jacket. That foolish gel's gone and ruined it." Then the innkeep saw the carcass. Her eyes narrowed to slits and she fixed Beth with a beady glare that had sent more than one drunken farmer scurrying for home. "Now who's going to pay for me chicken, eh?"

Derrick struggled to his feet, wincing at the pain shooting from his buttocks down his legs. "Never fear, Mistress . . . Smollett, isn't it?" he inquired with a charming grin that sent most women into a daze. "I'll pay for the damages."

His charm had the intended effect on the old woman—and the young one, too, even if Derrick was not aware of it. Beth stood mesmerized by that slash of perfect white teeth, and the lock of black hair that fell artlessly over his brow when he cocked his head. His eyes were the cerulean blue of the Atlantic off the Georgia coast and, Lord above, he even had a dimple in his right cheek!

Not wanting to attract any further attention, Derrick mollified the innkeep by placing several coins in her palm as he flattered her until she was blushing like a school miss.

"I do thankee, sir. Ye be the kindest gentleman I've ever met, even if yer an Englishman!" To that backhanded compliment, she added, "Just remember, Coey Smollett's always got a cool pint waiting whenever ye stops by her place, she has." With a malevolent glare at Beth, she reached down and picked up the dead chicken before waddling around the stable toward the inn.

Derrick turned to the girl, who had remained suprisingly mute through the exchange. Perhaps she'd been in trouble with the old crone before, since the woman seemed to know her. No doubt a local farmer's daughter. "I say, you don't look quite the thing, gel. Have you injured yourself?" he inquired as she continued to stare mutely at him.

"I . . . that is . . . I'm quite . . . quite the thing . . . that is, I'm uninjured," she finally managed to get out. "But Barnsmell's taken off for the city and he may be the one who's been hurt and I have to go find him before my brother does or else I'll be in terrible trouble and Papa will forbid my painting any more landscapes and I don't know what I would do if that happened!" It seemed as if once she began speaking, she could not stop.

He smiled again, which sent her heart into another frenzy of palpitation and stopped her babbling so he could get a word in edgewise. "I take it, er, Barnsmell is the dog who overran me and deposited Mistress Smollett's poor bird on my head?"

Beth felt her cheeks flame. "Yes, I'm afraid so. You must

let me repay you the cost of the chicken—not to mention the expense of replacing your clothing." Realizing she carried no money with her, Beth felt even more the fool. "Er, that is, my father will—"

"Please," Derrick interrupted, eager to be quit of the troublesome chit so he could check the documents in his ruined jacket. "I insist that you not give it another thought. I shall be sailing for home very shortly. And by the time I arrive, the jacket would doubtless have been out of fashion anyway," he added when she made as if to protest further.

Beth nodded bleakly. He obviously wanted to rid himself of her—and who could blame him? "Well, then, I do thank you, sir. I had better collect my horse and painting equipment and go after my dog." She backed slowly away, loathe to leave him even though she knew she was making an utter cake of herself. How her Aunt Barbara, that redoubtable Englishwoman, would laugh if she saw her niece in such a tizzy over a mere male.

Derrick watched, bemused, as she practically backed into the stable. To his utter amazement, she emerged a moment later riding a handsome Arab filly. She sat the beautiful roan with the practiced skill of one used to riding fine horseflesh. No matter her incredible garb or clumsy manner, she could not be a tavern wench or farm girl.

Most puzzling, these Americans. But then, the deranged were often a curious lot.

Musing to himself, he slipped inside the now deserted stable to check on the condition of the documents inside his jacket. Only on his ride back into Washington did he recall that he'd not asked the singular female's name.

Dolley Madison's Wednesday afternoon salons were considered by many wags in Washington to be the high-water mark of Jemmy Madison's administration. The president's lady was witty, charming and open-minded. Her salons attracted people of all political persuasions. A small orchestra played on a dais at one end of the ballroom, and servants moved through the press of guests carrying trays of sherry for the ladies and whiskey for the gentlemen.

Wanton Angel

Women in soft pastel gowns of sheer mull picked daintily at bowls of fresh fruit, while men in starched cravats cut wedges of strong cheddar cheese from a giant wheel. Dressed in her usual pale cream silks with an ostrich plume bobbing from the huge turban that had become her signature headgear, the First Lady moved through the room, breaking up disputes with her laughing chatter wherever voices grew strident.

Everyone argued politics. Quintin Blackthorne was in one corner mediating an argument between John Randolph and Henry Clay. His wife Madelyne was engaged in a heated discussion with the crude and annoying Representative Johnson from Kentucky. Beth sighed and looked around the room at the assembly of eligibles—congressmen, merchants, attorneys and diplomats.

Husband material. She knew that was why her mother had insisted she come to the capital. True, this session of Congress was debating Great Britain and France's violations of American shipping rights on the high seas. And true, her father, the senior senator from Georgia, was embroiled in the fight against war with either power, but her parents' major concern was finding a suitable match for their only daughter.

Beth admitted that she had not been very cooperative in that regard, scorning all the gallants in Georgia. Her art was her life and that left no time for husbands, babies or other such foolery. She intended to go to Italy and study painting. Unfortunately, neither her parents nor her brothers felt that was at all natural for a young miss.

Sighing, she looked across the room. Men were so boring. The only matters they could discuss were themselves and this accursed war—which prevented her from sailing to Italy. Even that perfectly gorgeous young Englishman she'd encountered at the post inn the preceding week would no doubt be a crashing bore if she but spoke with him for more than ten minutes. Beth had spent several restless nights reliving the humiliating encounter. Why, after making such an utter fool of herself, could she not seem to banish his face from her mind?

9

Probably because he would make such an excellent portrait subject. At least that was what she kept assuring herself. Of course, if she were ever to consider marriage ... he was English, and bother the old war, it was traditional for English gentlemen to take their brides on a grand tour of the Continent. What a delightful fantasy that was—but only for a moment until reality intruded. She shook her head at the absurdity of the daydream. Marry an Englishman indeed! Anyway, war had spoiled the opportunity to travel on the Continent for English or Americans since that wretched Napoleon had the whole of Europe in an uproar. Beth sighed. Best to forget the handsome mystery man.

"A penny for your thoughts, Miss Blackthorne," Aiden Randolph said wistfully. "You look quite vexed." Aiden was tall, pale and gaunt, with a strabismus of the left eye that made looking at him directly rather difficult. At present, his one good eye was fixed on her adoringly while its mate flitted vaguely around the crowded room. He was quite sweet and frightfully vapid.

"Actually, Mr. Randolph, I was just thinking about how I would much prefer to be outdoors on such a lovely day." She bit her tongue, fearing he would ask to accompany her on a walk after the salon. Eager to change the drift of the conversation, she launched into a description of her latest landscape sketches. That normally drove suitors away.

Across the room, Derrick observed the tall, striking redhead in the mint green mull gown. She was a bit on the thin side and too young for his tastes, but fetching with all that heavy auburn hair falling in artlessly arranged curls over her shoulders. Something about her gestures and posture seemed vaguely familiar, but he could not for the life of him place her.

A hoarse chuckle from his companion drew his attention away from the girl. "A pretty bit of fluff, Blackthorne's daughter, but I'd not trifle with her, my boy," Roarke Kenyon cautioned. Kenyon, a short stocky fellow with merry hazel eyes and an ear for gossip, had proven an invaluable source of information regarding the sentiments of pro-British Federalists in his home state of Massachusetts.

Derrick wished to satisfy his curiosity about the girl and learn more about the illustrious Blackthorne family. Brushing an imaginary speck of dust from the ruffled shirtcuff spilling from the sleeve of his new bottle-green jacket, he inquired, "Is she the merchant's daughter or the planter's daughter?"

"The planter, Quintin. Quite opposed to a war against your country. A sensible fellow, even if his reasons are not the same as ours."

"And his reasons would be?" Derrick prompted.

"Relates to his cousin Devon."

"Ah, he runs a large shipping enterprise, does he not?" Derrick had heard about the two patriarchs of the fabulously wealthy Blackthorne clan. "Old Devon would have a deal to lose if war breaks out."

"True, but Devon has an English wife. His son's been living in London for the past year, as a matter of fact. Married an earl's niece, so rumor has it. Then, too, Dev and Quint were raised together, more brothers than cousins, and Dev's part Creek."

Derrick paused incredulously in the ritual of opening his cloisonné snuff box. "You mean red Indian?"

"None other. Quite the scandal some years back, but no one much remembers his origins now that he's become bloody rich."

Derrick nodded, piecing together what he had painstakingly gleaned over the past few months. "I understand the Indian confederacies are pro British because they want to halt American expansion into their lands in the west. Do tell me more about this fascinating family."

Kenyon's expression grew crafty. "Wouldn't be thinking about taking an American heiress for a wife, would you? Rather a turnabout on the way the Blackthornes have done it." He chuckled heartily at his own wit.

In order to learn more about the influential Blackthorne family's politics, Derrick nodded, searching the crowd for the redhead. "As a second son with modest prospects, I must confess, there is a certain appeal . . . if she's rich enough."

Shirl Henke

"Oh, Elizabeth's rich enough all right." Kenyon's chuckle set his ample belly to rolling beneath his brocade waistcoat. "But the gel's got bats in her belfry. Wants to be an artist, if you can believe that. Dabbles in paints, running around the city dressed like a ragamuffin. It would take a strong hand to straighten her out, I tell you."

Derrick was flummoxed. Never taking his eyes off Elizabeth Blackthorne, he choked out, "A painter, you say?" It couldn't be his harlequin . . . could it?

Kenyon proceeded with an embellished description of the girl's disgraceful attire. It *was* she.

"She doesn't look the hoyden, I must say," the Englishman said uncertainly.

"Appearances can be deceiving, my boy," Kenyon replied gravely.

When Beth saw him walking across the floor she nearly sank to her knees with embarrassment. He was heading directly toward her! Would he remember their awful encounter from last week? How could he not? Of course, she had looked much different in her painting togs. She was suddenly grateful for the way Mama had insisted on tricking her out for this affair.

"Beth, you look ready to pick up your skirts and run," Madelyne remonstrated, trying to discern the reason for her daughter's panic. Then she saw him, quite the handsomest young man in the room, moving in their direction along with Roarke Kenyon. Beaming, she looked back at Beth. "Oh, do try to smile, dear. I daresay he won't bite you."

When they approached the ladies, Roarke introduced his companion as Derrick Jenkins, late of Manchester, England. Elizabeth Blackthorne curtsied to him rather stiffly. The awkwardness of her normally graceful daughter was not lost on Madelyne. Derrick bowed with an affected flourish that he'd found most American females adored. Before Miss Blackthorne could do more than smile woodenly, Quint motioned to his wife and political ally Kenyon from across the room. They made their excuses to the two young people and went to join him.

12

"You look far better without paint on your nose," he teased when they were alone. "In fact, I wouldn't have recognized you if Kenyon hadn't mentioned that you dabbled at painting."

Her eyebrows arched sharply and her wide green eyes narrowed imperceptibly, a sure sign of danger, as her brothers could have warned him. "Dabbled?" she echoed sweetly.

"His word, not mine, but you must confess it is rather unusual for a lady of your background to go about the countryside in the company of a chicken thief." His grin was infectious.

She was not certain whether she should be amused or incensed. If only he weren't so damnably good-looking! He quite unsettled her. She decided incensed was safer. "I'm sure I prefer the company of an honest thief to that of a condescending Englishman," she said with frosty dismissal, turning away from his penetrating blue eyes before she drowned in their depths.

"Just because our countries may one day be at war does not mean that we need be," he said. "Besides, I'm given to understand that you have English relatives on both sides of the Atlantic."

"Aunt Barbara is an American now and Cousin Alex's wife Joss will be too. They do not laugh at the idea of a woman wanting to be an artist." Actually, having never met her new cousin, Beth had no idea how Joss felt.

Elizabeth Blackthorne sounded so young and earnest in her righteous anger that he reconsidered his earlier impulse to use her as a source of information. There were many other older and wiser women on whom he could work his charms, women who knew far more about military and political matters than this backcountry miss. Magnanimously, he decided to let her go.

"My dear Miss Blackthorne, I wish you every success as an artist, and please note that I am not laughing as I do so," he replied with feigned boredom.

"You are every bit as insufferable as Cousin Alex described the Earl of Suthington!"

13

Having met Suthington, Derrick understood the magnitude of the insult better than she. As he watched her stalk away, a most peculiar sense of something lost squeezed his chest. The sudden pang was akin to how he had felt when his family disowned him.

Chapter Two

The Quay, Bay of Naples, Fall 1814

Derrick Jamison stood on the deck of the brigantine *Mayfair*, surveying the sparkling aquamarine depths of the bay. Small fishing skiffs and sloops with their characteristically curved sails skimmed across the water, nets heavy with the morning catch. The high tenor voices of the fishermen echoed along the quay. In the distance Mt. Vesuvius released a lazy curl of smoke, teasing the deep purity of the azure sky. Along the shoreline steep tiers of stucco buildings gleamed white as snow, their seemingly pristine appearance given the lie by the harsh odors of fish and animal dung blending with the sickly aroma of sulfur, all wafting on the balmy breeze.

It was an invigorating sight to the Englishman after the icy rain of the North Atlantic. Feeling the warmth of the autumn sun beating down on his shoulders, he studied the wide sandy stretch of beach where rude vendor's stalls boasted a colorful array of fresh produce—aromatic bins of golden figs, the deep crimson of halved watermelons,

15

piles of hairy tan coconuts, bright splashes of lemons and oranges.

That was when he saw her—or rather, heard her. A low rich voice vibrating in a loud burst of staccato Italian, which was generously interspersed with cursing, some of it so idiomatic he could not comprehend the specifics. Her tone of voice combined with the Italian words he did know clearly gave him the gist of it. She stood surrounded by a gaggle of older, lower-class women, dressed as she was in brightly colored skirts and loose white blouses. They appeared to be encouraging her in a diatribe against one of the local fishermen whose catch lay in piles on the sand.

Derrick struggled to keep up with the argument. The woman was a redhead, a good foot or so taller than any of the other females. When the crowd parted, he could see her great mass of deep russet hair spilling in unruly curls down her back, stopping just short of a tiny waist that rounded out to a pair of beautifully curved hips and a lush derriere. Her Amazonian form was outlined through the thin cotton of her short skirt as the breeze whipped the bright green cloth around slender ankles. He leaned forward on the deck's railing and peered at her, willing her to turn so he could see her face.

If it's half as good as her backside, I want her tonight, he thought with a sudden tightening in his groin. In service of king and country Jamison could be more abstemious than most, but he saw no reason to deny himself one brief night's pleasure before getting down to the business for which he'd been sent.

Just then she bent down and seized a large mackerel from the fisherman's pile and smacked him roundly across the face with it. This action seemed to incite the rest of her companions to take up arms. Before the hapless man could beat a retreat, the rest of the women picked up scaly cudgels and pelted him with his offending wares. Seemingly satisfied, the redhead spun on one sandaled foot and strode down the beach.

"Bloody hell, she's magnificent," he breathed as the wind molded her soft blouse against high, generously rounded breasts. The strong clean lines of her face in stark profile would have been the envy of a Greco-Roman goddess.

"You may quit your embarrassing salivating any time now, old chap. It quite unbecomes a gentleman to behave like his spaniel," Alvin Francis Edward Drummond remonstrated.

"Do not remind me of that accursed beast," Derrick said, gritting his teeth.

A slight smile curved Drummond's lips, then quickly vanished as he recalled how he had spent the previous evening, picking dog hairs from a kerseymere jacket. "Would that I had the luxury of such blissful forgetfulness."

The dandy's slight stature and effete mannerisms belied a core of sinewy toughness, and his cool green eyes missed nothing. He was utterly calm under fire, which was precisely why he had been chosen to accompany Derrick Jamison on this assignment.

Derrick returned his attention to the girl on the beach. "I suppose she's *lazzaroni*. Shouldn't be too difficult to locate her, hmmm?" he mused.

"And aren't they the local riff-raff who, according to our briefing, sleep with a crucifix on one side of the bed, a rifle on the other and a stiletto beneath their pillow?" Drum reminded him. "She's probably got a man, some great hulking fellow who shall slit your gizzard in one of those noisome and narrow alleyways."

"I'll take my chances," Jamison replied with a grin.

"Don't you always, old chap?" Drum murmured.

Beth Blackthorne sighed and tossed the letter down on the Dante chair. "How can they be so . . . so obtuse! So provincial!" She had come straight from the market, flushed with victory over Signore Begani, only to be laid low by this. She paced across the marble floor of the villa's portico, oblivious to the musical call of the fountain or the warm sunlight streaming down through the wisteria-covered pergola overhead.

"Another missive from America, I take it," Vittoria,

Contessa di Remaldi, said with a smile. The contessa was a striking woman of middle years, voluptuous of body, with heavy black hair lightly threaded with silver. Her olive complexion was lined with the tiny crinkles that came from much laughter. "Who writes to scold you this time, your mother or one of your now reformed brothers?"

"My father. He's heard the rumor about my posing for Signore Pignatelli."

"Oh, my . . . the whole rumor?" the contessa asked delicately.

"Just because I posed au naturel for an artist with Pignatelli's gift—why, his nudes are considered the finest since Tintoretto—my provincial father demands to know how I could debase myself in such a manner!"

Chuckling gently, the contessa asked, "And will you explain that such was the price of the master so that he would tutor you in portraiture?"

"I might as well have sold myself in the Porta Capucina cribs. It would be no worse by my father's lights. How on earth did that tale travel all the way to Savannah?"

"You have become quite the toast of the court, *cara*. An American female, single and living independently, studying painting . . . becoming successful at it." There was a note of pride blended with concern in Vittoria's voice.

"You are very kind, but you well know that without your sponsorship I would have had no entrée to local artists' circles, not to mention all the wealthy patrons at court. I don't know how I should have survived without your friendship, Vittoria."

"Come here, child," the contessa said, patting a cushion on the chaise beside her. When Beth walked over and took a seat, Vittoria said, "Mark my words, you shall always survive, with or without me. You crossed the wide Atlantic all alone, with nothing but a small inheritance and your dream of painting to sustain you. American courage has always been considered dauntless. Once I saw you standing on the quay, pale and nervous to be sure but with your back so straight, I knew you were going to be someone formidable."

18

"I was frightened as a hare surrounded by hounds that day—and my Italian was atrocious," she added, chuckling as the memories of those harrowing days three years earlier came back to her.

"Well, you speak like a native now, and barter like the *lazzaroni* on market days."

"And who taught me to enjoy the freedom of peasant garb and the fun of haggling with waterfront vendors?" Beth reminded her friend.

"What fun it can be, although I must confess I never had the flair for it that you have exhibited. But now, enough of reminiscences and recriminations from across the Atlantic. I shall write your father assuring him that you are under the most proper chaperonage of the Contessa di Remaldi—tomorrow. Tonight is Queen Caroline's ball, and your gown has just been delivered by the dressmaker."

Beth made a face, "You know how I detest dressing up in court regalia. High-heeled slippers pinch my feet."

"Duke Umberto d'Aquino will be in attendance, and I hear he's looking for an artist to paint his family."

"I shall be most winsome and charming to him, then," Beth said with a grin. "But the slippers will still pinch my toes."

"Not a bloody trace of her." Derrick stared out the window of the handsome quarters Drum had let for them. "I made inquiries all about the waterfront. Even ventured into the *fondachi.*" He shuddered, remembering the Neapolitan version of English slums, with their tiny airless rooms, noisome and dark as caves.

"Ah, my boy, your lust will one day see you dead in an alley. Of course the beggarly classes around the waterfront wouldn't talk with you—even if, mind, you could converse in passable Italian, which you cannot."

"Neither can you."

"Ah, but being a rational man, I have no desire to communicate with *lazzaroni,*" Drum retorted as he continued unpacking their trunks. "His Britannic Majesty's English is all I aspire to speak."

"Scarcely a practical attitude for a man sent to the Continent to spy for that very same Britannic Majesty," Derrick replied dryly.

Drum shook out a pair of doeskins and inspected them critically, saying, "I am not the spy. You are. If it weren't for some slight misunderstanding with my creditors in London, I would never have departed fair Albion's shores."

Jamison gave a snort of laughter. "A slight misunderstanding in the neighborhood of twenty thousand pounds. Actually, I thought it rather generous of the Foreign Office to buy your way out of Newgate."

"Generous indeed. In return I must risk my life on this absurd venture, acting as bodyguard to a reckless madman," Drum said with a sniff.

"Not just bodyguard, body *servant,* my dear Drum, body *servant.*" Derrick chuckled.

The little dandy stiffened and dropped a pile of starched neckcloths into the drawer of a huge *armadio*. "I shall remember this humiliation whilst I'm guarding your backside against Calabrian thugs. My aim might be a bit off."

"Your aim is never off," Jamison reminded him, returning to brood as he stared out the window at the narrow cobblestone streets six stories below their quarters. What had become of the stunning woman with the russet hair and Boadicean stride?

His reverie was interrupted by a knock at the door. The landlord's pudgy young son stood panting after his sprint up the steep stairs. "For the signore," he said in broken English, handing a sealed note to Drum, then waiting for a reward for his swift delivery.

Derrick crossed the room and flipped a coin into his grimy fingers. Swift as a thief, he took off. Drum closed the door, then handed Jamison the missive. Breaking the seal, he read, scowling. "You'd best hurry with the unpacking. I've just been summoned to an audience with the queen."

*   *   *

Wanton Angel

Caroline Bonaparte Murat had never been a beauty like her sister Pauline, but rather favored their brother, with plump pouty features and a heavy mien. Like Napoleon, she also took her role as head of state very seriously. Her husband, the dashing and handsome Joaquim, tried to be a good ruler but was far better at leading cavalry charges. With the exile of Napoleon to the not too distant isle of Elba, both Queen Caroline and King Joaquim of Naples walked a tightrope between British naval power and Austrian land forces.

Thus the gaiety of their court appeared a bit strained during the autumn days of 1814. But the decadent Spanish Bourbons, who had held the kingdom before the French interlopers arrived, had known how to live like royalty, and the soaring towers and vast stone walls of their palaces were tangible proof of it. Inside, the number of rooms and lavishness of appointments boggled the mind of northern visitors.

Not wishing to be outdone by their predecessors, the Murats threw masques, balls and carnivals for the Italian nobility, currying popularity, if not loyalty. But now, with the fate of Europe on the negotiating tables of Vienna, the Murats intrigued to gain advantage from all quarters.

The English had traditionally found Italy a favorite haven from dank north Atlantic winters, and when the war ended, a flood of wealthy and bored British expatriots once again took up residence in Naples. Ostensibly, Derrick was the wastrel younger brother of an earl, frittering away his income under the warm Italian sun, a perfect cover from which to observe the comings and goings between Naples and Elba.

Everyone in the grand alliance that had defeated the little Corsican was certain he would try to escape and turn Europe into a battleground once again. Derrick could feel the tension in the air as he was presented to her majesty, Queen Caroline. Since her English was worse than his Italian, they exchanged the formalities in French, a language in which he had become fluent over the past few years.

Across the crowded room, standing beside the flickering

tapers of an ornate gold candelabra, Beth observed the tall
Englishman from a distance. The light was poor, the room
smoky, but she would never forget that arrogant profile or
the wayward lock of inky hair that tumbled over his brow.
What is he *doing here?*

"You look as if you've seen a ghost, child. Whatever is
wrong?" Vittoria asked, her dark eyes searching Beth's
face. Then she followed the path of the younger woman's
gaze to the tall foreigner. "My, my, he is a beautiful devil,
isn't he?" she said more to herself than to Beth.

"*Devil* being the operative word," Beth murmured beneath her breath. For all that, she could not keep her eyes
from him. He was tall, a head above any of the Neapolitan
courtiers surrounding him, taller even than the smattering
of Frenchmen and other foreigners in the vast room.

A light gleamed in Vittoria's eyes as she watched Beth's
reaction. "You have met before, I take it? Is he American,
then? They are a strapping, reckless breed, I hear."

"He is English."

The words were spat out like a malediction. More and
more curious. The contessa would have licked her lips in
anticipation, but she knew how stubborn and proud Beth
Blackthorne was. If there was the faintest hint that she was
matchmaking, the girl would refuse to say another word
on the subject. "Of course, your countries are at war." She
sighed theatrically. "And with good reason, too. The Royal
Navy simply assumes it can sail anywhere on earth and set
up a blockade."

"I doubt very much Derrick Jenkins has anything to do
with the Royal Navy. He's simply a foppish boor I was
unfortunate enough to run into in Washington several
years ago." Beth winced at her all-too-literal choice of
words.

"I imagine he's on his grand tour, just as so many other
young Englishmen are, now that the war is finally over,"
the contessa said dismissively, not believing it for a moment. Vittoria's keen instincts had been honed surviving
two disastrous marriage alliances, then making her way
through the imbroglio of Italian politics to emerge an in-

dependent woman of some influence in court circles, as well as an arbiter in the world of art and letters. There was something about the way the Englishman worked the crowd, smiling charmingly at introductions, listening more than he spoke. Her senses hummed with curiosity.

"You must excuse me, Vittoria. I find I suddenly have developed a headache. Perhaps a bit of fresh air will clear it."

"But my dear, the duke and his vulture-faced wife have just arrived. You must be introduced to them if you are to get the commission. Albeit, the work will be more like painting wildlife than portraiture, but it will be quite a coup for you," Vittoria said lightly. Whatever the reason, her young friend was disturbed by the Englishman, for surely that was the reason for this sudden flight. The contessa knew Elizabeth Blackthorne never suffered from headache in her life.

"I shall be in the gardens. Perhaps later?" she pleaded, rubbing her temples.

"Sit in the gazebo near the fountain of Pan. That way I shall be able to find you once I've run the ducal couple to ground." Beth nodded, then fled. Vittoria smiled to herself. It was not the Duke d'Aquino whom she planned to run to ground.

Derrick listened intently as two of King Joaquim's royal guards discussed strategies for invading Sicily, a long-cherished goal of Murat. Amazing what one could learn simply by eavesdropping right out in public. Perhaps this assignment would not be as fruitless as he had first believed it to be.

He scanned the room, looking for a cabinet minister who had been pointed out to him prior to his presentation to the queen. Within a quarter hour, he made the acquaintance of the minister, who was as tight-lipped and disdainful as a High Churchman at a Methodist prayer meeting. Noting a number of people drifting out onto the portico and into the gardens beyond, especially those who were imbibing liberally, he followed, still sipping from his first glass of champagne.

The gardens by torchlight were impressive indeed in the feudal, decadent manner of Spanish Bourbon excess. The lush vegetation lent a heady fragrance to the night air. Flickering lights seemed to cast each person's face in sinister shadows. *If ever there was a night for intrigue—or a place—this is it.* Recalling how he had on occasion unintentionally overheard conversations through the dense shrubbery in Vauxhall, he decided to stroll down a deserted pathway close to where he'd seen the reticent cabinet minister with a French officer.

He took a swallow of champagne, then quickly spat it onto the ground. Warm and flat, and a poor vintage at that. He heard the faint buzz of voices farther down toward the garden wall. Perhaps his quarry? No, what he heard were sounds of a breathless struggle between a man and a woman.

"If you don't release me this instant, I shall scream the palace down around your ears, you drunken, stable-mouthed scum!" hissed a female voice in fluent Italian.

"Considering your reputation, it would reflect far worse on you than on me if you did, but I don't believe you will." The man, who spoke Italian with a heavy French accent, sounded arrogant and more than a bit drunk. Then the sound of fabric ripping was followed by a loud grunt.

Tossing his glass into the grass, Derrick sprinted down the path toward the struggle. He found a man dressed in the showy uniform of a royal guards officer struggling to maintain his grip on a woman whose sheer silk gown had been torn from one milky bare shoulder. Since the guardsman was armed and he was not, Derrick called out no warning, simply came up behind the man, wrapped his arm around the fellow's neck and yanked back hard.

"I believe the lady is unappreciative of your attentions," he said in French, applying pressure with his forearm to the soldier's throat until the man gave up his attempts to draw his saber and began to wheeze, choking for air. Derrick gave him a hard shove, knocking him onto his hands and knees, where he remained, coughing violently until he suddenly rolled over and passed out cold.

"You are most noble, Mr. Jenkins, but I could've managed the drunken lout quite handily," a husky contralto voice said in English.

Derrick's head swiveled from the guardsman to his victim. The disheveled female revealed a small jeweled stiletto in her hand. "For someone whose clothing has been half ripped from her body, you appear remarkably calm, madam," he replied as warning bells sounded. Where the devil did she know him from? And the name, Jenkins—why, he had not used it since . . . Washington—over three years earlier, when he was a green beginner.

But it was exceedingly difficult to concentrate on the dangerous puzzle while every nerve in his body sizzled as he watched the pink tip of one lush breast spilling from her torn bodice. Then his tormented gaze swooped lower, watching her bare a creamy thigh and a seemingly endless expanse of leg as she slipped the deadly little weapon back in its sheath on her garter. When she straightened up once more, he got his first good look at her face. "You!" He had been unable to discern the color of her hair in the moonlight or he would have recognized that magnificent body at first sight.

One delicate eyebrow arched. "Then you recognize me after all these years?" she said, forcing her voice to remain cool, her fingers not to tremble as she refastened the torn bodice of her gown with a brooch.

"Scarce that long. I saw you on the beach early this morning. What the devil are you doing at the palace?" He sounded utterly baffled, oddly wary.

Beth deflated a bit. Of course he would not remember their first meetings. Perhaps it would be best if he never did. She'd been a skinny, provincial miss then. Judging by the way his eyes devoured her now, he obviously found her mature form attractive, to say the least. "This morning? Ah, yes, this morning when I had that slight, er, altercation with the wretched fishmonger Begani."

He threw back his head and laughed. "Slight altercation? You flogged him with a fish!"

"He had it coming, selling rotten mackerel to women whose families can afford no other meat."

"Mayhap, but what were you doing dressed as a *lazzaroni*? You're obviously educated, with sufficient connections to be received at court."

"How typically English," she replied angrily. "If I'm one of the 'better sort'—even if that sort is American—then I could never dress comfortably, walk about unchaperoned or consort with poor people!"

Still trying in vain to place her, he replied, "Even in America ladies do none of those things."

He had her there. A vision of Quintin Blackthorne's stern countenance flashed in her mind's eye. Quashing it, she tossed the shambles of her once elegant hairdo back over her shoulder and tried to step past him. Arrogant English lout!

Derrick reached out and took her arm proprietarily. "Please, I didn't intend to be rude—just typically English," he said with a devilish grin that normally sent female hearts fluttering. She made no attempt to pull away as he continued, "I know we've met in America, but for the life of me I do not recall it—and I never forget a beautiful woman. Am I losing my mind?"

His disarming charm and the warmth of his touch worked their magic on Beth. *He thinks I'm beautiful!* her heart sang. *He disapproves of everything I am and do*, her common sense reminded her. Still, she could not think straight standing so close to him, with those fathomless blue eyes sweeping hungrily over her body. "Your mind is quite intact, Mr. Jenkins. I was a girl when first we met—or perhaps I should say 'collided' behind Mistress Smollett's stables."

"My god, the Blackthorne girl! Elizabeth. You've . . . you've grown!" *How the deuce do I explain being called by another name in Washington? And how the deuce do I get her to trust me enough to entice her into my bed?*

26

Chapter Three

Collecting himself, he bowed politely, saying, "Not Jenkins, I fear. Derrick Jamison, at your service."

"Jamison?" A frown marred her forehead.

This was no longer an easily flummoxed school miss. "Yes, Jamison, the younger son. My brother Leighton is now the earl. I was sent to America to escape disgrace over a dueling mishap."

"You killed a man in a duel?" Her father had fought a duel over her mother long ago. As a girl Beth had thought it romantic, but now it only seemed dangerous and foolish.

He shrugged. "I didn't intend it, but he turned to fire before the count was complete. I had no choice." The event was no fabrication, only the rest of the tale. "The family of the man I killed was so powerful that I was forced to flee the country and assume another name until the matter died down." In truth, his father had easily bribed the greedy young baron's relatives. "So," he added with another boyish grin, "I stand before you an utter scapegrace, the family black sheep, whiling away my life in exile."

"You might consider my country an exile, but from

what I've seen of Englishmen in Italy, you should quite enjoy life here. Heaven knows enough of your countrymen do." He had the oddest effect on her. Suddenly she realized that she felt at ease and charmed. *Be honest. You feel much more than just charmed.* She shoved the niggling thought aside and returned his flirtatious smile.

"Too true, but I only just arrived this very day. I've no one to show me the city." He waited a beat, hoping she'd volunteer.

"And since I'm an expatriot who knows every nook and cranny, who better to teach you about Naples?" She inclined her head, returning his bold stare.

"And perhaps there is something I might teach you in return?" He took her hand, raising it to his mouth.

Vittoria had tutored her well in playing saucy games. A woman had to use every weapon at her command in order to succeed in a world controlled by men, the contessa had explained. Beth, much to her own amazement, had discovered that she excelled at such games. She allowed him to brush her fingers with his lips, then withdrew her hand before he could move in farther. "Unless you're really J. M. W. Turner in disguise, I doubt there's anything you have to teach that I wish to learn," she replied with a sparkling laugh, then turned and began retracing her footsteps up the pathway.

He followed her as he knew she expected him to do. *A brazen wench, but beguiling.* He'd desired her when he'd thought she was merely an Italian peasant, but knowing that she was educated and had connections at the court made the prospect of a liaison with her doubly appealing. *I let you escape when you were an innocent miss, but not this time,* cara. "You still have not said if you will show me Naples."

"La, sir, you are persistent, even for an Englishman."

"And you are bold, even for an American. We should suit."

"Might I remind you that our nations are at war?"

"But Italy is neutral ground and we are both expatriots. What are politics to us?"

28

She appeared to consider, slowing her steps as they neared the flickering torchlight at the outskirts of the palace. "Your point is well taken, Mr. Jamison."

"Please, call me Derrick."

She stopped, suddenly realizing that her gown was torn and the elaborate coiffure Donita had labored over was hanging askew. "Very well, Derrick," she replied while checking the opal brooch holding her torn gown together. The clasp had not caught securely. She started to readjust it, but he reached out, placing his warm hands over hers. "If you'll allow me, please?" he said.

Suddenly her heart was pounding furiously once again. Beth prided herself on her control with men. But this Englishman was different from any other. As his fingers deftly worked the clasp, gathering the ends of the fabric on the sharp pin, she reached up and attempted to secure the combs that had held her coiffure in place.

"Your hair is marvelous," he whispered, inhaling the tantalizing musky fragrance of the heavy mass. "Lush, and the color . . . rich as fine old claret. That's what I first noticed when I saw you on the shore this morning." He finished the repair of her gown, but instead of stepping away, he raised his hand and took a loose tendril in his fingers, tugging on it ever so gently, drawing her lips nearer to his.

"Not my Amazonian height or loud voice?" She stood her ground.

"All the above made a most enticing picture, Miss Blackthorne," he murmured, lowering his mouth ever so slowly to hers.

"Please, call me Beth."

"It would be utterly shocking for a gentleman to kiss a lady if he did not use her given name . . . wouldn't it, Beth?"

Her eyelids fluttered downward. "Shocking . . . utterly . . ." She could say no more before his lips brushed against hers, lazily at first, then with deepening intensity.

Since moving to Italy, Beth had allowed a good number of men to kiss her, more out of curiosity than real attraction. She had actually become quite proficient at technique but had never much cared for it . . . until now. She melted against him as he tightened his arms around her.

Derrick could feel the soft fullness of those lush breasts pressing against his chest. He opened his mouth over hers, waiting to see if she would allow his next liberty. When her lips parted, he plunged inside, tasting of her, his tongue probing, dueling with hers.

Beth spun out of control, feeling a thousand sensations all at once, things she had never experienced before. Her breasts tingled, rubbing against the hardness of his chest. His tongue was mating with hers, dancing in and out of her mouth, leaving her breathless. A deep ache pooled low in her belly, throbbing with the furious beat of her blood. *This is madness!*

His hand cupped the lush milky breast he had so admired when it was unveiled, rubbing the hard tip between thumb and index finger until she moaned, arching her hips against his. Requiring no further encouragement, he slid his other hand over the deep indentation at the small of her back, then spread his fingers around one firm buttock, kneading it and pressing his hips in sync with hers, rocking them slowly to the rhythm he set with his plunging tongue.

Beth had participated in some heated embraces over the past three years, but she had always kept a distance in her mind, assessing the situation, planning her next move, deciding when to break away before things got out of hand. This was definitely out of hand, and she had planned nothing at all! Derrick seemed as powerless to resist their passion as she. Beth could feel the obvious pressure of his erection straining against the sheer fabric of her gown, pressing near the juncture of her thighs.

Lord above, I want to take her right here on the grass by torchlight, in clear view of any accidental passersby! If they were discovered by anyone of account at the court, it could jeopardize his mission. He should stop while he still could . . . *if* he still could . . . but he did not. Instead he ground his hips against hers with fierce possessiveness and lowered his lips from hers to trail hot wet kisses down her throat, slipping her bodice from the very shoulder where he had earlier repaired it, eager to take that lush pink nipple in his mouth and feast.

The faint scratching of the brooch as he slid the bodice free of her breast brought Beth back from the edge of the abyss. She took a deep shuddering gulp of cool night air and removed her hands from where she'd buried them in his thick black hair. Pressing her palms against his chest, she stopped him from placing the searing heat of his mouth on her breast. If he'd done that, she intuited that nothing would have enabled her to say him nay.

Standing on the stairs of the portico overlooking the garden, Vittoria observed the lovers faintly visible in the distance. Beth's heavy mane of hair and statuesque body were easily identifiable, and she was returning Jamison's kisses with an ardor that greatly pleased the older woman. At twenty, the contessa had been already well experienced in the joys of the flesh. It was time her young protégée took a lover.

Of course, a lover was all the Englishman could ever be for Beth. The son of an earl, even the younger son who had not inherited the title, could never consider marriage with an American. But this was acceptable. Her mentor knew that Beth had no interest in shackling herself to a man. Her career as an artist was the driving passion of her life. And the contessa bitterly understood that there could be no room in any woman's life for two passions.

But a little dalliance now and then . . . well, that was another matter. Vittoria had always believed Englishwomen were the most painfully inhibited on earth until she met Beth. She had spent nearly three years trying in vain to convince the girl that she could enjoy her sexuality without having to abandon her art. Then tonight, observing Beth's reaction to that handsome devil in the audience room, Vittoria had made it her business to learn Derrick Jamison's identity. Above all she would protect her surrogate daughter.

Something about his manner had set her suspicions humming when she'd first watched him. Ever since Joaquim Murat had been given the Neapolitan throne by his brother-in-law Napoleon, spies swarmed around the court, thick as flies on overripe fruit. But Jamison apparently was a member of one of the richest and most prestigious families in England. The late Earl of Lynden would never have permitted his son to do anything so tawdry as spying. From what various courtiers knew of Derrick Jamison, she surmised that he was either an indolent wastrel enjoying the warm Italian sun or, more likely, a rogue banished for some infraction in London society. In either case, he would be recalled to make the requisite marriage in due course, leaving Beth in no danger of leg-shackling.

Yes, the contessa could not have arranged matters better herself. When Beth finally pushed him away and stepped back, Vittoria chuckled. Beth might be young, but she had a solid head on her shoulders. That was precisely what most men feared in a woman, but Jamison would not be daunted since he had no thoughts of marrying her. The course was set now. Let nature do its work. If it did not, Vittoria would simply lend it a hand.

"You look like a kitten in cream, darling girl. What has put that slumberous expression on your face, eh?" the contessa asked as a servant pulled out a Chiavari chair at the table laden with ripe figs, sliced oranges and crisply browned anise cakes. Vittoria raised a cup of black coffee laced with goat's milk to her lips, staring at her young protégée over its steamy rim. "Well?"

Beth had been up since just past dawn, a crassly American habit according to her friend, who always slept until at least eleven. For her this was an early luncheon, for the contessa, breaking her fast. Even though the light was excellent, Beth had not done much painting this morning, contrary to her usual habit. In fact, all she had done was think about Derrick. She could see Vittoria was waiting her out, one elegant sable brow arched in that sardonic way the older woman had.

"Oh, all right. As if you did not already know. I was thinking about the Englishman. He kissed me in the gardens last night. It was . . . rather intense."

32

"I thought the Englishman was, how did you put it, 'a foppish boor'?" The hint of a smile whispered around her lips as she sipped her drink.

"Perhaps I was mistaken . . . or perhaps . . ."

"At last a man who takes your fancy as much as you take his. This is a refreshing change. Tell me about him—I mean everything from when you first met in America."

Beth outlined that first disastrous encounter with Barnsmell, then the second equally unpleasant meeting at Dolley Madison's salon. "So that's why I suddenly developed an acute case of headache upon recognizing him last night."

"Then what changed your mind—other than the very obvious fact that he's quite the most dashing figure of a man I've seen since Prince Metternich returned to Vienna?" A faint niggling of unease once again pricked the contessa. She made a mental note to check further into Jamison's background.

Beth blushed faintly, something she had schooled herself to avoid. "I must confess that I fancied him even back in Washington. But I was only a naive schoolgirl of seventeen. What did I know of men?"

"What indeed?" the contessa echoed, biting into a plump, juicy fig.

"I would probably not have even spoken to him if he had not rescued me from Evon Bourdin."

"The king's captain of the guards?" Vittoria made a small moue of distaste.

"None other. He was drunk and must have followed me to the gazebo in the garden. I was about to give him a set down with my stiletto when Derrick came up behind him and seized him about the neck."

"An intelligent move if the Englishman was unarmed. Even drunk, Bourdin can be quite dangerous. I can imagine what Jamison must've thought when he saw your weapon . . . and where it came from." A look of sly amusement lit her eyes.

"He was, er, interested in where I keep it. I was quite brazen, showing him the blade, then replacing it on my garter while he watched. You would have been proud of

33

me," Beth replied, grinning. Then her expression grew serious. "He devoured me with his eyes. I felt . . . unlike any time before . . . warm, breathless, as if the world was spinning out of control. Is that the way it's supposed to be when you're attracted to a man?"

"Yes, but only if you're careful you don't lose your heart in the process of losing your virginity."

"I understand about European nobility and arranged marriages, Vittoria. You above anyone should know what my art career means to me. But how am I to paint about life unless I experience it?"

The contessa gave a fatalistic Latin shrug of agreement, but her thoughts were still troubled. *Why is Jamison in Naples?* She intended to find out.

"I tell you, old chap, this is intolerable, simply intolerable. I shan't be responsible for my actions if Sir Percival remains," Drum said, eyeing his sterling-headed sword cane. He held up for Derrick's inspection a pair of riding boots, with the toe chewed off one, a heel demolished on the other. "Forty pounds! The finest shoemaker in London fitted them to my feet. Deuced hard to find a craftsman who can do this sort of work."

"Especially when you fail to pay him," Derrick replied.

"Articles of *my* apparel were not the only casualties of this guerrilla war," Drum replied with silky smugness. "Only this morning I found that bottle-green jacket of yours covered with hair. I still have not managed to remove it all. Doubt I shall. Sir Percival must go."

Just then the object of Drum's ire trotted into the sitting room and jumped onto the settee, where he promptly proceeded to groom his unmentionables with a long red tongue.

Jamison narrowed his eyes at the King Charles Spaniel, whom he liked no better than did his companion. "Sir Percival is a highly trained courier. He's been assigned to us and there's an end to it. You'll just have to apply yourself to keeping clothing and footgear out of his reach."

Drum quit the room, muttering beneath his breath, "I

warrant he'd reach a deal less high if I cropped off his demned legs at the first joint."

Derrick looked over at the spaniel, who returned his gaze with guileless liquid brown eyes. "No need to look at me as if you were innocent as a newborn foal. I know better." The dog hopped from the settee and padded over to him, sitting at his feet.

Sighing in resignation, Jamison patted the dog's head. Bloody hell; how had he come to be saddled with a clothes-chewing canine and a debtor dandy? He had been perfectly content working alone across the capitals of Europe for the past three years. Been damned successful at it, too. Owing to his information, several crucial battles on the Peninsula had gone to Britain and her Spanish allies. And his assistance to incompetent Austrian military had been considerable. Perhaps if he hadn't described the fighting capabilities of the Austrian army by writing that the best that could be said was that they had the prettiest uniforms on the field, he might not have been sent down from Vienna. *How the bloody hell was I to know the idiot British chargé d'affaires would share that dispatch with Metternich?*

He returned his attention to the Italian newspaper in his hand. His Italian needed work, but he had a natural affinity for languages and felt certain that within a few weeks he would be able to comprehend passably well. Beth Blackthorne would doubtless be an excellent teacher. He grinned, recalling their encounter last night, then glanced up at the ormolu clock on the mantel. He had an appointment at half past the hour . . . and he could almost justify his dalliance because her Italian was so skillfully idiomatic.

Later, after he had dressed for his outing with Beth, he watched in the mirror as Drum fussed with his cravat. "No, no, my dear fellow. You simply must hold still. It does not quite stand to your chin properly," the little dandy said.

"If the damned thing stood any higher, my neck would be stretched tighter than a Tyburn felon's. And you must desist in calling me 'old chap' and 'my dear fellow.' Remember, you're supposed to be my body servant."

Shirl Henke

"As the Honorable Mr. Jamison wishes, sir," Drum replied curtly, looking up the narrow blade of his nose at the much taller man. Cool green eyes met amused blue ones. "I see nothing of humor in this ghastly situation."

Derrick suppressed another chuckle as he turned to inspect himself in the glass and nodded approvingly. "You're getting to be a passable dresser, I must say, my good fellow. I look . . . er, what is it the Beau would say—all the crack, I believe."

"Not quite the crack. You're over tall. That Scots blood, I suspect." Drum sniffed, shaking his head as he folded a stack of cravats and replaced them in the *armadio*.

"Give us Scots our due. We've successfully infiltrated the whole of the English bureaucracy and run the bloody government now." Derrick turned to leave, then paused to deliver his departing sally. "Oh, by the by, I just received word while you were engaged drawing my bath—this afternoon Sir Percival begins earning his dog bones. You're to walk him along the Via Roma toward the Piazza Dante where you will—"

"*I'm* to walk him! I? Whyever not you? The beast is supposed to be your dog," Drum interrupted.

"This is merely a trial run, to see if the dog can find his trainer and messages can be easily exchanged in his collar without anyone taking note. I've placed a brief report regarding what I gleaned at court last night inside the collar. All you need do is place it around his neck and be off. Slip his leash when you reach the piazza. He should return to you when his mission is accomplished."

"I might better wish that the accursed hellhound runs off, never to be heard from again!" Drum replied with an indignant wave of his hand. "I, who trod the streets of the Great Wen with the Beau, reduced to walking a dog!"

Derrick could not resist tweaking the little dandy. "It will raise less attention if the locals believe a mere servant is walking the dog."

Drum huffed. "A mere servant indeed—"

"Be a good chap, Drum. See to Sir Percival," Derrick said, suppressing another chuckle as he closed the door.

* * *

"Do I look all right?" Beth asked worriedly, turning this way and that to check her appearance in a looking glass, although she normally concerned herself little about clothing.

Vittoria inspected her charge, who was a vision in a pale spring green gown and spencer, sprigged with darker green leaves. The short jacket was cut cunningly, with a clasp holding it together just below the curve of her breasts. The color brought out the green in her hazel eyes. Her hair was wound in a simple heavy chignon at the crown of her head with soft tendrils escaping around the edges of the tiny confection of her bonnet. To add just a hint of sophistication, the contessa had insisted she borrow an emerald necklace and earrings set in antique filigreed silver.

"You're exquisite, child. Ah, to be twenty once again, with handsome men flocking about."

Beth smiled and kissed the older woman on the cheek. "You still have handsome men flocking about you and well you know it—just not this one particular Englishman."

"Speaking of whom, I do believe I hear his curricle in the drive," Vittoria said, slipping over to the open window to look down into the front entryway. "My, he does cut a dashing figure. Matched bays with white stockings and blazes."

"Must all Neapolitans judge people by their horses?"

The question was rhetorical and Vittoria knew it. "Next to the English, we're the most horse-mad race on earth."

"You haven't met my Creek Indian cousins, else you'd never say so." Beth smoothed her hands over her hips nervously, then licked her lips, which had been glossed with berry juice so they glowed a soft pink. A hint of kohl darkened her eyelids and lashes, but her sun-kissed face was smooth and golden, innocent of the artifice of cosmetic whiteners. Derrick was from England, where the standard of beauty was blond and pale. Would she compare unfavorably? Throwing her head back, she went to meet him, but her confident stride belied the butterflies dancing in her belly.

He watched her descend the curving staircase, a statuesque Juno in a soft, clinging ensemble that beguilingly hinted of delectable breasts, hips and long sleek legs. Ah, how well he remembered that firm creamy expanse of thigh when she'd replaced the stiletto in her garter. Did she carry it today? The thought was a bit unsettling, but she had not offered to use it on him last night.

She was followed by an older woman of more than passing handsomeness. Derrick knew she must be the Contessa di Remaldi, the notorious widow who owned this magnificent old villa. Twice widowed, Vittoria di Remaldi lived life as she pleased, taking lovers by the score, if international gossip was to be believed. She was rich as the Romanovs and a serious patron of the arts, sponsoring numerous young painters, among them Beth Blackthorne.

She was also nobody's fool, having been raised amid cutthroat Italian politics. His sources said she supported Murat's bid to unify the smaller Italian states, something Britain and her Austrian allies were dead set against. He would have to tread very lightly around the contessa. But if he were careful, he might be able to glean from Beth all manner of information about court intrigues, especially any contact the king and queen had with the prisoner on Elba.

Beth made the introductions and he bowed, kissing the contessa's hand, which was suprisingly bare of jewelry. Last evening she, like every other Italian noblewoman, fairly dripped with rubies and diamonds. "It is a pleasure, Contessa. I have heard much about the charming and lovely patron of the arts."

"Then you are quite ahead of me. I have heard little of the Honorable Derrick Jamison, other than that he is the younger son of the late Earl of Lynden. Why are you here, sir?" she asked in musically accented English, adding, "Other than to enjoy the company of our beautiful women, that is?"

"Need I have any other reason for coming to Italy? It's been second home to my countrymen for generations," he countered smoothly, adding, "But none of them ever beheld ladies as breathtaking as I do now."

"You are a flatterer, signore. And in a handsome man, that can be a dangerous thing."

"As is intelligence in a beautiful woman, Contessa."

After they had departed, Vittoria stood on the portico watching the curricle vanish amid a stand of olive trees. He had been gallantly glib. Perhaps a bit too much so?

They rode through the glorious open countryside, following an ancient cobbled road that overlooked the bay to the west. Derrick handled the ribbons with considerable skill. As he drove, Beth observed his face in profile. His look was hawkish, intent—dangerous was the word Vittoria chose. She studied him silently. They had spoken little since driving away from the villa on the outskirts of the city. It was as if each was too aware of the other and the sudden and powerful sexual chemistry that had charged their meeting and prompted their rash behavior in the royal garden.

"Am I frightening you?" he asked, turning his attention from the road as he reined the bays to a slow trot.

"I know how to protect myself," she replied.

"Ah, yes, the stiletto. I was wondering if you would wear it today, but I was referring to my driving."

Beth laughed, a warm throaty sound that she was unaware he found incredibly stimulating. "You drive no more recklessly than any of my brothers or cousins. I come from a family of horse-racing men. Georgia planters and Creek Indians are notorious for their weakness for fast horses."

And fast women? He did not voice the question aloud, but somehow it hung in the air between them. "Tell me about your family and why you ran away."

"I didn't run away," she said defensively, then sighed. "Well, perhaps I did, but not because I don't love them or they me. Everyone expected me to marry and settle down to raise babies, but I wanted so much more out of life."

He nodded. "I understand that. The prescribed life for

a second son is either the Church or the military. I chose neither because I, too, wanted much more out of life."

"Then possibly we can understand each other," she said tentatively, wondering if she dared ask what was on her mind. She plunged ahead. "I can understand why the life of a country curate might not appeal, but I would imagine the army to be just the sort of adventure you would thrive upon." A haunted expression darkened his eyes for a flash, then vanished. Or had she simply imagined it? When he spoke, his dazzling smile was in place once more.

"My father naturally assumed I'd buy a commission, especially considering the war on the Continent, but I'm really a worthless scoundrel, you see, enamored of sleeping late, dressing well and spending my time with beautiful women. The army would quite interfere."

"I imagine your father was not pleased. Is that why you left England again?"

He shrugged rather carelessly. "Why remain on a damp cold island when one can bask in the warm sun of Italy? Especially when Naples draws the most beautiful women on earth."

"I think you are like Naples—drawing women to you, that is. Shall I allow myself to be the latest in a long list of conquests, I wonder?" The question was rhetorical, but she still struggled to keep the heat from staining her cheeks.

"Shall you, Beth? I wonder, too. I find it difficult to imagine a young woman from good family turning her back on the conventional life as easily as a man might. A man naturally avoids leg-shackling, but women seem to thrive on it. Why would a beautiful, passionate woman reject the idea?"

"Most men, certainly the male members of my family, share your opinions. I'll give you the same answer I've given them. My life's passion is to be an artist. I don't mean a lady of leisure who dabbles at watercolors while her maid puts the children down for their nap. I mean a real painter who earns her own way by her talents. Men

40

have been doing it for centuries. Why, if she has the talent, should not a woman have the same right?"

He smiled again. "Perhaps she should, but are you certain you would not be happier in Paris than Naples? Such revolutionary ideas would suit better in France than Italy."

"I confess to being an admirer of French thought during the Enlightenment. A bit of it even rubbed off on the English."

He grinned. "Touché, mademoiselle. And so did a bit of it on our American kin, else there would have been no break with the mother country."

"Do you find my idea of independence unnatural?"

"Nothing about you, my dear, is in the least bit unnatural." His voice was a husky purr as he leaned closer. "You're an enigma, yes, but a most pleasant one, whose mysteries I fully intend to unveil." With that, he stopped the already slowing curricle and leaned over, taking her in his arms.

Chapter Four

Their eyes met and held for a moment, measuring each other. Then she said, "Last night was rash . . . reckless."

"Yet you accepted my invitation to ride in the country and brought no chaperone," he countered as his fingertips lightly caressed her cheek.

He wore no gloves and she was surprised to feel slight calluses on his hands. She'd expect that of her father or brothers, but not of a self-confessed English dandy. Her thoughts spun crazily at his touch. His intense gaze mesmerized her until all she could think of was melting into him like wax in the Italian sun.

Rather than make reply to his teasing retort, she raised her lips to his, initiating the kiss with a boldness that surprised her more than him. She had never done such a thing. A small voice warned, *You're being drawn in too deeply, too quickly. He will hurt you.* That voice was silenced when he deepened the kiss.

One hand splayed across her back while the other slid around to the opening of her jacket, insinuating clever fingers through the clasp and stroking the peak of her breast through the sheer fabric of her bodice. Her nipples burned. When she emitted a small, sharp gasp of pleasure, he growled deeply into her mouth, working his firm sculpted lips over hers with such hunger, he left her breathless, dizzy. Clinging to his shoulders was not enough. She reached up, threading her fingers through his night-dark hair, pulling him closer . . . closer.

She was a witch, an enchantress, knowing just what to do to drive him wild. He pressed her backward against the soft velvet of the curricle's seat, knowing full well they could not satisfy their desire in the small vehicle. He cursed the desperate impatience that led him to murmur against her mouth, "I want to touch every inch of you . . . caress . . . lick, taste . . . I can't get enough of you, Beth."

Beth moaned her assent as his knee moved between her legs and rubbed intimately against her thighs. The ache that throbbed wickedly in her blood now centered low in her belly and moved to that most secret place, which was untried but eager . . . so eager. His hands were swift, certainly practiced, as they unfastened hooks and clasps, sliding her jacket off and opening the front of her gown, baring her breasts to the wet heat of his mouth.

Derrick was near to bursting, buttoned into fashionably tight doeskins, but just as he started to unfasten his fly, the sound of bleating goats and voluble Italian curses echoed in the distance. Distractedly he turned his head and saw an old man brandishing a shepherd's crook as he scrambled in a crab-legged gait after half a dozen runaway goats. The farmer was followed by two youths who appeared more interested in the fancy curricle ahead than in rounding up the recalcitrant livestock.

Doing a bit of cursing himself, Derrick quickly covered Beth and seized the reins, slapping them so the bays took off at a smart clip.

As they passed the old man and his helpers Beth pressed herself against the velvet squabs of the curricle, turning her head away from their curious eyes. Good lord above, she was practically undressed—in broad daylight in the middle of a public road! Still, it was a very remote road, she rationalized to herself, trying to collect her scattered wits as Derrick concentrated on driving.

"I apologize for what just happened," he said as she rearranged her clothing.

"For undressing me or for being interrupted?" some imp made her ask.

"For your embarrassment and most definitely for the untimely interruption, but for wanting to make love to you, never."

A slow smile bowed her lips. "We do seem to lose all sense of decorum, not to mention practicality, when we come together."

His eyes blazed hungrily. "We have not come together . . . yet."

"Inevitable, I fear." There was no question in her mind, but what of her heart? "It might be wise to spend a bit of time becoming better acquainted first . . . in some more public places."

Now a grin tugged at his mouth. "You mean places where probable interruptions would ensure my good behavior?"

She nodded, also grinning. "Let me show you my Naples, the one proper English gentlemen never see."

"No one has ever accused me of being a proper English gentleman, but I accept your offer anyway. For now, the sun is sparkling on the waters of the bay and the scent of lemon trees wafts on the breeze. Let us enjoy the countryside this afternoon."

They laughed and talked, both striving to ignore the tension that sung between them with every glance and touch. Savoring what was to come only added to the delight for the novice Beth. Knowing full well what was to come, Derrick felt anticipation fraught with considerably more impatience and discomfort, but he found she was a witty and charming companion. Expecting her to be well versed in the arts, he was surprised that she had also received an education in philosophy, politics and the sciences the equal of any man of his acquaintance.

There was much to recommend intelligence in a beautiful woman. As a callow youth, he'd had a few mistresses who were only marginally more intelligent than their lap-dogs. He had found such women tedious in the extreme, especially when it came time to part. An intelligent woman realized sulks and tears did not work on a man such as he. Would it be all that easy to say good-bye to Beth—or would she be the one to bid him adieu?

"What do you make of the new Englishman Jamison?" the contessa asked, sipping the Conde di Ruvo's finest Madeira from a crystal goblet.

The shrewd old man was a born gossip who knew all there was to know about the expatriot community in Naples. Derrick Jamison was probably just another indolent Englishman wanting only to enjoy warm weather and beautiful women. But she had taken his measure and seen how smitten Beth was with him. She needed to be certain he would not hurt her young friend.

"Jamison, old Lynden's boy. He is the younger son. His elder brother Leighton inherited a year or two ago," the conde said, rubbing his pointy chin and staring contemplatively at a DaVinci hanging on the wall of the sitting room. "Why do you ask about him—interested in some young meat, are you?" His swarthy complexion was whitened with arsenic powder, giving the impression of a lecherous corpse.

"Not at the moment, Enrico," she replied, brushing aside her distaste. "I merely observed him at her majesty's ball last evening and something about him seemed . . ." She searched for the proper words, then shrugged. "Something just told me that he is not what he appears to be."

"Woman's intuition?" the conde asked lightly.

"Call it what you will. He is too charming by half for an Englishman."

Enrico cackled. "You might just be right. I've heard whispers about the court regarding exchanges between here and Elba. The British certainly wish to see that Napoleon remains in exile. It is logical to assume they would send an agent to Naples. I've heard rumors young Jamison came here from Vienna."

"That does put a disturbing complexion on it," Vittoria mused, knowing the reactionary allies were convened in the Austrian capital to divide the spoils of Napoleon's empire. "I had thought the son of an earl above spying."

"Never underestimate the vulgarity of the British, dear one," the conde replied.

"Keep your ears open, will you not?" she asked. *As if you ever did aught else.*

In the distance Mt. Vesuvius rose majestically, outlined in a sunrise of pink, aqua and orange. The rhythm of waves lapping against the shore gave an aura of tranquillity to the otherwise bustling commerce on the waterfront. The air resounded with the cries of gulls and songs of fishermen blending together, much as the pungency of sulfur from the mineral fountains blended with the briny smell of the fresh squid and mussels being unloaded from the men's nets onto the shore. In vociferous clusters, women of various classes haggled with fishermen and produce vendors, crowding around sailboats and crude wooden stalls. Here and there a group of old men gathered around the cheery glow of charcoal braziers set out to ward off the early morning chill.

Beth took a deep breath and sighed in contentment, rising up on tiptoes to stretch like a cat. Standing beside her on the quay, Derrick admired the curves of her breasts outlined against her sheer white cotton peasant's blouse. He allowed his eyes to roam down her body, pausing at the indentation of her tiny waist, the gentle swell of her hips, then moving to the slender ankles revealed below the hem of her simple tan skirt.

"You love this place, don't you?" he asked, noting the sparkle in her eyes and the glow of her cheeks, the way the wind lofted her curling hair, sending it flying wildly around her shoulders.

"Always, but especially at dawn."

He shuddered. "I can't believe I actually agreed to arise at such an unholy hour."

"When do you normally arise, sir? Noon?"

"The Beau and his fashionable crowd in London make their appearance around fourish. Of course, one must allow several hours to dress for any occasion."

"Of course," she replied drolly, looking at his attire. She had explained that fine wool and linen would not do for the day she had planned for them. "I fear 'the Beau' would scarce approve of your present attire."

"As long as you do, what matter?" His tone was intimate, his eyes hot, dark.

"Oh, I do." She returned the smoldering look, allowing her eyes to roam boldly up and down his tall frame. He wore a pair of loose cotton pants with the legs rolled up, as was the custom among the working classes, revealing strong brown ankles and long narrow feet encased in a pair of leather-strapped open sandals. Both the shoes and pants were a bit too small for him, although purchased from the tallest fisherman on the bay, as was the gray cotton shirt, open to the waist where it was tied carelessly in a knot. His wide shoulders strained at the seams of the shirt and his darkly tanned chest with its mat of black hair invited her fingers to weave through it.

"My man had the very devil of a time getting the aroma of cuttlefish out of the shirt and pants. He fair boiled them until I feared the cloth would dissolve," he said with amusement, recalling how Drum had cursed and carried on about his partner's "cork-brained escapades." "After all he suffered, it heartens me that you approve. He was aghast when I left on foot this morning, dressed like a common laborer."

She dimpled. "Nothing about you, Derrick Jamison, is common."

"I'll take that for a compliment and not press the issue," he replied as they began strolling down toward the gathering crowd.

Jacomo, a boy in Vittoria's employ, followed with a large basket in which Beth would place her purchases. "I

47

think we shall have mussels for dinner if they are large enough," she murmured as they approached the fishing nets piled high with the morning's fresh catch. "Do you enjoy shellfish?"

"Oysters and mussels are my particular favorites. The idea of teasing a sweet juicy morsel from deep inside its shell holds a strong appeal," he replied suggestively.

"Naughty fellow," she scolded, marching ahead of him toward old Diomede Corenzio, whose sons brought in the finest catch of any fishermen on the bay.

Derrick watched as she haggled and exchanged good-natured insults with the wizened old man whose face resembled a raisin. Once satisfied with the bargain, she moved on to a shy young woman so swollen with child, she looked ready to birth the baby at any moment. The girl sold her half a dozen fragrant fresh oranges. Next was a toothless hag whose stall was piled high with deep green stalks of brussel sprouts and red ripe tomatoes. Beth enjoyed the bargaining as much as did the merchants, who called her "Bella Signorina."

He struggled to follow the local dialect, in which she was so proficient, catching more of the idiom as they moved along. Having always prided himself on his linguistic skills, he asked, "You have a natural way with languages. What others do you speak so fluently?"

She considered a moment. "Other than English and sundry Italian dialects, French, Spanish, Muskogee and some Cherokee."

Derrick was impressed. "The latter two I'm unfamiliar with—Indian tongues?"

"Yes. My uncle Dev is a quarter Muskogee, or Creek, as outsiders call them. The Cherokee I picked up when I went on some trading expeditions into the Carolina mountains with him and my brothers and cousins when I was young. Alex was always my favorite cousin. I tagged along behind him and my brother Rob until they were ready to drown me in the Tallapoosa River. But I fooled them and learned to swim instead."

"You've certainly led a . . . colorful life, Beth. I'm surprised you wanted to leave it behind. There must be a deal more freedom for women in America than in my country."

Her expression turned sad for a moment. "I do miss my homeland at times, but I had no choice. And, Englishman, I have no intention of ever going to your country." The words held a ring of finality.

Derrick did not wish to spoil the fun of the day, so he followed without comment as she wended her way expertly down the twisting narrow streets. By this time Jacomo's basket was heavily laden with fresh food. "What else do you need to purchase?" Derrick asked.

"You'll see," she said with a saucy toss of her long, unbound hair, her good mood once more restored.

He wanted to reach out and grab a fistful of the riotous russet curls, to bury his face in their fragrance, but instead he trudged dutifully along, taking in the sights, sounds and smells of the bustling seaport city. The cobblestone streets were twisting and narrow, enclosed on both sides by six-story buildings. Wash lines were strung across from window to window overhead, with wet clothing flapping in the breeze as it dried. Taking advantage of the beautiful autumn morn, craftsmen worked at their trades in front of their shops, right out in the midst of foot traffic.

Finally they came to an open plaza, which the natives called a piazza, where he stepped gratefully into the sunlight once more. The dry dusty earth was sere and brown, with only a few sparse clumps of grass, owing to a small herd of tethered goats that munched contentedly. Most were nannies, with a few scattered kids either nursing or gamboling around unfettered. Several ancient-looking crones sat nearby hunched on stools. Two of them haggled with customers who brought their own pails, while the others filled the containers with foamy yellowish-white milk from the nanny's teats.

While Beth was occupied paying one toothless old farm woman for her wares, Derrick wandered across the piazza, stopping to scratch the chin of a particularly winsome kid who nuzzled against his hand. "My, my, aren't you the affectionate one," he said with a chuckle. Bending over to better reach the young goat, he murmured, "If only the bella signorina proves as accommodating."

From a distance Beth watched him with the kid, charmed by his way with animals. Just then the kid's nanny, protective of her young one, broke free of her tether and took off at a dead run, head lowered. Derrick's rump presented a splendid target as he patted and wrestled with the kid. Beth started to call out a warning, but it was too late. Instead she raised her hand to her mouth to stifle a most unladylike guffaw when the nanny made contact, pitching him forward with enough force to tumble him over the kid and into the side of another nanny. The startled goat jumped sideways to avoid the human cannonball, giving a loud bleat as she kicked the filled pail of milk beneath her.

Derrick hit the hard-packed ground with enough force to jar his teeth just as a deluge of white liquid drenched his head and shoulders. He sat up, dripping milk, which mixed with the clay to form a slippery mud. Shaking his head to clear it, he started to rise. The kid trotted up once again, but before he could touch it, Beth's laughing voice called out, "I wouldn't do that. His mama is quite put out with you."

"I am not exactly in charity with her either," he said, combing his fingers through his hair, sending droplets of milk down his face and neck.

He started to climb to his knees just as Beth cried, "Look out!"

The nanny made another pass, this time butting him square in the center of his back. He lurched forward onto all fours in the mud. Beth approached, doubled up with laughter now. She exchanged a few coins with the old woman whose goat's milk had been spilled, then extended her hand to him to help him stand up. She was still laughing uncontrollably.

A grin split his face as he laced his mud-slicked fingers through hers, pulling her down alongside him. "Laugh at me, will you, wench?"

Beth started to sputter, but the humor of their situation

got the better of her and she joined his rumbling bass chuckle. Then, suddenly, the amusement faded as they stared into each other's eyes. With his index finger he painted a yellow line from the tip of her nose around her lips, then down the column of her neck to the swell of her breasts.

"Mmm, I've never used mud for this . . . works as good as oil, I'd wager . . ." he murmured as he continued caressing her with his fingertips.

Beth closed her eyes for a moment, savoring the tingling sensations his clever fingers aroused, but the bleating of goats and the chiding voices of the farm women and their customers quickly broke the spell. "You're covered with milk and mud," she said, realizing at once how idiotically obvious that was.

"And you?" he countered with a grin.

"Thanks to you. I was helping you and look what you did."

"You were laughing at me and look what I did." He got gingerly to his feet and pulled her up after him, ignoring the titters and smirks of the locals, who mouthed the word *amore* frequently as they watched the young foreign couple with amusement.

"We'd best wash this stuff off before we draw flies—or worse yet, harden like statuary. I have a large tub at my apartments," he offered.

"I have a better idea. Our day's outing isn't over yet," she replied. After sending Jacomo home with her morning's shopping, Beth took Derrick's hand and said, "Come with me."

"I plan to," he murmured under his breath.

She tried to ignore the frisson of heat deep in her belly as they walked back into the maze of narrow streets. At length they emerged near the waterfront again, in the district where fishermen made their homes. The smell of sulfur wafted on the warm morning air, blending with the ripe odors of the bay. A large plaza opened out on the quay, with a series of fountains spilling from one to another down the hill. Water gushed from the largest one at

51

the top, giving off a smell that suggested it would be brown as sewage but was clear as crystal.

"What is that stink?" he asked, wrinkling his nose.

" 'Tis the mineral waters. They come from underground springs. People come from all over Europe to partake of them, drink them and bathe in them for good health."

"Drink and bathe in it? It reeks of rotten eggs . . . of sulfur."

"Come, don't be such an Englishman," she said, pulling him down the hill to the largest of the series of circular stone tanks holding the overflow of water from the fountain at the top of the hill.

"You make that sound as if all Englishmen are imbeciles."

She shrugged as she sat on the low lip of the fountain and swung her legs over into the water. "Sometimes you are. Take the matter of the war you foisted on my country . . ."

"I foisted nothing on your country. I'm a pacifist at heart."

She gave him a measuring look. "Odd, but I find that difficult to believe. You look quite the warrior when you're angry," she said.

"I'm a lover, not a warrior," he replied, watching in fascination as she submerged herself beneath the lapping water. Her unbound hair floated on top, a deep ruby curtain. All around them men and women sat in the water, unconcerned with their drenched clothing. Children, wearing none, splashed and squealed in delight. But Derrick was oblivious to everyone else when Beth stood up. Her thin cotton skirt and blouse clung almost translucently to her body. "God, you're magnificent," he whispered hoarsely.

"Plunge in, Derrick," she invited.

"I intend to, m'dear, I intend to," he murmured. He stepped into the cool water and knelt, dipping his head beneath the surface and scrubbing milk and mud from his hair.

"Brrr, it's always chilly. They say it comes from deep underground," Beth said.

He could see the pointed tips of her nipples through the soft cloth clinging to her breasts and his mouth went dry. "There are ways I could warm you up," he suggested.

"But, sir, I am not cold," she replied, skimming her arm across the water and splashing him.

He blinked his eyes to clear them, then went after her with a growl. "I'll teach you, minx—or is it otter?" he added as she slipped smoothly from his grasp and splashed him once more.

They laughed and played until they were breathless, tumbling around in the water until he finally subdued her, pinning her arms to her sides as they knelt, submerged almost to their shoulders. All laughter died. He lowered his mouth to hers as she tipped back her head, raising her face for his kiss. His thigh slid between her legs and hers clamped around it, clinging with strong, sleek muscles. He released her arms and ran his hands down to cup and lift her buttocks as her fingers dug into his back, urging him closer.

The tittering of a small boy finally interrupted them. Breathing hard, they broke apart, looking over at the urchin, who grinned and chattered at them in rapid Italian.

"What is he saying?" Derrick asked, the local idiom still impossible for him to completely decipher.

"He's asking if we would like a place to be alone. He has a very nice house just down the Via San Luca."

"What is he charging?" Derrick asked with a rakish grin.

"Not nearly enough for it to be up to your standards, I'm certain," she replied.

"Well, in that case, you can always consider my original offer and return with me to my apartments."

"I'm hungry," she announced suddenly, standing up.

"So am I and well you know it." He watched as she wrung the water from her hair and her clothing, then attempted to straighten herself.

"I mean for food," she replied impatiently.

Sighing, he followed her from the fountain to a stall

where a pretty young woman was taking sizzling hot rounds of flat bread from an oven using a long wooden paddle. The bread was topped with chopped tomato, anchovy and cheese. "That does smell good," he conceded.

They bought two of the scalding hot pizza pies, as they were called, transferring them from hand to hand to keep from burning themselves until the bread cooled enough to eat it. "This is one of my favorite things about Italy," she said, wiping a string of cheese from her chin.

"Unusual," he conceded, taking another hearty bite.

"Delicious. Admit it."

"Not half as delicious as you," he replied.

"But you haven't tasted me yet."

"True, only an hors d'oeuvre or two," he teased. "Just enough to whet my appetite."

"And after you have had the entrée, then what, Derrick? Will I become table scraps?" Her tone was light, but her eyes were serious.

Chapter Five

Derrick stopped and looked directly into her eyes. "Table scraps? My fear is that I shall never have my fill of you, Beth." He had not planned to say that, but now that he'd blurted it out, he realized that it was true. No, there was something about Beth Blackthorne that touched a part of him no one had reached before.

His expression was almost grave. *He looks surprised. He did not expect to say what he said!* She felt the most pleasurable rush of . . . of triumph surge through her. To cover her own reaction, Beth started strolling again. "Ah, easily enough said after less than two days' acquaintance."

"Not true. We have been acquainted for over three years," he corrected.

"I shudder to remember our first meetings," she said with a nervous laugh.

"You do seem to have a remarkable propensity for wreaking mayhem on my person. Another day and you may well have me in my grave."

"Do you wish to be a coward and cry off?" she asked, polishing off the last bite of her pie and licking a smear of tomato sauce from her fingers, all the while watching him from the corner of her eye.

"I'm willing to take a risk . . . and you, my Amazon warrior . . . ?"

The lazy taunt in his low husky voice sent shivers down her spine. "Is that a challenge, sir?" she replied.

" 'Twas you who issued the challenge, madam. I but answered it. My choice of 'weapons' is dinner tonight."

He was daring her and she wanted to take that dare, but she could not. Sighing with genuine regret, she replied, "Tonight I am committed to accompanying the contessa to a masquerade at the Duke di Arcovito's palace. She went to some little trouble obtaining an invitation for me."

"I thought you disliked the social whirl of the nobility. Why would you importune her to get you an invitation to a gathering of court sycophants?" He was surprised at his sudden blaze of disappointment, and perversely angry with her for causing it.

"Because only last evening did I learn that your illustrious J. M. W. Turner will be present, and I'm dying to meet the finest landscape painter of our generation . . . even if he is an Englishman!"

He threw back his head and laughed, pulling her into his arms beneath the shade of a shopkeeper's canvas awning. "There's much to be said for we Englishmen! But I'm relieved to know the reason for your refusal has to do with your art," he replied, bending down to kiss her, heedless of the press of people on the busy waterfront street.

Derrick stood in an alcove partially hidden by a huge potted palm, observing the scene on the polished marble floor of the Duke di Arcovito's ballroom. Men and women dressed in costumes every color of the rainbow whirled around the floor to the lively strains of the Viennese rage, the waltz.

Everyone wore masks, from simple black silk dominoes such as his to incredibly elaborate sequined and feathered affairs that covered most of the wearer's face. He scanned the dance floor, searching for a tall russet-haired woman amid all the jeweled headdresses and turbans. Then he saw her, dressed in a fantastical costume made of softly tanned white leather, elaborately worked with tiny shells and beads. Around her head she wore a matching beaded band, with her hair plaited into a fat gleaming braid that hung all the way down to her waist. Not a woman in the room could compare. She stood in a far corner, deep in discussion with a slight, fair-haired man who must surely be English judging by his pallor. Turner, the painter. Their conversation was animated.

Derrick smiled faintly. *Always so predictable, puss. Art before pleasure.*

Of course, he also had a professional reason for wangling an invitation through the English chargé d'affaires office. He had mixed and mingled, listening and convincing several of Queen Caroline's ladies-in-waiting to reveal with whom her majesty had been corresponding in recent weeks. If the exiled Napoleon planned to foment an uprising in Italy, Lord Liverpool's government in London would be advised of it well in advance.

That was how he'd justified his presence at the masquerade to his snappish "manservant." Drum had fumed about Derrick being tricked out like a Bartholomew baby when he dressed all in black from domino and swirling cape to thigh-high leather boots. The idea of masquerading as a highwayman had a certain ironic appeal for a spy, he'd told Drum, who merely scoffed, saying that Jamison's only reason for the costume was to appeal to his latest paramour. Although he vehemently denied it, Derrick was forced to admit that Beth Blackthorne had taken hold of his imagination . . . and more physical parts of his anatomy.

Was she right? Did he desire her because he had not yet had her? Or was this fascination something more complex? There was only one way to find out. He began wending his way across the room to her, but before he could get through the press, a man dressed as a Turkish sultan swept her onto the dance floor. The long fringes on her costume swayed in time with the music, parting enticingly to reveal flashes of sleek long arms and legs. His mouth was dry as he watched her laugh and banter with the "pasha."

"Might I cut in, old chap? There's a good fellow," he said to the elderly Neapolitan gentleman who was left standing flummoxed in the middle of the floor as Derrick whirled Beth away.

"I don't believe Signore Valpolicino understood a word you said, and it was rather rude of you to cut in that way," she said with no apparent displeasure. The tiny white silk domino she wore shadowed her eyes, but her lips were tilted in a delighted smile.

"I doubt the relations between Naples and England can be set back much further than the Royal Navy has already done," he replied, also smiling as they glided around the floor. "You are dressed as a red Indian. Tell me, do the women take scalps as well as the men?"

"No, but we're justly famed as skilled torturers."

"Oh, I know well how skilled you are at torture, madam," he whispered against her neck.

The heat of his breath sent a shiver racing through her body. "How did you gain admittance to the palace?" she asked, shifting the conversation to a safer topic.

"I had an invitation. Of course, it was issued to Sir Edmund Osgood, who works for the British chargé d'affaires. I've known Eddie since school days."

"How convenient. Did you come just to dance with me?" *What made me ask that?*

"What other reason could I have?" he murmured, holding her far closer than propriety allowed.

Her laugh was low and seductive. "I do believe I like the obvious reason very much." *What a dangerous game I play,* she scolded herself, then stopped. No. *I'm not the childishly rebellious young prude who arrived in Naples so long ago. I am a woman dedicated to my painting, but that need not mean that I cannot enjoy life's other pleasures as well.*

Her fingers glided over the satin of his cape, which flew rakishly behind him as they danced. She could feel every muscle in his shoulder and her fingertips flexed, digging into the steely hardness. Her eyes were at a level with the broad column of his neck, but she could glance down at the crisp black hair peeking out of the white linen shirt he wore open halfway to his waist. She wanted to bury her face against the wall of flesh, inhale the maleness of his scent. "You make a most convincing highwayman, Derrick. I can imagine you thundering over the moors on a big black stallion, terrorizing the local gentry and making all the ladies swoon even as you rob them."

"I've never owned a black stallion, but I thank you for the compliment nonetheless." He could feel her heart beating in time with his as they whirled about the floor. The high color staining her cheeks and the delicate little pulse at her throat revealed that she was his for the taking. He would take her, yes, but he would not use her, he vowed.

This is the second time I've made exception for you, puss. What is it about you, hmmm? He knew she was certainly not the virginal miss he'd met in America, but then again, what did he really know of Americans? Of her? Perhaps his assessment of her innocence had been wide of the mark even then. She had been alone in the wilderness with only a dog for chaperon. If she had been an amoral free spirit from her childhood days, all the better for this evening's agenda, he assured himself.

When the music stopped, he took her hand, and they made their way across the floor to where the Contessa di Remaldi waited watchfully. Derrick knew the worldly older woman could see what was going on between him and her young charge. He could not imagine that a woman of her reputation would object to Beth's dalliance with him—unless the cunning contessa suspected that he might be a spy using Beth.

I shall simply have to charm her mistrust away. A task easier vowed than accomplished, he knew. Her smile was wide and appeared genuine as she greeted them, offering a hand dripping with sapphires this night, the gems matching the heavy royal blue border on her elegant Grecian robe. She was dressed as the goddess Athena, a most appropriate choice, he thought with wry amusement.

"A notable turnout," the contessa said, scanning all the important court officials around the room, then returning her penetrating black eyes to him as he raised his head after saluting her hand.

"I understand the duke is one of the most ardent supporters of the king among the Neapolitan nobility. It would make sense that everyone of import would attend if invited," he replied with a smile.

"Even though you are a gentleman of some import, how did you receive an invitation, having just arrived two days ago?"

"I went to Eton with a chap who's now working for the chargé d'affaires here. He fell ill and gave me his invitation."

"How convenient," the contessa murmured.

"Precisely what Beth said," he returned with another blinding smile. "Would you be shocked if I confessed that I put an emetic in his afternoon tea in order to be here to dance with Beth?"

The contessa's eyes grew merry. "You are a rogue, sir."

"I am a man who knows what he wants," he replied, his gaze traveling to Beth.

"Ah, but how ruthless are you in obtaining it . . . and to what end?" Her words hung on the air and her expression was once again wary.

Beth had watched the fencing between Vittoria and Derrick with a bit of bemusement. Whyever would her mentor, who had so long urged her to take a lover, object to a man like Derrick Jamison? She must assure her friend. "I shall confess something myself," she interjected into the pregnant silence. "I am flattered that a gentleman would go to such lengths for the pleasure of dancing with me."

"What greater pleasure could there be?" His words were suggestive. "And since they are striking up another waltz, would you do me the honor, Beth?" he asked, bowing as he extended his hand.

Sure of himself, the cheeky devil, the contessa thought, amused in spite of herself. "You had best start dancing lest trouble interrupt. Here comes Bourdin, his majesty's illustrious captain of guards."

"How dare he even approach me after his conduct at the palace the other night?" Beth seethed with fury.

"The Frenchman who attacked you in the garden?" Derrick asked, eyes narrowed on the tall blond wending his way toward them. He was accompanied by a companion, also dressed in the elaborate gold braid uniform of Murat's palace guardsmen.

"Evon Bourdin, late a captain in Napoleon's Grand Army during its ill-fated invasion of Russia. He's a particular favorite of the king. I would not further antagonize him were I you," the contessa cautioned.

"Even if he's an animal who tears the clothes off women in fits of drunken lust?" Derrick asked, clenching his jaw.

Vittoria was silent, but she eyed the Englishman with increased interest.

"As I tried to explain the other night, Derrick, I could have handled him, especially because he was drunk. The first time he attempted it, he was sober, and I put a six-inch gash across his right arm. It quite spoiled his lovely white uniform," Beth said with equal parts disdain and loathing as she stared at Bourdin's pale narrow face. Turning back to Derrick with a smile, she added, "Although I thank you for your gallant dispatch of him in the garden, Vittoria is right. Further antagonizing him would be imprudent."

"You could take his scalp, I suppose," he suggested, attempting to cool his fury. He had been instructed by the British ambassador in Vienna to keep a low profile at Murat's court and make friends among his sycophants, not engage them in duels, he reminded himself.

"I'm wearing my weapon tonight," she replied, her hand resting lightly on a beaded sheath cleverly concealed on the waistband of her dress.

"Good evening, Contessa, Miss Blackthorne," Bourdin said with an oily smile. When neither woman offered him her hand, his insolence remained undaunted. "Surely you do not still hold my impetuosity against me, fair ladies.

61

Beautiful women must be used to driving mere men to rash behavior. May I have the honor of presenting my superior officer, Major Carascossa?" The older man bowed politely as Bourdin continued. "He has been an admirer of the contessa for many years. Perhaps while they become acquainted, you will do me the honor of dancing with me." His words were couched as a demand.

"Major Carascossa and I are already acquainted," Vittoria said with a cool lift of an eyebrow.

"I would not dance with you, Captain," Beth replied, "if my only other choice were to stand still on burning coals."

"Such spirit," he said, reaching for her hand in spite of her clear refusal.

"I believe the lady has made her wishes known in no uncertain terms," Derrick said in perfectly idiomatic French, stepping between them.

The captain turned to Jamison with a brisk nod. "I do not believe we have been introduced, sir."

"Ah, yes, since you were groveling on all fours in the dirt at our last encounter, introductions seemed rather pointless. I am Derrick Jamison, late of London, at your service." He watched with perverse pleasure as the Frenchman's pale complexion reddened with anger. So much for his low profile.

"You were the cur who slipped behind me—"

"As you were forcing yourself on a lady. And as for *cur,* you were the one on all fours. In any case, I'm facing you now, Captain." Jamison's voice was a deadly purr.

"Captain, Mr. Jamison, this is neither the time nor the place for such a display," Major Carascossa said, his French thickened by a Calabrian accent. His eyes moved meaningfully to the Duke di Arcovito and several other important Neapolitan nobles and French favorites at court.

"As always, dear Etore, you are nothing if not discreet," the contessa said to Carascossa, ushering Beth and her Englishman away from the still red-faced Bourdin. "You have made a deadly enemy, signore," she whispered to Derrick.

62

"One the two of you have already made as well," he replied.

"You know nothing of Neapolitan politics. We are women, and women can manage things quite differently. I could have sliced his arm off right in the midst of that waltz and no one at court would have done anything but applaud me," Beth said in an angry whisper. "Bourdin has a filthy reputation with women, which Murat ignores, but the queen would protect me. You she would feed to the *lazzaroni*."

"She is correct. As an Englishman newly arrived in Naples, if you were to have an altercation with one of the king's favorites, the best you could expect would be for their majesties to send you packing immediately."

Derrick smiled at Vittoria. "Then I am in your debt, my lady, since the last thing on earth I wish at this time is to leave your beautiful country." As he spoke, his eyes moved to Beth. "Perhaps it would be wise if we departed while the king's illustrious captain of guards is otherwise occupied?" he suggested to her, adding, "that is, if you and Mr. Turner have concluded your earlier discussion?"

"We have arranged to meet at sunrise the day after tomorrow at the Duomo so that I might see how he paints the light against stone," she replied in acquiescence.

Vittoria, seeing which way the breeze wafted, silently sighed in resignation. With an amused smile, she said, "Take very good care with her, Signore Jamison."

They took his curricle back to the apartments he had let on the Via Roma. The view from his sixth-story window commanded the full sweep of the bay from the Castel Dell' Ovo directly below to Vesuvius smoldering on the southern horizon. A full moon bathed the city in soft white light and silvered the tips of the waves on the water.

"It is quite remarkable. I can see why you love it here," he murmured in her ear, looking over her shoulder as they gazed out the octagonal window in the main salon.

Beth had always admired the handsome old building but never seen the interior of it. The main salon was furnished with spartan elegance, a sofa and Savonarola chairs, a few eclectic occasional tables and a large Venetian tapestry on one wall, but she was far too nervous and excited to take note. Instead she remained by the window, staring out at the bay as he poured them each a brandy from a cut-crystal decanter.

When he handed her a glass she willed her hand to remain steady and took a sip before replying, "I felt as if it were my home within days of arriving. I think I shall never leave . . . except perhaps to visit my family one day."

"But you would return?"

"Naples calls to me. How could I not answer?" she replied.

"You called to me . . . that first morning on the shore . . . like a siren of the sea conjured by my imagination." He punctuated his words with soft, brandy-sweet kisses on her neck and shoulder, moving her heavy plait away for better access to the sensitive nape.

She shivered, growing increasingly uncertain of what she should do next. Heated kisses exchanged in a garden she had experienced with numerous men since coming to Italy, but she had never allowed matters to progress further than that. Never had she wanted to . . . until now. *Remember what Vittoria taught you,* she repeated to herself as he turned her into his arms.

She took a sip from her glass, then offered it to him, turning the rim so he could drink from where her lips had touched. His eyes never left hers as he accepted the brandy, cupping his larger hands around her smaller one, guiding the rim to his lips. He kissed the edge of the glass before he drank deeply. When he returned it to her, Beth, too, kissed the rim where his lips had been, then drained the last sip, her other hand massaging his.

They stood swaying to the sound of a distant mandolin strummed by some lover serenading his lady on the streets below. He took the glass from her and threw it against the stone fireplace, murmuring, "No one else will ever share what we have this night."

With that, he swept her into his arms and carried her

from the salon down a narrow hallway lit by flickering wall sconces into the large bedroom at the end. Moonlight spilled in from a set of small windows overlooking the large round bed, which sat on a dais elevated by three steps. Pillows were piled in front of the ornately carved walnut headboard. He sent them bouncing every which way as he pulled down the coverlet with one hand, holding her tightly against his body with the other arm.

"Lie back," he commanded, easing her onto the snowy softness of sheer linen. Then he moved about the room, lighting dozens of creamy white candles, arranging them in a semicircle around the bed until the room glowed with rich warm light. If she had hoped her inexperience would be obscured in the dimness of moonlight, she now realized he would be able to see every inch of her naked body. Of course, she could see every inch of his as well. The thought sent fire singing through her veins.

Beth watched light and shadow play across the chiseled planes and angles of his face; he was strikingly beautiful in a completely masculine, virile way. Derrick's deep-set eyes were rimmed with long black lashes and punctuated by heavy slashes of eyebrow, his mouth firm and wide, his jawline bold and faintly darkened by his heavy beard.

When he bent over to remove his boots, that errant lock of black hair tumbled onto his forehead. Moving with pantherish grace, he approached the bed, pausing at the first step, one bare foot resting on the top of the dais as his hungry eyes swept over her. Although Beth had posed as a nude model, she felt self-conscious lying back on a mound of pillows, still fully clothed. Did he expect her to disrobe in front of him? As if in answer to her question, he stepped onto the platform in one swift stride and sat down beside her, reaching for her foot.

Raising it slowly, he slid her buckskin skirt up her leg, then unlaced the thongs on her high moccasin, sliding it off her foot and tossing it to the floor. His hand curved around the arch of her bare foot, massaging it. "I feel like purring," she breathed softly.

He chuckled, repeating the process on her other foot.

"Oh, I intend to make you purr, puss." His fingers caressed the delicate flesh of her inner thighs until she gasped in pleasure. "Such a responsive pussycat," he murmured, taking her hand and pulling her up into his arms for a soft series of kisses across her face and neck. Then he leaned back and whispered, "Unplait your hair for me."

Trembling with excitement, she reached up and tugged the fat braid over her shoulder, unfastening the beaded thong and working her fingers through the heavy silken mane until it blanketed her shoulders. She could feel his hot eyes burning her even though she did not look up until she had completed the task. "Is this what you wish?" she asked softly, daring to raise her eyes to his once more.

"God, yes," he said hoarsely, then knelt on the bed and pulled her up against him, his arm holding her tightly as his mouth claimed hers in a deep, hungry kiss.

Beth was dimly aware of her belt being removed and the shoulder ties of her gown being unfastened, but when he slipped the top of the heavy buckskin down her arms, baring her breasts to the cool night air, her lethargy evaporated. Once before she had felt the heat of his mouth on a nipple. In anticipation, both globes tingled, their tips hardening into nubs that ached for his touch. Ever so lightly, he cupped one in each hand, lifting, running his thumbs over the incredibly sensitive nipples until she cried out incoherently, arching against his caresses, desperate for more. "Your mouth . . . I want your mouth . . ." she said with a boldness she never imagined she could muster.

"And I will taste; but you as an artist understand that first my eyes must feast," he murmured before lowering his head to take one deep pink bud into his mouth, teasing it with the tip of his tongue, suckling deeply until she moaned and dug her fingers into his hair, pressing him closer. He moved between her breasts, murmuring praise for their perfection.

Beth's head dropped back, her eyes closed as she arched into his caresses. At length he slid his hands over her ribs to span her waist, pushing the buckskin gown lower. His mouth followed, the tip of his tongue swirling and teasing her navel as he worked the soft leather over the flair of her hips. As the gown pooled around her legs, they knelt facing each other on the bed. He cupped her buttocks in his hands, kneading their firmness, murmuring, "Is it an American custom for ladies to wear no undergarments—if so, I heartily approve."

"Only the Indian women," she gasped as he buried his fist in her hair and tugged gently, nuzzling her throat.

"Then I heartily approve of your red kinswomen," he replied between kisses.

She could feel the crisp abrasion of his chest hair against her bare breasts, and lower where his hips rocked hers in gentle rhythm, she could feel the pressure of his erection. That male mystery she had studied in art anatomy books but had never seen in an aroused state, although Vittoria had described it in considerable detail. Some primal instinct led her to rub her pelvis against the protuberance until he growled a low oath.

"I think we're finished with seduction, or I'll not be able to contain myself for your pleasure, love," he whispered as he laid her back on the bed, then stood up and began to disrobe.

She watched as he tore off his shirt, and the muscles of his upper arms and chest flexed and rippled. A light dusting of black hair covered his forearms and a much heavier pattern of it veed down from his chest to vanish beneath the waistband of his pants. Her eyes followed avidly as he unfastened the buttons of his fly and started to tug off the tight breeches. The sun had bronzed his upper body as darkly as the olive-skinned men of the Mediterranean, but his lower parts were much paler. Every inch of him was lean, powerful and graceful. He was utterly magnificent. Her eyes traveled to his engorged staff, jutting proudly from the thick black hair at the base of his pelvis. He reached down and stroked it lightly, murmuring, "A poor thing, but mine own."

She could see one pearly drop of semen glistening on the tip. Licking her lips, she replied in a raspy whisper, "Not poor . . . beautiful . . . oh my, yes."

Derrick grinned, looking into her heavy-lidded eyes. The candlelight brought out the golden flecks in their depths. Her mouth was slightly parted and her breath erratic, her body writhing on the sheets, eager for him to join her. He placed one knee on the edge of the mattress and then leaned over her, arms straight, bearing his weight as he gazed intently into her face. "This is going to last all night," he vowed.

Chapter Six

His weight bore her into the soft mattress as his mouth claimed hers. This time the kisses were not gentle but deep, his tongue plunging in and out of her mouth, a harbinger of that other more intimate penetration to come. Beth felt his knee press between her thighs. Vittoria had explained to her that the first time could hurt a woman a bit, especially if her lover were not careful to make her fully ready to receive him. After his long seduction she could not imagine how she could be made to want this coming together more. "Now, Derrick, now . . ."

"Your every wish . . ." he murmured, rising up, trembling with his own long-suppressed need. She opened her legs, clamping them instinctively around his hips as he pressed the head of his shaft at her portal, rotating it to spread the creamy moisture on her nether lips. She was so hot and ready.

Slow. He had promised it would take all night. Well, perhaps the first time might go quickly, but the night was long and he would not leave her. He plunged inside of her with one smooth, slick glide, feeling her incredible tightness . . . and just the faintest hint of a barrier being breached. Did he imagine her body recoiling the slightest bit? When her arms and legs clung to him, nails digging into his shoulders, thighs pressed against his hips, all thought ceased and pure animal instinct took over. He began to stroke deep and strong, holding an even pace to prolong the exquisite pleasure of their joining.

The first penetration did hurt. But it was little more than a swift pinch, instantly forgotten in the wonder of being stretched and filled with his hard hot flesh. *So this is the mystery of men and women, the two becoming one, an end to the ache caused by desire.* Beth gloried in his powerful body laboring over hers, hard against soft, dark against pale, hairy against smooth. She sought his mouth for another kiss, this time catching the rhythm of his thrusts above and below, kissing him back even as her hips began to arch and rotate in the dance as old as nature itself.

What began as pure wonder over new sensation, joy in intimacy, soon changed as the heat of slick flesh gliding over slick flesh created a growing pleasure that defied any description, was unlike anything she had ever before experienced in her life. Slowly, gradually, it built . . . and built. Had he not said it would last all night? As the ecstasy grew stronger, she became uncertain if she could sustain such a surfeit of pleasure without dying of it. Yet there was something . . . just out of her reach . . . something she strained toward, worked for, craved with every fiber of mind and body.

Derrick crooned, growled, groaned low words of love and sex, praise for her beauty and the pleasure she was giving him, all the while holding off, waiting for her to reach culmination. Then at last he felt the first faint tremors quivering through her body and with a lusty sigh gave in to his own release.

The craving intensified until Beth was certain she would go mad, and then the contractions began, wrenching her with their incredible sweetness, searing her with their intensity. Her whole body shook and bucked. She cried out his name and dug her nails into the bunched muscles of his back, suddenly aware that his body was shaking, too. His spine stiffened as his staff swelled even more tightly within her, releasing life deep against her womb, intensifying her pleasure a thousandfold.

They lay, spent and panting, their skin slick with perspiration despite the night's coolness. He rolled to his side, carrying her with him. She rested her head against his chest, feeling the strong, swift beating of his heart gradually slow.

"That was . . . wonderful." She had started to say, *even more wonderful than I had imagined it could be,* but caught herself. Perhaps he would not notice that she had been a virgin. Beth certainly did not want any offers to "do the honorable thing." She had entered into this seduction with no expectations of anything more than learning the pleasures of coupling, having a brief liaison before returning to the isolation and discipline of her work.

Are you sure that is all you want? some tiny voice deep within her whispered. When his hand cupped her chin gently and raised her face so he could gaze into her eyes, she was almost undone. She could have drowned in the depths of his dark blue eyes if not for the troubled expression on his face.

"Yes, it was exceptional, quite extraordinary, as a matter of fact . . . but why, puss, do I suspect I'd be considerably better able to assess that than you, hmmm?" His hand moved from her face down between their bodies, sliding between her thighs.

She flinched, not in pain but embarrassment. There it was, that faint smear of blood Vittoria had warned her about. "Do you mind terribly?" she asked, trying to read his expression.

He raised himself up on one elbow, looking down at her. "It has been quite a while since I deflowered a virgin. I never expected you to be one."

"I did not intend to mislead you," she replied, her earlier euphoria quickly turning to misery.

"You did much to mislead me—dressing like a peasant

wench, traveling unchaperoned, allowing me to take liberties, returning my kisses with considerable fervor, not to mention skill."

"I've practiced kissing with other men," she said stiffly, never expecting to be so hurt by his words.

"But quite obviously never allowed any of them what you allowed me."

"Don't preen overmuch." She struggled to keep her tone light. "I decided it was past time I had a lover. I'll make no claim on you, Derrick—you do not have to marry me."

"I did not offer," he replied, his voice cool, flat.

"I cherished no hope that you would," she snapped back, hurt giving way to anger now. She rolled away from him and started to climb off the bed, but he caught her wrist and pulled her back down beside him. "Let me go." She bit off each word.

"Not until I'm satisfied."

"I may be new at this, but I'm reasonably certain you have been quite 'satisfied,' " she replied sarcastically.

He caressed the pulse on her wrist with his thumb, feeling the thrum of her anger. "Let me rephrase that. I only want to understand why you chose me to bestow your virginity upon—not that I did not greatly enjoy it," he hastened to add, still massaging her wrist, refusing to release her.

"You appealed to me more than any of the other men I've met at court. 'Tis as simple as that."

He chuckled, laughing more at himself than at her. "Nothing about this or you is simple. I take it your decision to take a lover was made after you came to Naples, not back in America—or did none of the backwoods bumpkins appeal?"

"You are an arrogant lout." She tried to pull away again. And again he refused to release her. If only he would cease that maddening caress with his thumb!

"It's part of my charm. You are a bold vixen, which is also part of your charm. I imagine your interest in the amorous arts began at the contessa's urging?"

"I told her I had no desire to tie myself to a husband

who would forbid me to paint and live my life as I choose. Men, here or in America, are mostly the same."

"And you speak from such vast reservoirs of experience," he replied, his tone growing lighter.

"The only way to obtain the experience and see if Vittoria's descriptions of what I was missing were correct was to take a lover."

"I wait with bated breath for you to give me your evaluation." Now his teasing grin was unmistakable.

When he began to pull her back to him, she did not resist. How could she when he looked at her that way? She reached up to brush that lock of hair from his forehead, returning his grin. "Vain man. Yes, she was right. I was missing something quite delightful. Are you satisfied now?"

"Oh, no, not satisfied at all . . . remember, I gave my word this would last all night . . . and the word of an Englishman can never be broken. . . ."

"I must say, you look inordinately pleased with yourself . . . or mayhap you are pleased with your new bit-o-muslin," Drum said sourly as he unleashed Sir Percival after returning from their morning walk, a chore he considered slightly above cleaning privies but below sweeping chimneys.

The spaniel quickly trotted over to the gondola chair in the corner and climbed onto it, his nails snagging in the expensive velvet upholstery. Feeling utterly sated and mellow, Derrick ignored the infraction. Dressed in a navy blue silk banyan, he leaned back against his chair and stretched contentedly, then picked up his mug of steaming black coffee and took a sip. "I am pleased, and yes, 'tis because of her, but the term 'bit-o-muslin' seems inadequate."

"She is quite a fetching piece, I'll grant, if one prefers the Amazonian sort." At Derrick's quizzical look, Drum explained, "I witnessed your fond adieu from across the plaza." Drum cocked one eyebrow in sardonic amusement. "It must have been quite an entertaining evening . . . judging by the lingering farewell."

73

"Oh, it was . . . she was."

"I say, old fellow, surely you aren't smitten?" A look of consternation flashed across his face.

"Hardly anything that would involve leg-shackling, no. Beth Blackthorne is an utter free spirit who—"

"Blackthorne?" Drum interrupted. "Of the Georgia Blackthornes?" His tone was incredulous . . . and deadly.

Derrick set down his cup and studied the little dandy's inexplicable expression. "As a matter of fact, yes, she is, but how the devil would you know about them? They're Americans."

"As it happens, Alex Blackthorne, late of London, is a very dear friend . . . who has fondly mentioned a time or two over the years the only daughter of his uncle Quint. She is his favorite cousin, an innocent from a very prominent family, not at all some 'free spirit' for the likes of a bored aristocrat to despoil!"

"I am not a bored aristocrat," Derrick shot back.

"Ah ha! But you did despoil her, did you not?" When Derrick made no immediate disclaimer, he huffed, "I thought as much. Well, you shall simply have to wed her, old chap, and there's an end to it."

"Are you insane!" Derrick jumped up from his seat and glared down at the much smaller man. "I shall do no such cork-brained thing."

"Do not make me call you out, sir. I assure you I am a far better swordsman or pistol shot than you." Drum looked up his nose at the thunderous expression on Derrick's face, utterly undaunted.

"Don't be absurd. We are on a mission for his majesty's government. Enough blood's been spent between England and the thrice-damned French without one of us killing the other while Bonaparte escapes to resume the war." Derrick fought to rein in his temper, although what he truly wished to do was throttle the arrogant little dandy, whose boast about dueling skills was not at all idle.

Drummond appeared to consider for a moment, stroking his chin. "No, I imagine that would be sapskulled. If I killed you, your Miss Blackthorne would have no husband, would she? Hmmm. Perhaps I should merely lame you. Then you could not run from your duty."

"There is no 'duty' from which to run, you chuckle-headed fool," Derrick gritted out. "You're completely misjudging the circumstances—"

"Pray, enlighten me then." The little man crossed his arms over his chest and waited, his foot tapping on the rug impatiently.

"She has spent the past three years under the tutelage of the Contessa di Remaldi." At Drum's horrified expression, Derrick said dryly, "It would seem you've heard of her."

"Considering that female's reputation, I am considerably amazed that Miss Blackthorne remained a virgin for you to despoil—although the fact is that you were the one to do the deed," Drum reiterated stubbornly.

"She wished to be relieved of her innocence and knew precisely where our relationship was headed from the moment it began. Beth is a painter of some skill who wishes to earn her own way, shackled to no man."

"How convenient. If she cannot support herself by painting, she can always fall back on the skills you have taught her." Drum's tone was more appalled than angry now.

"Whatever the young woman does, it signifies nothing to you." Turning his back, Derrick stalked from the room. Sir Percival growled very softly as he passed.

"We shall see about that, old chap . . . we shall just see," Drum murmured to himself.

"I cannot imagine why you don't like him, Derrick. He's an absolute dear," Beth said, scratching Sir Percival's ears.

"It is not so much that I dislike him as that he dislikes me, but since he was a gift from my best friend at Eton, I dare not give him away."

"He reminds me of Barnsmell."

"I rest my case," Derrick replied with a mock shudder. "He nearly broke my neck."

" 'Twas the chicken's neck he broke, not yours." Now she could laugh about their first meeting. "But this noble

Shirl Henke

beast"—she gave the black-and-white spaniel an affectionate thump—"has broken nothing whatever."

Overjoyed with her attention, the dog began beating his
tail on the floor and jumping around. Just as Drum stepped
down onto the terrace carrying a heavily laden tray, the
spaniel gave a loud bark and lunged backward, directly in
his path. A Sevres coffeepot, a pitcher of cream and a loaf
of sugar all went sailing from the tray as the startled Drum
tried to regain his footing. Pieces of china shattered on the
flagstones of the terrace balcony, which was now liberally
coated with coffee, cream and gritty sugar.

The dog beat a hasty retreat, tracking the muck into the
house as Drum cursed creatively under his breath while
kneeling to scoop up the broken dishes. Derrick laughed
uproariously, turning to Beth. "I believe you were saying
something about this noble beast . . ."

She put her fingers to her mouth to stifle a chuckle as
the servant's smothered cursing grew louder. Poor man
could have broken *his* neck, and here they were laughing
about Sir Percival! "Oh, Derrick, you really place too
much burden on Drummond. I'm certain the contessa
knows some reliable maids who could help with cleaning
and such about the place. Do you want me to inquire for
you?"

"I require no assistance whatever, save for someone to
resurrect Lucrezia Borgia so she may poison that cursed
hellhound," Drum snarled, tossing the last of the china on
the tray and stomping back into the house.

"I do not believe your manservant approves of me,"
Beth said, her good humor evaporating like bay fog. In
truth, vestiges of her strict Episcopalian upbringing in a
close-knit family still made her uncomfortable about her
relationship with Derrick.

" 'Tis not you of whom he disapproves but me." He
raised his wineglass and sipped lazily. They had spent the
late morning abed after Beth had given the sunrise hours
to painting under the critical eye of J. M. W. Turner, the
preeminent English landscape artist. Glowing with his
praise, she had come rushing to Derrick's place to share

76

the good news. He had spent the preceding night at the villa of a French officer, pretending to be drunk while gleaning information about how Murat and Napoleon exchanged correspondence, not returning home until well past four. Beth had teased him about being a lazy slugabed before he had pulled her into his embrace. That had been several delightful hours ago.

When they finally emerged from his bedroom, after what Derrick was certain was a rather noisy romp, he had ordered Drum to serve them a light repast. For the past several days since their appalling argument about marriage, the little dandy had said nothing more regarding the unsettling matter. But his disapproval oozed from every pore, while at the same time he gave off an aura of sly satisfaction, which might have worried Derrick if he had not been so occupied with Beth and his mission.

"Whyever would you employ a servant who so openly dislikes you?" she asked, more puzzled than upset. She would gladly have taken Sir Percival if Derrick could have given him away, but as to Mr. Drummond, that was another matter entirely. When they had walked into the salon that morning, obviously disheveled and sated, the servant had done little to conceal his disapproval.

How to explain that one? "Er, he has certain skills that are invaluable."

"Such as?" she asked, raising one eyebrow, now more interested in teasing him than in learning about the stuffy little Englishman. Lord, but Derrick Jamison was the most splendid figure of a man she had ever seen. Nothing, not even her own puritanical qualms, could for long daunt her delight in being with him.

A bit of the truth would not hurt if generously leavened with fabrication. "I fear my family insisted. He's a crack shot and quite deadly with a foil. I have a penchant for trouble, which you may have noticed that first evening at the palace . . . not that you don't share it."

"I can understand how you might drive a man into a killing rage, but Drummond a bodyguard? That gnat of a man?"

Just as she said the words, Drummond appeared at the door. If he had overheard, he gave no indication, except to Derrick, who noted the imperceptible narrowing of his cool green eyes. "A message for you, sir." He presented a small silver tray with a note on it, then turned and left the terrace.

As Derrick scanned the missive, Beth looked out over the balcony at the city below them. She had everything now. Naples, her work and a man to love. But did *he* love *her*? Where had that thought come from? Of course he was not in love with her—any more than she was in love with him! Being lovers implied just that, a physical relationship, nothing more. *Then why do you want more?*

Her troubling thoughts were interrupted by the cause of them. "You're in a brown study all of a sudden, puss. What were you thinking to mar that lovely face—not still brooding about Drum, I hope?"

"Oh, no. It was nothing really, just a bit of homesickness," she prevaricated.

"It's been three years since you've seen your family. That is a long while," he murmured, thinking fleetingly of his own family.

She shrugged. "Eventually I will return for a visit, but they own a fleet of ships. If Papa weren't so disapproving of my desire to paint, they could have visited me in Naples long before now." Visions of Quintin Blackthorne's reaction to her relationship with Derrick were more than a little unsettling. She changed the subject. "What about your family? You have never spoken of them, other than to say you are a second son."

His expression turned from warm and smiling to grim. "I said I was a scapegrace; in fact, nearly a scapegallows as well."

"And the old earl did not approve," she guessed.

"He was a rigid man of the old school . . . duty to king and country, to family, to the Church . . . to everything which, according to him 'holds civilization together.' At least, the English definition of it."

"That sounds little different than the way Americans

view life. But you put me in mind of another irredeemable rascal, my cousin Alex."

"It greatly lightens my mind that you Americans have produced some rogues equal to me." Drum had mentioned his friend Alex, although Derrick certainly had no intention of explaining that to Beth. Instead he asked, "Alex is the one with the English wife you've referred to, is he not?"

"My favorite cousin. We got into all sorts of scrapes together as children. I imagine he's leading Joss a merry chase. I would love to meet her, but they sailed for America just as war broke out. What of your brother, the new earl?" she asked, hoping he had some redeemable family relationship left now that the old earl was gone.

"Leighton gave me the cut direct the last time we met in London. I'm no longer received at Lynden Hall." He was unable to keep the bitterness from his voice.

"And he is your only brother? Have you no other family?" Coming from an enormous extended family with siblings, aunts, uncles and cousins by the dozens, Beth found it difficult to imagine being once alone in the world.

"Oh, a few cousins once or twice removed. The direct Jamison line will die out, I'm afraid, unless Leighton does his duty and provides an heir for the title."

She snorted. "That is the way a man would think of it."

"And how, pray, does a woman think of it?"

"It is the countess, not the earl, who must perform the difficult duty of providing an heir."

It was his turn to shrug now, his mood lightening. "I will concede that the man's role is considerably less difficult than the woman's."

"But a woman may certainly enjoy the initiation of the process equally as much as a man."

"Only if the man is a skilled initiator," he said smugly.

"You are insufferably vain," she replied, rising to leave. "I promised to meet Vittoria and I am already late."

She kissed him quickly and started for the door as he called after her, "The very reason you are late is reason enough for me to be vain."

*   *   *

"Gnat of a man, indeed!" Drum huffed. He had been in high dudgeon ever since Beth departed. "I've a good mind to suggest to Alex when next we meet that he should take that impudent young baggage and paddle her backside." He looked over at Derrick, who remained seated at the table on the terrace staring out at the bay. "By the by, old fellow, what are you going to do about the Oil Merchant?"

"You read the message before bringing it to me." It was not a question.

Nor did it require an answer. "I don't trust the froggies, and I trust their Italian minions even less. How do we know his information is reliable?"

Jamison grinned. "Spoken like a true Englishman. My sources in Naples vouch that he's expert at breaking codes and reading sympathetic ink. If he wants to meet with me, I think it worthwhile."

Drum shrugged. "It may be your funeral."

"Since you'll be covering my back, it had best be yours first, old chap."

The "Oil Merchant" was his code name. He was known to the British Foreign Office, even though he was in the pay of the restored Bourbon monarchy in France. A short, rotund man with an ever-ready smile and the unctuous manner of a street peddler, he waited in the deep shadows of the old church, Santa Maria del Carmine. The flickering lights from hundreds of votive candles gave off a reddish glow, faint in the small alcove where he hid, pretending to pray at the small altar. His ear remained alert for the sound of the Englishman's footfalls.

"Will the Eagle soar once again?" Jamison used the agreed-upon passwords.

Alessandro Forli spun around, crossing himself in reflex, surprised at how silently such a big man could move. "You are late," he whispered angrily to cover up his unease.

"That is not the appropriate response," Jamison replied, turning to leave.

"Not if we clip his wings." The Englishman stopped but remained standing. "Even if you are a heretic, kneel beside me so we may talk without drawing attention."

"No one is about. It's the middle of the bloody night," Derrick replied but knelt all the same. "What do you have for me?"

From a choir loft high in the back of the church, Drum observed the conversation taking place between his countryman and the Italian. He kept a pair of Egg pistols cocked and ready to fire should the need arise.

After an exchange that lasted a good quarter of an hour, Jamison rose and left the fat man in front of the altar. By the time he reached the church door Drum was waiting for him, weapons nowhere in sight. "Was it worthwhile?"

"Quite. A bit of spiritual uplifting would do wonders for you as well, my man. You should try prayer sometime."

"Quite amusing," his companion drawled as they set out down the steps and crossed the piazza just as a light drizzle began to fall.

"The Polish Wife paid a visit to Napoleon last week," Derrick said.

The Polish Wife was the derisive title given to a young Polish noblewoman who had become the emperor's mistress during his earlier triumphs against Russia. Unlike his other paramours, the Countess Maria Laczynska Walewska remained fiercely devoted to Napoleon after his fall from power. She moved freely around the capitals of Europe and was a trustworthy courier for her lover.

"So, the plot does thicken. Hmmm," Drum said as Derrick finished his summary.

"Murat's backwater country is not the key to the conspiracy. Forli agreed with me. That crafty Corsican is going to head straight for Paris, Italy be damned. If only those buffleheads in the Foreign Office would see it," Derrick said in frustration. "I should be in Marseilles or Monaco, or in Livorno if I must remain in Italy. At least there I could observe the ships coming and going from Elba."

"Leaving Naples would mean leaving Beth Blackthorne. Are you certain you could do that?" Drum asked.

The question took Derrick by surprise. Of course he

could . . . couldn't he? "I would regret it, naturally," he said.

"Naturally," Drum echoed. Was there just a hint of a smirk in his voice?

"Normally when a relationship is this new, neither partner is ready to cry off—if they suit, that is."

"And you and she do suit, don't you?"

"Not in the manner you mean," Derrick snapped. "I do wish—"

"Quiet," Drum hissed. Without another word he dropped back into the shadow of an awning.

Derrick continued walking down the long narrow street. It was nearly three in the morning and all the taverns and public houses had closed hours ago. Other than the occasional bark of a stray dog, not a sound could be heard . . . but for the pad of soft-soled shoes over cobblestones.

He rested his hand on the butt of the pistol he wore at his waist beneath his cloak. A wicked knife was concealed in his boot as well. It might be a good idea to rid himself of the long outer garment if he was forced to fight in close quarters. Just as he began to unfasten his cloak, the footfalls suddenly accelerated. Derrick reached down and slipped the knife into one hand while his other withdrew the pistol from his belt. He whirled around, sending the cloak flying at the first attacker, stopping the assailant's progress when the man's dagger became entangled in the voluminous cloth.

As he stumbled back trying to free himself, the second thug shot but missed. Cursing, the assassin withdrew a second pistol, but before he could raise it to fire, Derrick ploughed into the first man, knocking him back into the arms of his comrade. From up the street Jamison could hear the crack of a single shot. Drum. He must be dealing with still more assassins.

"I could use some help here, old chap," he called out as his two attackers quickly disentangled themselves and faced him, pistols and knives gleaming in the moonlight.

There was something familiar about the taller one, although his face was obscured by one of the broad-billed straw fedoras worn by the peasantry. With no time to consider that, he fired his own weapon, and the tall man dropped his pistol, turned and fled into an alleyway. Derrick could see that his shot had found its mark; the man held one arm. The first attacker, armed only with a wickedly long stiletto, faced him since his path into the alley was cut off by Derrick.

The two antagonists circled each other, knives at the ready, each feinting, testing the other's strengths, looking for an opening. The assassin was smaller, his reach not as long as Derrick's, but his agility was considerable and he was lightning quick, grazing his opponent's arm the first time they crossed blades. Trapped, he wasted no words, concentrating with single-minded intensity on the task of killing. Derrick knew that made him doubly dangerous.

Back down the street, Drum stood over the body of one dead assassin, looking at the other as he withdrew the length of his sword from the man's heart. He had intended to take this second one alive for interrogation, but it was not to be. Hearing Derrick yell for help, he turned and swiftly darted down the street toward the sounds of a fight in progress.

The deadly ballet played out before him. He had never seen Derrick work before, and was curious to learn if he was any good. He was. So was his opponent; an even match, Drum observed, holding his sword ready to intervene if the fight turned against his countryman. Derrick parried a lightning-swift strike to his left, then feinted to the right, high but scoring in a lowering arc that sliced through the assassin's shirt, bloodying his sternum. The Italian grunted, seeming impervious to what must have been considerable pain. Both men were cut, neither dangerously . . . yet.

Derrick had seldom seen a man fight so ferociously. His muscles screamed and numerous nicks and slices stung, his breath coming out in low pants, matched by those of his foe. *He's tiring, too . . .* Derrick backed off, moving his blade back and forth at waist level, as if trying to retreat. *Come on . . . come on . . .*

The thug took the bait. He had seen Drum standing in the background, and desperation made him rash. He lunged forward, trying to thrust over Derrick's blade and sink his own in his foe's throat. Just as the killer's arm extended with blurring speed, Derrick dodged to the left while seizing the Italian's right arm, jerking him off balance. The thug's blade sliced harmlessly over Derrick's arm as his own knife plunged directly into the assassin's gut. A harsh swift hiss of agony accompanied the sound of the knife as Derrick shoved it upward toward the heart, then allowed the corpse to drop onto the cobblestones, which quickly grew red with gore.

"Done to a cow's thumb, old chap. Couldn't have handled it better m'self," Drum drawled, fastidiously cleaning the blood from his slim sword before sliding it inside his polished walnut walking stick. He rolled the dead man over onto his back with the toe of one boot. "Pity you had to kill him."

"You could have intervened."

"I would have rescued you if need occurred. Besides, I wanted to take your measure first. From what I have observed, the Blackthorne women expect courage from their men."

"Will you cease and desist with that!" Derrick hissed angrily.

Drummond did not deign to reply, instead looked around the deserted street. "Two others lie dead under the awning. What happened to the fourth man?"

"I hit him, but he got away down that alley."

"Any idea who they might have been? The dead ones look like *lazzaroni.*"

"The other did not seem so . . ." Derek replied.

Drum looked up to where a candle had finally been lit in a fourth-story window down the street. "We'd best be away lest we end up answering to the local constabulary— or worse, some of the king's Frenchie guardsmen."

Derrick gathered up his cloak and they slipped quickly down the street. "The man who escaped looked familiar to me. Taller, muscular, clean shaven . . . there was something I recognized in the arrogant way he moved—Bourdin! I'd bet my last guinea on it. Your mention of Murat's guardsmen must have triggered the association."

"The rotter from whom you rescued Miss Blackthorne? He'd certainly have reason enough," Drum mused.

"If it was that simple, why not call me out? He's purported to be quite the deadly duelist."

"You think he plays a deeper game, then? That would mean Murat is aware of your mission. Things could get rather sticky for us in Naples, old chap."

"Perhaps he works for the king . . . or someone else . . . We won't be leaving Naples just yet—and I'll have to send a report to our contact via Sir Percival tonight. You'd best change into dry clothes before you set out, old chap."

"How solicitous of you," Drum groused as they trudged through the rain toward their apartments.

Chapter Seven

Beth sat back and looked critically at the scene she had just sketched. Her hours spent with Mr. Turner had proven invaluable. But then, so had the hours spent with Derrick, she thought as her mouth spread in one of the dreamy, foolish grins about which Vittoria continually teased her.

The warm golden days of autumn were now blending with the slight nip of what passed for winter in the Mediterranean. The weeks had flown into months and she had been painting more productively than ever. Perhaps having a lover was as conducive to her art as instruction from the famous J. M. W. Turner. She was deliriously happy . . . as long as she kept busy and did not think about the time when Derrick Jamison would return to England and their magic interlude would end.

"He is the son of an earl, and as such he will sooner or later be forced into making a suitable marriage," the contessa had warned only a week ago as they were sharing an early evening meal at the villa.

"And you have made me more than aware that I am not

'suitable,' " she had replied, striving for a light and unconcerned tone.

"*Cara,* it is never my intention to hurt you, but I do not want him to hurt you either." Vittoria sighed. "Perhaps with a first love it is inevitable."

"Do you still love Piero?" Beth asked softly.

The contessa sipped from her wineglass, considering her words. She had confided about her first lover, a goldsmith's son, deemed unworthy by her family because he was a commoner and a Jew. The unthinkable misalliance was quashed by arranging her marriage to an older nobleman whose vast estates adjoined their own when she had barely turned seventeen. Piero Torres had left Naples for America, and although she had never seen him again, a small part of the practical Vittoria would always mourn for what might have been.

"Sometimes I think of him and wonder if he prospered in your country . . . he had kinsmen there, I think."

"You have not answered me," Beth chided gently. "I asked if you still loved him."

Vittoria shrugged and smiled. "Who is to say what that means, that much used word *love.* I prize many things and people . . . I do not think of love in the way you define it."

"Oh, and how, pray, do I define it?"

"Being *in* love, completely wrapped up in one person upon whom your entire happiness depends, needing to spend the rest of your life together, bound by marriage vows and children," Vittoria replied, studying Beth's expression.

"If you think that is what I want with Derrick Jamison, or with any man, you could not be more mistaken. I would have to give up painting and become someone who lives by society's rules, someone who is not me, someone I would grow to hate . . . and in the process I would come to hate my husband as well. No, I shall not do that, Vittoria."

"Ah, *cara,* why do I fear that you have already taken the first step?" the contessa had murmured sadly, more to herself than to Beth.

Shirl Henke

Giving herself a mental shake, Beth returned to her sketching and tried to put that troubling exchange with her friend out of her mind. Did she truly, in her heart of hearts, want to spend her life with Derrick, bear his children?

"Well, it's not possible, so I'd best content myself with enjoying our time together, however brief. There will be other men after he is gone." *Liar*, a voice deep within replied.

"I simply cannot credit it! Our Elizabeth, behaving like a common . . . courtesan." Quintin Blackthorne struggled for a word not quite so harsh as the one that first sprang to mind when he read Drum's letter.

His wife Madelyne, sitting calmly while he paced furiously, tried to soothe his raging temper, something she had spent the major portion of her life doing. "In the first place, Quint, Beth is not selling her favors to Mr. Jamison."

"Oh, no? What would you call it, then?"

He threw down the letter, which she had read before he returned to Savannah, since it had been addressed to both of them. She had taken the time to read between the lines and consider what Alex's friend had really intended to convey. "Beth is in love with the Englishman, who is certainly from a good family. They do things differently in Europe than—"

"They damned well do," he snapped furiously. "They are decadent lechers who would take advantage of an innocent's virtue and laugh at the consequences. Well, there will be consequences—consequences that the Honorable Derrick Jamison will not find amusing!"

"Now, Quint, calm down!"

"I am quite calm, darling," he replied, moderating his tone with gritted teeth, as he pulled on his greatcoat.

"Where are you going?" Now Madelyne was alarmed.

"To the city to check Dev's sailing schedules. I will be on his next ship to Naples."

* * *

88

"Now, hold still—no, no, not like that. You look as if you've just taken a seat on a sharply pointed stick!" Beth burst into laughter as Derrick's face darkened thunderously.

"Mock me, will you? And yet you dare to ask that I sit for a portrait." He reached over and grabbed her sketchbook from her hand. "Let me see if—"

"Oh, no, you don't," she cried, seizing back the pad and shoving him firmly down onto the ancient oak limb lying across the mossy floor of the glade. "Now, lean back as I showed you, there's the way . . . just relax . . ." Her voice faded as she tried to concentrate.

Beth recalled vividly when she'd finally worked up sufficient courage to ask him to pose for her. One morning she had awakened in his bed, drowsy and sated from a long and lovely night of making love, to observe him as he slept, bathed in the soft, golden glow of the rising sun. He lay on his side, facing her, one powerful leg thrown possessively over her thigh, a hand warm against her breast. She had eased slowly away, careful not to awaken him so that she could study the sheer male beauty of his naked body.

Thank God, the superficial nicks and cuts he had received during the attempted robbery outside that gambling den had disappeared weeks ago without adding to the scars he already bore. Still, even those scars only added to his virile allure. His long lean frame filled the bed, skin dark against the pristine whiteness of the sheets. How, she had wondered, did an Englishman living in cold northern climes get so deeply tanned? Her fingertips traced the pattern of black hair on the back of his hand and forearm, marveling at the slim strength and beauty of his hands, hands that could control a powerful team of horses or caress her flesh with consummate skill.

He stretched and rolled over onto his back, affording her a better view. His shoulders were wide, his chest thick and powerful, covered with an even heavier growth of black hair, which then tapered into a narrow line toward his navel and arrowed to the black bush where his phallus lay dormant in repose. His body was contoured with lithe muscles that rippled more than bulged when he moved. But most of all she loved his face. The shadow of his black whiskers should have given him a piratical air, and would have had he been awake. But asleep his expression was younger, almost boyish, as she brushed that always errant curl of inky hair from his brow. She studied the arch of his eyebrows, the high planes of his cheekbones, the straight clean line of his jaw, but most of all, his mouth. The heat of it had the power to scald her. When he kissed her it had the power to draw her very soul from her body.

The ancients, so she had read, believed that when a person's likeness was captured in a picture, a part of his soul was owned by the one who possessed the likeness. *You own my soul, Derrick . . . why should I not claim at least a small part of yours?* Her disturbing and bold thought had been interrupted at that very instant when he awakened, capturing her wrist in his hand. He brought her palm to his mouth and kissed it. Before she could lose her nerve, Beth found herself blurting out, "I want to paint you, Derrick."

He had refused at first, but she had cajoled and teased until she finally agreed to allow her to do some sketches. To her surprise and secret amusement, the bold, self-confident Englishman was decidedly uncomfortable about posing as an artist's subject. One of the reasons he had finally given in was that she had bribed him with the promise of a picnic in this secluded woodland glade, beside a small stream with a waterfall and a pool.

The moment she had described the background she wanted to use for the portrait, he had asked if she knew how to swim. Beth had been raised in the Georgia backwoods where being unable to swim was tantamount to courting death by drowning. Everyone, female as well as male, swam in the Blackthorne family. Derrick was pleased. He would pose for her during the morning in return for her spending the afternoon in the pool with him.

Just thinking about that swim made her hand tremble

as she focused on her sketch. "This is going to be wonderful . . . if I can only capture . . ."

"You're mumbling as though you have a mouthful of feathers, puss," Derrick could not resist teasing. Her look of intense concentration was arrestingly erotic in a strangely innocent way. He loved the way the tip of her tongue lightly glossed those lush pink lips, the way small white teeth bit the lower one when she was deep in thought. Her eyes flashed to him, then back down to her work, and a long coil of dark red hair bounced back and forth over her shoulder.

She's still an innocent . . . in spite of me. That thought had considerable power to disturb him, and he had been plagued with it often. Beth had known full well what she was doing when she had come to his bed. Good family or no, she was American, living the unfettered life she had chosen, far from the strictures of the proper English society in which he had been raised.

And what would happen to her when he left? For all her youth and trust in the goodness and beauty of the world, she was a strong woman who would accept the inevitable and get on with her life. He had reassured himself of that repeatedly whenever his conscience—usually a Greek chorus of one, namely Alvin Francis Edward Drummond—chided him for their liaison. What he refused to consider, kept buried in the deepest recesses of his heart, was what would happen to *him* when he must go.

And go he would, all too soon. He had used a variety of means to intercept correspondence between the Murats and Napoleon. The exiled emperor was planning an escape. As soon as Derrick learned his destination, he would deliver the critical information directly to the heads of state assembled in Vienna, then await orders that, he hoped, would at last allow him to purchase a commission in the army and fight openly.

"Your expression has changed again, Derrick," she scolded. "Such a brown study. Perhaps I could capture that pensive quality in the finished oil," she mused more to herself than to him.

Shirl Henke

"Enough. My leg's gone to sleep and my neck most probably will never turn to the right again," he said, standing up and stretching, then striding over to her. "Put down the charcoal and paper, puss. 'Tis noon." He pointed toward the sun high overhead. "Time for a nice, cooling swim."

" 'Tis unseasonably warm today, I agree, but the water will be a bit more than just cooling, I warrant."

"The bold Georgia frontier woman, afraid of a bit of cold water?" he teased, pulling her into his embrace. "Then I shall just have to warm you up first . . . 'til you're so warm you'll be burning . . . eager to plunge into the depths . . ." He punctuated his words with kisses, running his hands over her body, slipping the drawstring at the neckline of her blouse and freeing her breasts.

The moment his mouth tugged gently on a nipple she moaned, burying her hands in his hair, then running them down to his chest, where she seized his shirtfront and began pulling it open. She tore off several buttons in feverish haste when his hands glided beneath her skirt and caressed the sensitive skin of her inner thighs, murmuring his pleasure at the moisture already dewing on her petals.

Her skirt dropped with a soft slither, pooling around her feet, followed by her loose blouse. He shrugged off his shirt as she worked on his fly, her fingers clumsy with need, yet once his sex sprang free, the deft delicacy of her artist's touch made him the one to moan with pleasure.

"You drive me mad, Beth. I don't think I can wait—"

She released him and spun away with a husky laugh, kicking off her sandals so she was completely naked in the noonday sun. "The last one in the water has to feed peeled grapes to the winner!" she shrieked with glee, dashing toward the small tumbling waterfall while he struggled to pull off his pants.

"That's cheating and you know it," he called after her. Long used to swift summonses to dress in haste, he had already rid himself of his boots and made quick work of the pants, then tore out after her.

His long strides caught up with her just as they reached

92

the water's edge. Derrick scooped her up in his arms and stepped into the pool, which was cold. Then he tossed her into the deepest part, where she landed with a loud splash and a high-pitched squeal of dismay.

"It's freezing!" Her teeth chattered as she treaded water in an attempt to warm herself. "But I won the contest," she crowed triumphantly.

"Not so, puss. I was the one who first touched water. I win." He pointed to his feet, around which the clear water lapped, turning them decidedly blue.

She splashed him with icy droplets, crying, "That *is* cheating!"

"That cooks your goose," he shouted, diving in after her as she turned and swam away. The cold nearly stole his breath, but he cut though the water with clean powerful strokes until he caught up to her, no easy feat since she was quick as an otter. Seizing her from behind, he pulled her against him, murmuring, "I'm freezing, thanks to you. So you shall just have to warm me."

Beth turned her face up to his, knowing he would kiss her. "You warm me, Derrick," she said as his mouth claimed hers, hot and fierce in spite of his protests about freezing. Their combined body heat made them impervious to the temperature as the kiss deepened. She levered her body higher by wrapping her arms around his neck as his tongue plunged rhythmically in and out of her mouth. His erection pressed between her legs, stone hard and hot as the sun. And she melted like wax over him, clamping her legs around his hips, opening to his second invasion.

They rocked in the water, he thrusting back and forth, she gliding up and down while he fisted his hands in her long wet hair and she dug her nails into the rippling muscles of his back. They finished in one swift, breathless spasm of bliss, then grew still. His feet were planted on the mossy bottom of the pool, steadying them as she slithered down his body, standing on tiptoe to brush her lips against his playfully.

"I warrant the water's risen a degree or two by now . . . what do you think?"

Shirl Henke

"I think you owe me some peeled grapes, dropped one at a time in my mouth," he replied, pulling her toward the bank, where a large picnic hamper sat beside their hastily discarded clothing.

" 'Tis you who owe—"

"I overtook you before you—"

"We shall compromise," she interrupted, opening the hamper to take out a large fluffy towel, which she offered to share with him. Laughing, they dried each other, tugging on the cloth, trying to make it reach. Then all laughter died and they were once more in each other's arms, cocooned in white linen, looking deeply into each other's eyes.

"What is it about you . . . that I can never get enough?" he murmured as his lips descended on hers.

They slowly sank to the ground, rolling on the crisp dry winter grass, kissing, caressing. Then she rolled up on top of him, her thighs straddling his torso. "Just to show you what a sporting woman I am, I shall go first." With that, she reached into the hamper and pulled out a fat bunch of sweet yellow grapes and began to peel one, making a slow production of it. Then she held it over his mouth, commanding, "Open for me."

He obeyed. She popped the grape inside, then began peeling another. His hips moved restlessly beneath her as he chewed and swallowed. She could feel his staff brushing against her buttocks and wriggled provocatively. He groaned.

"Witch, you enjoy torturing me, don't deny it."

"Deny it! Why should I? You . . . are . . . such a . . . delight . . . to torture . . ." she replied between kisses.

As she fed him another grape, his hands cupped her buttocks, kneading them in a slow sensuous rhythm until he could feel her thighs quiver. "Naughty puss. I can feel your wetness on my belly," he scolded.

"And I can feel your great club striking my backside . . . who is the naughty one, hmmm?" As she spoke, she arched his spine, throwing her long wet hair backward until it teased the sensitive tip of his phallus.

He muttered an oath of endearment as the swift jolt of pleasure rocketed through him. Her breasts, nipples hard and rosy, stood erect, jutting out as if inviting his hands. Unable to resist, he complied, cupping them around the soft globes, lifting and teasing them. She shook her head, sending the weight of her hair brushing back and forth over his shaft, then reached back with one hand and stroked it, using the other to cup his sac.

"Now you go too far," he gasped, trying to unseat her so he could roll on top and plunge deep inside.

"Ah, no, not nearly far enough," she murmured in reply, easing up, then back on her knees, guiding him to the portal.

"Now!" he cried, arching up.

But she only raised herself higher, continuing to tease him with her hands, then rub the pearl-dewed tip against the creamy softness of her outer lips. When her legs began to tremble so greatly that she knew they could no longer support her, she sank slowly down onto the steely length of him, taking him deep, deep inside.

They moved slowly, she riding him as his hands held her hips, setting a rhythm together, unhurried this time. The sun beat down on them and the towel tangled around their legs, but neither noticed as they took their pleasure, savoring every moment as if it were their last.

And well it might be, he thought as he looked up into her radiant face. "You shine brighter than the sun," he whispered, *and I shall miss the sun . . .*

"I mislike this," Derrick said, tossing down the latest report from the British emissary on Elba assigned to watch Napoleon.

"I take it you've also read the dispatches from the latest group of Royal Navy officers to visit Boney's 'capital,' " Drum said as he laid out Derrick's court clothes for the evening's gala.

"A pack of gullible fools. Bonaparte simply tells them he's resigned to ruling over a tiny island a mere skip from France and they swallow it whole." He took a sip from his cup of thick steamed coffee laced with cream, a pleasure he had learned to enjoy in Naples . . . one of the many pleasures to which Beth had introduced him. Tonight might be the last they spent together. *Don't think of it.*

"You heard the reports regarding Boney's 'spring planting' and his orders for refurbishing his summer residence in the hills. A smoke screen?" Drum speculated.

"Most likely. The Oil Merchant believes he'll sail by March first. I concur, especially since hearing the rumors of supplies being loaded on his ships at night."

"Something is afoot, little doubt," Drum agreed, balefully picking up a well-gnawed riding boot from behind the *armadio* and holding it in front of Sir Percival's unconcerned nose. "You shall be the death of me . . . or I of you once this ghastly misadventure is over," he added darkly.

Used to the running battle between Drum and the dog, Derrick ignored them, his thoughts torn between Beth and the fast-moving events on Elba. "If I pick up nothing useful at court tonight I'm for Livorno tomorrow to see if the Oil Merchant has any hard evidence with which to convince those dunderheads in London. Failing that, I shall go to Elba."

Drum paused in his selection of Derrick's cravat, a serious consideration for the little dandy, and said, "You most certainly cannot leave without explaining to Beth."

"I fear I shall be forced to do just that. If I tell her in advance that I'm leaving, she will speculate with her friend the contessa, who you well know is closely connected to Murat's court. Vittoria would go to the king with her suspicions and I might never be allowed to leave."

"Beth would not betray you if you explained the circumstances," the little man argued stubbornly.

"Just because the Peace of Ghent has ended hostilities between her country and ours does not mean she would take it well if she were to learn that I have been a spy since first we met in her nation's very capital. No"—he shook his head determinedly—"this is a matter of our country's security—the very peace of Europe hangs in the balance. I can ill afford to moon about like a schoolboy. Nor can you continue to play marriage broker."

Muttering imprecations, Drum returned to his task as his mind raced ahead, re-forming plans. *Just wait. You may run away, but if Quintin Blackthorne is half as formidable as Alex says he is, you shall one day be forced to face up to your obligations.*

"Is the English princess really as awful as they say?" one of the queen's ladies-in-waiting whispered to Vittoria as she scanned the door to the grand ballroom, where the Prince Regent's estranged wife Caroline would enter as honored guest of the Murats.

"Not so much awful as just a bit on the homely side and really quite sad," the contessa replied.

Always the charmers, King Joaquim and his Queen Caroline had made Princess Caroline welcome when she deigned to visit their small country during her long odyssey to escape her disastrous marriage to Prinney. However, Vittoria's attention was not fastened on the royals, but rather on her young charge and Beth's handsome escort, who stood talking with several Neapolitan nobles on the opposite side of the crowded room.

The contessa had marked how Derrick Jamison's fluency in Italian had improved in the few short months he had spent in Naples. She had cautioned Beth to no avail, for even when he would break engagements with her and send no word for days on end, Beth would defend his inattentive behavior. She was utterly besotted, Vittoria concluded with resignation.

Vittoria knew he could not be trusted. But how to prove it—indeed, did she really wish to destroy Beth's happiness? Now that the war between the United States and the British Empire was over, did it really matter? Perhaps not for Beth, but if Jamison was working toward his country's goals of keeping Napoleon on Elba and overthrowing Murat as king of Naples, then it mattered a great deal to the contessa. What she wished and what Beth wished might be quite the opposite. What would she do if faced with a decision that would cost Beth her first love . . . and perhaps destroy Beth's love for her friend as well?

Across the room, far from those troubling thoughts, Derrick and Beth whirled about the dance floor, she floating on a cloud of delight with the music, the warm spring air and the man holding her, he preoccupied by the courier he had seen ushered quietly up to the dais a moment earlier. Murat had read the message while smiling broadly, then handed it to his queen, who was considerably more skilled at hiding her emotions.

What the deuce is going on? He knew he had to get his hands on that message, which the queen had now given to Maria Walewska. Napoleon's "Polish Wife" also smiled unabashedly. Just then the music stopped and Princess Caroline was announced. Every head craned to see the English regent's unwanted wife, a pale, plump dumpling of a woman, as their Polish guest quietly absented herself from the festivities.

"Such deep thoughts. Are you on her side or your awful Prinney's?" Beth asked.

Pondering how he could learn the contents of the message the Countess Walewska had taken with her, Derrick did not immediately reply. "Oh, er, I suppose I've never given it much thought. The Brunswick royal house always ran to lantern-jawed women; but then, Prinney's no Brummel himself."

"Spoken like a true male. I imagine your fastidious man Drummond shares that unenlightened opinion."

Derrick barked a laugh. "No, I daresay he would take up the poor princess's cause without a moment's hesitation." *As he has yours.*

"Then perhaps I've misjudged him . . . even if he *does* dislike dogs."

"So do I—at least King Charles spaniels." As he spoke, his eyes strayed to the small anteroom into which his Polish quarry had disappeared.

"If you ever decide to rid yourself of him, do remember that I should love to have him."

Before Derrick could reply, his opportunity to pursue

Bonaparte's mistress arrived in the person of Francisco Fiore. When her old friend asked for the honor of the dance, Derrick excused himself and quickly made his way through the press to find Napoleon's mistress.

As he slipped through the door and closed it behind him, Derrick did not see Captain Evon Bourdin watching him.

Chapter Eight

Derrick found himself in a small, lavishly appointed antechamber. No one was about, but the faint trace of her musky perfume indicated that the Polish wife had just passed through. Another door stood slightly ajar. He followed his nose down the corridor, hoping he could run Napoleon's mistress to ground before becoming hopelessly lost in the maze of the old palace.

Then, about halfway around the second turn, he heard women whispering in a Slavic language he took to be Polish. He paused in front of the door, recognizing Maria's voice. Improvising quickly, he knocked. Speaking in French, he inquired, "May I enter, my lady?"

"Who is there?" a soft voice inquired nervously in atrocious French.

Derrick opened the door and bowed politely. "Ramon DiMiglio, my lady, a member of his majesty's security."

Maria was quite pretty in a pale blond way, with wide Slavic cheekbones and deep-set blue eyes, although her mouth was a bit weak. She motioned him inside uncertainly as her maid, a stolid Polish grandmother in a babushka, stood guard beside her chair. "I do not recognize you," she said haltingly, obviously confused.

He gave her his most winsome smile as he saluted her tiny hand. "That is because my position requires that as few people as necessary know that I guard the king and queen." He spoke slowly so that she could follow his words. Although he was fluent to the point of being able to pass himself off as a Parisian, her French was sketchy at best. "His majesty bade me follow you because he is concerned about your safety . . . and that of our emperor."

At the mention of Napoleon, she grew agitated, biting her lip. "I would do nothing to endanger him," she said, garbling the idiom because she was upset.

"The king knows that, but when he realized that her majesty gave you the emperor's message, then allowed you to leave with it, he grew worried that an English or Bourbon spy in the palace might harm you in order to steal it, thus jeopardizing the escape plan as well."

"Ooh! No. I did not mean—that is—did not think," she stumbled for the words, then, red-faced, she turned and retrieved the note from the bodice of her gown. "I should have . . . destroyed it, I know. It was"—she groped for the word— "sentimental of me, but it was written in his hand . . ."

And she had carried it against her heart. Feeling a surge of pity, Derrick almost wished he could return the missive to her after reading it, but that was not possible. When she extended it to him, he took it, bowing once more. "His majesty profoundly regrets the necessity of taking it from you, my lady." He turned and left the room.

As he walked, he quickly perused the message. Napoleon had sailed two days ago! His destination was the south coast of France.

Derrick's mind raced as he stared down at the almost illegible signature of the emperor. Even those fools in the Foreign Office would believe him when they saw this. He would have to leave at once, on horseback. Busy calculating how many days it would take him to reach Vienna, where the delegates for the peace conference were assembled, he did not see the guardsman. Bourdin had hidden behind a suit of fourteenth-century armor in a dimly lit section of the corridor.

The sudden prickling along the back of his neck, a sixth sense honed over the years, alerted him to the menace. He whirled around just as Bourdin's sword came hissing at him. Derrick jumped back, barely avoiding the powerful slash intended to decapitate him. Before the guardsman could lunge with the heavy saber, he moved out of reach, slipping the note inside his pocket with one hand while removing the dagger from his boot with the other.

"I believe you have something that belongs to his majesty," Bourdin growled, scoffing at the uneven contest between his saber and Derrick's knife. "I will return it and drag you before him right now, Englishman!"

" 'Twas you that night outside Santa Maria's, wasn't it? I recognize you by the way you strike . . . at a man's back," Derrick taunted, careful to keep out of reach of Bourdin's slashing saber. Although much longer, it was a heavy and clumsy instrument intended to be swung from the back of a horse, not employed fighting in close quarters.

"You are a dog of a spy, running with your tail between your legs," the Frenchman replied.

"I thought we had already established which of us crawled on all fours, my fine French cur. Besides, last time 'twas you who ran with my lead ball lodged in your right shoulder. Slows the sword arm down a bit, eh?" Derrick noted that Bourdin's strength was quickly waning and sweat beaded his forehead.

Come on, one more swing . . . waste it . . . yes! As soon as his foe made another pass, Derrick used the instant's respite to shove the top-heavy suit of armor forward with all his might, toppling it over onto the Frenchman.

The crash echoed deafeningly in the deserted hallway as over a hundred pounds of rusted steel broke apart, striking Bourdin's body, knocking him to the ground and pinning him. Derrick would have taken the time to finish off his enemy, but Bourdin's right arm remained free and he reached inside his tunic for a small pistol before Derrick could get close enough to deliver a killing blow. As soon as he saw the weapon, the Englishman spun away.

This time Derrick was not able to move quickly enough. The ball sliced a savagely burning path across his right side, knocking him against the wall. He could hear Bourdin calling for help and struggling to get out from under the crushing weight of the armor. The pounding of footsteps sounded in the distance, coming from the direction of the ballroom. No time to lose; he must escape before the hall was swarming with guards.

He forced himself to run down the hallway, holding his side to slow the flow of blood. *St. George for England, help me find my way out of this maze!* He twisted and turned, opening doors along the way until at last he found one leading into the gardens. He looked back, checking the rug for bloodstains, cursing when he saw how clearly he was marking his own trail. He could hear yelling in French and Italian not far behind as he darted across the open grass and slipped behind a topiary hedge.

After running through the formal gardens for several hundred yards he stopped. In the darkness the trait of blood was not easily visible in the grass, but he would pass out from light-headedness soon if he did not staunch the flow. He probed experimentally at the ugly gash. There might be a cracked rib, but no vital organs seemed impaired. Unfortunately, the shot was just deep enough to cause a damnable lot of bleeding. He had been shot before, had the scars to prove it, scars that he had explained away to Beth as the results of his wicked life and history of dueling.

Beth. How could he leave her this way? She remained in the ballroom, probably by now searching for him, wondering why he had deserted her. He doubted Murat would want it bandied about that an English agent had intercepted a message from Napoleon, so no one in attendance at the ball would know he was a fugitive. She would not know. Small consolation, he thought, forcing himself to concentrate on staying alive long enough to complete his mission.

Grimacing, he pulled off his jacket, then cursed some more when he saw that the pocket in which he'd shoved Napoleon's message was blood-soaked. He carefully extracted the slip of paper but could not ascertain the extent of the damage in the dark. All he could do was attempt to dry it out later. He removed his shirt and tore it into strips, using them to bind up his side as tightly as he could stand it, then put the jacket on once more and started loping toward the farthest perimeter of the garden. There was a wall, if memory served, which he could scale . . . at least, he hoped he could.

"Where do you imagine Derrick could be?" Beth asked, chewing worriedly on her lower lip as she scanned the crowded room.

Vittoria made a noncommittal reply. Not too long after Jamison had excused himself, the contessa had heard the faintest echo of what might have been a shot, followed by angry shouting. Some sort of commotion had drawn away a number of the royal guards, and the king had left the dais after a terse exchange with his now grim-faced wife. All did not augur well for Derrick Jamison. " 'Tis late and the press is thinning, moving into the dining hall. Do you wish to stay for supper?"

"Not if I must make my entrance without Derrick. I cannot credit that he would simply leave without explanation."

"Well, it would appear that he has done precisely that," Vittoria replied. "Come then, let us repair to the villa and I shall send Georgio to make an inquiry."

"Derrick will have a deal of apologizing to do before I forgive this."

"Perhaps he was summoned away on one of his mysterious trips," the contessa suggested as they made their way through the crowd.

"Honestly, Vittoria, you are not still suggesting that he is some sort of spy?" Beth had scoffed in disbelief the first time her friend mentioned it, and she still found the idea absurd in the extreme.

Her Derrick, an agent of the British government? Why, he had been forced to flee London with officers of the crown in pursuit. He was a rake and a wastrel who enjoyed the sybaritic life of idleness here in Italy far too much to be slinking about after Bonapartists. Of course, until a few months ago when the war ended, he could have been after Americans as well—*if* he was a spy, which, she stoutly assured herself, he was not.

Neither was he *her* Derrick, she was forced to concede. He made no claims on her, showing not the slightest hint of jealousy when she flirted with other men or spent inordinate amounts of time at Signore Pignatelli's studio. Even when she had let slip that she was again posing in the nude for the famous portraitist, Derrick had only raised one eyebrow sardonically, inquiring if he might attend one of the sessions as an observer. She was forced to admit that she had done the unthinkable—she had deliberately baited him, as if she were a green miss fishing for a marriage proposal. Small wonder he had slipped away without a word tonight! He was teaching her a lesson, the rogue.

On the carriage ride back to the villa, Beth fell silent. Her thoughts were troubling. She reviewed the course of her relationship with Derrick, trying to pinpoint just when she had started attempting to make him jealous. She could remember the day, early in the new year, as if it were yesterday. . . .

They had gone riding down the coast. She had been eager to show him the magnificent ruins at Pompeii, beneath the shadow of Vesuvius. After viewing the ruins they had found a small inn on the road to Amalfi, where they spent the night. Their hostess, noting the absence of a wedding ring on the finger of the foreigner, had been suspicious and unfriendly, in spite of Beth's fluency in the local dialect.

"Signora Varola thinks I am your kept woman," she had said after the scowling matron deposited hearty portions of osso bucco simmered with winter vegetables on the small table in their upstairs quarters.

"Well, I did pay for this," Derrick replied, grinning as he held up a meaty end of the veal knuckle, then licked his fingers with relish. "She may be a prude, but she is an excellent cook."

"I shall pay for tomorrow's lodging and meals," Beth said, her appetite suddenly gone.

He looked up, wiping his mouth on a much-mended but clean napkin. "Your greatly vaunted independence is duly noted, m'dear, but wholly unnecessary. I know I have no claim on you simply because I happen to have paid a simple night's lodging."

She forced a smile. "Would I have a claim on you if I paid—is that what you fear?"

The barb must have struck because he replied tersely, "Call it simple male vanity and leave be. A man does not allow a woman to pay his keep."

"Even if he sleeps with her?" What had made her ask such a thing!

He threw down the napkin and leaned back on the crude cane chair, studying her intently with his arms crossed over his chest. "What is it, puss? Do I stand stud for you, hmmm?"

"Scarce that, since the purpose of a stud is to beget offspring." The instant she blurted out the words, Beth wished to call them back. "I—I did not mean—"

"For a woman who professes to want no leg-shackling, you have an odd way of looking at a bare fact of life," he interrupted. "I've sensed for some time your unease when we began taking measures to prevent . . . an accident."

She could not argue that stopping before they made love so that he could apply a "French letter" had broken the mood for her. Nor was it much better when she employed Vittoria's remedy, vinegar-soaked sponges inserted in the vagina. She shrugged helplessly. "I know we must be careful, but it just seems so . . . so calculated. We didn't use anything at first and I did not conceive. I suspect I am barren."

"I would not wager on that. Acting as impetuously as we did was insane . . . but I wanted you quite badly. You know I had no idea that you were a virgin. I assumed you'd taken measures. When I realized you had not . . ." It was his turn to shrug. "You are quite the little Puritan after all, aren't you, puss?" A flicker of amusement lit his eyes then.

She smiled, conceding, "Scarcely Puritan, but I suppose I never realized how much my strict Episcopalian upbringing has influenced me. Vittoria was appalled when I admitted that we had not been taking precautions." Beth knew her face had grown pink in the candlelight. "She explained what I needed to do long before you and I met."

"Do you want children, Beth?" His mood shifted once again, became expectant, tense.

She could feel his discomfort and it more than equaled her own. "No." That was the answer he wished, but a sudden epiphany told her that it was not the one she wanted to give him. "If I was to have a child, I would have to give up painting, wouldn't I?"

Do you want him to say that you need not? That he would not ask it of his wife? Such pretty dreams. She knew they were nothing more. And her heart broke . . .

After those days on the coast, she had begun to test him, although not consciously at first. She had danced with ogling admirers in the homes of Vittoria's noble friends, spent even more time down on the waterfront in her scandalous peasant clothing, given in to Pignatelli's importuning and again posed for him.

Her reputation in Naples was utterly wicked. The old women of the nobility gossiped, saying that the young American was even worse than her mentor the contessa. And none of it seemed to matter a fig to Derrick Jamison.

The subject of Beth's late-night ruminations stood hunched in the noisome squalor of the *fondachi,* waiting for Volio, the self-styled "King" of the cutpurses, prostitutes and other rough elements of the city. Derrick had little time before Murat's guardsmen alerted the watch and every nook and cranny of the twisting streets and back alleys would be crawling with armed soldiers. He'd paid a runner to deliver instructions to Drum.

He could not take the time for a circuitous escape route from Naples. The information he possessed regarding Napoleon's flight from Elba must be delivered to the heads of state assembled in Vienna by the swiftest and most reliable messenger. He dared trust no one but himself. He waited inside the door of what looked like the very gates of hell, a warren of small filthy rooms from which emanated the stench of unwashed bodies, human waste and rotting garbage.

Derrick could hear the cries of the watch. Soon they would begin their systematic search and he would never be able to get out of the city. If Volio lived up to his reputation, and for the price Derrick was paying him he had better, then he would soon be hidden in a small skiff on the bay. He heard the stealthy sound of footfalls on the cobblestones and the small wiry *lazzarono* seemed to materialize out of the murky air. At least the weather had begun to cooperate as a heavy night fog settled over the city.

"Come with me, signore. It is all arranged," Volio whispered in the guttural dialect of the lower class, looking over his shoulder. "Hurry!" The flicker of a torch cast shadows at the end of the street.

They slipped down the hill in the opposite direction, heading toward the bay. Several times they were forced to backtrack to avoid the watch, but Volio's boast about knowing every inch of the waterfront sections of the city was not an idle one. Within the quarter hour Derrick was lying in the wet musty bottom of a small boat that reeked of fish.

"I wish to land as close to the Piazza Sannazaro as possible," he reiterated in serviceable Italian. He kept his hand on the hilt of his dagger, not trusting the *lazzarono* any further than he could throw the Duomo. Although he had already paid Volio an exorbitant sum, the fisherman would not receive a coin until he arrived at his destination. *If only Drum is waiting . . .*

Derrick was relieved to see they were indeed headed in the right direction. In moments he was on a deserted stretch of beach to the north of the city and the skiff had vanished into the fog once again. If he had been betrayed, surely the guards would be upon him by now . . . but where was Drum?

Just then a black-cloaked apparition materialized, leading a four-footed creature that could most charitably be called a nag. "Bloody hell, Drummond, surely you don't expect me to cross the Apennines riding that beast?"

"From the looks of you, I don't expect you to cross the street. You must see a physician or you'll bleed to death by dawn."

"I don't have time to bleed to death, much less to waste with a leech. You have only one horse. I instructed you to bring two. You'll have to leave Naples or Murat will arrest you as well."

"I'm not bouncing about on horseback after you. Even if I had been able to secure a second mount, I confess to being the world's worst rider. I shall make arrangements to travel by sea after you're taken care of."

"What of the dog?" Derrick asked as they walked toward the shelter of a thick stand of cypress trees.

"I placed a summary of what has transpired in his collar and gave the command. Considering how he obeys orders regarding the upholstery, not to mention our clothing, I have my doubts he will reach his destination, but there you have it, old chap. One does what one can."

"Let's hope good old Percy earns his dog bones this time." Derrick stopped short, wincing in pain.

"You can't ride, man—bloody hell, you can barely walk." Drum looked at the widening red stain around Derrick's waist.

"I'll make it," Derrick gritted out. "There's no choice."

"Stow the king-and-country balderdash. How will it serve either if you lie dead by the roadside?" Without waiting for an answer to his rhetorical question, Drum took Derrick's arm and slung it across his own narrow shoulders, supporting the much larger man as they walked through the trees. Leading the horse, he struggled back to where his small rig lay hidden in a swale.

"We can't . . . go driving about the . . . countryside,"

Derrick protested, laboring for breath as Drum shoved him into the vehicle.

"Quite so. That is why I have devised a plan," Drum replied, tying the reins of the nag onto the rear of the rig.

Within ten minutes it became apparent to Derrick where they were headed. "You can't take me to Vittoria—are you mad? She'll turn me over to Murat in a trice."

"I am not taking you to the estimable contessa, but to the young woman who happens to be in love with you."

"Who happens to live with Vittoria. Everyone in Naples knows of our liaison. Bourdin himself is probably waiting outside the villa for another shot at me."

"That is the fly in the ointment, old fellow, I confess, but there simply is no other way. You must have medical attention and we can trust no one else. We shall have to sneak into her quarters . . . you do know where in that great sprawling place Beth sleeps, hmmm?"

"Of course," Derrick replied, ignoring the sarcasm in Drum's tone. " 'Tis next to her studio in the east wing."

"Wait here while I scout around," Drum instructed after pulling the rig off the road into a thicket of olive trees.

Derrick would have protested that he should lead the way, but suddenly he felt quite woozy. The way his luck had turned this night, he would probably stumble into Bourdin's gunsights before he got within a hundred yards of the villa. He leaned back against the squabs and waited. The next thing he knew, Drum was shaking him awake and whispering.

"There are two of those buffoons from the palace guard nattering about the front drive, but if we approach from the rear, there is an open door leading from the portico into the first floor of the east wing. I say, are you up to climbing through a hedge or two?"

"I shall have to be," Derrick replied, gritting his teeth against the pain. As they made their way to the east wing, he described what had happened at the palace in greater detail, concluding, "So you see, we have no time to waste. Bonaparte is already halfway to France. I shall cross the Apennines and sail from Pescara to Trieste, then ride directly to Vienna. But in case I do not make it, you must leave for Rome immediately. The Austrian ambassador to the Papal States will move the very Alps to alert the allies."

" 'Tis to be hoped Sir Percival has succeeded in his quest and a third messenger is already enroute to Leghorn to alert the Royal Navy. Perhaps they'll catch Boney before he sets foot on French soil."

Derrick grunted. "That damned little Corsican has the devil's own luck. I wouldn't count on it."

They made their way through the contessa's gardens, which were lushly overgrown with willows and almond trees, providing ample cover as they slipped silently toward the portico. The guards must have awakened the household some time ago. A dim light flickered in the main salon, and they could hear a servant complaining because he had been dragged from his bed at such an ungodly hour. The east wing was dark.

"Do you suppose Beth is with the contessa?" Drum whispered as they hid in the blackness of an alcove off the main rooms.

"No matter. I can make my way to her quarters from here. You must head pell-mell to Rome."

"I mislike leaving you to stumble about in the dark, dripping blood."

"The bleeding's stopped." Derrick was not at all certain of his welcome now that Beth knew of his deception. She might scream the house down, and then both of them would be arrested.

Without answering, Drum once again seized Derrick's arm and started toward the stairs to the second floor.

Beth lay in her bed, drowsing, unable to return to a sound sleep after being awakened some time earlier by what sounded like hoofbeats on the front drive. She'd had considerable trouble getting to sleep, tossing and turning for over an hour thanks to Derrick Jamison.

Just then a soft click broke the silence. Beth looked at the window near her bed. Nowhere near false dawn. None of the servants should be stirring yet. She sat up and started

111

to swing her legs from beneath the light cover when a familiar voice spoke from the darkness near the door.

"Hello, puss. Will you forgive me for deserting you tonight?"

Chapter Nine

Beth peered into the blackness, her heart suddenly hammering, her mouth gone dry. "Derrick?" Her eyes strained against the darkness, now seeing two shadows moving toward her. Derrick was slumped over, being supported by someone much smaller than he. His manservant Drum?

" 'Tis I, Beth." His voice was a hiss of pain.

She recognized Drum's voice as he said, "Slowly, old boy, have a care you don't start the bleeding again."

Bleeding! She seized her robe with unsteady hands and slipped it on as Drum helped his master to the opposite side of her bed, where Derrick took a seat. "You've been injured?" she asked, knowing something was horribly wrong as she fumbled to light a candle. Seeing the blackened crust of dried blood that covered his midsection, she gasped.

"He's been shot," Drum said matter-of-factly. "Just scraped a rib or two, but he's lost sufficient blood to make him quite loggerheaded."

"What is going on?" she asked, kneeling beside Derrick to see the extent of his wound as Drum began unwrapping the makeshift bandage. As his companion pulled the dried cloth away, Derrick cursed beneath his breath. "Here, let me. You're too clumsy," she said, steeling herself as the long ugly furrow across his side began to seep blood.

"Cow-handed? I? Not likely. 'Tis this buffle-headed maggoty-brain who is guilty of that, else he'd not be bleeding over your bed linens," Drum replied.

"We'll need yarrow to stop the bleeding and clean bandages," she said in a businesslike manner, reaching for the bellpull to summon her maid.

"No, puss," Derrick replied, his hand shooting out with surprising strength and steadiness to grasp her wrist. "You cannot disturb the household unless you wish to bring the king's guards from without to arrest me."

"Arrest you?" She looked from Derrick's to Drum, her shock and fright giving way to anger. "I will personally drag you to King Joaquim's gaol if you do not explain at once."

"You had best be on your way, Drum. I will handle matters from here on," Derrick said to his companion.

"I can see how swimmingly it's going thus far," Drum replied dryly, showing no sign of leaving.

"You aren't a servant, are you?" She had noticed from the first time she'd met the little man that he did not act the way servants—especially English servants—acted in the employ of an earl's son.

"The Honorable Alvin Francis Edward Drummond, at your service, Miss Blackthorne." He executed a most proper bow, which should have seemed ludicrous with her in her night clothes on her knees beside the bed. Somehow it did not. "I have the honor to be a good friend of your cousin Alex."

"Alex? You knew Alex in London? But why—" Then it struck her with the force of an avalanche. "Vittoria warned me, but I didn't want to believe her," she said, turning back to Derrick. "You're spies—she was right, wasn't she? You've used me to get to her."

"Go now, Drum." There was steel in Derrick's voice, but his eyes never left Beth's face.

The little man looked between them for a moment, then reached his decision. "Do be the one who exercises some modicum of intelligence, Miss Blackthorne, and see that he neither hangs nor rides away to die. I'm off then." With that pronouncement, he vanished into the blackness.

"He's right about one thing, Beth: If Murat captures me, he shall hang me. After a bit of . . . interrogation. His emperor has escaped from Elba. If Bonaparte reaches the French army, all Europe will go up in flames again." He studied her face, trying to read her expression.

Pain lashed at her as she asked, "Three years ago in Washington, were you spying on my country, too?"

"I was sent to learn about American incursions into Spanish territories," he admitted.

"You used me—from the first time we met! Was that gallant rescue in the palace garden arranged for my benefit? What a blind, trusting fool I've been."

"I did *not* use you—neither when that pig Bourdin attacked you nor back in Washington, although it would have been child's play if I'd chosen to charm you at Dolley Madison's salon. Instead, if you'll recall, I let you off the hook, puss, albeit not very gently," he said softly, realizing for the first time that he still held her in his grasp, and that she had not pulled away in spite of her anger.

She followed his eyes to where his large dark hand encircled her slender wrist, then jerked free with a colorful oath she'd picked up on the Neapolitan waterfront. "How very charitable of you, Derrick. Oh, it is Derrick Jamison, isn't it—or is the name a sham, too?"

"No, the name's all too genuine," he replied darkly.

"Well, then, I warrant 'tis the only thing about you that is genuine." *Did you care for me even a little bit, Derrick?* She wanted desperately to ask, but pride forbade her. He knew what she wished to hear . . . if only he would say it, she would risk the world for him, even betray her best friend.

There was no time to waste and he had already told her more than his superiors would countenance. "I must get out of Naples. It was cork-brained of Drum to bring me here," he said, struggling to rise. But the room began spinning as soon as he tried to take a step.

Beth rose with him, reaching out when he started to crumple, throwing her arms out to break his fall, then easing him back onto the edge of the bed. "Drum's right— you are maggoty-brained. Now you've started the blood flowing again. Only a madman—or an Englishman— would think to ride in this condition."

"We're a stubborn lot," he said with a faint smile that quickly turned into a grimace.

"Let me remove that jacket," she said, pulling the ruined garment from his good side, then reaching around to tug more gently on the other until he was bare from the waist up.

He had not the strength to argue. The least bit of movement not only hurt like bloody hell but caused the gash to bleed more rapidly. He cursed beneath his breath. There was no time to lie unconscious while Bonaparte was on his way to Paris!

"Lie down so I may take a look at your injury," she commanded.

"And you shall ascertain the extent of damage from your vast reservoir of experience with gunshot wounds," he said through gritted teeth as she probed the raw flesh.

"Not gunshot wounds, no, but I've a deal of experience with deep gashes. My brothers and cousins were forever getting into scrapes with everything from mountain lions to wild pigs to each other. I shall need to fetch clean water, bandages and medicines. Lie still until I return."

He said nothing as she stood up and lit another candle, only studied her with those compelling blue eyes. "I will not betray you, Derrick."

Even though I *betrayed* you, he thought.

There was no need to say the words. They hung in the air, heavy as the fog outside. He watched her walk barefooted into the hallway, regretting the loss of her trust . . . and something more . . . something to which he would not put a name.

He must have dozed, for when he looked up she was

seated on a stool beside the bed, pouring water from a pitcher into a bowl. He nervously licked his lips as he watched her thread a nasty-looking curved needle with black suture. "Are you certain you can sew me up?"

She studied his dubious expression and arrogantly cocked an eyebrow. "Are you certain you can endure while I do?" she replied sweetly.

"It will not be the first time I've been stitched . . . only the first time by a woman. Perhaps your sex is better suited to the task than the leeches."

She focused on the job at hand, carefully cleansing the caked blood away from the wound to see how deep it was. Although she had assisted as her Aunt Charity sewed up numerous cuts and gouges, she had never been forced to perform the delicate task herself. Could she do it on her lover's flesh? Her gaze roamed over his long body and powerfully muscled bare chest. His breathing was ragged. She almost reached out to place one palm against his crisp black chest hair to feel the reassuring thump of his heart as she had done so often after they made love.

He watched the play of emotions on her face, so enigmatic and lovely in the flickering candlelight, so intent with concentration. When she reached over to the bedside table, her robe gaped open, revealing the lush swell of her breast, the pale pink tip of a nipple clearly visible through the sheer silk of her night rail. He felt his body harden in spite of the pain in his side. " 'Twill be difficult to leave you, Beth," he said aloud before realizing it.

"I doubt you will be going anywhere soon," she replied tartly, daubing the coagulant paste into the ragged edges of the wound, so intent on what she had to do that she remained unaware of the growing bulge in his breeches. He sucked in his breath on a hiss of agony, then gritted his teeth and remained silent as she completed the task. "The yarrow will stop the bleeding, but the gash is deep. 'Twill not heal properly unless I sew it."

He watched her pick up the already threaded needle. "I take it you are not asking my permission," he said dryly. "Pray proceed."

She could tell that he knew this was going to be exceedingly unpleasant. "How many times have you been stitched before?" she asked as the needle punctured skin, knitting one side to the other. "I have seen only one other such scar on your body." The moment she said the words she wished to call them back . . . and with them all the memories of the two of them lying entwined, naked and sated.

"There were three others, not counting direct punctures. I heal quite well. Don't tend to scar much, so the leeches tell me. Something that runs in my family."

"Like lying?" she muttered, concentrating on the rhythm of stitching, in and out, pierce and pull.

His hands dug into the bed linens, clenching in fists, but he did not otherwise move, nor give her the satisfaction of crying out. For all her anger, she still had a far more skilled touch than any of the medical practitioners who had tended him. As she tied off the last stitch, he managed to say, "You would have made as fine a physician as an artist, puss."

"Don't call me puss," she snapped.

"I never intended to hurt you, Beth," he said simply, knowing no way to excuse the pain he had inflicted.

"And what did you intend, Derrick? To just ride away without a word, never to return, leaving me to wonder if you were dead in some back alley?"

The accusation struck too close to the truth. If not for his being wounded and Drum's insistence, he would have done as she accused. But would he have returned to her when the war was over? If she had never learned of his subterfuge, she would still love him. That sudden thought shocked him to the core of his being.

Beth is in love with me. Or she was.

He knew it beyond certainty. But was he in love with her? Perhaps so. Having never experienced that tender emotion before, he found it difficult to decide. But it did not signify either way, for he was who he was and she hated him now for his betrayal. He had killed her love.

When he did not respond to her question, Beth stifled her sigh of resignation and said in a flat voice, "In order for me to bandage you, you must sit up. I'll help you."

When she leaned down to place her arm around his shoulders, he could smell the light floral fragrance of her skin. The weight of her unbound hair fell around him like a cloud of burnished silk and he fought the desire to bury his fists in it and pull her down into a fierce kiss. Madness! The pain helped him to break her spell. When he sat up, the agony in his side felt like a hot poker thrust against his midsection.

She felt his reaction to the pain. "Sit still and move your arms away from your sides, like so." She demonstrated, helping him to brace himself upright by pressing his palms against the mattress behind him. Then she reached for the pile of bandages and took one end of the linen, placing it against his uninjured side, pressing his hand to it and saying, "Hold this." When he complied, she began coiling the cloth around the stitched side. He trembled but made no sound as she pulled the bandage around his back and repeated the process, tightening the linen with each turn.

Derrick was grateful for the pain. It helped him get past the soft pressure of her breast pressing against his chest as she reached around him. When she finished tying off the bandage, he swung his legs over the side of the bed and straightened up. More pain, but it was bearable after a few steadying breaths. The light-headedness was fading as well. She had done a good job. The bleeding would not resume now that the slash had been sewn shut.

Beth poured a spoonful of the liquid from the bottle in a glass of water, then turned back to him. "Drink this."

He looked at the bottle. "What is it?"

"Laudanum. 'Twill help you to sleep."

"I have no time to sleep," he said, pushing the glass away. "Every hour counts. Bonaparte may have already landed on French soil." He stood up, not without considerable difficulty, but steadily enough to satisfy himself.

Not enough to satisfy her, however. "Are you mad! You can't ride in this condition. Drum was right; you'd bleed to death before you got anywhere near Vienna."

Shirl Henke

He looked at her with narrowed eyes. "I don't recall mentioning Vienna."

She scoffed. "You've already made a fool of me once. Do not further insult my intelligence. I know that the congress of allies is meeting in the Austrian capital to carve up Europe now that Napoleon has been vanquished."

"Not vanquished yet," he replied, taking an experimental step, then two, to see if his legs would support him.

"Let your friend Drummond see to it. You're in no condition to—"

"I must go, Beth," he interrupted. She blocked his path, pressing her palms against his bare chest. He took her hands gently and raised them to his lips.

The heat of his mouth on her fingers made her feel faint with wanting him. The very idea was detestable. He was her enemy, a spy who had used her, deceived her . . . and did not love her. But she loved him still and would not see him die. "No, Derrick, you cannot go. I'll raise the alarm if you try."

"And see me dance on Murat's gallows? Two of his guardsmen stand ready to arrest me in the courtyard out front. Your friend the contessa would turn me over to them. I know she's a patriot who wants Murat to unify Italy with Bonaparte's help."

"Have you reported her to your English masters, too?" Her voice was cold.

"They have little interest in Murat, even less in Vittoria di Remaldi."

"How fortunate for her," she replied.

" 'Tis only Bonaparte who concerns them."

"And you. Will you die because of him?"

"To stop him . . . if I must. But I shall endeavor to live through this," he added lightly, attempting to reassure her. He realized that he was still holding her hands. "Ah, Beth, I do hate to leave you this way."

She pulled free and wrapped her arms protectively around herself. "But you always intended to leave me. What shall you do if you accomplish your mission?" What had made her ask that?

"I never intended to be a spy, Beth," he replied as he gingerly slipped on the blood-encrusted jacket. "My family has disowned me for cowardice. Perhaps I can redeem myself . . . if the war reopens, I should like to purchase a commission in the army . . . fight Bonaparte with honor on the battlefield. God, I've hated this sneaking about in back alleys!"

"Your family doesn't know you've been risking your life for your country?"

He could hear the shock in her voice. "My orders explicitly forbade telling anyone. What could be more convincing than to be shunned as a coward by one's own family? My father went to his grave thinking I was unfit to bear the Jamison name."

Beth could hear the desolation in those words. He had sacrificed everything for his country and been disgraced for his devotion. By comparison, her desertion of her family to pursue her own dreams seemed shallow and selfish. She did not know how to console him. They lived in such different worlds . . . and they always would.

She looked so vulnerable standing there, pale and ethereal in white silk. He interpreted the pain he saw in her eyes as accusation. "I made you no more promises than you did me," he said sadly, feeling like a cad and hating himself for it.

"I asked nothing of you when we became lovers," she said, swallowing the lump in her throat. *So it has come to this at the end.* "Good-bye, Derrick."

He ached to take her in his arms one last time, but if he did, he feared he might not leave ever . . . and that could not be. "Good-bye, Beth." He bowed stiffly and turned away.

She watched at the window as he slipped silently through the gardens, moving with startling speed for a man who had been so gravely injured. As she suspected, he made his way into the stable, where Vittoria's prize horses were kept. As the sun rose over the distant ridges on the eastern horizon, he rode the contessa's swiftest stallion into its brilliant light.

121

Against the odds, Derrick made it over the Apennines and took ship across the Adriatic. During the voyage he lay abed trying to prepare his report to the Austrian authorities when he reached Trieste. The note signed by Bonaparte's own hand was so hopelessly stained with Derrick's blood that it was crumbling and illegible. Having dealt with the Austrians before, he was not optimistic regarding any effective response from them.

At night he tossed in restless sleep, dreaming of Beth Blackthorne. Seeing her face in front of him had been the only thing that kept him riding the cold and rugged trails with his side throbbing wickedly. Her stitches had held. If he had started bleeding while in the wilderness, he would be dead now. To her, he already was. His betrayal had killed her love. Impossible though that love was, he mourned its loss nonetheless.

Derrick arrived in Vienna on March 5. He found that Foreign Secretary Castlereagh had returned to London, leaving Wellington in charge of the British delegation to the peace conference. At least the allies' most able commander was present to take the field against Bonaparte. After a terse interview with the duke, a man noted for his brusqueness, Jamison was instructed to deliver his information to their Austrian allies.

Derrick cooled his heels in the antechambers of Prince Metternich's palace for several hours before being granted an audience. He seethed, for every moment the allies dithered, Bonaparte drew another mile closer to Paris.

As charming as he was ruthless, the prince listened to Jamison's report, delivered in flawless French. Although he gave no indication, Derrick understood every word exchanged in German between Metternich and his ministers. As instructed, he imparted these juicy details to Wellington, using the opportunity to request that he be allowed to serve under the duke in the upcoming conflict. The request was denied.

By March 9, Napoleon was once again at the head of a rejoicing French army that had eagerly deserted its hated

Bourbon king. Not until the thirteenth was a formal declaration of war announced by Britain, Austria, Russia and Prussia. Wellington departed to take command of his troops in Belgium. All of Europe girded for another war. And Derrick Jamison was given his new assignment.

"What you need is a bracing bit of sea air to clear your mind, *cara*," Vittoria said to Beth. She had come upon her young friend once again standing at the window of her studio, gazing at the eastern horizon like a lost soul. Beth had not painted since Derrick Jamison had fled two months before. All she had done since was mope about her studio, playing at sketching but doing no real work.

"You cannot go on this way. I vow, no one has ever died of a broken heart, but you may be the first. You do not even eat!" She pointed an accusatory finger at an untouched plate of oysters sautéed with ripe olives and sweet pimento. No delicacy seemed to tempt Beth's palette and she was losing weight. Vittoria was alarmed.

Beth set down her charcoal and turned from the half-finished drawing. "I don't mean to worry you . . . it's just that I can't get my bearings. Perhaps I should go home and spend some time with my family."

"Who would immediately barrage you with eligible young bachelors. I do not believe that would solve your problem—only create new ones."

"You mean I might succumb to marriage."

"Wed in haste, repent at leisure," Vittoria replied. "You're particularly vulnerable right now. The last thing you need is to be placed in a situation where you might make a life-altering decision."

Beth sighed and paced across her cluttered studio to her only view of the bay. "A sea voyage might be a good idea. I've heard that Sicily has some marvelous ruins, and the Baleric Islands are said to be wild and enchanting. Perhaps they might inspire me to paint again."

"There have been ugly rumors about Algerian corsairs being sighted off the coast of Sicily. . . ." Vittoria's voice faded as she considered the danger.

"I have heard those rumors ever since I arrived in Naples," Beth said dismissively.

"You are right. If we cower in port every time a Barbary galley is sighted, we shall never leave Naples again!" Vittoria rubbed her hands eagerly. "I shall book us passage immediately. Once you gain some perspective on the matter, you will see that the world does not begin and end with Derrick Jamison."

The salt spray was invigorating. Beth stood on the deck of the brigantine *Sea Sprite,* breathing in the dawn air as the bow pitched and rolled with each swell. She was the only passenger aboard who had not spent the night wretched with *mal de mer.* Vittoria was also an excellent sailor, but an infected tooth had forced her to remain behind. She had insisted that Beth go ahead and they would rendezvous in Palermo at the end of the month. Meanwhile, Beth had visited several of the lovely little islands off the coast of Spain. Three finished landscapes were already carefully stored in her cabin below.

In truth, Beth had enjoyed this time to herself, away from Vittoria's constant fretting. Her friend had become an overprotective surrogate mother, which was the last thing Beth needed. But the contessa had been right about leaving behind Naples and its haunting memories of Derrick. Beth began to feel the earlier zest and passion that had fueled her art. The ocean was a magical place, especially the Mediterranean in the spring. She was up every morning with the dawn, paint palette and canvas in front of her, ready to work.

The rough storms of last night had ended just short of daybreak and she was eager to begin. Beth turned from the railing back to her easel, but a loud cry from the crow's nest high over her head distracted her. The lookout was pointing to the southwest. As one sailor scrambled belowdecks to summon the captain, the others grew increasingly agitated, jabbering among themselves in a patois of Calabrian and Genoese dialects.

A trio of sails grew larger and larger on the horizon.

Beth took out her own glass from the paint box at her feet and looked through it. She saw a small swift brig flanked by two schooners, all flying a flag she recognized instantly. She had seen one of those flags on display in Washington when she was a little girl. President Jefferson had dispatched an American fleet to end the demands for tribute. They were Barbary corsairs—slavers and pirates—and they were swiftly gaining on the *Sea Sprite!*

Chapter Ten

The ships approached like birds of prey, the brig in the lead, with the two schooners spreading out to encircle the wallowing old brigantine. They bristled with cannon, and the decks were filled with men whose blood lust seemed palpable across hundreds of yards of pitching ocean. Beth steadied her trembling hands and readjusted her glass to study the lead ship. A tall man with curly red hair appeared in command.

The *rais*. She had heard that many European men turned renegade for the booty, converting to Islam and attacking their former co-religionists with horrible ferocity. The captain towered over his swarthy, slightly built crew. She could not decide which looked more daunting—the crew with their glowing black eyes and drooping mustaches or the *rais* himself, a strapping giant with a flaming red beard. He brandished a wicked-looking scimitar, and his belt was laden with two braces of ornately engraved pistols.

His men carried all manner of weaponry, from Moorish fishtail muskets to the fearsome bows with which they were reputed to be able to fire thirty arrows in the time it took an experienced man to load a musket and fire a single shot. The crew hung over the railings as the *rais* ordered a warning shot fired across the bow of the *Sea Sprite*. The deafening report drowned out the cries of panic from the brigantine's crew, whose captain was trying, in vain, to control his frantic men.

We shall all be enslaved!

Beth had heard stories of the *bagnos* or slave markets of Barbary. Most prisoners were ransomed, she assured herself. The Algerian flag flew boldly from the mast of the *rais's* ship, and was not Algiers known as "the city that bankrupted God" because of the exorbitant ransom fees paid to its dey? But Beth knew female captives were subjected to horrifying indignities prior to their release. Worse yet, if they were young and nubile, they might vanish into a seraglio, never to be seen again by Western eyes.

Your father is a United States senator and a wealthy man, she repeated to herself as the captain of the *Sea Sprite* struck his colors. She debated returning to her cabin, then decided it was better to put on a bold front.

Beth had not counted on the speed with which they would be boarded. The heavily armed corsairs, brandishing scimitars and daggers, swarmed over the railing of the *Sea Sprite* like army ants, knocking the Neapolitan sailors to the deck and placing booted feet on their throats. She stood at the bow, partially obscured by casks of wine that had been lashed against the mast.

Beth watched silently, her dagger hidden in the folds of her skirt, as corsairs began herding the terrified passengers onto the deck. Several fat old merchants' wives were bleating like terrified sheep, much to the amusement of the corsairs, who plucked at their clothing and poked them with the tips of their weapons while relieving them of their jewelry. The male passengers were also stripped of any valuables and then forced to lie flat on the wooden planks like the crew.

Then one of the corsairs, a taller rangy fellow missing all his front teeth, spotted Beth's bright hair as it blew in the breeze. With a guttural cry he dashed toward the bow of the ship and reached for her with a large beringed hand. He pulled her against his body, which stunk of garlic and sour sweat. His skin was clammy in the early morning damp, and he wore only frayed leather breeches cut off at midcalf. His feet were bare and callused like horn, but when Beth stamped with all of her weight on his instep, he howled in pain and released her.

His companions erupted with laughter. Angrily, the corsair withdrew his heavy curved blade and pointed it menacingly at her throat. Beth raised her head haughtily, making no further protest as he once again took her arm roughly. When he lowered his large clumsy weapon and began fondling her breasts, the others now cheered him on, each man eager for his turn at her.

As they crowded closer and her captor began tearing open her blouse, Beth hoped to die quickly. Better that than being torn apart by this filthy mob. She slipped the stiletto from her skirt and plunged it into her attacker's gut, driving it deeply, then ripping upward. With a startled oath, he stumbled back, blood flecking his lips as he watched his entrails spill onto the deck.

As he fell, she grabbed his scimitar and held it in one hand, her bloody dagger clutched in the other. "All right, come and get me, but before you do, I guarantee a high price for my life," she gritted out as they stood for a moment, gaping in shock. The stunned reaction did not last long. One wizened old man missing an eye raised his fist and yelled. They advanced as she retreated toward the end of the bow.

Her last thoughts as she felt the splintery wood press into her back were of Derrick. A profound sense of regret washed over her as two men rushed her from opposite sides while a third came at her head on. She swung the scimitar in her left hand, opening a slash down her frontal attacker's right arm, then caught the fellow at her left with her dagger, puncturing his Adam's apple. Every instant she waited for the shot or thrust that would end her life.

Several balls whizzed around her, missing all but her flying hair. She fought like a cornered wildcat, slashing and thrusting high and low against enemies who suddenly had far greater respect for a mere female as an opponent. Three men were down and two others sufficiently bloodied to withdraw from the fray when a voice boomed out a command in Arabic, then laughed heartily as the corsairs sullenly withdrew, leaving her alone at the bow. She was bleeding from several superficial cuts and her skirt and blouse were rent severely, revealing tempting expanses of pale skin untouched by the sun.

"By Allah's one true Prophet, you are a magnificent wench!" The big redheaded *rais* strode around the wine casks and approached her, then paused just out of range of the scimitar. He stood with his fists on his hips, arrogantly grinning down at her.

At least his teeth are not rotted, she thought in relief. He wore a white linen shirt unlaced, revealing a muscular chest covered with more red hair. His clothing was clean and expensively made. Heavy gold chains hung from his sunburned neck, big gold loops pierced his ears and all manner of gems winked from every finger on his hands as he raised them, palms out, in a placating gesture.

"Be a good cat and sheathe your claws. I'll not harm you, nor let my men have you," he crooned, speaking English with a distinctive Irish lilt.

"Are you in charge of these animals?" She did not yet lower her weapons.

"Aye, that I am. Captain Liam Quinn, at your service, my sweet vixen." He made a courtly bow, sweeping the broad-brimmed, plumed cavalier's hat from his head.

"I am not your vixen, and most certainly not sweet, as you can clearly see," she replied evenly, nudging a dead corsair with the toe of her slipper.

This elicited another burst of hearty laughter. "By Allah, so you are not. But I can also clearly see that you are a rare beauty. It would be a great waste to feed the fishes with such splendid pulchritude, eh?"

"Better fishes than corsairs," she replied. "But I can be ransomed. The Contessa di Remaldi will pay any price you set." At his dubious look, she continued, "My family is wealthy—my father is a United States senator. He will reimburse her the redemptionist fee."

"Ah, so that is the accent. I did not place it at first. I took you for English. So much the better that you're not a member of that bloody race."

"You, a renegade pirate who enslaves Christians, dare to call the English bloody?"

He shrugged in supreme indifference. "My family fell on evil days courtesy of the British army when I was but a stripling. My father was murdered in his bed, my mother died of a broken heart and my elder brother Conal fled, a hunted outlaw forced to hire out his sword to the Spanish king."

His eyes, a green even more vivid than those of Drum, narrowed on her for a moment. She tried to read his enigmatic expression. He might yet turn her over to his crew . . . after he took his fill of her. Beth waited, turning over her options—sure death versus the chance to survive Liam Quinn. "Then you will ransom me?"

"For the right price, yes, I would." He looked her squarely in the eye as he said it, one big hand slowly reaching for the scimitar.

At least she would not be torn apart by a crazed mob. She gambled on Liam Quinn, perhaps a foolhardy thing to do. Had Beth been English, she would never have considered it, but perhaps because she was not one of his hated enemy, he might only use her, then turn her over to the redemptionists for repatriation.

At least he was clean, if not civilized, she thought, forcing back a shudder as she handed him the scimitar and stiletto. She still had a second, smaller dagger hidden inside her soft kid boot, but if she was treated like most captives, it would avail her nothing. En route to Naples, Beth had learned from the American sailors that all prisoners were stripped naked by the corsairs in order to steal their clothing and to prevent them from concealing any weapons.

If he lays one hand on me to take my clothing in front of his men, I'll gut him, she vowed.

But he did nothing of the kind. Extending his hand with

a gracious smile, he took hers and escorted her over the gangplank and aboard his vessel. At Quinn's command, the sweaty, fearsome crew with their motley assortment of weapons, peg legs, eye patches and hooks in place of hands returned to plundering the *Sea Sprite* and securing the hapless prisoners.

"Will any other of the captives be ransomed? I'll vouch that most of them can well afford the price of their freedom. They're wealthy merchants," Beth said with a tinge of guilt as the fat old Genoese spice trader's haughty wife knelt, attempting to cover her naked body with naught but her hands, too frightened and humiliated to cast hateful glances at "that shameless Americana" as she had before.

The *rais* grinned. "I do appreciate your information, but after all these years, I can tell when a pigeon's ripe for plucking with one look at its plumage. The lot of them should make me a tidy sum, even after the dey takes his share."

"You are utterly without conscience," she said, realizing that beneath his charming exterior lay a ruthless will that would be most deadly to cross. The thought of giving her body to him made her ill . . . but the thought of refusing him was even worse.

"And you are utterly foolhardy," he replied. His seeming unconcern with her insult was belied by the slightly increased pressure on her hand as he held it in his grasp.

Beth stared straight ahead as they passed by his crew, ignoring their leering expressions. They were somewhat cleaner and more orderly than the corsairs from the schooners who had first boarded the *Sea Sprite* but still a very rough-looking lot.

Dear God above, what is going to happen to me?

"Are you virgin?"

Quinn's question startled Beth. They were dining in his cabin, a small but luxurious room appointed with the booty from his piracy—golden wall sconces, Venetian glass, silk cushions. As she picked at a hunk of mutton with her fingers—the *rais* dined without utensils, as was

131

the Arab custom—she debated lying, but his next words startled and puzzled her even more.

" 'Twill do no good to lie—the palace midwife is most skilled at making such determinations."

The palace? "No. I had a lover in Naples." She felt it prudent not to share with Quinn that he was English.

"Had?" He cocked his head, waiting as he toyed with the heavy silver wine goblet. "Do I detect a note of sad parting in those words?" He took a sip of the sweet port, studying her over the rim. "What was his name, this Neapolitan lover?"

Beth felt it safer to volunteer as little as possible. Just thinking of Derrick made her ache with sadness. She searched frantically to come up with an Italian name. "Piero," she replied, as the name of Vittoria's long-lost love flashed into her mind.

"A pity. The dey's son is particularly fond of deflowering virgins." He shrugged negligently, then grinned. "But perhaps there will be some . . . other compensation for me . . . not of a monetary nature."

The sinister comment hung on the air while the spicy mutton pitched nastily in her stomach. "What has the dey's son to do with me—you said I was to be ransomed." She dreaded the answer.

"I lied." He grinned rakishly and shoved another chunk of mutton in his mouth. "Little matter what your family so far away in America could pay. 'Twould take too long, even if the dey had not declared war against your prickly young republic for being rather . . . contentious on the subject of tribute."

"Something for your dey to think long and hard on," she replied with building anger—and horror. "My father is a man of great power in President Madison's administration."

"Ah, but if he does not know where you are . . . there is nothing he can do. No, a rare beauty such as you will command a lavish reward from my sovereign. The old dey is too long of tooth to use a woman, but his favorite son and heir, Kasseim, will be delighted to add you to his harem. Since you are already damaged goods, he will not care if I partake of the sweetness first."

The dagger was still in her boot and she ached to plunge it directly into his black Irish heart, but she considered what would happen if she succeeded in killing the *rais*. His men would tear her apart. *Think, think!* she admonished herself, forcing down the red rage blurring her vision.

He studied her with his unnerving eyes of brightest green, leaning back against the deep pile of silken cushions, rubbing his hand over his chest absently, disturbing the patterns of thick red hair. Save for their difference in coloring, he was built much like Derrick, only on a larger scale. That this renegade Musselman was the fair one and her love the dark one was an irony that did not escape her. How could the one man so utterly entrance her, the other so thoroughly repulse her?

"I've always fancied dark women, never been interested in the pale, puling Northerners we've captured ... until now." He rolled up in one lithe motion and reached across the foot-high lacquered table upon which they had dined.

His big hand curved around her forearm, enveloping it, but before he could pull her up, she slipped from his grasp and scooted back against the wall. "You would enjoy it far more if I were willing ..." she said in a low, husky voice.

"Ah, colleen, that might be, but I'll not bargain your freedom for your body when I can possess it without." He sounded almost regretful.

"No, that is not what I meant." She knew that ploy would be hopeless. "I do not wish to conceive ... or to be given the sailor's disease." Rather than risk slow death by the pox, she would kill him or herself. She slipped one hand inside her boot, hidden beneath her skirt, and felt the tiny dagger.

Beth never knew whether or not Quinn would have agreed to her terms, for at that very moment a loud cry sounded abovedeck, followed by the boom of cannon fire. The *rais* jumped to his feet with a snarled oath and ran from the room, not even taking time to lock the door to

133

his cabin. She heard the babble of voices speaking excitedly in Arabic mixed with the rumble of artillery and the splintering sounds of cannonballs smashing wood. Hope seared her like a flame. If those attacking were European, she and all the other captives might be rescued! Beth climbed the small narrow stairs leading abovedeck.

The scene that greeted her was like a painting of hell by Bosch or Brueghel. Quinn's ships were engaged in a battle to the death. The main mast of his brig had been shattered halfway and broken off, groaning in the wind as it hung by its lines, the sails shredded and blackened by gunpowder. Men lay sprawled grotesquely, some dead, others dying. Blood ran red on the planks. Beth peered through the smoke-blackened air to see the attacker's flag. Her heart sank when she recognized it as Maltese. The corsairs of Malta were bitter rivals of Algiers, but every bit as infamous for being cutthroat slavers.

There would be no salvation if Quinn lost. Just then the Irishman ordered his port battery to fire on one of the brigs that was attempting to flank them. She watched, fascinated in spite of herself as his seamanship and daring began to turn the tide. His shots struck the flanking brig at the waterline, nearly cutting it in two. As it began to sink, he signaled his sloops to reopen fire on the remaining Maltese brig now that he had directed them into position.

Before the crew of the sloops swarmed aboard, the Maltese ship managed to fire off one final salvo, which was enough to wreak even more havoc aboard Quinn's brig, smashing into the quarterdeck and sending men flying like bits of kindling. A jagged piece of railing struck the *rais*, knocking him to his knees as blood began to spread across his bare chest. He continued to bark orders, then slowly crumpled to the deck. "Better the enemy I know than one I do not," Beth muttered to herself as she raced toward the stricken *rais*.

"Tell them to fetch my trunks. I need the medicines in one of them," she said to Quinn as she began slicing off a big piece of her skirt with the dagger from her boot, then applying it as a compress to his side.

Eyeing the small blade, he grinned crookedly in spite of the pain. "Would you have used it on me, colleen?"

"We can discuss that later—if you don't bleed to death dallying."

He gave several commands in Arabic, and two of his men scurried to retrieve her belongings while three others carried their fallen leader below. Within a few moments he was lying in his cabin while Beth dug through her trunk for the medical supplies she always carried. "I'll need yarrow . . . the needle and suture . . ." she murmured more to herself than him as he watched from the large pallet in the center of the room.

"I take it you've done this before," he remarked.

She looked up, then snapped tersely, "Altogether more often than I care to discuss."

He was a more obliging patient than Derrick had been, passing out halfway through the suturing. The corsair's injury was far deeper and required that she dig ugly shards of wood from his flesh before she could cleanse the area and stitch it. She hoped he would not die of blood loss or fever . . . at least not 'til she could get free of his ship.

As she watched through the night, Quinn did grow feverish, tossing and crying out in delirium. All she could do was sponge his body with cool water and wait. All the while her thoughts turned to Derrick. Had he fallen from his horse somewhere in the cold reaches of the Apennines . . . lain bleeding on the hard earth? Was he long dead?

Shuddering, she tried to push the ghastly images from her mind. *No, if he were dead, I would know. Some part of me would feel it, I am certain.* Even that reassurance was cold comfort, for her love was lost to her.

Quinn came out of his feverish stupor on the second day but remained too weak to do more than allow her to spoon broth into his mouth and issue a few brief orders to his second in command. The scowling Algerian Selim understood not a word of English, or at least pretended not to. Beth knew her safety, probably her very life, rested on Quinn's survival. An odd sort of companiate relationship

135

developed between them over the next few days as they sailed toward his home . . . and her destiny.

The Barbary port of Algiers was a suprisingly large place, appearing from a distance much like other European cities in the Mediterranean. But on closer inspection, Beth could see that it was indeed the bastion of an alien civilization; it extended in a crescent three miles across with two massive walls fortifying it, nearly a hundred feet high in many places. Three hundred brass cannon were positioned on those walls, facing the harbor. Crenellated towers at several points had numerous narrow windows from which the famed Janissary archers could fire a hail of arrows on any invaders fortunate enough to get past the cannon.

From slender high minarets across the city the sounds of muezzins calling the faithful to prayer echoed eerily over the waters of the harbor as they sailed in. Beth stood beside Liam Quinn studying the largest building, a monolithic structure in the center of the walled city . . . the dey's palace. *Will I ever leave once I enter it?* She shivered in spite of the warm sun.

As if intuiting her thoughts, Quinn said, " 'Twill not be so bad, colleen. A woman with your beauty and intelligence can rise far in the hierarchy of the harem."

"I can think of nothing more abhorrent than spending my life cloistered in some man's seraglio."

"Kasseim is well favored, young . . . once you give him children, he will be generous."

"Will he give my freedom?"

"Ah, Beth, you are too single-minded for your own good," he replied with a shaky sigh, taking a seat on the rail. This was his first time abovedeck since his injury and he was still weak. "Only have a care that you curb your outspoken American tongue in front of the dey. You would not like his methods of punishing insolence."

"So you have described in gory detail. I have not survived this far to perish at the hands of some petty tyrant."

He looked at her dubiously, then shrugged in regret. "If only we had been able to share one night together . . ."

"It's not too late. Just turn about and sail for Naples."

"So single-minded," he chided again.

Chapter Eleven

From the outside, the Dey of Algiers's palace was a large pile of limestone, plain and unprepossessing. However, the interior was truly amazing. In its labyrinth of open courtyards tropical birds with brilliant plumage sang from the branches of lemon and orange trees; and gardens lush with myrtle, jasmine, roses and tropical flowers of every hue surrounded burbling fountains full of brightly glistening fish. Highly polished marble floors gleamed in hues of pink and green. The slippered footsteps of servants seemed to hiss through the corridors.

On a dais four steps above the vast hall the dey reclined on an enormous high-backed throne of beaten gold. He was a small man, his face pale and shriveled. But the hard black light of his narrowed gaze indicated that he was a wily and dangerous man.

Derrick Jamison waited for his audience with the dey, all the while studying the undercurrents between the fish-eyed Janissaries and quick-tempered locals. He had languished for nearly two months in the opulent capital, making friends with the dey's eldest son and heir, Kasseim.

137

This had been the last place he wished to be when Bonaparte's army took the field against the allies to decide the fate of Europe.

But he had been dispatched to keep an eye on the war between the United States and Algiers. At the end of May, England's old nemesis Commodore Stephen Decatur had been dispatched to North Africa with a fleet of nine American warships. When Decatur's upstart nation had refused to pay the customary tribute to Algiers, the dey foolishly decided to use the young republic as an example. Having followed Decatur's career during the late war between their countries, Derrick had not been surprised by what transpired, all of which he reported in detailed dispatches to London. The commodore was wreaking even more havoc on the dey's corsairs than he had on the Royal Navy.

Damned if he didn't admire the Yankee. *Just as you admire Elizabeth Blackthorne.* In spite of the hopelessness of it all, he could not help replaying their last night together and brooding over the possibility of returning one day to Naples.

He knew he only deceived himself with wishful dreams. He had spent his life on the edge, a man without a country who could never reveal the truth of who he was. Leighton might provide him a meager stipend on the condition that he never set foot in England again, but pride forbade him from asking for that. He had few prospects if he left the Foreign Service. None of which would allow him the luxury of supporting a mistress—much less a wife. Beth's family was rich. He could have lived off her, but that was even more galling than crawling to his brother.

The thought of marriage still gave him shudders. He would far prefer resuming the freedom of their old relationship, but at the end neither of them had been happy with that arrangement. She had tormented him by lying naked in front of lecherous old Neapolitan painters, dancing indecently close with handsome noblemen and walking about the public markets on the waterfront teasing burly young fishermen until they fair drooled. He had become increasingly jealous, an emotion no other woman had ever succeeded in arousing in him.

But Beth had made it clear that she would never wed. Her painting would always come before home and hearth. She would allow no husband to demand attention and loyalty that she did not wish to give. She had told him she wanted no children. Since his elder brother had the duty to provide the Jamison heirs, he had never given the slightest thought to the idea of children. Yet, bizarre as it seemed, seeing Kasseim with his young sons and daughters had made him reconsider the idea of being a father.

His melancholy reverie was interrupted by one of the Janissaries, who informed him that the dey would grant him the honor of a brief audience. Grateful to turn his mind to something productive, Jamison approached the throne.

"What news of the great battles in Europe?" the dey inquired as a Nubian slave wafted a fan over his sovereign's turbaned head. Although he understood English, the arrogant old man refused to speak it, insisting that all court matters be handled either through translators or in Arabic. Derrick's Arabic was adequate to the task.

Hate to disappoint you, old boy. Derrick knew all the Barbary states considered the conflict between Napoleon and the allies to be a great windfall that they hoped would not end any time soon. As long as it continued, they had free rein to loot the Mediterranean. Smiling after he made the customary bow, he replied, "Excellency, the great battle has been concluded in the Low Countries, near a place called Waterloo. The French have been defeated decisively and their emperor will be well and truly banished this time."

"That is good news indeed," the dey said after a pregnant pause. His sour expression indicated that he thought it was anything but.

Then the dey's chief of eunuchs slithered up from behind the dais and whispered something in his ruler's ear. The old man smiled slyly and dismissed the slave. Waving his ministers to silence, he said to the Englishman, "I am informed that one of my *rais* has returned with captives to be ransomed . . . a rather large group including several of your countrymen—and women. I would, of course, be pleased to allow you to speak with the English prisoners and make arrangements for their repatriation."

The dey's attempt to curry favor with his government was transparent. "You are most gracious, Excellency. When might I be permitted to see the prisoners?"

"They are being brought to the palace right now. Hammet will escort you," he said, indicating the burly eunuch, who bowed obsequiously.

Derrick followed the giant from the audience room through a twisting labyrinth of corridors to the courtyard where a dozen heavily armed Janissaries stood guard over around thirty men. As was the Islamic custom, the women had been separated from the men as soon as they reached shore.

Poor blighters. They looked starved and filthy, not to mention frightened within an inch of their sanity. As soon as he identified himself, he was assaulted by a babble of languages: Italian, French and even German, as well as English. After explaining that he himself could only assist British subjects, he assured them that their own legations would be informed and ransoms arranged.

In the middle of the discussion, Jamison heard the sounds of an altercation echoing through the latticed partition of the courtyard. Female voices were raised in high-pitched squeals—no, he amended, not all female, at least one was a eunuch attempting unsuccessfully to restore order amid the female prisoners, who apparently had not as yet been ushered into the women's quarters.

"I am an American and we grovel before no one—nor strip naked to be inspected like cattle! If you want my clothes, you try to take them—then try to make me press my face in the dirt!"

Beth! Derrick could never mistake her voice. He stood frozen for a moment as the men around him stared at him uneasily. An English merchant named Binghamton volunteered, "That must be the Blackthorne baggage. American," he sniffed. "A hussy with a frightful reputation. Took straightaway to the pirate captain's bed without a moment's hesitation. About time she received her come-uppance."

"Really," Derrick replied coldly.

The pompous merchant might have embellished his tale further if a loud Italian oath had not interrupted them, followed by more sounds of scuffling and the high-pitched wail of the eunuch. Beth, disheveled and flushed with fury, came flying into the open courtyard where the men were clustered, pursued by the hapless eunuch, who sported what would soon be a beauty of a black eye.

Expecting no help from the wretched male prisoners, she ignored the lot of them and made for the large tree growing beside an exterior wall. But before she could get more than a foothold in the lower branches two of the Janissaries were upon her. Hauling her down, they struggled to subdue her. Derrick stood watching in horrified disbelief, knowing that if he exhibited any undue interest in her, the Janissaries would immediately report it to the dey. That would significantly hinder his options for getting her out of here. He was grateful that she had not recognized him standing at the rear of the crowd of men.

She was magnificent, making the tough, wiry Turks expend considerable energy before they finally succeeded in getting her to the entrance of the women's quarters, where a phalanx of eunuchs had now assembled to take charge. Elizabeth Blackthorne, of the illustrious Georgia Blackthornes, was dragged unceremoniously by her hair to meet her fate in the harem of the Dey of Algiers.

Her head ached from those savages in pantaloons dragging her by her hair. She was filthy from wrestling with the oily slavers who had tried to force her to salaam. In spite of their efforts, she stood up straight, glaring back at them. Beth noted with satisfaction that it had taken four of the strange attendants to hold her down while a fifth stripped off her clothing. But that was small consolation as she stood shivering naked in front of her emasculated captors, cursing Liam Quinn with every fiber of her being.

By the time the eunuchs had subdued her, the other female captives from the *Sea Sprite*, who were to be ransomed with their menfolk, had all been ushered away. She stood alone surrounded by the eunuchs, who treated her as nothing more than a commodity, much as butchers would regard a slab of meat. It was eerily unnerving, but nothing compared to the inspection she received when a mysterious woman walked into the room.

The apparition was cloaked head to foot in black silk, dripping with jewelry. The old crone must be someone of import, although from what little Beth knew of Islamic society, females were always subservient. Who was she? Someone to decide the fate of a lone American woman? Beth met the old woman's assessing eyes, trying to gauge what was going on behind them.

The eunuchs all scraped and bowed before her as if she were the dey himself. She was tall for an Arab woman. Her face resembled a pitted date, long and narrow, the nose faintly hooked at the tip, the lips compressed as if they had never smiled. Her eyes were the most arresting thing about her countenance, black as a starless night, deep set, sweeping up and down the tall voluptuous foreign female.

Ignoring the arrogance of Beth's returning glare, the stranger studied the younger woman's high, firm breasts, slim waist and long, perfectly sculpted legs. "My son will enjoy her . . . once we break her cursed infidel pride," she said in flawless French to one of the eunuchs.

A retort to the hag's nasty remark sprung to her lips, but she suppressed it. If they believed she spoke nothing but English it might work to her advantage. She stood still, waiting to see what would come next, bracing herself.

"You will learn to obey," the old woman said in thickly accented English.

"I am not an animal to be poked and examined for defects," Beth replied evenly.

A thin smirk animated the old woman's lower face for a moment. "Fortunate for you that you have none—physically. As for your behavior . . . you will learn the way of Islam for women . . . or be sold in the *bagnos* to some Berber camel driver." Motioning to the eunuchs to seize Beth, she turned and walked imperiously away.

The thought of their plump, asexual hands on her body made Beth shiver. She shook them off and followed the old woman into an immense vaulted room filled with the miasmic vapor of sulfur, wet and dense as Neapolitan fog. High windows ringed the domed ceiling, their light barely penetrating through the gloom. Small wonder, for the entire blue-tiled floor was under an inch or more of water, which splashed from huge brass spigots. The water spilled over the edges of the big porcelain tubs around which clustered naked women of all races.

While still standing in the doorway, Beth was given a pair of pattens, much like those worn by European women in inclement weather to protect their shoes and the hems of their skirts, wooden platforms fitted in this case to the bare feet of the bathers and their servants. Not knowing what ichor might lie in the bubbling water sluicing across the floor of the chamber, she put them on willingly while glancing nervously around the crowded room.

Nubians with skin like glowing ebony chattered with gold-haired Circassians and exotic-looking Orientals. The rankings were readily discernible when Beth observed that those seated on bamboo stools were being bathed by the others, who scrubbed vigorously with pumice stones and huge loofahs. At a glance she could see that the most comely of the females were being waited upon by those less favored. The only exceptions were a few older women, probably the wives of the dey and his ministers who lived at the palace.

From her position at the entry, the black-robed harridan who was the dey's chief wife directed the eunuch to take Beth to the closest tub of running water. She dismissed the women nearby, who were curiously gawking at the newcomer. One of the bamboo seats was produced and the eunuch indicated that Beth should sit upon it. Never in her life had she taken a bath while a crowd of people watched her. Still, she was filthy and desperate for some clothing. If cleansing was a prerequisite, so be it.

She reached for the loofah and a bar of the scented soap the eunuch held. He began chattering in Arabic, pointing to the chair. Beth shook her head. "Don't be ridiculous. I can wash myself quite adequately," she said, again trying to take the soap.

"You will be seated. My personal slaves will bathe you," the chief wife commanded in English as the eunuch handed over the soap and loofah to a thin sallow-complected slave woman whose eyes were sullenly downcast. A second one took the big sponge while a third stood back, holding a bowl filled with some vile-smelling paste.

Beth stifled her angry retort. Sitting passively while two women lathered and scrubbed every inch of her skin, even the most intimate places, was mortifying. They applied pumice and loofah with puritanical zeal, as if dirt and sweat were tantamount to original sin itself. Taking particular time with her hair, they sudsed the long curly mane with floral-scented shampoo, then beaten egg yolks.

"For shine," the girl called Naime explained in French.

Beth pretended not to understand as they applied the golden foam. Once satisfied that the job had been completed satisfactorily, they filled big clay urns with the clean mineral waters from the spigot and poured them over her head and entire body until she was fair drowned in the deluge.

The dey's chief wife had assembled a "work crew" of slaves while this process went on. She issued crisp orders to them in Arabic, then departed with a swish of her shroudlike skirts, the eunuchs all following except for one hapless soul left to see that her commands were carried out.

The oldest of the three slaves, whom the others called Zehra, a gnarled dark-skinned woman with oddly pale eyes and large brown teeth, issued instructions to her young charges. She approached with the vile-smelling bowl and dipped a brush into the paste.

"*Rusma,*" was all she said, indicating that Beth should

stand up. When she did so, the two younger women each raised one of her arms. Zehra applied the paste to her armpits.

At first it tickled, then it began to burn like Hades. Beth broke away and almost dived into the tub in her haste to remove the evil stuff. To her horror, faint bits of reddish underarm hair floated away with it. Well, that was not too bad, she supposed, although best gotten over with quickly. Then they applied it to her legs, where it did not burn as fiercely on the less sensitive skin, but when they indicated that she was to allow them to do the same thing to the red triangle at the juncture of her thighs, she balked.

"Good God, what kind of barbarians are you! You'll ruin me!" she shrieked, kicking the bowl from Zehra's hands.

"Sit quiet. Will not harm you," Zehra said in crude English as the other two quickly gathered up the broken clay and scooped up most of the glop around it, then scurried away to procure more, casting exceedingly hateful looks at the new captive.

"I'll break your scrawny neck if you try to burn away my woman's parts—do you understand me?" Beth gritted out, red-faced with fear and fury.

Zehra shook her head, as if dealing with a child. "Hair on woman body . . . ugly. Kasseim not like." As if that was all that mattered.

"Good! Already I do not like him one whit and I've yet to meet him!" To these poor benighted creatures, doing what men found pleasing might have been all they lived for, but she would be damned if she abided by their rules.

After three more tries and a truly awful mess of *rusma* around the bathing tub—Beth was certain it must have been enough to eat the pattens off their feet by the time they cleaned it up—Zehra abandoned her attempts to "beautify" the wild American savage in the proscribed manner. Shaking her head in frustration, she led Beth to an adjacent room, where a vast pool of clear aqua water was populated by yet more women, a few swimming, others playing and splashing each other like children. And

145

there were children, too. Girls of all ages and boys, although none of the males were much past weaning age. "Swim?" she asked.

Unable to believe the beneficence of Zehra's offer, Beth kicked off her pattens and dived into the cool water. After her days of confinement on Quinn's brig, then sitting through the ministrations of the slave girls, any activity other than fighting was pure heaven. She swam until she was exhausted, then crawled to the edge of the pool and fell asleep on the cool tiles.

There was method to Zehra's madness. When Beth awakened, she was being carried by two of the eunuchs to a private chamber where the chief wife awaited her, seated on a luxurious pile of cushions, smoking from a hookah. Vittoria had some Magyar friends who were addicted to the Turkish water pipe, which could be used for tobacco or a combination of narcotics, usually hashish and opium.

As she was deposited on the floor, Beth observed the old woman's heavy-lidded eyes and slack mouth and decided that the faint sweetish aroma of the pipe was certainly owing to opiates of some sort. The chief wife pointed to a loose caftan of sheer white linen, indicating that Beth was to don it. Relieved to finally be clothed, she complied.

As she was slipping it over her head, the old crone said, "Now, we begin your instruction in pleasing a man . . ."

Derrick learned through sources carefully cultivated in the palace that the fire haired American female was destined to become the slave of the dey's son. Right now Kasseim was scouring the hills with his Janissaries in search of raiding nomadic tribesmen who had attacked one of the dey's outposts. He was expected back within a few days. Derrick wracked his brain for some way to get the prince to give up his new concubine.

If you were given Elizabeth Blackthorne to do with as you wished, would you relinquish her to please a diplomat?

A ridiculous question. But then, Kasseim had dozens of beautiful women in his harem, and Derrick knew he preferred them sweet-tempered, meek and obedient. He smiled grimly. After Beth's demonstration in front of the Janissaries, it must be abundantly clear to everyone in the palace that those were qualities she would never possess.

If only he could find a way to reach her and secure her cooperation. Such an undertaking was not only personally risky but would endanger his mission and British relations with the dey if he were caught. Still, he knew he could never leave Beth to spend the rest of her life as a harem slave. A free-spirited American such as she would whither and die in a gilded cage.

Nola, a lovely Circassian woman with bright yellow hair and exotic high cheekbones, had been provided by the dey to amuse Derrick during his sojourn in Algiers. She had been raised as a slave and would unquestioningly do anything asked by her master . . . who at this point in time happened to be the Englishman. He formulated his plan.

Chapter Twelve

Beth sat alone in the small garden alcove, shaded by an acacia tree, her heart beating wildly as she looked around surreptitiously to be certain no one was watching her. She slipped the note from the pocket of her caftan and read it.

Beth,
   Do everything you can without endangering your life to infuriate old Fatima, the dey's chief wife. Refuse all instruction and show that splendid American temper. It will work toward winning you your freedom. No time to explain. Keep hope alive. Destroy this message as soon as you read it. If we are discovered, the dey will have both of our heads.
   Derrick

The message had been slipped to her with the greatest secrecy as the harem women were allowed the respite of fresh air in the seraglio gardens. Beth did not recognize the striking blonde who had delivered it but knew that any communication from the outside was strictly forbidden.

She had hidden the tiny scrap of paper until she was able to find a place where she could read it without anyone seeing.

Derrick! Alive! Here in Algiers! But why—and how had he learned that she was a prisoner? *Foolish questions,* she berated herself. He was an agent of the English king, a spy. Lord only knew what intrigue had brought him to North Africa, but whatever kind fate had intervened, she would not question it. This could mean swift deliverance . . . or a slow, horrible death.

Trembling, she tore the note into tiny scraps of confetti, hiding the evidence beneath the richly tilled soil with her hands. Beth considered the stories she had overheard regarding punishments for harem women who were caught communicating with men who were not their masters. The kindest fate was to be tied alive in a heavy sack weighted down with rocks, then cast into the harbor to drown.

Shuddering, she pushed the thought aside and dreamed of her English lover. Not a day had passed since he'd left Naples without her thinking of him, missing him, desiring him. What would he expect of her when they were reunited? That she would fall into his arms in gratitude, once more becoming his mistress? Or, worse yet, might he simply be doing his duty as an English gentleman in rescuing her—would she be of no further interest to him after she was free?

That is a bridge to be crossed when this nightmare ends. If *it ever ends.*

Pushing her disquieting thoughts aside, Beth began to plot her strategy for becoming the worst pupil old Fatima had ever attempted to train in the arts of pleasing the almighty Kasseim. A slow smile spread across her face as she contemplated it.

"Ah, my friend, your barb is splendid, but there is nothing like sitting an English Thoroughbred," Derrick said, patting his big bay's neck as he watched the light in Kasseim's eyes dance. They rode side by side through a fertile river valley, a few miles outside the city.

"I do not think so. We must race them when they are fresh to see who is right," the prince replied.

His coal-black Arabian stallion was small and fine-boned compared to the Thoroughbred, but Derrick knew the breed to possess tremendous strength and stamina. Kasseim was a handsome man, slim and swarthy with liquid black eyes and a wide sensuous mouth.

Derrick did not reply to the prince's offer of a race immediately. Palm trees swayed in the lush moist breeze as they neared the city after a day of hunting in the foothills. "A race, you say?" He feigned disinterest, knowing Kasseim, like most of his countrymen, was an inveterate gambler.

"I believe Prince Tarak is swifter than your stallion. Would you be willing to wager him?"

Perfect! "I might . . . if we could agree on something worth my while." He shrugged, as if the idea were of no great import to him. Kasseim ticked off a list of his Arab racers, several of which Derrick actually would have loved to own. " 'Tis risky transporting horseflesh by sea. I shall most likely be returning to England during the winter, when the Atlantic is roughest. In fact, I have been considering leaving Excaliber behind when I depart."

That remark pricked Kassein's interest mightily. "Then you would, of course, allow me the first opportunity to purchase him . . . if I do not win him, that is," he added with a chuckle. "Ah! I have it. Something that might induce you to the contest . . . a beautiful woman, a new one from my own harem."

Derrick smiled inwardly. For the past several days the palace had been abuzz with rumors about the incorrigible American female slave whose shrewish temper and blatant defiance could not be curbed even with frequent applications of the bastinado. Beth was playing her part to the hilt—too much so for his comfort. He must rescue her soon else old Fatima might have her maimed or drowned.

"This new female would not be that wild American, perchance?" he asked with a chuckle.

"I see you have heard of her," Kasseim replied sourly.

"She will never be a true daughter of Allah, I fear, but she speaks English and is magnificent to look upon—great clouds of red hair the color of a desert sunrise, a waist so tiny." He demonstrated with his hands, going on to describe her breasts, hips, legs, until Derrick found himself grinding his teeth with jealousy.

"If she is such a hellion, it must be dangerous to bed her. She might take it into her head to lop off your cock while you sleep some night," he said, fishing to find out if his friend had indeed taken Beth—a subject that the palace gossips dared not discuss.

"I have entertained such misgivings, believe me," Kasseim replied, laughing. "My mother wishes to sell her to the *bagnos,* but that seems a waste of such lush flesh."

"Perhaps that might be the safest solution," Derrick said helpfully. If Beth was taken from the palace and sold in the open slave market, he could purchase her, by far the easiest and surest way to free her. He noted that Kasseim had not indicated whether he had used Beth yet. *The rais has already had her. What matter if Kasseim has or not?* But it did matter. A very great deal, although Derrick refused to admit it even to himself.

"Then you are not interested in winning her?" Kasseim studied the Englishman's face. Western men had strange and often fascinating ideas about women.

"I did not say that," Derrick replied casually. He'd better tread very carefully. Kasseim or his mother could just as well have Beth killed as sold. "If she is truly so beautiful, I might be tempted. She has not been scarred?" He was terrified of what the dey's vindictive chief wife might do, since Beth had been playing her part with such zeal.

"No. We are not barbarians," Kasseim replied stiffly. "The bastinado is painful, but it leaves no permanent injury."

"Just very sore feet," Derrick replied with a forced grin. "I shall agree to the wager. Even allowing for . . . ah, some slight exaggeration, the creature you've described must be exceptional."

"Good. It is my understanding that European men do

151

not require the same . . . er . . . serene qualities in female disposition that we do. Perhaps she might please you greatly, my friend," Kasseim said with a laugh. "But first you would have to win the race—something I do not believe Prince Tarak and I will allow!"

When Derrick returned to his quarters in the British legation, he had a surprise visitor. Alvin Francis Edward Drummond slumped petulantly on a Dante chair, fanning himself in the humid late afternoon heat.

"Drum, what the devil are you doing in Algiers?"

"Precisely the question I've been asking myself ever since setting foot on this accursed heathen shore. 'Tis a veritable viper pit. I was forced to sail from Sicily aboard one of the corsairs' ships, and the captain had the unmitigated audacity to feed me camel meat—camel meat!" He shuddered at the memory.

"Camel is considered a delicacy in some parts of the east," Derrick replied, suppressing a grin. "But you still have not explained what compelled you to come here. I expected you'd be sipping port at White's by this time."

"So did I," Drum said glumly. "But fate in the form of Lord Exmouth intervened."

Jamison knew Exmouth by reputation in the Foreign Office. "He's cunning and utterly ruthless when he wants something. What has happened to merit sending a personal messenger all the way from Europe? I received the dispatches from Brussels regarding Wellington's victory. Surely there's been no further problem with Bonaparte."

"Old Boney's goose is cooked," Drum replied dismissively. "No, this pertains to that rash American chap you so admire, Decatur."

"The commodore has put on quite a show of force along the North African coast," Derrick replied with some relish.

"So your dispatches indicated. That was why the Foreign Office saw fit to send me here," Drum replied accusatorily. "It would seem Lord Exmouth is interested in mounting a British expedition to achieve the same results for jolly old England . . . once Decatur actually gets the old dey to sign on the dotted line. I'm to report the details of the treaty between the United States and Algiers after it's signed. Then all British subjects here are to make arrangements to depart before Exmouth's fleet comes a-calling."

Jamison whistled low. "No small order. What am I to do then?"

Drum smiled broadly now. "A task you should relish—return to Naples and keep an eye on the Bourbon restoration to the throne now that Murat is dead."

Derrick paced across the floor of the cluttered room. Beth was not in Naples waiting for him as Drum assumed. He looked over to Drummond and said, "I have some disturbing news regarding Beth . . ."

After Derrick had finished imparting the details of Beth's capture, Drum was aghast. "And you believe you can win her freedom in a horse race? Can that heathen prince be trusted to keep his word?"

"I believe so, but if Decatur comes sailing into the harbor beforehand, matters might get a bit sticky."

Drum huffed. "I daresay Decatur would demand the repatriation of all American captives."

"There are still dangers—the dey and his son are proud men. Rather than see the sanctity of their harem breached, they might have Beth killed. Our safest course would be for me to win her from Kasseim . . . if possible . . . but just in case, I have a backup plan."

Early the following morning the laughing, boisterous crowd of men, mostly Kasseim's brothers and friends from the court, rode with their prince and the Englishman. Having observed many such races since his arrival, Derrick was expecting that they would head toward the flat grassy plains of the river valley where such contests were usually held.

However, Kasseim veered from that course and rode instead into the rocky hills that ringed the city to the southwest. "We are not going to the racecourse where you defeated Al-sedac last week, my friend?" Derrick asked innocently.

153

Kasseim chuckled. "I prefer to test Prince Tarak's mettle over a longer course. Surely you feel your English horse equal to such a challenge, do you not?"

"As you wish, my friend." Derrick cursed silently. The young heir was his father's son in cunning. His Thoroughbred was fast as lightning on a straightaway over a mile or so but would not be as sure-footed and long-winded on rough, uneven terrain. There the sturdy little Arabian would have the advantage.

His only hope for victory was to save Excaliber's speed for a final burst at the finish line. It was well that they had agreed to race early in the day, before the heat became oppressive and gave Prince Tarak yet another advantage.

"To show my sporting blood, I will not make the course overlong. Say from the shepherd's hut to the ridge," Kasseim said, pointing to a rocky outcrop looming in the distance. He directed several of his guards to take positions at the opposite end of the course, which was easily two miles distant.

A dicey chance at best. Derrick nodded as they turned and retraced their path to the rude hut on the side of the hill. One of Kasseim's brothers dropped his arm, signaling the riders to begin, and they kicked their mounts into a swift gallop. As he expected, the little Arabian held to a steady ground-eating pace. He allowed him to maintain a slight lead while eyeing the stretch of rock-strewn ground coming up.

This was where Kasseim's advantage would really come into play. The desert horse picked his way effortlessly over the rough, uneven ground while the Thoroughbred stumbled, forcing Jamison to slow or risk injury to his mount. As they began to ascend the slope toward the finish line, Derrick kicked the bay hard and leaned forward, redistributing his weight as he had seen red Indians race in America.

Whispering in the stallion's ear, he crooned, "You can do it, yes, that's the way, faster now, yes!"

He pulled abreast of Kasseim's fleet Arabian . . . a nose after they passed the finish line. As everyone gathered around the prince, congratulating him on his splendid victory, Derrick was forced to follow suit.

"My felicitations on such splendid riding. A pity 'tis you, not I, who will ride the beauteous American as well as the English Thoroughbred."

Everyone shared in the raucous laughter, congratulating Derrick on being such a fine sport. The group was in an exuberant mood, something on which he had counted as he proposed a time-honored English custom.

"A toast to the victory of your future ruler—and to his good health!" He produced a jug of "lion's milk," handed to him by the groom who had accompanied him. Although Islamic law prohibited the consumption of alcoholic beverages, in North Africa the custom was often observed in the breach, especially when a group of friends gathered away from the prying eyes of religious authorities. Lion's milk was made from grapes distilled with anise and tasted rather like Greek ouzo, a potent enough drink on an empty belly in the heat of the day with a long ride back to the city ahead of them.

The celebrants quickly seized upon the idea, passing around not only Derrick's offering but several other leather jugs brought along for just such a happy occasion. Now, if only his fallback plan would work . . .

Beth heard the frightened whispers of the women, many of whom eyed her with open hatred since she was one of the accursed American infidels. Always fearful of being displaced by a newcomer, Maya, Kasseim's favorite odalisque, particularly detested her and had done everything in her power to make Beth's life in the harem even more hellish than old Fatima could. Now Maya vented her spleen.

"We shall all die in our beds, buried beneath tons of rock, when the American dogs destroy the city and the palace with it. Not a stone will remain standing and it is all *her* fault," the beautiful little Abkhasian blonde said, pointing a hennaed finger at Beth.

Maya spoke in Arabic, but Beth understood enough to realize that her deliverance might be at hand. Imagine, her father's old friend Stephen Decatur, here in Algiers, forcing the dey to sign a peace treaty and free all Americans held captive! The news had spread through the palace like wildfire shortly after a fleet of American warships under the command of the feared commodore sailed right into the mouth of the harbor.

From what Beth had gleaned during the past week, Decatur's brilliant tactical skills had destroyed most of the Algerian corsairs' ships and taken prisoner their surviving crews. Now he menaced their very citadel with his powerful cannon, which had already reduced the lesser pirate strongholds to little more than heaps of rubble. Even the fortress of Algiers could not stand against the assault.

The dey was negotiating for an end to his rashly declared war against the distant republic. Beth knew that the terms of any treaty would include the repatriation of all American prisoners—but she had not been taken from an American ship and no one in her country knew of her plight.

Only Derrick knows.

But where was he? It had been days since his message, and following his instructions had cost her dearly. She had refused to use depilatories and henna on her body or to wear the voluminous but translucent pantaloons of an odalisque. She would not give even lip service to Islamic prayers as the rest of the Christian slave women did, and worst of all, she would not learn the skills required to please her lord and master, such as playing the lyre, dancing and reciting Arabic poetry—not to mention a vast repertoire of erotic tricks.

For her obduracy she had been forced to go without food and clothing for days at a time, and when that did not break her spirit, Fatima had ordered her eunuchs to hold her down so the slave women could perform their cosmetic foolery on her body. But Beth had become enraged beyond the basic resistance Derrick had suggested. She fought with teeth and nails, kicking and gouging until Fatima's puny "not-men" had fair quaked in terror whenever the chief wife ordered them to approach the wild foreigner.

When all else failed, Fatima had had her dragged from the women's quarters to a dungeon where the Janissaries had applied the feared bastinado—beating the soles of her feet with a truncheon. The pain was excruciating, but she refused to give the hateful old crone or her sadistic minions the satisfaction of crying out. Twice she had passed out during the administration of punishment. But after all she endured, there had been no further word from Derrick.

Then two days ago Kasseim had returned from his journey into the interior and requested the defiant female be brought before him. Quinn had not lied about the prince's looks—at least that much was true—but Beth hated the way he studied her with his keen dark eyes. North African men had elevated male arrogance to an art form. Rather than lowering her lashes as Fatima had instructed her, Beth had met his stare boldly, which perversely seemed to amuse him.

Although his mother insisted that the infidel be educated properly first, Kasseim had decided to take his chances. Beth had been desperate that afternoon when the women were all rewarded with a few hours in the gardens—all but the disobedient one.

While left to languish indoors, she had filched some opium powders from Maya. Beth had observed the prince's favorite hiding them in a secret compartment inside the silk coverlet on her pallet when Maya believed no one was looking. Beth concealed in the lining of her caftan enough of the vile narcotic to knock down a camel.

That night Kasseim was surprised to find her compliant, even offering to pour his sherbet and serve him. She had acted just reluctant enough to hold his interest and not arouse his suspicions, sipping her own drink while he downed several goblets of the lemon-sugar drink that she'd laced with opium.

When she finished serving him the meal, he reached for her and then she turned coy, playing teasing games just long enough for the drug to take effect. As his eyes started to lose their focus and he slid down on the pile of cushions, she slipped off her caftan and went into his arms. He ca-

157

ressed her breast once, then fell asleep with a smile on his face.

Last night Maya had retaliated with the connivance of two of her Abkhasian friends, who attacked the American rival. Rather than fighting back and knocking the plump weaklings unconscious, Beth had allowed them to win the contest before the eunuchs dared to interfere. Scratched and bruised, Beth had been allowed to retire to the baths while Maya had been sent to the prince. Apparently that had not been sufficient to quell her jealousy. Today, with the latest news of Decatur, the favorite had begun venting her spleen until the entire harem was ready to claw out Beth's eyes.

"Perhaps if the dey were to deliver me to my father's old friend, I could intercede for your safety," she replied to Maya's diatribe, knowing old Fatima could hear her. The chief wife sat behind the lattice screen by the pool, as was her custom, so that she might eavesdrop on her son's concubines.

The ploy did not work. The women were herded into the baths for their late-afternoon ritual. The eternally boring order of harem life was not to be disrupted, even by the threat of enemy bombardment. Beth walked proudly on her bruised feet, refusing to give her tormentors the satisfaction of limping.

Fatima had abandoned her attempts to have Beth properly groomed. She wondered if Kasseim had ordered his mother to desist, preferring the way she looked when she removed her caftan—that is, if he could remember anything at all from their first night together. *What will I do if he sends for me again tonight?* she thought as she stripped and dived into the tepid pool. Beth had not enough opium to drug him again and if she took any more from Maya's hiding place she risked discovery. If Kasseim ever found she had put anything in his drink, she would die.

As she cut through the water with strong clean strokes, she could think of no way to save herself. Had fate spared her from Liam Quinn only to deliver her into the bed of another heathen stranger? *Derrick, where are you?*

Drum paced furiously across the quarterdeck of the American warship, cursing the sweltering heat that caused him to perspire like a common laborer, not to mention the salty humid air that had quite wilted his last fresh cravat. "No way to be presented to that colonial, no way at all," he muttered beneath his breath.

If only Derrick's cork-brained scheme worked. What if the commodore refused to see him after he'd risked life and limb to get here? He had slipped from the fortified city and paid a ghastly cutthroat to row him out to the American position at the mouth of the harbor, a dangerous feat that had nearly gotten them blown out of the water before he was able to identify himself as a British subject.

Just then a tar motioned for Drum to follow him below-deck. Commodore Stephen Decatur was an imposing man, even for a colonial, the little dandy was forced to admit. Tall and muscular, he wore his elegant dress uniform with true dash. Wavy light brown hair faintly flecked with gray framed a handsome face whose large blue eyes were keen and penetrating as he studied the Englishman from behind a desk filled with charts and papers.

"Jorgensen tells me that you're here on a mission of some great urgency you can only divulge to me directly, Mr. Drummond—is it not?" Decatur said.

"The Honorable Alvin Francis Edward Drummond, your obedient servant, sir," Drum replied, clicking his heels and bowing smartly.

"Then you'd best get on with it as I have a fleet waiting to attack Algiers at dawn if the dey refuses my terms," the American officer said impatiently.

"Does the name Elizabeth Blackthorne mean anything to you, sir?"

Decatur's eyes narrowed. "Pray explain yourself at once, Mr. Drummond."

Drum proceeded.

* * *

Shirl Henke

The dey sat as straight on his throne as his arthritic spine permitted, watching the big arrogant American enter his audience room. If only Kasseim were here—if only the accursed infidels had not appeared without warning scant hours ago demanding he sign a treaty that would effectively put an end to his rich Mediterranean enterprise—not to mention freeing a fortune in slaves from the *bagnos,* even a few men who labored in the palace itself!

Allah had indeed cursed him, he concluded as the presentation of Commodore Decatur was made. Perhaps if he stalled enough, his riders might yet locate his son. But what could Kasseim do against nine warships with their cannon trained on the city? The infidel dogs had already all but wiped out his fleet. No, he would be forced into the humiliating treaty . . . which would only leave the European powers sniffing the air like the greedy curs they were. All because of the Americans, Allah curse them. He inclined his head ever so slightly, noting the mere sketch of a bow the commodore made before him. "My ministers have looked over the treaty. All is in order. I have signed it." He motioned for his chief adviser to hand the document to Decatur.

"There is one more matter that must be resolved before I may sign for the United States, Your Majesty," Decatur said, waiting as the interpreter translated, maintaining the fiction that the dey did not understand English, even though both men knew he did.

"And what is that?" the dey asked ingenuously.

"We have reviewed the listing of prisoners and find one missing person."

"The *bagnos* have been searched diligently, as have all households in Algiers. Every one of your countrymen taken by our corsairs has been freed," the dey's adviser replied indignantly.

"I do not speak of an American man, but a woman . . . the daughter of an American senator. Elizabeth Blackthorne is being held prisoner right here in your palace."

A murmur went up around the crowded room as Decatur's words were translated. Algerian men bristled in outrage, and the dey's advisers circled around his throne like angry hornets. This time the old man did not bother with a translator. In thickly accented but quite serviceable English, he replied, "Our religion demands that we keep the sanctity of the harem. No woman who has been placed under protection of my household may be taken from that sanctuary. The one you speak of is now a concubine of my son Kasseim. She is dead to you."

Derrick stood in the shadow of the hallway, listening to the exchange. He had left Kasseim and his friends collapsed in celebratory inebriation after the race and ridden hard to reach the city before Decatur signed the treaty. He was determined to make certain Beth was rescued, even if it meant upsetting British diplomatic relations with Algiers, but the dey's words rocked him. *The one you speak of is now a concubine of my son . . .*

She had not been able to stave off the inevitable, he thought with bitter regret, all the while realizing that one more man could make little difference. He had been the first, but he had always known that he would not be the last. She had done what was necessary to survive. At least she would be free to pursue her life's dreams once again. But Derrick had not expected reality to hurt so much.

He watched as Decatur took a step forward, his hand on the hilt of his ceremonial sword, his expression cool and grim. The dey's Janissaries also reached for their weapons. The American was backed by several dozen heavily armed marines whose ferocity under fire had already become legend along the Barbary Coast.

He said, "The sanctity of your slave women be damned, Your Majesty. You will produce Miss Blackthorne or I shall dispatch my men to tear your harem apart silken sheet by silken sheet."

"This is an outrage! An affront to Allah himself, may the Prophet curse you!" The cries went up from around the throne, but Decatur's words cut through the babble of protest.

"I will have Miss Blackthorne or by the Almighty, I shall order this city bombarded until it makes the Roman's treatment of Carthage seem merciful by comparison. You may choose, Your Majesty," the commodore said with steel in his voice.

Derrick's hands rested on the pistols in his sash, praying the dey would not be so foolish as to provoke a bloodbath. The Englishman was grateful that Kasseim was not present. The young prince's pride might well have led him to act rashly.

The dey motioned for silence, his eyes never leaving those of his American adversary. Slumping back in his seat, he said, "Bring the wench. My son is well rid of the infidel baggage."

With a huge sigh of relief, Derrick slipped his hands from his pistol butts and waited as a pair of eunuchs were dispatched to fetch Beth from the seraglio. He did not see Drum glide up to his side until the little man spoke.

"Done to a cow's thumb. That Yankee certainly came up to scratch. Now, we can spirit Beth to safety—"

"What do you mean, we?" Derrick snarled. "She'll be reunited with her countrymen. They shall see to her safety."

"Ah, no, old chap. 'Fraid not. That task's been set for us . . . or rather you," Drum replied with a beatific grin. "I arranged everything with the commodore."

Chapter Thirteen

When the eunuchs took hold of her to drag her from the women's quarters, Beth feared she was going to her death. *This is the end of it, then.* Regret for the loss of her young life seared through her, for all the painting she had not done, for all the times she had not told her family how much she did love them in spite of her choice to live abroad, for not being able to tell Vittoria good-bye . . . but overshadowing everything was her regret over Derrick.

Derrick, whose children she would never bear, whose life she would never share. She would never again feel his hard, lean body pressed against hers, his hands caressing her, or hear his low voice teasing her. Derrick, whom she loved.

There was no longer any use denying the truth. In these last few moments of her earthly existence, Beth openly admitted to herself what she had been afraid to consider during the time they had spent together and the time after he had betrayed and deserted her. She would gladly have given up the life she'd built for herself in Naples in exchange for being his wife.

But he had not even attempted to reach her in this prison after that one mysterious note. Then the thought came unbidden—if she was being taken to her death, perhaps the same fate had already befallen him. That would explain why he had not rescued her after she did as he asked and received such painful retribution from old Fatima.

Perhaps we will be together again . . . in a better place. She was delivered to the two grim-looking Janissaries, who held her in their steely grip as they walked swiftly through the twists and turns of the palace, taking her to her fate.

When they reached the dey's audience chamber, Beth was stunned to see Stephen Decatur standing boldly in front of the throne, in full dress uniform, flanked by dozens of heavily armed American marines. The Janissaries released her at the doorway, giving her a rough shove toward the dey. In a daze of disbelief, she stumbled and would have fallen if the commodore had not stepped forward to assist her.

"Miss Blackthorne, are you all right?" he asked with formal solicitude.

"Yes . . . yes, of course I am now. I heard that your ships were in the harbor, but I never dreamed you would be here—that I was being brought to you . . ."

"You're safe now, my dear," he soothed.

"How did you know that I was a prisoner?" Derrick! It had to be.

Suddenly one of the dey's advisers spoke angrily in Arabic. "Please forgive me, but I must see to this treaty. Lieutenant Granger will escort you to my flagship," the commodore replied, motioning forward a young man with a round, florid face and pale ginger hair.

"Your servant, miss," Granger said stiffly, offering her his arm.

Beth guessed that his high color was not entirely due to being a redhead. *He thinks I'm a ruined woman debauched by Algerines,* she thought with faint amusement. If only he was aware of her reputation back in Naples!

Derrick stood hidden behind a screen where he could observe Beth being led to safety. It was his duty to see that friendly diplomatic channels remained open for the time being between his government and the dey, but as a man he wanted nothing so much as to take her in his arms. He had heard the rumors about her punishment for disobedience and was relieved to see that she bore no permanent injuries.

Beth would be too proud to limp if they broke all the bones in her feet.

He smiled sadly, knowing the truth of it. What had they done to her? What had his supposed friend Kasseim done to her—not to mention the corsair Quinn? He cursed the turmoil in Europe and Napoleon for separating them, then realized how foolish that was. If not for his assignment spying on the exiled emperor, he would never have met Elizabeth Blackthorne. But he did wish mightily that he could have been her deliverer instead of Decatur.

As to what had passed between Beth and the prince . . . he would not think of it. She had survived. Still, the images of her locked in intimate embraces with other men ate at his guts. He felt guilty and jealous. And he did not like himself for it one bit.

Aboard the U.S.S. *Guerriere,* Beth waited in the commodore's cabin, scarcely able to believe that she was free at last. Lt. Granger had politely offered to have a meal brought to her and asked if she required anything else, since his commander might be several hours finalizing the treaty arrangements in the city. She had declined the food but inquired about how Decatur had known she was being held captive.

"You'd best discuss that with Commodore Decatur when he returns, miss," was all he would volunteer.

"Did a man named Derrick Jamison come to him?" She held her breath.

"I couldn't say."

Beth would have stamped her feet in aggravation if they had not still hurt so much from the bastinado. "He's English, tall, black-haired, arrogant, rather difficult to miss. He was the only foreigner who knew that I was there."

Granger seemed to be weighing his answer, as if the security of the republic hinged on it. "Well . . . there was an Englishman." He sniffed at the word as if it were rancid cheese. "He came aboard while the commodore was preparing to meet with the dey. An arrogant devil, but neither tall nor dark. A scrawny little runt, if you'll pardon my saying so, miss."

"Dressed to the nines, light tan hair and cat-green eyes, about so high?" She raised one hand just above her shoulder. At his nod, she exclaimed, "Drum!" What was he doing here? For that matter, what had Derrick been doing here?

Before she could question Granger any further, he said, "This is a United States naval vessel, miss. My apologies that we have no"—his face turned brick red now as he fumbled for words—"that is, no proper accoutrements for a lady." He eyed the bedraggled caftan that hung like a shroud over her tall frame. Although it covered her from neck to ankles and was made of heavy cotton, the indication that she wore nothing beneath it obviously disturbed his sense of propriety.

"I understand the limitations, Lieutenant. Please do not concern yourself. What I'm really interested in is—"

"I really must go, then. With your permission?" he asked. Not caring if he had it or not, he sketched a quick bow and backed out of the room.

"I might as well have some contagious disease!" His American provinciality would have been amusing if not for her concern about Derrick. Drum had been the one to approach Decatur. Did that mean that Derrick was unable to do so? Or unwilling? The longer she waited, the more she stewed.

Toward evening, the commodore returned. She watched through the porthole of his cabin as he boarded his flagship. He was followed by two civilians, both of whom she recognized immediately. By the time the cabin door opened, her aching foot was tapping impatiently on the polished walnut flooring.

"I do apologize for keeping you waiting, my dear," Decatur said with fatherly concern after entering alone. "But the treaty is now duly signed and that thieving riffraff will never prey on innocent Americans again."

"I quite understand. You cannot know how grateful I am that our government sent you to deal with them," she replied, then asked, "The two Englishmen who accompanied you aboard—"

"I asked them to wait outside for a moment, my dear. As you know, I have been fast friends with your father for many years."

Beth had an inkling of where this conversation was going and she did not like it. Men were such imbeciles when it came to their protective instincts toward women. "And my father would wish me returned safely to Savannah after my ordeal," she supplied helpfully. Decatur appeared relieved for an instant, then took note of the look in her eyes and realized his mistake. "Although many women might wish that, I do not," she said with gentle finality in her voice.

"I was given to understand by Mr. Drummond that you would prefer to return to Naples, where you were residing prior to your . . . misfortune."

"Yes, I would. My home has been in Naples for nearly four years now. It would serve nothing and greatly distress my parents if they were to learn that I'd been a prisoner of the dey. May I beg you never to speak of this misadventure again?"

"As far as I and my crew are concerned, it has never happened, Elizabeth," he reassured her. Decatur lost a bit of his parental composure then, as if uncertain how to proceed. "My orders are to set sail for home directly, so I cannot see you safely to Naples on any of the ships under my command."

"I know you do not wish to leave your friend's daughter unchaperoned with two young Englishmen, but I assure you that I have known both gentlemen for some time."

Decatur's face did not become as red as Granger's had, but he was nonetheless feeling his tight dress collar pinch as he replied, "Mr. Drummond gave me to believe that you and Mr. Jamison were affianced. Is that not so?"

Drum, matchmaking? She suppressed a smile at the unlikely behavior from the gruff little dandy. "Well, not exactly, no. Although we have spoken of marriage," she added vaguely. "But I do trust him and he can be relied upon." *Yes, to lie and deceive you,* a voice berated her.

Decatur drummed his fingers on the polished surface of his desk for a moment, then reached a decision. "Very well, if you are certain," he said, looking at her to see if she remained adamant. When she nodded calmly, he opened the door of his cabin and asked the Englishmen to enter.

"Hello, puss," Derrick said in that husky voice that always melted her bones. He was dressed in dusty tan riding breeches and high boots, as if he'd just spent the day in the countryside. He bowed over her hand, and that errant black curl fell across his forehead. Beth ached to brush it with her fingers and fall into his arms. Instead, she said in a cool, controlled voice, "I was fearful something had happened to you when I heard nothing after that one note."

Ouch! It was as bad as he had feared. " 'Twas too risky to send another. If Nola had been intercepted, she would have been put to the torture to reveal that I had sent her—and you would have been punished severely as well."

"Nola?" she inquired with raised eyebrows.

"I say, Miss Blackthorne, you do look quite well after such an ordeal," Drum interjected with false cheeriness, attempting to head off an argument over Derrick's "gift" from the dey.

Beth turned to the little man with a smile. "I've learned that I have you to thank for my rescue, Drum. How shall I ever repay you for alerting Commodore Decatur?"

Derrick's expression darkened, but Drum ignored him, saying smoothly, " 'Twas nothing, m'dear. So glad to be of service. After all, Alex would have my head if I let anything befall his favorite cousin."

"I think it might be best if we saw Beth safely aboard the *San Marcos,*" Derrick said to Decatur, fighting the urge to throttle his companion.

The commodore looked at Beth. "If that is your wish, my dear." He appeared anything but happy about the prospect.

"I take it the *San Marcos* is bound for Naples?" she asked.

"She sails on the morning tide under an English flag, bound for Naples, with a brief stop in Sicily," Derrick replied.

He was standing too close. Beth could smell his scent, faint male musk combined with perspiration and horse. He had been out riding while Drum arranged her rescue and the Americans stormed the palace. But nothing mattered except that he would be taking her home to Naples. As they were rowed across the bay to the waiting English ship, Beth could not help thinking how grateful she was that her father would never learn about this episode.

As soon as they boarded the *San Marcos*, Drum explained that he would not be sailing with them. "Someone must remain behind to close the British legation. Now that your countrymen have so gallantly led the way, all the European powers will follow suit, driving those demned pirates out of business."

Beth took his hand and looked into his eyes. "I thank you, my friend, for all that you have done. Perhaps we shall meet again in Naples?"

"Possibly. Who knows what joyous event might occasion my return, hmmm?" he said mysteriously.

After Drum had departed, the captain bowed obsequiously and introduced himself as Liro Calvara. Although he and his crew were from Genoa, the old brigantine was under the protection of the English flag, headed for the Royal Navy stronghold of Palermo, heavily laden with a cargo of wool and spices.

"But we will go from Sicily to Naples?" Beth asked the rotund, beetle-browed old man, casting a suspicious glance at Derrick.

"As soon as we unload our cargo, signorina." He shuffled about nervously for a moment, clearing his throat, then continued, "There is little room for passengers—I only take you on because of Signore Jamison . . ." He looked to Derrick for support.

"What he is trying to tell you, Beth, is that there is only one cabin free—his. He has agreed to sleep with his men.' "

"Oh, and pray where will you sleep?" she asked sweetly. *Not so easy as that, Derrick. You cannot desert me, then reclaim me as if I were no more than a traveling trunk.*

"I think we could better discuss the matter after the captain has shown us the cabin," he replied smoothly, ushering her toward the belowdeck stairs.

The light pressure of his palm against her spine sent shivers through Beth. Rather than argue in front of Calvara, she followed his lead. Her sore feet and long caftan made negotiating the crude ladder difficult. She bunched the garment up in her hands and hobbled down, holding on as best she could.

From below her, Derrick watched the curve of her derriere wriggle as the cotton cloth pulled tightly across its rounded contours. His mouth went dry. Small wonder, he thought wryly, since all the juices in his body were now centered much lower. When she took her foot from the last rung, he could not resist placing his arm around her waist to assist her. She looked up into his face, startled by the contact, and he almost drowned in the golden flecks floating in her eyes.

When she tried to move away, she stepped on an uneven plank and winced. "Are your feet still sore from the bastinado?" he whispered.

She pulled away without answering and walked stiff-spined down the dark narrow passageway to the door where Calvara waited. The cabin was small and the furnishings well worn but clean. There was only one bed, of course: a narrow bunk fastened to an interior wall. As if sensing the tension between the two of them, the captain bowed again and excused himself.

"There is but one cabin free and one bed in it, puss. Are you so angry at my deception in Naples that you refuse to share it with me?" he asked baldly. *No use waiting. I might as well know.*

She surveyed him as he leaned against the sash of the doorway, arms crossed over that broad chest, one booted foot crossed over the other, a study in indolence if not for the tight set of his mouth and . . . was there a haunted look deep in those blue eyes? Subtle signs, difficult to interpret. Always the consummate spy, Derrick Jamison gave little away. Her heart began to pound in her chest and the pulse at her throat raced. She fought the urge to throw herself in his arms as if nothing had happened to estrange them.

"When you left me that night I felt betrayed, yes," she admitted, dying to know what was truly going on behind those magical eyes.

"Yet you bound up my wounds and allowed me to steal Vittoria's best mount," he said with a touch of the old bravado. Perhaps all was not yet lost.

He knew she had watched him take the horse—knew that she could not bring herself to sound the alarm. His sheer male arrogance galled her. She felt used all over again. "You never lacked for nerve, Derrick. That was one of the reasons I assumed that you would find a way to rescue me when I received your note."

"But I failed," he said, slumping against the doorframe. "I am sorry, Beth. I heard how Fatima had you punished."

"From Nola? The women in the harem gossiped about how the dey bestows odalisques on visitors whose favor he wishes to curry."

He was amazed at the sudden flash of fury that surged through him. "You're jealous of Nola after Kasseim!" He advanced on her, all the fear and anger bottled up inside him exploding. "I never touched the vapid little chit—I was too busy trying to devise a way to get you out of that sink of depravity before they killed you!"

He had been jealous of the prince, but more importantly, far more importantly—he had remained faithful. And she sensed he was telling the truth. Such joy suffused her that she did not realize what he had implied about her and the prince. "You did not sleep with her? Oh, Derrick, I am sorry for my accusations—for everything! I'm sure you would have rescued me if you could have. Just receiving your note gave me hope to survive," she said, moving across the cabin and throwing her arms around his neck.

The moment she smiled and ran to him, his anger vanished like fog at sunrise. His arms enveloped her and he held her long slender body against his, savoring every soft, lush curve, so dearly familiar, so dearly missed for all the hellish lonely months they had been separated.

He reached down and swept her into his arms, carrying her over to the bunk where he knelt and laid her on the mattress, leaning over her as he lowered his mouth to hers. Her arms came up, encircling his neck, pulling him to her as her lips opened for his invasion. Their tongues touched like lightning sparks, twining, dueling as hungry mouths glided and pressed together, fitting and refitting, accommodating in old, well-remembered ways that thrilled and delighted anew.

His hands caressed her breasts through the soft cotton of the caftan, feeling the tips harden as she arched upward eagerly. She writhed desperately, wanting the barrier of cloth between them removed, on fire with the need to feel his bare skin on her own. Her fingers worked the fastenings of his shirt, tearing the front open so that she could press her palms against the crisp springy hair on his chest. When she felt his hand gliding up her leg, baring it from ankle to calf, then up over her thigh, she cried, "Remove this accursed sack from me."

"Your wish is my command," he murmured as she wriggled the bunched cloth over her hips and sat up, raising her arms so that he could pull it over her head. He threw the voluminous robe across the cabin. It floated to the floor as he cupped a breast in each hand, teasing the nipples, then raising them to his mouth one at a time, feasting in pure delight.

The heat, the sweet suckling pressure of his mouth sent frissons of ecstasy through her, pooling low in her belly. Beth worked with clumsy fingers at his belt, sliding it off, then unbuttoning his fly and reaching for the hardness imprisoned inside. When it sprang free she wrapped her hand around it and stroked until he moaned.

"You'll unman me if you don't stop that," he growled, stilling her busy fingers. Sitting on the edge of the bunk, he tugged off his boots and pulled down his breeches. As he kicked them away, she peeled the sweaty white cotton shirt from his shoulders and threw it onto the growing pile of clothes.

Desperate in their need, they wasted no time, tumbling backward onto the hard, narrow mattress. As he lay on top of her, her legs opened, wrapping around his hips. Derrick plunged deep inside her welcoming heat. She was wet and tight and blissfully sweet, but his long celibacy denied him the patience to savor that as he pumped furiously. Her own hunger matched his. She rode with him, maddened by each long hard stroke, her hips arching, her fingers digging into his back, the nails scoring it as she felt the swift completion begin.

It was too soon, too soon, and yet it was such blessed release after the long bitter separation from this man, from the wild hunger he evoked and only he could quench. She gave in to the climax. Derrick could feel her body spasm, feel the furious pounding of her heart, hear her sharp cries muffled in his mouth as he kissed her and followed her over the edge to fierce, draining surfeit.

They lay collapsed and panting, sweat-soaked and utterly sated, his body pressing hers into the mattress, hers enveloping his while they both let the universe spin away. If the dey had opened fire with all the cannon on the city walls, neither of them would have noticed. Finally, Derrick rolled off her and onto his back, pressed against the wall on the narrow bunk. Still breathing hard, he raised himself up on one elbow, resting his head against his hand and looking down at her, letting his eyes travel from her flushed face to her slender feet and back, enjoying all the creamy curves along the way.

"Woman, you are a wonder," he breathed, touching her lightly with his other hand, letting it rest on her hipbone.

"I'm filthy and disheveled, my hair is a tangled rat's nest

and I have nothing to wear." Looking up into his eyes, she did not seem the least bit concerned about any of those problems.

"You're the most beautiful creature I've even seen. I'm the one who's filthy. I warrant this mattress is gritty with half the sand in the foothills."

"You were out riding, weren't you?" She was curious about why he had been away while so much was going on in the city.

"My original plan was to win you from Kasseim."

Beth was flummoxed. "Win me?"

He shrugged one shoulder, not sure how she would take it when he replied, "In a horse race."

"A pity you did not arrive in time to collect your prize," she said with some asperity. A horse race indeed!

"I lost. But at least I had a contingency plan. Whom do you think sent Drum to Decatur with word that you were being held by the dey?"

"How did you know that I was there in the first place?"

He grinned and ran his hand over her belly, caressing the concave surface. "I was interviewing the male prisoners taken from your ship, assuring them that they and their families would be ransomed, when I heard some remarkably familiar oaths. Then you exploded out into the courtyard pursued by several very unhappy Janissaries."

"I'd heard stories in Naples about Barbary, but nothing prepared me for being enslaved. I'm glad Commodore Decatur taught them what it means to interfere with American rights—also glad he was there to get me out when your original plan failed."

That still rankled. "If Kasseim hadn't changed from the usual race course, I would have won you, but either way I had to get him out of the city while his father was negotiating with the Americans. He's too much of a hothead to have given in as easily."

"You know him then?" she asked, biting her lip. The night she'd spent in his bed as he lay drugged still made her ill.

Not as well as you, I fear. The treacherous thought came

unbidden. He suppressed it and replied, "I was sent to Algiers several months ago to watch Decatur when we learned his fleet was headed there. Cultivating the young heir was a good way to learn the mood and workings inside the power structure."

"Always patriotism, Derrick?" she whispered, wondering sadly if everything he cared about was related to his sense of duty.

"Enough talk," he murmured, letting his hand glide lower, covering her mound, massaging it as he said, "So lovely, it matches the hair above."

"Arab men find women's body hair unattractive. There would have been nothing to compare if I hadn't fought like a wildcat when Fatima ordered my nether parts beautified."

His hand froze and his breath hissed sharply before he could control it. "Let us never again speak about your time in the harem," he said.

She could sense the anger he was holding inside. "What is it, Derrick? What's wrong? You act as if it was my fault that those animals enslaved me."

"That accursed corsair Quinn would never have captured you in the first place if you'd stayed at home," he blurted out angrily.

Beth bolted upright, furious and amazed. "And pray where is 'home'? Naples? You left me there, riding away on your sacred mission to stop Napoleon—you could've bled to death in the mountains for all I knew! Was I to pine away staring out at the Apennines for the rest of my life? Or is home America? Then we should never have become lovers in the first place—a capital idea now that I think on it!"

She swung her legs from the bed and started to rise, but he reached out and seized her wrist, roughly pulling her back into his arms, muffling his own angry oaths in her mouth. As he savaged her lips, she started to claw at him, but her nails did not dig in. Rather her fingers clamped over his shoulders, holding fast to him as she returned the fierce possessive kiss.

175

They tumbled back onto the bed, lost again in a maelstrom of passion, flesh slick against flesh, hungers flaring, demanding appeasement after the long abstinence of so many months. This time he lay on his back, placing her over him, staring intently into her eyes as she impaled herself and rode him like some splendid pagan goddess. His hands cupped her breasts while she arched her back, flinging her tangled hair over her shoulders. Then he teased her nipples, urging her to bend toward him so he could feast. When she did so, the milky globes hung like ripe fruit for him to taste as his hands held her hips, guiding their wild ride.

This time he slowed their rhythm, prolonging the glory of the joining, as if sensing there would be a reckoning once their passions had been sated. Each time they neared the brink, he would clamp his hands over her buttocks, stilling her gyrations as they both strove for control, until they could endure the sweet torture no longer. Then they spent themselves utterly once more.

Chapter Fourteen

Beth lay with her head on his chest, feeling the furious beating of his heart gradually slow to an even thrum. She had never loved him more . . . and never been angrier with him than at that moment. Still, in spite of her hurt, her fingers played with the mat of hair on his chest and she nuzzled her face in the curve of his shoulder, unable to stop her body from reveling in physical contentment as he held her tightly while his hand played with a lock of her hair.

Derrick hated to break the spell. But they could not make the voyage to Sicily joined together without respite. Then again . . . ? He could not help smiling against her hair, stroking the wild curls. "This is good, isn't it, puss?"

Once there had been so much more—laughter and companionship, the enjoyment of simple things such as walks on the quay, rides in the countryside, sunsets on the bay, even arguments about politics and Italian unification. "Yes, it's wonderfully good . . . but only this, Derrick? Is passion all we have left?" she asked sadly, raising her head.

He sighed. "I don't know. What do you want us to have, Beth?"

The question hung in the air between them. He wished he could take it back. *Am I afraid of what she will answer? Or of what I will?*

She knew what her heart longed to reply, but that could never be. He could never marry her, she who had so long protested that she would never marry. What irony. There would be no vows, no children, no growing old together. "Only now, Derrick," she replied simply, turning into his embrace. "I only want us to have now."

They spent the following days aboard the cramped quarters of the ship trying not to think of what lay ahead, living moment by moment. And the moments were good. The weather was golden and the leisurely pace of the overloaded old brigantine gave them time to walk on the crowded deck, laughing and exchanging jests with the sailors whose Genoese dialect was often difficult to understand.

They talked about everything . . . and nothing. By tacit agreement, neither raised the subject of what would become of them once his assignment in Naples was complete. He told her that the restoration of the Spanish Bourbons had been smoothly facilitated by the Royal Navy. Joaquim Murat had been placed before a firing squad by his own Neapolitan troops and Queen Caroline and their children had fled to France. There would be no reason for Derrick to remain in Naples after he made his initial report. But he never spoke a word about his plans and Beth did not ask.

Instead they talked about Naples and what she would paint when she resumed her place in art circles there. With lavish spenders such as the Bourbons at court again, commissions would be plentiful. Her future was assured. And bleak. But she revealed nothing of her feelings to him, only going along with his glowing predictions about her brilliant career.

There was an air of uncertainty and desperation beneath

their laughter, even in their loving. They came together nightly, even in the afternoons, slipping into the privacy of their cabin during the heat of the day to make love. The hot, sultry day they arrived in the beautiful Sicilian port of Palermo, Derrick stood staring out at the harbor, ringed with British warships of all sizes, gazing past their masts to the enchanting town set amid jewel-like green hills. The houses, great and small, were painted soft pastel blues, greens, pinks and yellows. Flowers abounded everywhere.

" 'Tis lovely," she said as she walked up to join him.

"Calvara says it will take the rest of the day to unload his cargo. We don't sail 'til morning, so we could find a local inn and wash the itch of saltwater from our skin . . ." He turned to her with heavy-lidded slumberous eyes.

"I would like that very much," she replied, already feeling the fire lick through her veins.

They found a small inn on a hillside overlooking the waterfront. The elderly man who owned it smilingly ushered them past a splashing fountain in the courtyard and up a narrow outside staircase leading to a second-story room that was airy and spacious, with floor-to-ceiling glass-paned doors that opened onto a balcony with a view of the bay.

Derrick made arrangements for them to stay the night and ordered a large wooden tub filled with scented water to be delivered immediately. They sat out on the balcony and ate a light repast of fresh melon and rich goat cheese washed down with crisp white wine as the servants scurried up and down the stairs bringing pails of water.

" 'Tis so peaceful here," Beth said dreamily, looking over the verdant hills surrounding the city.

"Appearances can deceive. Only look to the British flotilla in the harbor. This has been the Royal Navy's major outpost in the Mediterranean since the war began. All of Sicily is rife with political intrigues."

"What a perfect place for a spy," she replied lightly. "Will you keep at it now that Napoleon is no longer a threat?" She had not asked until now. Perhaps it was un-

179

wise, but she longed to know what he would do after they reached Naples tomorrow.

He stared out at the distant sky, billowing with fluffy white clouds, saying nothing for a moment. "I honestly don't know. I would probably not have ended up in this life if not for Bellingham."

"The peer you killed in a duel—or was that just a Banbury tale made up for me?"

"I was in bad loaf over the duel, true, but Bellingham was just a baron of little consequence with greedy relatives who felt a deal more warmly about my father's money than they did him. My father summoned me to Lynden Hall after that incident . . ." He paused for a moment, as if the memory was too painful to speak of, then sighed and went on, "He was furious with me for besmirching the family name and demanded that I purchase a commission. I had been a wastrel, bored with my aimless life. Killing a man changes one. I agreed to do so, thinking the army would be a way to redeem myself, but Colonel Sir Wilton James introduced me to two senior members of the Foreign Office instead. It seemed they'd heard of my difficulties— and my facility with foreign languages and, er, other things." They'd heard of his reputation wheedling his way into the beds of noblewomen, a useful skill in their line of work, but Derrick did not choose to mention that.

"And you were allowed to tell no one what you were doing—not even your father. I can only imagine how terrible that must have been."

"When he became ill . . . several years later, I intended to return to the Hall and explain. But then there were rumors that Bonaparte might invade Russia and I was sent to Paris. By the time my assignment was completed the earl had died and my brother succeeded him. I believe I told you that he gave me the cut direct the one time I attempted a rapprochement in London. I never tried again."

"You should return and try once more," she said, her conscience forcing her to suggest it, even as her heart broke at the thought of losing him.

"Lee and I were never close. No, I will continue working for the government. 'Tis an atonement of sorts, serving my country to make up for disgracing my family." He shook his head sadly, breaking the melancholy spell, then smiled and took her hand. "Enough of brown studies. I believe our bath awaits, puss."

They undressed each other slowly in front of the huge wooden tub, inhaling the fragrance of sandalwood blended with the musky essence of their own arousal. She was dressed in a loose peasant blouse and skirt much like those she had worn in Naples. Derrick had purchased the items on the waterfront while she waited aboard the ship, clad in an oversized sailor's shirt and trousers, which were much like what he wore now. The simple clothing dropped to the floor, piece by piece.

He unfastened the drawstring of her blouse, easing it off her shoulders, then suckled her breasts while he worked the ties at the waist of her skirt. Her busy fingers pulled his shirt free and tugged it over his head, then began to unbutton his fly. When he kicked away the pants, she knelt before him on the soft pile of clothes and took his pulsing phallus in her mouth, teasing at it with her tongue until he growled and dug his fingers into her hair.

"Stop, before it's too late!"

She looked up at him with a wicked smile. "As if you cannot recover quickly enough under my ministrations."

"At least let me bathe the salt away," he said, picking her up and holding her over the rim of the big tub until she squealed.

"Derrick, don't you dare drop me!"

The splash was resounding. She came up from beneath the water sputtering as he stood leaning over the rim, doubled up with laughter. Until she wrapped her arms around him, toppling him into the tub. They splashed and laughed as they settled into the bath, but when their eyes met, their expressions turned serious.

He cupped her face with his hands, studying it. "You are a rare work of art, far better than any master could ever paint or sculpt." As his fingers traced the contours of her cheekbones, eyebrows, lips and chin, she closed her eyes and let her head fall back, luxuriating in his soft caresses. She let her entire body go lax, leaning against the wall of the tub with her arms stretched out on the rim. She felt a faint ripple in the water when he moved. His fingertips glided down the slender column of her throat and over her breasts, holding the buoyant globes ever so slightly while he suckled them.

Then his hands slid over her waist and down to her hips, holding them firmly as his head vanished beneath the water. She felt his mouth, far hotter than the bathwater, pressing the most intimate caress on her. A gasp of ecstasy tore from her lips as he worked magic with his lips and tongue. Beth writhed with pleasure, then fiery need when his head broke the surface and he gulped a breath of air.

"I've discovered a more precious underwater treasure than pearls," Derrick rasped wickedly. He then returned to pleasuring her, coming up to breathe several more times as she held on to the rim of the tub with white-knuckled little fists.

Feeling the ever-deepening frissons of delight radiate from the core of her body, she undulated beneath the water's gentle lapping . . . and his. When the contractions began, she stiffened and cried out his name. In an instant he rose up like Poseidon and thrust into her. Her sheath tightened around the steely hardness of his staff, enveloping it as she bucked and swayed in the water, holding on to the edge of the tub, letting him carry her away into another world of such bliss that it was oblivion.

As the sweetness gradually subsided, she reached out to him, unclasping her hips from his as she gently pushed him back to the other side of the tub. "My turn," she whispered hoarsely, reaching beneath the water to grasp his still unsatiated phallus with one hand while cupping him with the other.

"Aaaah!" His strangled gasp of pleasure echoed in the afternoon stillness when her head dipped beneath the water. He held on to the rim, watching her hair float across the surface, glimmering like drowning flame. Drowning, just as he was, lost in the almost unbearable ecstasy. He had taught her to give and receive physical love this way, and Beth proved the most exquisitely skilled pupil he had ever tutored. He could never last long with her. When he felt his body swelling for that final release, he pulled her up into his arms and thrust inside her.

He refused to consider his need to be completely joined with her, to have her come with him as he climaxed. She trembled in his arms, brought to a second shattering completion as she felt him hold himself back, teetering on the brink until she could do nothing but helplessly go along. Afterward, they sat in the cool water, holding each other, saying nothing as the sun dipped low on the western horizon, bathing the room in a soft golden haze.

That same warm sunset reflected off the bay at Naples to the north as the *Lady Barbara* sailed into the harbor bearing two passengers, both nervous but for very different reasons. Quintin Blackthorne was desperate to see if the corruption of the European nobility had done irreparable harm to his beloved only daughter. Beth simply must return home with him. He would allow nothing else. He would, in fact, drag her from that accursed villa and tie her to the masthead if necessary.

His companion, an old friend and long-time business associate of his foster brother Devon, had a far different agenda. While arranging Quint's passage, Dev had mentioned his friend from Charleston, who happened to be a native of Naples. Once Dev reached the Neapolitan, he had quickly volunteered to accompany Quint. Although born in Naples, he had moved as a youth to Savannah, where his cousin Solomon was engaged in a highly successful dry goods business.

His cousin's family had been eager to expand their enterprise up and down the coast of the new nation. When he exhibited such industry and initiative that the store he managed in Charleston flourished, they brought him into full partnership. Within a decade he owned stores and warehouses stretching all the way to Baltimore. That was when he formed a partnership with the Blackthorne family and entered the shipping business as well. At the age of forty-six, Piero Torres was a rich man.

He had never married, although his striking good looks and smooth Neapolitan charm had won him many lovers over the years. The bright blue eyes of his Sephardic ancestry combined with deep olive skin and curly black hair from a mysterious Hungarian Gypsy rumored to be a branch on the family tree. A succession of mistresses and ill-fated affairs had convinced him that he would never be able to forget the love of his youth.

Blackthorne had described the life his daughter was living and the remarkable woman who was acting as her sponsor in the art circles of the city. Vittoria di Remaldi. Piero did not recognize the surname and Vittoria was a common enough Christian name, but the descriptions of Beth's mentor struck a chord. Could it be? If so, Vittoria was twice widowed and lived in independent wealth, at last free of her scheming family. Free to rediscover the passions of youth? He feared to hope for too much. After all, their love affair had been so many years ago. She would be a woman in her prime now, no longer the innocent girl with whom he had first tasted love. Would she still desire him? His troubling yet hopeful ruminations were interrupted as Quint strode across the deck to where he stood alone, watching the city washed with the softness of twilight.

A tall commanding man with hawkish features and streaks of gray at the temples of his black hair, Blackthorne looked every inch the owner of a vast plantation, an American patrician who oversaw his agricultural empire and other business enterprises with meticulous care. The same way he safeguarded his family. Torres remembered his cousin Solomon's tales about Blackthorne's heroism during the American War of Independence. He had ridden with the legendary Swamp Fox, General Francis Marion, whose guerrilla campaign cost the British dearly in the southern theater of the war. Piero decided he would not want Quintin Blackthorne for an enemy.

Join the Historical Romance Book Club — and GET 4 FREE* BOOKS NOW!

A $23.96 Value!

Yes! I want to subscribe to the Historical Romance Book Club.

Please send me my **4 FREE* BOOKS.** I have enclosed $2.00 for shipping/handling. Each month I'll receive the four newest Historical Romance selections to preview for 10 days. If I decide to keep them, I will pay the Special Members Only discounted price of just $4.24 each, a total of $16.96, plus $2.00 shipping/handling ($23.55 US in Canada). This is a **SAVINGS OF AT LEAST $5.00** off the bookstore price. There is no minimum number of books I must buy, and I may cancel the program at any time. In any case, the **4 FREE* BOOKS** are mine to keep.

*In Canada, add $5.00 shipping/handling per order for the first shipment. For all future shipments to Canada, the cost of membership is $23.55 US, which includes shipping and handling. (All payments must be made in US dollars.)

NAME: _____

ADDRESS: _____

CITY: _____ **STATE:** _____

COUNTRY: _____ **ZIP:** _____

TELEPHONE: _____

E-MAIL: _____

SIGNATURE: _____

If under 18, Parent or Guardian must sign. Terms, prices, and conditions subject to change. Subscription subject to acceptance. Dorchester Publishing reserves the right to reject any order or cancel any subscription.

The Best in Historical Romance!
Get Four Books Totally FREE*!

A $23.96 Value! FREE!

PLEASE RUSH MY FOUR FREE BOOKS TO ME RIGHT AWAY!

Enclose this card with $2.00 in an envelope and send to:

Historical Romance Book Club
20 Academy Street
Norwalk, CT 06850-4032

"Has Naples changed since last you saw it?" Black-thorne asked.

Piero shrugged. "More ships in the harbor, here and there a new building along the outskirts, but no, the city remains the same. It is very ancient, you know, nothing like the growth and newness of America."

Quint studied the man he now called friend. "You've become quite Americanized, yet Dev worries that you might decide to remain here in Naples. Do you still have family here?"

"No. They all died many years ago. As to whether I might remain here . . . that depends . . . on many things," Piero replied with a faraway look in his eyes.

When they debarked, Quint oversaw the unloading of their luggage while Piero made arrangements with a driver to transport them to one of the city's finest inns, a place that a Jewish jeweler's son had never been allowed to enter. But that had changed now. He had become a wealthy American merchant. What had Vittoria become?

When they reached their lodgings, Piero obtained directions to the villa of the Contessa di Remaldi. "Perhaps it might be best if I went first to speak with the contessa, to see how Beth will react to your coming to fetch her," he suggested to Quint when they were at last alone in their spacious fourth-story apartment.

"I've not known a moment's peace since receiving Drummond's letter. No, my friend, I must see my daughter at once."

"I was afraid you would say that," Piero replied wryly. "I feel there is something I should tell you before you go storming off to the contessa's villa."

"You've been quite preoccupied ever since we came in sight of the city. What is it?" Blackthorne asked warily.

"I may know the contessa. I've told no one in America the reason I left Naples as a youth . . ." He outlined the story of young love thwarted by class and religious differences and the hope that the wealthy widow might indeed be his long-lost lady.

"Incredible," Quint said when Piero finished his tale. "If

185

she is who you think she is, will she attempt to stop me from taking Beth home?" The one matter that had worried Blackthorne was running afoul of the Neapolitan authorities if the contessa tried to stop her young protégée from leaving.

"If she is the same romantic she was then, she might see you as she did her own father."

"And that would not be to my benefit at all, would it, hmmm?" Blackthorne replied, thoughtfully. "You would suggest I remain here while you scout out the enemy . . . if she is indeed the enemy, eh?"

And so, Piero Torres took a carriage to the elegant villa alone. It was full dark when he arrived, but he could see that it was a splendid home. *She has done well for herself.* But then, so had he, he reminded himself as he grew increasingly nervous. Ignoring the churning deep in his gut, he walked up the stairs of the entry and knocked.

He was greeted by a grim-faced servant who ushered him down a wide marble hallway into a large sitting room with glass-paned doors opening onto the portico that encircled three sides of the mansion. The contessa might or might not be available to a stranger at such a late hour, the sour old man had said. The name of Piero Torres had meant nothing to him. What would it mean to her?

He studied the room's decor, trying to see her hand in it, but the sophisticated furnishings, almost spartan with their clean lines and cool, pale colors, spoke nothing of the passionate girl who had loved bright pink and deep violet. Then he sensed her presence. Holding his breath, he turned and gazed into the fathomless dark eyes of his lover.

He could see a few silver strands in her lustrous raven hair, faint crinkles from laughter around her eyes and mouth. Her body, once girlishly slender and coltish, had fulfilled its early promise; now it was voluptuous yet sleek as she stood frozen in the doorway, her figure outlined by the sheer mull of her gown, which was raspberry pink.

"You are even more lovely than I remembered." He whispered, but the sound carried across the silence stretching between them, echoing in the big room.

"And you are an incredible flatterer," she managed, although her voice was breathless. "I cannot believe it. Piero."

She inspected him as he did her, their eyes mutually devouring. He was still whipcord lean and sinewy, swarthy dark with those same unbelievably blue Torres eyes, eyes that had haunted her dreams for too many years to count. "I heard you went to America. It must be true that talent and industry are richly rewarded there." She could see by the cut of his clothing, the gold watch chain suspended at his waist, the very way he carried himself, that he was a man of consequence now. Her knees felt weak and she was forced to clutch the doorframe to steady her trembling.

"America is a remarkable country. I'm accounted a success, yes." He tore his eyes from her for a moment and looked around the room. "The same might be said of you. There was a second husband after Nicolo?"

She shuddered, remembering the vile old man her family had forced her to wed. "Nicolo died within a year of the marriage, but I was still underage. My brother Luciano made the arrangement with the Conde di Remaldi, a boon companion of his university days."

"And you did not love him either." It was not quite a question, more like a secret wish that he could not keep from voicing aloud any more than he could keep from moving slowly across the room to where she stood in the doorway.

Vittoria realized that they could not continue this very private conversation with servants eavesdropping. Taking a deep breath to steady herself, she stepped into the room and closed the door behind her. "No, I did not love him. He was not a depraved brute like Nicolo, but neither was he what one might exactly call a devoted husband. He went his way and I was allowed to go mine."

"And then he died, leaving you a wealthy widow." *You do not mourn him. Did you mourn me?*

When he reached out and took her hands, she knew he must be able to feel her pulse racing madly. "He gave a good account of himself trying to bankrupt my estates as

187

well as his own, but fortunately his profligacy caused his death before we became destitute. Since I was of age by then, I learned to manage my own affairs."

"And what of your parents, your brothers, the rest of your family?" As he spoke, he continued to hold her hands, massaging the fine bones of her wrists with the pads of his thumbs.

"My parents are dead . . . the rest are dead to me." *But never you, Piero. You have always lived in the deepest part of my soul.* "I have told you much of my life. What of yours? I knew your parents were gone, but surely in America you have married, had children."

His eyes met and locked with hers as he brought her hands up to his mouth. "No, my beloved, I have never wed," he said as he pressed his lips to her sensitive open palms, then to her wrists, where he could feel the blood beat. "You see, I have never found a woman to match you," he murmured, raising his head once again.

The look in his eyes took her breath away. "Piero, my darling," she whispered, her voice breaking as she melted against him, feeling the hardness of his body, inhaling the scent of him, still the same and yet not the same. The boy had become a man. All thoughts were swept aside as his mouth covered hers and she opened to him, cupping his face between her hands to meet the onslaught of his hungry kiss.

When he swept her into his arms and demanded, "Which way to your bedchamber?" she did not hesitate.

"Up the stairs and to the right, the first door," she replied between kisses.

Chapter Fifteen

They lay in her big soft bed, entwined, satiated. Piero's body had not felt so at peace since the last time he had been with Vittoria. They had been little more than children then, she even younger than he, although both had been virgins. "Amazing, that after all this time we should be brought together once more," he whispered, stroking her cheek as he leaned over her.

She reached up and placed one palm against the hairy wall of his chest, feeling the steady rhythm of his heartbeat. "After so many years . . . why did you return? Why did you wait so long?"

He took her hand and pressed kisses on the sensitive pads of her fingertips. "Fate brought us together, I suppose . . . no, that is not an honest answer. I was afraid—afraid to find you still wed and surrounded by children . . . or worse, dead. I was a coward, wanting to hold my memories of you inviolate."

She smiled sadly, yet a bit of mischief lit her dark eyes. "Perhaps it was a fear that you would find me fat and wrinkled and shrewish, not at all the smiling slim girl of your dreams."

"You will always be the girl of my dreams."

"But you built a life, made a fortune, became an American. That must have taken a great deal of time and energy." When he did not deny it, she felt her heart go cold. He was no longer Neapolitan. His life was in the New World now. Where did that leave them?

Piero was too preoccupied to sense her disquiet. How could he tell her about Quintin Blackthorne? He had not intended to seduce her this way, for them to move so quickly to their old intimacy, but once he had seen her standing in that doorway, there had been no way to stop. Now he realized that it might have been a mistake. Gently, he withdrew from her embrace, kissing her hands. Then he sat up and said, "You asked why I came back after so many years and I replied fate. In a strange way, fate did force my hand. My business partner in the shipping trade is Devon Blackthorne."

Vittoria felt as if icy water had splashed over her. "Beth's uncle," she said flatly.

"Yes. Quintin came to him with a letter that accused an earl's son of dishonoring Beth."

"And you were sent to investigate?" She willed herself to remain calm, sensing his anguish as he searched for the words with which to explain.

"No. When Dev sent for me, I was asked to accompany her father to Naples as an interpreter. Then they told me Beth was being chaperoned by a countess named Vittoria who was a widow . . . I could not be certain it was you, but I dared to hope."

"And what does Quintin Blackthorne intend to do about his daughter?" she asked with growing dread.

"He is intent on taking her home, but I'm not sure that is the best course," he said carefully. "We were torn apart by our families. Perhaps the wiser course would be to follow the advice of the author of the letter and see that they are wed."

She swallowed the tears. "Oh, Piero, if only that could be."

"You mean the cad would refuse—or that Beth herself would not wish to marry him?"

"I mean that Beth is not here to wed anyone. She was captured by Algerine corsairs two months ago. All the other captives from the ship on which she was sailing have been ransomed, but she has vanished. The rumors are that she was taken to the dey's seraglio." She blinked back useless tears. She had wept and prayed and spent a small fortune sending redemptionists to Algiers.

Piero took her in his arms and she drew strength from him, telling him of the hellish nights and days since word of the *Sea Sprite*'s capture reached Naples, of everything she had done to find Beth and the guilt she felt for agreeing to the trip, then being unable to accompany her young charge.

"*Cara, cara,*" he whispered, rocking her and stroking her hair. "This was not your doing. Beth came to the Mediterranean knowing full well the dangers, but do not despair. My country has dispatched a fleet to stop Algerine depredations and force the dey to return all American captives. Stephen Decatur is in charge. He is not a man to take no for an answer," he said wryly.

She raised her eyes to his, daring to hope. "You know this Stephen Decatur?"

"Quite well, yes. He's a remarkable fellow who would not hesitate to march his marines right into the dey's seraglio with swords and muskets."

"I must speak with the redemptionists about this," she said as she slipped from the bed and reached for a robe.

"First we must break the news to Beth's father," Piero replied grimly. "She is his only daughter and he's been on the verge of distraction ever since that letter reached him in Savannah."

"Yes, I suppose we must," Vittoria said sadly, knowing the anguish she already shared with Quintin Blackthorne . . . and the guilt she alone bore for allowing Beth to sail without her.

191

Once he recovered from the devastating shock of the news, Quintin Blackthorne was a veritable tornado of energy, rousing all of Vittoria's household in the middle of the night, sending messages to the Neapolitan authorities, even to the British chargé d'affaires and the commander of royal naval forces in Palermo. Then he set about arranging to purchase a ship to take him in search of Decatur's fleet.

By mid-afternoon of the following day, everything had been set in motion. An unshaven and utterly exhausted Quint sat on the contessa's portico, sipping a cup of the heavy black Turkish coffee so favored around the Mediterranean. He grimaced at the bitter undertaste of the sweet drink and stretched his long legs out in front of him, combing his fingers through his hair as he looked at Vittoria.

"Tell me about this English lordling my daughter has become involved with."

"Derrick Jamison is the brother of the Earl of Lynden . . . and a British spy."

"A spy!" Blackthorne sat bolt upright in his sgabello chair. "How the gods do mock us, Contessa. In the late war between his country and mine, I, too, was a spy. It does not endear him any the more to me. What was his mission here?"

Quint knew little of Italian politics beyond what Beth wrote in her letters, which were mostly filled with fluff to soothe her fretting parents. Vittoria explained what she had gleaned about Jamison's work.

"Then the wretch was using Beth," he said in a quiet but deadly tone of voice.

Vittoria, like Piero, decided quickly that it would not be wise to cross Quintin Blackthorne. But prudence be damned; Beth's happiness came first. "He may have been . . . at first," she conceded. "He came here grievously wounded the last night Beth ever saw him. Murat's guardsmen were scouring the city for him."

"I find it difficult to credit that you did not turn him

over to the soldiers, *cara*," Piero interjected softly, for he had always known her politics.

"I might have, but Beth was quite desperately in love with him. Even if I had known of his presence, I do not think I could have hurt her that way. She stitched up a terrible bullet slash on his ribs; then he stole my fastest racer and left before dawn."

"You let her lose her innocence to him in the first place. That was the beginning of the hurt," Quint accused.

Piero started to remonstrate, but Vittoria placed her hand over his and answered, "We do things differently here, signore. That is part of the reason Beth wished to come here—to be free to pursue her dreams, to—"

"To give away her virtue like some waterfront prostitute!" Blackthorne interrupted tightly.

"You are unfair, Quint," Piero said evenly, trying to mediate what was becoming an ugly confrontation. "You are both too exhausted to think straight."

"I can think well enough, Piero," she replied, staring intently into Blackthorne's cold green eyes. "Her virtue, as you so quaintly put it, is Beth's alone to bestow, but that was not what brought her to Naples. She came to paint. To create a life for herself in a place where people would understand and appreciate her for what she is—a very gifted artist."

"And you imply, madam, that her family did not understand or appreciate her."

She ignored his deadly tone. "You love her—and she you, but that alone cannot make her happy."

"And taking an English lover did?"

Before Vittoria could reply, Beth's maid Donita came scurrying from the main salon onto the open porch, breathless, her face flushed with joy. "Oh, Contessa, Contessa, she's alive—she's here! My mistress is here!"

Piero and Vittoria understood what the maid had blurted out in Italian and leaped to their feet as the contessa attempted to calm the hysterical young woman. Quint could only intuit that the news was good, but it was he who first saw his daughter walking down the hallway to the portico door.

"Beth!" He strode eagerly across the marble floor separating them.

"Papa!" Beth flew into his arms. "How wonderful to see you. What are you doing in Naples?"

"I've come to take you home, daughter."

It was then that Quint noticed the tall Englishman. Mutual recognition flared instantly. A second later, Blackthorne's fist connected with the younger man's jaw, knocking him to the floor.

Derrick Jamison had spent years learning to sense danger and protect himself from it. He had seen Blackthorne's fist coming. Yet he made no attempt to avoid it. Had guilt and some perverse need to be punished turned him into a damned punching bag? What a coil, he thought as he rolled instantly, albeit a bit unsteadily, to his feet. His hands were still at his sides.

The explosive violence had been so completely unexpected that it took a moment for Beth to react. "Stop this at once!" she shrieked as she rushed to Derrick. Shielding him from her father, she daubed at the blood trickling from the corner of her lover's mouth.

Blackthorne did not fail to note his daughter's protectiveness. Then, glancing over her head, he met the steady, calm gaze of the dark-haired Englishman. Damn, this was not going to be easy.

Vittoria broke the tense silence. "As to what your father is doing in Naples, *cara,* he has heard some unfortunate rumors about your romantic involvement with Signore Jamison." The contessa's eyes flicked to Derrick with a faint hint of amusement. *Let him sweat.*

"Rumors? From whom? Some Neapolitan busybody?" Derrick asked, noting for the first time the presence of a stranger standing beside the contessa.

"A countryman of yours, chap named Drummond. Indicated that he's a friend of my nephew Alexander," Blackthorne growled, daring the bastard to deny the allegations.

"Drum!" Derrick cursed silently, employing every epithet he knew to the devious dandy. "So that was what the scrawny little wretch meant when—" He stopped before he dug himself a deeper hole.

"And just exactly what did you hope to do when you found me with Derrick?" Beth interjected. These two arrogant males were not going to decide her fate or fight a duel or commit any other tomfoolery while she had a tongue in her head!

"Jamison, consider yourself fortunate that I'm more concerned with seeing my daughter returned safely home than I am with you," Blackthorne replied, directing the answer to her question to his opponent.

"I'm relieved to hear that, sir, but perhaps your daughter does not wish to return 'safely home.' Will you drag her aboard ship?" Derrick asked with the lazy arrogance of an English toff.

"Kicking and screaming, if necessary, to save her from the likes of some damned bored lordling such as you." Blackthorne's voice was colder than ever now.

Derrick stiffened at the insult. It was too close to the opinion shared by his family. "You have an ill way of repaying kindness, especially considering that I have risked my life to free your daughter in spite of the fact that it was her own impetuosity that landed her in danger in the first place," he snarled.

"Just a moment!" Beth said loudly, forcing herself between the two bristling men and placing a palm on the chest of each one, shoving them farther apart so she could speak her piece. "How dare you both speak of me as if I were not even present!" Rounding first on Derrick, she said, "It was not some flight of *impetuosity* that sent me sailing, but the opportunity to paint in the Baleric Islands." She would have bitten off her tongue before she admitted that she'd taken the journey as a nostrum to forget him. Then she turned on her father. "And I will do a deal more than kick and scream if you even think of forcing me to return home!"

Vittoria placed her arms around Beth's shoulders and removed her from between the two glowering men. "As

Piero suggested earlier, everyone is too exhausted and overwrought to make any rational decisions."

"Piero?" Beth echoed, looking at the handsome older man who had said little during the exchange but remained steadfastly at Vittoria's side. "Not your Piero—the one who . . ."

He bowed gallantly to her, saying, "Yes, the very one. I accompanied your father to act as his interpreter, hoping to find the Vittoria of Mr. Drummond's letter was the lady of my heart."

"Enough of this," the contessa interrupted, feeling almost giddy from Piero's words. *The lady of his heart!* "I'm going to see that Beth has a hot bath, a quiet meal and some rest. I would recommend the same for you, gentlemen. I'll have my servants see to your needs," she said firmly, ushering her young friend from the room with a warning glare in Derrick's direction. As soon as she saw to Beth, she would dispatch a trusted servant with instructions to see that the Englishman did not once again slip away.

After the women had departed, Piero looked from Blackthorne to Jamison and back. " 'Tis good advice."

"Bugger it!" Derrick snapped, his patience at an end. "I'll not see Beth dragged back to some provincial wilderness. She chose her course and you have no right to change it at this late date."

"Are you challenging me to a duel for exercising my fatherly duty?" Blackthorne asked in a deadly quiet voice.

Piero's patience was beginning to wear decidedly thin. Anglo-American propriety was oppressive in the extreme. "Perhaps I am not as Americanized as I thought. Italians possess infinitely more sense when it comes to matters of the heart. It would seem that Beth loves you both . . . although I cannot see any good reason for it," he added beneath his breath. "I would imagine there is a very good chance that you would both acquit yourselves expertly on a field of honor. A dead father. A dead lover. Now there's a fine solution to everything."

The antagonists were forced to see the logic in his words.

"Perhaps a duel is not wise," Blackthorne conceded.

Jamison nodded. "Yes, I agree."

"But there are matters that must be settled," Quint said, turning to Piero. "If we give our word not to go at each other with any lethal instruments, will you trust us alone to discuss the matter?"

Piero considered for a moment, then reluctantly agreed. "Only remember that the ladies will have a say in anything you might decide." On that disquieting note, he went indoors in search of the bath and meal Vittoria had promised. Once rested, they, too, had much to discuss.

"Beth's reputation is in shreds because of you and because of her abduction. She cannot remain here in Naples. The only solution is for her to return home."

"She won't go," Derrick replied wearily, with a sigh of defeat. *Ah, puss, what are we to do with you?*

"What if she's pregnant?" Blackthorne's words hung on the air. "I assume you . . . sailed together from Algiers?"

The implication was not lost on Derrick. "Yes," he admitted. "I brought her safely back where she wished to go. After your friend Decatur secured her release, he urged her to return to America with his fleet." He could not resist adding, "She refused."

"That has nothing to do with the dilemma now. She is here. She has been compromised—by you. And it is your duty as a gentleman to wed her." Exactly how he had leaped to this unpalatable conclusion completely on his own stunned Quint as soon as he had uttered the words, but before he could reconsider, Derrick surprised him by nodding in defeat.

The guilty realization that they had done nothing on the voyage to prevent conception had struck him the moment Blackthorne raised the question of possible pregnancy. Of course, there was every good chance that any child she might carry was not his but the corsair captain's or Kasseim's. But for all the willfully foolish risks she had taken, Beth did not deserve to be left without the protection of a husband's name. "I will marry her . . . if she'll have me."

*   *   *

Shirl Henke

"I will not marry him!" Beth was so frustrated, she would have hurled the bust of Julius Caeser across the sitting room if she could have lifted the immense hunk of marble. She stood beside the chair she had just jumped out of, ready to bolt. If she could not make Vittoria understand, how would she convince her father?

After speaking with Quintin Blackthorne, Vittoria had convinced him that it might be best if she broke the news of Derrick's proposal. She had ordered a light repast for the two of them in her quarters and urged Beth to talk about what had befallen her during her captivity and rescue. Only then had she explained Derrick's offer. "Be reasonable, *cara*. You love him—"

"Ah, yes, I love him, no matter at all that he does not love me," she interrupted Vittoria.

"How do you know that he does not? It seems to me he risked a great deal to save you in Algiers, then bring you back here instead of leaving you with the Americans."

"You don't understand," Beth said miserably.

"Then explain, *cara*," the contessa replied gently. "We have all night. That is why I asked your father to leave us alone."

"I'm amazed my father agreed. In fact, I'm amazed he even considered my marrying Derrick. And don't tell me that it was Derrick's idea." She wanted desperately for Vittoria to reassure her but could see at once that her hope was vain.

"No, it was not, although apparently he did agree quite readily."

"And my father did not even have to point a pistol at his head to extract the offer from him? I should feel thrilled by the romance of it!"

"It was not that way at all," Vittoria remonstrated, not one bit certain what actually had transpired.

"Oh, then what way was it? Why couldn't Derrick come to me himself and propose?" Saying the words hurt.

"After the scene you witnessed between him and your father, he felt it best if I broached the subject to you first. He has been summoned to speak with the British chargé d'affaires. He is still in the employ of their Foreign Office, you know."

"You are in great charity with him, considering how you felt when you first learned he was a spy. Then you wanted to cut out his heart and feed it to the gulls on the quay. What has changed your mind about him?"

"You, *cara*. After he was gone and you believed you'd never see him again . . . how you grieved and could not paint . . . I knew then that you loved him as I loved Piero."

"You always told me that you didn't believe in that kind of forever love."

Vittoria smiled sadly. "I lied . . . to protect you from the hurt I felt. Perhaps I lied to myself as well all these years. My life has been good, yes, but a part of me was always empty. I never knew how empty until I saw Piero standing in this very room yesterday evening."

Beth felt her chest tighten with emotion—joy for her friend . . . and what for herself? "You think that I will always love Derrick that way—that I will never get over him?"

Vittoria took her hand, smiling. "You don't have to get over him—or pine away alone. He's here and he wants to marry you. I doubt even your formidable father could force him if he did not want to. All you have to do is say yes. Father Vivalde will perform the ceremony as soon as I speak with the bishop regarding waiving the banns."

"This is all happening too swiftly. I must discuss this with Derrick before I'll agree. We have many things to sort out first."

Beth waited for Derrick to return that night, pacing nervously in her quarters. She was afraid to hope that they could build a life together. Would she be forced to spend the rest of her life as Vittoria had until Piero returned? Her friend, usually cool and aloof, now radiated the glow of a well loved woman, blissfully happy, almost girlishly giddy when she looked at or spoke with her lover.

Is that how I appear around Derrick? she wondered. If so, she had certainly been wearing her heart on her sleeve.

Not so her spy. Physical desire for her was the only emotion he had ever revealed. Why had he agreed to leg-shackling? For that matter, why should she? Hearing the tall case clock down the hall strike midnight, she realized he was late. Still conferring with the officials from his government? Or had he repented his offer and fled Naples in the night once again?

Derrick stood in the outside doorway to her quarters, watching her while she was unaware of his presence. After the ordeal with Blackthorne, followed by a lengthy session with Sir Richard, he was past being exhausted. His mind felt as numb as his body—until he looked at her. Ever since that day when he'd first seen her in peasant's garb on the quay, she had entranced him to the point of obsession. As a mistress he had desired her beyond all reason . . . but as a wife? He was not certain how he would feel when the priest pronounced them bound together for life.

Dammit all, he had never intended to marry. That was Leighton's duty, not his. But when he gazed at the strong, vibrant planes of her face, the lush curves of her body . . . She seemed to sense his presence like a doe sensing the approach of a predator. He watched as she turned and looked at him without saying a word.

"Hello, Beth. Sorry I'm so late." *Too stiff by half, Jamison.* He strode into her sitting room and took her hands, raising them to his lips as he tried to read her expression.

"Vittoria told me you were with the chargé d'affaires," she replied, withdrawing her hands and turning to the table, where Donita had set out a cold collation and a bottle of claret. Her hands trembled as she poured two glasses of the ruby liquid. Forcing them to hold steady, she handed him a glass.

He accepted it, taking a sip while studying her over the rim. "So, puss, what's it to be—will you marry me?"

"At least you have the good grace to ask. Everyone else simply assumes I'll fall in step with the arrangements, which appear to be moving along briskly. Father Vivalde was here earlier to assure me that the bishop has granted a dispensation so that we may be wed on the morrow!"

He shrugged. "Tomorrow would be fine with me. What of you?"

"You must first tell me why you wish this. The only time you have ever spoken of marriage was to call it leg-shackling and shudder at the prospect."

"So did you, if you recall. Your art was your life . . . or so you told me."

His coolness was palpable, as if he'd removed himself from emotional involvement. How could he ask her to bare her soul when he stood so aloof, a handsome stranger with the unreadable face of a spy. "What are you fishing for, Derrick? Do you want me to tell you I would abandon painting for love of you?"

"I expect not," he said, a rueful half-smile touching his lips fleetingly as he sipped at his wine again. "I'll not forbid you to paint, Beth—as if forbidding you to do anything would signify. You may pursue your art career as you wish. After all,'tis not as if I were the earl and you my countess."

The offhand comment wounded her painfully. How careless were the barbs of the aristocracy. "I would be a scandal in London," she replied, taking a large swallow of wine for courage. "My father believes I'm one here, too."

"He doesn't understand Naples." He did not deny that she would be a fish out of water in London society.

"He doesn't understand you. Neither do I. Vittoria's right. Even Quintin Blackthorne could not coerce you into what on our frontier is called a 'shotgun wedding.' "

He stiffened angrily for an instant, then brought his temper under control as Piero's words echoed in his head. *A dead father. A dead lover. Now there's a fine solution to everything.* "I am no more afraid of your father than he is of me. That is not why we reached an accord."

"You still have not answered my question, Derrick. Why are you willing to marry me?" *Just say you love me.* The words echoed in her head, but she knew they were foolish even before he replied.

"Dammit, must everything be spelled out for you as if you were still a school miss!" His angry outburst made her pale and the wine splashed over the rim of her glass. At once he repented. "Ah, puss, I'm sorry. I did not mean to rail at you."

"What did you mean then?" she persisted doggedly.

He reached out and took the glass from her whitened fingers, setting it on the table, then drew her with him to the Grecian couch and sat down beside her. "I'm offering you the protection of my name. Beth . . . there might be a child. It could be mine . . . or that corsair Quinn's or Kasseim's—"

She leaped to her feet angrily, her head spinning with the sheer pain and rage of the practical arrangement her father and lover had made for her. "How noble that you concede it *might* be yours—this imaginary child!"

"I know for a fact that you have not had your courses since we left Algiers," he said, gritting his teeth as he rose. "How long before that?"

She had gone through hell to keep another man from touching her, working her fingers to the bone nursing Quinn, stealing Maya's opium to drug that thrice-cursed Kasseim! And now Derrick thought one of them might have gotten her with child. It had hurt when she realized that he believed she'd lain with them, hurt even worse that he blamed her for being captured in the first place. But even then, she'd wondered if it had been a prideful mistake not to reveal the real reason for her voyage. Now she was glad she had not confessed that it was despair over losing him that had driven her to risk sailing in Barbary waters.

Beth swallowed back her tears, unable to voice a painful denial, which he would not believe anyway. Instead, she replied, "My courses have always been erratic, Derrick. I think it best if we wait a while before leaping into a marriage that we may both regret. There may be no reason for it."

She looked so vulnerable and brave at the same time. His heart softened, but the memory of the steely glint in Quintin Blackthorne's eyes made him say, "Waiting may not be a wise idea, Beth. Your father wants this matter settled. He has the rather traditional view that his daughter's honor has been compromised, and the only thing that will satisfy him is a wedding."

"You aren't afraid of him." She was certain of that.

"I would not want to kill him either."

Then she understood. The ground seemed to evaporate from beneath her feet. "Dear God, he really did threaten a duel."

"As a matter of fact, the possibility was mentioned," he said with a wry smile that did not reach his eyes. "Piero reminded us that it would please you ill if either or both of us ended up dead. So, I think, puss, that you shall simply have to marry me," he announced, taking her in his arms and pulling her against his chest.

The world was spinning out of control, everything moving much too fast. Perhaps she *was enceinte*. Her dizziness was certainly not due to a few sips of wine. *It is Derrick.* Beth quashed the thought. "There must be another way to settle this," she said reasonably, pushing against his chest. "I shall speak with Papa."

Her resistance should have heartened him. Instead it only seemed to rub salt into what was already a fiery wound. He had fled the marriage noose repeatedly during his days as a London rake. Women had always tried to entice and entrap him. But this woman, a totally unsuitable American whose body had been violated in unthinkable ways, refused him. "You said yourself, Beth, your courses are erratic. What if we wait another month, two—and then learn that you are four months with child? Do you think your father will be willing to allow that?"

When he put it that way, reasoning with Quintin Blackthorne did seem a bit ridiculous.

"Look, puss, you shall marry me or I will kill your father . . . or he shall kill me . . . or we'll kill each other."

Beth was appalled. "Derrick Jamison, are you blackmailing me?"

Derrick cocked his head and stared down at her, an enigmatic smile slowly curling his lips. "Hmm, it does rather sound like it, doesn't it?"

Chapter Sixteen

Beth lay awake all night after Derrick left, tossing and turning until the sky pinkened with morning light. Wearily, she climbed out of her bed, which was large and lonely without him beside her. Even if her father's presence in the city was not a deterrent, it would have been unwise for them to sleep together until they settled this matter of marriage. What should she do?

Beth dressed hurriedly and went into her studio. Perhaps the familiar routine of work would soothe her troubled spirits, enable her to think more clearly if she focused on something other than this dilemma for a while. She readied her palette and brushes, dry and dusty from sitting so long while she was gone. The light was perfect. Now, what to work on? Several paintings in progress were propped about the room, covered with cloth. Some instinct sent her to the one farthest from her.

When she flung the cover off, Derrick Jamison's brooding countenance stared back at her: the portrait she had never completed. She studied the long lazy lines of his body as it reposed by the side of the stream, the tilt of his head, the deep blue of his eyes and that mouth . . . oh, yes, that mouth, sculpted as perfectly as if Michangelo himself had done it. But this man was not lifeless marble, the embodiment of some mythical figure. He was alive and warm. He was the man who would be her husband . . . if she agreed.

Perhaps . . . Her thoughts were broken by a knock at her door. Thinking that it was Donita with her morning coffee, she continued to stare at the painting as she bid the caller enter.

"So this is where you work," Quint said, striding into the large, cluttered room filled with canvases, paints, charcoal and paper. "I remembered that you were always up while your slug-a-bed brothers still slept."

When he approached, she started to cover the canvas, but he quickly stopped her, then stood back to study the portrait, which was almost complete. She had only to fill in the rest of the background. "It reveals much, Beth," he said thoughtfully.

"About him . . . or about me?" she asked nervously.

"Perhaps both. You've captured something elusive in his eyes, in the way he's looking out at the world—or at the one who's drawing him. You're in love with the rogue, aren't you, daughter?"

"Yes," she replied, seeing no use in denying it since he would not relent in his insistence she marry. "But he is not in love with me," she felt compelled to add.

Quint walked across the airy room to one of the large windows that overlooked the bay in the distance. The sun had just begun to clear the hills behind him and was gilding the water with flecks of gold and pink. He seemed lost in thought for a moment, then said, "Perhaps he is . . . perhaps not. When first we wed, I did not love your mother either." At her small gasp of shock, he turned. "I've never told a living soul what I am going to tell you now.

"Ours was an arranged marriage. Madelyne's father and mine had been compatriots in the war against the French. I did not wish to wed . . . but my duty to produce heirs for Blackthorne Hall made me consent to the match. Your mother was not . . . what I expected. I had wanted a plain, biddable wife."

"Mama—plain! Biddable!"

Quint smiled sadly. "I was mistaken about those matters . . . among many things . . ." he said, seeming to grope for words as his expression became haunted and grim. Beth sat spellbound as her father's tale of love and betrayal unfolded, stunned that what she had always assumed to be the most perfect love match ever made had in fact been a forced arrangement in which her father had treated her mother abominably. Almost too late he had realized how much he had come to love her.

"So you see," he finished at length, "women as remarkable as you and your mother have only to outlast and outwit male blindness and stupidity. I made it my business last night after Jamison and I had our discussion to make inquiries about him from some sources that Piero and the contessa have here in Naples. He is a man of honor and rare courage, in spite of the fact he's a bloody earl's son. And there is that unfortunate spy business . . ." he added with a wry grin.

"And you believe I can outlast and outwit him just by loving him?" she asked, afraid to believe it.

"Just by loving him, yes," her father replied simply.

Did she love Derrick enough for both of them? The thought tormented and tantalized her as she worked through the morning, filling in the background on his portrait. " 'Twould make a fine wedding gift," she murmured to herself, remembering the day she had made the first sketches for it, when they had made love in the water. At least that part of the marriage would work out splendidly. But passion alone was not nearly enough, as her parents had found out.

Sighing, she put aside her brushes and stood back to look at the finished work. His arresting blue eyes stared back at her, cool and distant, with just the faintest hint of mockery in them. Was it for the world around him . . . or for himself that his beautifully sculpted lips turned up in a melancholy smile? A bit of both, Beth concluded. She had captured a fleeting bit of the enigma that was Derrick Lance Jamison.

Thank heavens he was the earl's second son. What if he had been the heir? She shuddered at the thought, remembering her father's comments regarding Derrick's decidedly overdeveloped sense of duty. An American wife whom he believed had given herself to renegades and Algerines would scarce make a fit countess. Nor would a woman who dressed like a peasant and haggled with street vendors, posed in the nude for artists and, perhaps worst of all, sold her own paintings for money.

Her troubling reverie was interrupted when she heard Derrick's voice from down the hall. Hurriedly, she draped a cover over the portrait and walked to the door of her studio. He stood in the center of her small sitting room, seeming to overwhelm the dainty space with his masculine presence. He wore tan doeskins that clung to his long legs like a second skin, polished high boots and a white lawn shirt open at the collar, revealing a patch of the crisp black hair that furred his muscular chest. His skin had darkened even more under the hot North African sun, and she felt the heat of him leap across the room and scorch her.

"Vittoria said you had not been to the markets in a while. I thought we might go this morning. 'Tis one of my fondest memories of our first days together. That is, if you've finished your work for the day."

"Oh, yes; that is, I will have to change my dress," she replied, feeling foolish when he bowed formally.

"I shall await you downstairs," he replied and left her standing alone in her quarters.

When had they become so stiff and uncomfortable around each other? How she longed for the early days, when there had been no thought of permanence, no pressure from family—just two lovers laughing and enjoying life in each other's company. "I want that old Derrick back," she whispered to herself as she slipped into a pale yellow peasant's blouse and a dark green skirt.

Of course, the "old Derrick" had been a sham, a British

agent on a mission, only posing as a charming wastrel pensioned off by his family. Still, there had been real magic between them when first they met. She would not deny it. Neither could he.

It was late in the morning for the choicest fish on the quay, but since the summer harvests were bountiful, they bought ripe juicy melons and succulent peaches after appropriate haggling with the vendors. As in times of old, Jacomo followed behind to carry the bounty. She made a splendid bargain on a leg of spring lamb for the dinner table and would have felt inordinately pleased with herself if not for a hint of restraint on Derrick's part as he accompanied her.

This time when they reached the piazza where the goat milk vendors worked, he seemed to regain some of his old sense of humor, saying with a teasing light in his eyes, "I vow not to touch a hair on the head of even the most winsome kid." He eyed the tethered nannies warily as she chuckled.

Derrick watched her animated exchange in Italian with the old woman who owned the goats. Her artless American charm and free Neapolitan way of savoring life had delighted him when she had been his mistress. But everything had changed since his confrontation with Quintin Blackthorne. What kind of wife, and possibly mother, would she make? His own qualifications for being a husband and father were equally questionable; perhaps more so, he admitted to himself.

Yet here he was attempting to convince her that they should wed. *We will simply have to make the best of it.* More easily vowed than done, he realized, but there was no turning back now. He had given his word. They would remain in Naples, of course. The idea of returning to England was unthinkable. Beth would rebel against the social strictures of the ton and be wounded by the rejection of his family. Yes, here she could continue to paint and live the unconventional life she loved.

As to what he would do . . . therein lay the rub. The only life he knew was that of spying. Not exactly the sort of career compatible with wedded bliss. Blackthorne had indicated that Beth was an heiress and a sizable dowry would sweeten the marriage bargain, but the idea of living off a woman was more repugnant to him than accepting Leighton's offer to support him in exchange for his continued exile.

That left few choices. Piero had mentioned an intriguing possibility early that morning. He was considering expanding his shipping operations to the lucrative Mediterranean trade now that the Barbary pirates were being forced to stop their depredations. If Derrick was not averse to entering the world of business, he might become a factor for the warehouse here in the city.

The old earl would roll over in his grave at the very thought of it. Leighton would be apoplectic. However, the employment would yield a decent income. But he was loath to give up his work for the Foreign Office. He would miss the chase, the adventure of his old life. There was something addictive in the danger, an almost sexual thrill to outwitting his most cunning enemies in the game of intrigue.

The *baa* of a kid interrupted his tumbling thoughts, and without thinking he reached down absently and gave its head a pat, then jerked back his hand with a startled oath, stepping away before he could raise the ire of an overprotective mama again. He heard the old crone's tittering laughter. She remembered him from that last ignominious encounter. As he looked over at her, she raised a walking stick as gnarled as the fist that shook it, cursing as only the *lazzaroni* could. Her eyes were fixed on a ragged filthy mongrel who was lapping from an unattended pail of milk.

As the old woman scuttled toward the hapless dog, raising her cudgel, Beth suddenly darted to the rescue. Leave it to his softhearted love to save every starveling she encountered, he thought as she cried, "No! I will pay for the milk, please, Graciella." Beth knelt in front of the cowering dog who lay flattened on the hard-packed earth, seeming almost too weak to run. His long shaggy fur was so matted with filth that his color was not readily discernable, his

Shirl Henke

ribs practically protruded from his emaciated sides and there were raw sores all over his body, no doubt inflicted by irate merchants and *lazzaroni* children throwing rocks.

"Come, boy. It's going to be all right. No one will harm you. There's a love," she crooned as the dog bellied closer and she reached down to stroke his head. "Oh my lord, Percival, what evil has befallen you?"

"Percival?" Derrick echoed in stark amazement. Now that he looked at the poor creature, he could see that it was a spaniel—Sir Percival of Inverness! At the sound of Derrick's voice, the dog looked up with pain-glazed eyes, and Derrick recognized him.

Just then a half-dozen street urchins came darting furtively from one of the narrow alleyways leading to the piazza. Sticks and stones in hand, they caught sight of the quarry that had eluded them and took aim. Derrick jumped in front of the hail of fire, shielding Beth and the dog. Since he was not dressed as a gentleman, he was fair game for the young toughs, several of whom were as tall as he.

"Your fun is over," he said in Italian, standing his ground.

"What is it to you? We saw him first," one youth said arrogantly.

"Do not interfere in what is none of your business, foreigner," a second said with a menacing scowl, hefting a large sharp-edged rock in one grimy fist.

"He is a dog himself," the first said, mocking Derrick by barking. That move emboldened several of the smaller *lazzaroni* to draw closer to their ringleaders.

Beth started to rise, but Derrick motioned for her to stay back. As he did so he slipped the knife from his boot, letting the bright noon sun glint evilly on its blade. "Now, who wants to cast the first stone at this foreign 'dog'?" Derrick barked, advancing toward the larger of the two youths.

Indecision was written across his grimy face as he tensed, weighing his options. His instincts, sharpened by seventeen years of survival on the streets, told him that the tall fellow

210

with his cold blue eyes was very dangerous, in fact, spoiling for a fight. He, too, had a stiletto in his belt, but going one-on-one with the older man unnerved him. If the others would back him . . . he let the thought slide away. No, they would vanish into the *fondachi* the moment he crossed blades with such a deadly adversary.

He spit on the ground with a guttural oath, saying, "The dog will die anyway. There's no sport in killing him . . . or you."

As the bullies disappeared, Beth released the breath she'd been holding. She watched Derrick slip the knife back into its hiding place, as graceful and nonchalant as if he'd been cleaning fish instead of facing down a pack of dangerous ruffians. But she knew that none of them were half so dangerous as the Englishman. He walked over to her and knelt once more beside the dog, who raised his head and licked his former master's hand.

"Good boy, Percy," Derrick said, scooping up the injured animal, heedless of the dog's filthy condition.

Beth's heart skipped a beat at the gesture. This kind man was nothing like the deadly stranger who had faced down a mob only a moment ago. "Thank you for rescuing Percy. I assumed Mr. Drummond took him along when you left Naples."

"We sent him to his trainer with a message," he said to Beth. "I imagine Murat's men must have killed our man."

Beth blinked. "His trainer? I thought he was your dog." She quickly paid the nervous old woman for the milk, then turned back to Derrick with a puzzled expression on her face.

As they walked through the streets to where their carriage waited, Derrick explained about Sir Percival's training as a courier for the Foreign Office. She took the dog after he assisted her into the small curricle.

" 'Tis incredible. A spy dog," she said, crooning to Percival, trying not to think that everything she knew about Derrick Jamison had been a deception, right down to the animal she had believed to be his pet.

"His tail's wagging—or at least he's trying valiantly to wag it," he said softly.

She watched his large tanned hand stroke the dog's ears gently. The simple tenderness brought tears to her eyes. *I love you, Derrick. Papa is right. You're a man of honor and principle.* "I shall have to cleanse and stitch those wounds," she said, striving to be practical before she started blubbering.

"She's good at the task, old boy. I can vouch for it," he said, his eyes meeting hers as his smile was replaced by a serious expression. "I have never thanked you properly for saving my life that night, puss."

There was a warm light in his eyes. She was not imagining it. "You also saved me and now poor Percy as well. We are well met, Derrick," she said, meaning more than she was able to put into words.

"Perhaps we are at that, puss. Perhaps we are." He studied her face, looking at her as if he could see into her soul. He had hurt her with his lies, his desertion, but he knew intuitively that she possessed the power to hurt him even more. *I'm a fool to risk it.* But honor demanded that he do so. "Have you considered my offer, Beth?"

She had known he would press her sooner or later that day. Everyone seemed to wish that they wed. Indeed, it seemed that only she and Derrick had misgivings, but still his blasted honor made him agree with the others. What was she to do? Her breath was shaky as she replied, "Yes, Derrick. I will marry you."

"Stop fidgeting so I can straighten the combs. You've pulled them loose," Vittoria said, giving Beth's hair a final touch, then standing back to inspect Donita's handiwork. "You look enchanting, *cara.*"

The contessa had selected the fabric for the gown and engaged her own seamstress and several of her assistants to complete it in time. Made exactly to her specifications, it was palest peach silk shot through with glittery threads of gold. The color of the gown gave a rich glow to Beth's complexion and accented the lush burnished highlights in her russet hair. The low rounded neckline showed off the swell of her breasts, and the straight skirt emphasized the length of her legs. Gold-embroidered ribbon trimmed the sleeves and high waistline, and a train fanned gracefully from the back, light and airy as gossamer wings.

Beth's face was flushed with nervous excitement, but her eyes were haunted. Was she making a terrible mistake for which both she and Derrick would pay the rest of their lives? What if this was all for nothing and she was not with child? She'd had no real symptoms except for the cessation of her flux. Then again, what if she truly was carrying Derrick's baby? That could be even worse. He believed the child might be Quinn's or Kasseim's. *If I am pregnant, I will tell him the truth. Pray God he will believe me!*

That he might not believe her declaration had given her several bad nights since she'd accepted his proposal. She could only imagine what the passengers from the *Sea Sprite* had told him about her and Quinn, and apparently his "friend" Kasseim had lied about having her as well. Whose word would Derrick trust? After all, considering how they had met and become lovers in the first place, he had no reason for great confidence in her morals.

But I never lied to him as he did to me.

How could they build a marriage on such a beginning? "I don't think I can go through with this," she blurted out to Vittoria as soon as Donita was out of earshot.

The contessa looked at her young friend's flushed, tense face. "You're not just having bridal nerves, are you, *cara?* Oh, I was afraid of this when the men came to me with their assurances that things would work out and this was the only solution. But you are so in love with him, and he has pursued you . . . even courted you . . ." She shook her head uncertainly. "I've seen it with my own eyes."

" 'Tis just his sense of duty, not love."

"Oh, I'll grant you the young fool does not know he's in love with you yet," Vittoria said dismissively.

"What do you mean, 'yet'?" Beth asked, a faint flicker of hope rising.

"He's convinced himself that this is the honorable thing to do—and you know Englishmen and their honor," she huffed. "But that is because he's afraid to admit anything more. After all, he's spent his life very unconventionally for an earl's son—a spy, an adventurer moving from country to country, flirting with danger . . . and beautiful women," she admitted. "But you are different. He is afraid. He does not know how to show love. You shall simply have to teach him."

"Is this the same Vittoria who's always said marriage is a prison and love a myth? Piero has certainly changed your outlook," Beth said wonderingly.

An expression of great tenderness suffused the contessa's face, making the sophisticated woman appear almost girlish. "I confess,'tis true, but we had to wait half our lives to learn that truth. Do not waste half—or all—of yours to do the same. You have great courage, you Americans. You can win, Beth . . . if you wish it."

"Oh, I do wish it."

"Then I see little to stand in your way. After all, he's agreed to live here in Naples. Piero's already talking with him regarding the shipping business. You can continue your art career—what is to keep you from enjoying the same relationship you had before, now that he is no longer a spy who will vanish—poof!—in the night?"

Vittoria's flamboyant Italian gestures made Beth smile. "No, I suppose if he gives that damnable English word of his, he will not vanish—'poof!'—in the night."

"Then what are we waiting for? Your bridegroom has probably paced a hole in my best Turkish carpet by now. Come," she said, taking Beth's arm.

When they reached the bottom of the long stairway, Beth could hear soft music floating on the warm summer breeze from the portico. Her father and Piero stood in the hallway, engaged in conversation with a small handful of people while the jolly little priest, Father Vivalde, approached them, his round face beaming with smiles. The ceremony was to be simple with only a few guests, friends of hers and the contessa's from the art community.

214

"Ah, such a very beautiful bride!" Father Vivalde exclaimed with the inbred flirtatiousness that Beth had learned all Italian men possessed. He bowed over her hand, then greeted the contessa, who was a longtime friend as well as parishioner. But their conversation faded, as did everything else in Beth's sight when she saw Derrick step into the doorway. Everyone but her father began to file dutifully out onto the flower-decked portico as Quint led her toward her groom.

Derrick looked so splendid that she felt her chest squeeze tightly with joy. His wide shoulders filled out his dark blue cashmere coat, which was cut away to reveal an embroidered waistcoat of pale blue over a white lawn shirt and perfectly starched cravat. Fawn-colored breeches hugged his long powerful legs, and he wore Hessians polished to a high luster.

His piercing blue gaze locked with hers, transfixing her as she tried to read behind the set expression on his face. A faint smile touched those sculpted lips and seemed to warm his eyes . . . or was it a trick of the light? Did he welcome his bride—or accept his duty?

As her thoughts pitched and tumbled about, the keen longing for his love became an ache down to the very core of her soul. Then her father leaned down and whispered in her ear, "If you truly do not wish to wed him, Beth, I will take you home straightaway. Only say the word."

Chapter Seventeen

I will take you home . . . home. Where was that? Back in Georgia? The life she had worked so hard to create was here in Naples. Still, the comfort of her father's strong arm reminded her that she could once more be surrounded by loving family. All she need do was say the word. For an instant, Beth almost turned and fled the assembled guests—and her reluctant bridegroom.

But then she raised her eyes once more and fell under his mesmerizing spell. Derrick stood with his hands loosely at his sides, legs braced slightly apart as if they were still on the deck of the *San Marcos*. That single lock of hair fell across his brow as he tilted his head toward her, skewering her with his intense blue eyes. She felt like a sparrow stalked by a cat, powerless to fly away and escape its fate.

Her fingers tightened on her father's arm, but her voice was steady as she whispered, "No, Papa. I will wed him." *God help me, I can do nothing else!*

Her father said no more as they approached the beaming priest, flanked by the bridegroom, whose expression gave away nothing. With a sudden jolt of recognition, Blackthorne realized that it must have been precisely the way he had looked as Madelyne approached him for their marriage ceremony.

Would Derrick treat Beth as unfairly as he had her mother? He prayed not. *What have I done?* he thought helplessly as his daughter glided from his arm to that of her soon-to-be husband. Her cheeks were flushed, her eyes bright with emotion. She was not the innocent that Madelyne had been, he reminded himself. Beth and the Englishman had been lovers for some months and there could well be a child. Quint had no illusions about how headstrong and self-sufficient his daughter could be, nor did he doubt that she loved this man. He put aside his misgivings.

The ceremony went smoothly, with both bride and groom making their vows in strong steady voices. Derrick surprised Beth and her worried father by placing an antique gold ring intricately set with emeralds on her finger. Everyone could see that it must be a family heirloom. After the final benediction, the wedding party was served a light repast and sparkling wine on the portico. Everyone gave their good wishes, but after a few moments, Derrick and Beth found themselves with a moment's privacy in the shade of the bougainvillea arbor.

"To my bride." He raised his glass to hers in a salute, then took a sip. His eyes never left her face as he watched her drink. The ring sparkled delicately on her finger as she held the crystal champagne flute. "It fits quite perfectly."

" 'Tis lovely, Derrick. And very old." *An heirloom intended for a blue-blooded Englishwoman,* she thought disconsolately.

"It belonged to my maternal grandmother Celine. She was French, and ironically enough the only member of my family with whom I got on. She died when I was a lad at Eton. At least I did not hurt her as I did the rest."

"And this was to be for your English bride?" The moment the words slipped out, she wanted to call them back. Of course it was not for an American adventuress with a tarnished reputation.

"It was simply a keepsake, Beth. A lucky charm, if you

217

will, which I've always carried with me. It seemed appropriate to give it to you. The emeralds match the green flecks in your eyes."

When he took her hand and raised it to his lips for a soft kiss, she wished desperately to believe that he wanted this marriage to work as much as she did. "My eyes are drab hazel brown," was all she said in reply.

That called forth a flashing grin. "Not when you're angry . . . or excited."

From across the wide sunny portico, Piero and Vittoria watched the bridal couple. Her troubled expression led him to say, "Do not fret, *cara*. All will be well. Look at them. Whether or not they realize it, they are as much in love as we were."

"And that is supposed to soothe me?" she replied sharply. "Look what happened to us."

"We were separated by circumstances—family matters over which we had no control. These young people have nothing of the sort to concern them. They shall build a good life here in Naples. Only wait and see."

She smiled at him. "It was good of you to offer employment to the Englishman."

"It was good business. With the threat of piracy ended, Mediterranean trade will prosper, and with it, so will my expanding shipping business."

"Will you return to America once you've made all the arrangements here?" Her tone was watchful, guarded, even though she strove to make it sound casual and light.

Piero looked down at her with warmth sparkling in his bright blue eyes. "That would distress you, *cara*? To have me leave you once again?"

"I would not hold you from your new life," she said neutrally.

"Ah, yes, that is the crux of the problem. My life has been in America and yours is here in Naples. Here you are a contessa, from an old, powerful family, still welcomed at court, arbiter to the highest circles of belle lettres. And in America . . . you'd be but a Jewish merchant's wife."

A small gasp of surprise escaped her lips, she who had

trained herself never to reveal any weakness, any emotion, unless she chose to do so. "Are you asking me to marry you, Piero?"

"I've always wanted you for my wife, woman. Why do you think I never wed in all these years?" he replied, sounding almost angry.

"But we would have to live in America." She nodded gravely, considering the implications.

"Only part of the time. I know your life here means a great deal to you—"

"I don't give a fig for being a contessa or being welcomed by those depraved Bourbons . . . but . . ."

"But you do care a very great deal about being a patron of the arts, living outside conventional social rules, don't you, *cara?*"

She could not deny it. "You cannot imagine what my life was like married to Niccolo and Umburto—"

"And you compare me to those dogs?" he asked, incensed even though he knew her fears.

"Of course not! Oh, Piero, I did not mean to hurt you that way. I know, I am going about this badly, but I'm afraid . . . of losing myself. I have worked so hard to become who I am, to live as I please, to answer to no one. Here I may do that. But in America, Beth has told me a great deal about how things work. What if I did not fit in? What if your friends and family did not approve of me?"

"Or you of them? Do you honestly believe that after all we have endured I would choose anyone over you? I believe my family will welcome you—but even if they did not, it would not matter to me. You are the woman I have always loved and I would not change you."

She took comfort in the words, the earnestness of his voice. "You said we could live in America only part of the time?" she asked hopefully.

"I have a business that requires that I be there at least part of each year, but we could return to Naples for frequent visits—extended visits. I am an American now, *cara,* and I would like for you to see my new home and judge for yourself its merits. I do not believe you would find it all that oppressive a place if you gave it a chance . . . if you give me a chance."

She nodded slowly, her thoughts tumbling about in her head too rapidly to sort out all at once. "Yes, I—"

The sounds of good-natured revelry interrupted their conversation as Derrick scooped Beth up into his arms and carried her from the portico to the flower-bedecked carriage waiting for them at the entrance to the garden.

Derrick had purchased the small phaeton to have reliable transportation now that he was going to reside here permanently with his wife. *His wife.* He looked over at Beth as he reined in the matched bays at the entrance of the modest villa he had let on the outskirts of the city.

They had spoken little on the ride. He jumped lithely from the rig and reached up to assist her down as the servants who came with the villa filed dutifully out to greet their new master and his bride. When he placed his hands about her slim waist, she seemed to float from the carriage, a vision in peach and gold, lush and tempting as summer fruit ripening on a tree.

Thoughts of ripening led his mind to wonder again if she were indeed breeding. Would he recognize his own child? No difficulty if only Kasseim were involved, but since both Beth and the infamous Irishman had red hair, there would be no way to tell if Quinn had fathered her offspring. His troubling reverie was broken by the sudden sound of barking as a raggedy bundle of fur trotted around the side of the house, tail wagging excitedly.

Beth had felt the strange and disturbing undercurrent flow between them as Derrick lifted her from the phaeton. The sounds of Percy's barking were a welcome distraction. Derrick's hands left her body as he turned toward the dog, attempting to keep the spaniel from tearing their finery.

"Oh, Percy, you should not wear yourself out," she said, kneeling to pat his shaggy head and examine his wounds, which were healing nicely.

"Jacomo arrived early this morning with him in tow."

He did not sound pleased. Beth looked up at her scowling husband. "He is your dog now that his old master is dead, and I—"

"And you are my wife, so of course, the dog comes with you. Only let him sleep with the lad in the servant's quarters. He has wreaked quite enough havoc with the household already. I scarce had an unchewed pair of dress boots or a cravat the blighter hadn't slobbered upon when I went to dress for our nuptials."

She suppressed a grin. "You will behave from now on, won't you, Sir Percival?" she asked gravely of the dog, whose tail thumped furiously on the grass. The spaniel gave a sharp bark, looking from Beth to Derrick. "See there: He gives his word."

Derrick cocked one dubious eyebrow and nodded as he extended his hand to help her up. "We shall see."

Jacomo, who had been waiting with the other servants, stepped shyly forward at his new employer's summons and held the dog as Derrick made introductions to the staff, then escorted his new bride into the villa.

" 'Tis small, but comfortable, I think," he murmured as they walked from the trellised portico inside the main foyer.

On one side of it three stone steps led to an airy parlor. Its glass-paned doors opened onto the terrace at the opposite end of the room. Across the entryway through another arched doorway an enchanting dining area was filled with fresh flowers. The fragrance of a slow-simmered marinara sauce wafted from the kitchen to the rear. Two places were set on the polished walnut table, hers close at the side of his in the master's chair.

In front of them a stone staircase, its treads hollowed out by centuries of footsteps, curved upward to the second story. "Our sleeping quarters are above. I instructed the servants to draw you a bath before we dine . . . if that is your wish."

He sounded like a punctiliously polite stranger, not the teasing, carefree Derrick she had known. *He's trying. You must, too,* she reminded herself. "That would be lovely.

221

This gown is so stiff and uncomfortable, I should like to get out of it."

"I should like to see you out of it, too, my love," he murmured, sweeping her once again into his arms and climbing the stairs. Once in the spacious bedroom, he set her down, then showed her to the balcony overlooking the countryside. The villa was built on a small hillside, and a lush vista of vineyards and fig orchards stretched to the horizon.

" 'Tis lovely," she said.

"Yes,'tis, indeed," he replied, nuzzling her neck while his fingers began unfastening the silk-covered buttons down the back of her dress.

"The servants—"

"Have orders not to disturb us until I summon them."

She gave in to the heady rush of passion that his hands and warm lips evoked, leaning back against him, closing her eyes and remembering all the other times, the lazy afternoons and languid nights of loving him. *But this is different, irrevocable, this will make you his wife.*

As if sensing her hesitance, perhaps echoing his own, Derrick turned her into his embrace as he whisked the unfastened gown down her arms. It fell to her feet and lay in a glittering puddle. She stood in a thin white silk chemise and slip, both delicately embroidered with lace, the fabric so sheer that the warm tones of her flesh were almost visible through it. His seeking lips found the pulse hammering at the base of her throat. Her head dropped back and her arms draped over his shoulders, allowing him access to that which he so desperately craved.

Her quiescence only served to inflame him. Stand so languidly, would she? His desire was matched by a fierce need to have her want him as much as he wanted her . . . to have it be as it used to be when they had first become lovers. That seemed a lifetime ago now. He let his mouth travel across her collarbone, then down to the full high thrust of her breast, wetting the tip through the silk so that it stood out, a hardened little nub of deepening pink. When she moaned and drew his head closer, he swept her up and carried her over to the big high bed at the opposite end of the room.

He laid her on the bed quickly, almost dropping her on the soft pillows as he stepped back and began tearing off his own clothing. Beth's eyes flew open. She lay still, watching as he worked methodically and efficiently to rid himself of his wedding finery. How well she knew what lay beneath, the splendid male beauty of his flesh. He had undressed unashamedly in front of her often. But this was different. She could sense it and suddenly felt vulnerable, lying with her slippers and stockings still on, her dampened chemise clinging to her aching breasts.

It seemed but a moment until he was standing over her, completely naked, his staff hard and pulsing. The tip of it glistened with a pearly drop of semen as he placed one knee on the edge of the bed. He reached out wordlessly and took her hand, the left hand with the wedding ring on it, and placed it around him, shuddering when she stroked him, still saying nothing.

"Derrick—"

He reached down and lifted her up into his arms, his mouth smothering her entreaty, whatever it would have been. Kneeling on the bed, they shared a kiss of searing intensity. His tongue plundered deep inside, teasing forth a response from her, driving in and out as he held her pressed close against his hot, bare skin. The barrier of sheerest silk seemed to add a wicked enticement to their embrace. Then, without breaking the kiss, he began to slide the chemise straps down her arms, pausing when the garment caught on the tips of her breasts.

The soft rasp of the silk made her whimper with longing. She ached for his mouth on the sensitive nipples once more, but he only pulled the chemise past them, then untied the tapes of her slip and shoved all the undergarments down so they fell around her knees. Finally his mouth left hers, breaking off the kiss as if he were a drowning man struggling for breath. She could see the pulse pounding in the strong column of his neck. The muscles of his arms were taut as he guided her to lie back on the bed once

223

more, then followed her, looming over her like some dark and desperate god.

His bare skin gleamed with perspiration as he braced his arms rigidly on either side of her while his knee parted her legs. The silk undergarments were tangled about her ankles now, but before she could protest, he plunged deep inside her with a great shuddering sigh, murmuring her name as his eyes closed. The old familiar heat of this joining scorched her, and she moved her hips restively when he remained still. Then, with a soft murmur he began to stroke, swiftly, powerfully.

He felt her skin, softer than the silken things he'd torn from her body, felt the wet heat of her tighten around him, her hips writhing, imploring him. And all he could think of was the sheer exquisite ecstasy of making love to her. *Making her my wife.* No, he did not want to think of that. He only wanted to feel, to revel in the way they fitted together . . . the way she was his and only his, to exorcise from their consciousness the memories of Quinn and Kasseim and any other lovers she might have taken after he'd left Naples.

Any child she had would be his. He would think of it no other way. But that had proven impossible for him ever since Blackthorne had raised the issue. This then was his despair. But when he smelled her scent, touched her flesh, felt the searing need for her pounding through his veins, then all thought was obliterated. In loving her he found surcease . . . for the moments that the mindless bliss lasted.

He labored to make it last, gritting his teeth, holding back his completion as he felt her body spasm around his, the tight rhythmic contractions squeezing him as he held on, slowing down, waiting for her whimpers of pleasure to quiet, for her body to relax in satiation. Then he began again . . . and again . . .

There was an almost demonic frenzy to his lovemaking, a driven despair that frightened her. But in spite of it, her body, so hungry for his, could only give in to the pleasure he brought her. Her eyes opened as she looked up into his face, seeing the fierce grimace of concentration. He was holding back, letting her climax three times while he still did not allow himself satiation. She ran her hands up over his arms and chest, down his hard belly and around his straining back, feeling the sweat-slicked muscles bunch and flex, the blood pounding through his veins.

"Now, Derrick, fill me . . ." she murmured, arching high as her legs locked around his hips.

And he was lost. A deep guttural cry tore from him as he spilled his seed deep within her in the most intense, wrenching orgasm of his life. He collapsed on top of her, panting and sweat-soaked, his face buried in the sweet fragrance of her hair. One of the opal combs lay tangled in the ruins of her elaborate coiffure, winking at him. He rolled off her, closed his eyes and fell instantly into an exhausted sleep with his arm stretched across her waist just beneath her breasts. Holding her possessively, Derrick could not relinquish their closeness, even if it was only physical.

Beth lay beside him, looking at his face as he slept. She reached over and brushed at the black curl that fell across his brow, then stroked his jawline. His face appeared younger in repose, all the wariness evaporated, the harsh mocking gleam in those blue eyes gone for the moment. She felt his despair still hanging in the air, a palpable thing, and knew that what had just passed between them had everything to do with possession . . . and nothing to do with love.

Tears burned her eyes, but she blinked them back, staring up at the canopy overhead. Her body was satiated almost to the point of numbness, but her soul remained hungry. *Oh, Derrick, husband, what have we done?*

She gently removed his arm and swung her legs over the side of the bed, wincing at the tenderness inside her. He had used her hard, glorying in her helpless cries of release, yet trying to hold himself aloof. That he had not been able to do it gave her satisfaction. Only when she stood up did she realize that her torn silken undergarments still clung to her ankles. She kicked them away, looking down at her snagged stockings. One garter was pulled lower than the other. Both slippers had been lost in the bedclothes. Rather than search for them, she picked up the undergarments and walked from the bedroom into the dressing room, where she sat down on a chair. She felt in dire need of that hot bath Derrick had promised her when they first arrived.

Bright moonlight splashed across the bed, spilling inside the canopy curtains, which had not been drawn. Derrick awakened slowly, as if from a trance. At once his hand groped across the bed, searching automatically for Beth. She was not there. He rolled over and felt something prod him in the back. Reaching for it, he saw that it was one of her gold silk slippers. Its mate lay at the foot of the bed. Then the desperate interlude from earlier in the evening came back to him, and he clutched the slipper so tightly that he crushed it in his hands. Just as he had crushed her with his lust and despair. He had made her his wife, but he had treated her badly, perhaps even hurt her physically. Feeling sick, he tossed the slipper away and placed his head in his hands.

Oh, Beth, what have I done?

He looked at the wreckage of the room. His clothes were strewn hither and yon, but her beautiful wedding dress was not there. Other than the slippers, nothing else of hers remained. He remembered yanking the sheer silk undergarments from her body, not even bothering to remove her shoes or stockings. He was certain no servant had come in to take her clothing. She must have done it herself. *God above, please don't let me have injured her.*

He rose and pulled on his breeches, then went in search of his wife. The moisture from a bath hung in the dressing room air, fragrant with the faint essence of vanilla, her favorite scent. There he found her wedding gown, carefully hung on the wall rack. One hand reached up to touch the crisp brocaded silk, his eyes scanning it for damage. Only a couple of buttons were torn loose, thank heavens. Then he saw the dull gleam of white from one corner. Her chemise, slip and stockings lay hopelessly ripped and snagged, but at least there was no blood on them. He must find her and beg her forgiveness.

Derrick found her asleep in the guest bedroom at the opposite end of the hall. She lay on top of the covers, as if unwilling to disturb them and let the servants see that she was not sleeping with the master. Her body was coiled into a fetal position, wrapped in a heavy dark robe, and Percy lay cuddled in the curve of her legs. Swallowing the lump in his throat, he walked silently to the bed and sat down beside her. The dog watched him warily, not quite growling but very alert as Derrick reached over and gently stroked a few stray tendrils of hair from her face.

Were there traces of tears? In the dim moonlight he could not tell, but his puss was not given to tears. She was the bravest woman he'd ever known. When he leaned down to kiss her, the dog did growl, sitting up as if to protect her from his erstwhile master. "So,'tis apparent you've switched your loyalties. Can't say I blame you," he murmured.

She blinked and opened her eyes, rolling over and looking up at him. He could see no alarm or revulsion on her face and thanked God for that. But he did see confusion and a deep hurt. "Are you injured?" he asked, his voice a croaking whisper over the soft growling of the dog.

She shook her head, patting Percy to quiet him. "No, no, I'm not injured." He reached out then and gently touched one curl hanging over her shoulder. She felt his remorse even before he spoke.

"Beth, I am so sorry . . ." His voice cracked and he removed his hand from her hair and turned away, staring out the window at the night sky. "I only wanted . . . to make you belong to me, no one else. Can you forgive me?"

She scooted up against the pillows, then replied, "I do belong only to you, Derrick. You are my husband and I will try to be a good wife."

Percy sat at the foot of the bed, watching protectively as Derrick asked again, "Will you grant me your forgiveness? Let us begin anew?"

He held his breath. She could sense it. "Yes, Derrick. I

forgive you. I understand that you wed me out of obligation, to protect me." When he started to protest, she placed her fingertips over his lips, shaking her head. "No, my love, do not deny it, for 'tis the truth . . . I have something to tell you. . . ." Her hair dipped like a curtain, hiding her face in shadow as she explained, "My courses began tonight. I am not with child."

He felt as if the weight of the world had lifted from his shoulders until she added, "If you wish, you can obtain—"

"No!" Derrick surprised himself with the vehemence of his answer. Only later would he recognize that he was far more concerned with keeping her as his wife than he was with learning that she was not pregnant. His outburst startled Percy, who began to growl once more. Ignoring the dog, he took one of her hands in his, saying, "We'll not dissolve this marriage. You are my wife and I will have no other. I will try my damnedest to be a good husband."

And so the days passed as summer drew to a close. Derrick and Beth resumed a variation on their original relationship. She continued to paint, converting one of the extra bedrooms into a studio. Although it was much smaller than her quarters at the contessa's villa, the east light was good. She found that overseeing their small household was a pleasure and continued her old rounds with the fishermen and produce vendors, much to her father's dislike. His daughter had always been a tomboy, dressing unconventionally and running with her brothers, but that was back in the safety of Georgia, not in cutthroat-infested Old World slums!

Derrick completed his assignment with the British chargé d'affaires, then devoted his energies to helping Piero establish a shipping operation in the city. Quint Blackthorne stayed on, helping with the business, since he, too, was one of Dev's partners. When Derrick was not busy at the new office of Torres Merchandisers, he often accompanied Beth on jaunts to bargain for oysters and figs. Her commissions on portraits were lucrative and his business income began to grow steadily, assuring them of a comfortable—if unconventional—life. They had both vowed to make their unusual arrangement work. And it did . . . after a fashion.

Derrick found himself drawn into the contessa's circle of belle lettres, attending poetry readings and art exhibits with his wife. She, in turn, attended court functions with him whenever the British Government requested his presence. If their days were at times an uneasy compromise, their nights were unfailingly filled with heady passion. Derrick had never imagined that he could be content with one woman, but he was. Beth, relishing the permanence of a relationship that did not interfere with her art career, no longer felt compelled to test her husband's patience or stir his jealousy as she had earlier.

Within a few weeks of their marriage, they received the handsome gift of a sterling tea service from Drum, who congratulated their having the good sense to see reason and regularize their relationship as Alex and Joss had done. Derrick and Beth read his clever, witty missive, glad to know that he had survived the ordeal of a storm-tossed return voyage to "Albion's soil" after leaving them in Algiers. He also informed them that he had just had a run of good fortune at the gaming tables, winning some sort of tavern in the backwoods of Georgia, and he was off to America to visit his friends and inspect his new property. A chapter in their lives had ended with Drum's exodus. After all, it was his letter to Quintin Blackthorne that had changed their relationship forever.

Chapter Eighteen

"What am I going to do, *cara?*" the contessa asked Beth as they shared a late-morning meal one crisp day in September. "Piero says he will sail before winter comes. He demands an answer."

"As much as I would hate to lose my dearest friend, I think you should marry him and go to America," Beth replied gravely.

"It would mean giving up the life I've worked so hard to build," Vittoria protested, "but still . . ."

"What would you have to fear?"

"How about his family? Have you considered what they will think when Piero brings back a bride such as I? They're Sephardic."

"And they're Americans. The rules of the Old World no longer apply. Your noble blood, his lack of it. Anyone can wed anyone they choose, no matter their religion or station in life, something that certainly wouldn't have happened if Derrick and I had met in England."

"It did not happen here in Naples when we were young either." Vittoria sighed.

As if echoing her thoughts, Beth said, "You and Piero have waited too long to waste another moment."

The contessa's expression turned arch as she replied drolly, "Ah, but *cara,* we have not wasted any time at all since we've been reunited."

"You know perfectly well what I mean," Beth scolded. "You must marry him. Take the gamble."

"And it was worth it for you and Derrick?" Vittoria's smile was tinged with a faint bit of worry.

The question, coming out of the blue, unsettled Beth. She had gone to great lengths to assure her friend that everything was good between her and Derrick. It was, was it not? "I cannot imagine living without him," she answered honestly.

"Nor can I think of losing Piero again. . . . Men are such a bother, *cara.* Why do we put up with them?"

"Oh, I can think of at least one reason," Beth replied with a hearty chuckle.

With Beth, Derrick and Quint as witnesses, Piero and Vittoria were married in a quiet ceremony presided over with considerable misgivings by Father Vivalde. Performing a marriage for two members of the Church of England was one matter; performing one for his lifelong friend Vittoria and a Jewish American was quite another! Yet he could not help liking the charming outsider who had won the contessa's heart so long ago.

After the celebration, Quint planned to sail for home, finally satisfied that he had done the right thing leaving his child in the care of the Englishman. But then fate intervened when a black-bordered letter arrived from the Earl of Lynden's solicitor in London. Beth received the missive from a special courier who had been sent directly from the harbor. A feeling of dread swept over her as she held the heavy velum envelope in her hands. Although she knew Derrick was not close to any of his family, it boded ill that someone had died.

"What's troubling you, puss?" he asked, coming from

his office at the rear of the villa into the foyer after hearing the echo of hoofbeats.

" 'Tis for you," she replied gravely, giving him the letter with trembling hands.

He tore it open at once and began to read, then cursed succinctly beneath his breath. As he continued to scan the pages, he began pacing like a caged cat.

" 'Tis the earl, isn't it," she said, fighting the wave of dizziness that swept over her. Pray God that the countess had been safely delivered of an heir by now!

"Yes. Leighton is dead. He broke his fool neck when his mount went down during a foxhunt," Derrick snarled with an oath.

Beth sank into a chiavari chair, awash in misery, her whole world vanquished by this stroke of a pen. "And the countess?"

" 'Twas a girl." His eyes met and held hers. "I am now the ninth Earl of Lynden." The despair in his voice was mirrored in his eyes.

Beth understood better than anyone how strong was her husband's sense of duty. He would go to London and assume the title, look after his sister-in-law and infant niece, restore the honor of the family name—and his own. But Beth would be an albatross about his neck, utterly unsuitable. *'Tis not as if I were the earl and you my countess* . . .

"I must sail for London as soon as possible."

Thoughts tumbled about in her mind helter-skelter until his clipped words broke into her trance. He'd said *I*, not *we*. Beth fought back tears as she said, "Of course, I shall remain here in Naples."

Derrick was too engrossed in the enormity of the calamity that had just befallen him to think coherently. He knew Beth would hate London, hate giving up her life here every bit as much as Vittoria had. And lord knew, if the social arbiters of the ton found out about her shocking background, it would certainly put a period to any hope of redeeming his name from disgrace.

And still he could not imagine leaving her behind. "Of

course you will go with me to London," he snapped, feeling put-upon. He did not want to examine his feelings about her as his countess any more than he wanted to think about being the earl.

Beth stood up on shaky legs, taking a deep breath to clear her spinning head. "I do not think it wise, Derrick."

If he had hinted that he did not give a fig for the opinion of the ton, declared that he cared too much for her to leave her behind—if he had said anything at all conciliatory, matters might have proceeded differently. But Derrick was not feeling particularly conciliatory at the moment. "What you think—or what I want—do not signify at this time, m'dear. Duty calls."

"And we both know how seriously you take your duty, don't we, husband?"

The stark pain in her voice seemed nothing but bitterness to him. " 'Twas your father who forced the issue, puss," he replied in a low, deadly voice.

Beth recoiled as if he had struck her. "And I agreed after your most dutiful importuning. More fool I for giving up my freedom!"

"A fate worse than death—becoming a countess. Many of your countrywomen would sell their souls for English titles."

"While I only had to sell my body?" she asked icily.

"You've given it readily enough in the past—Quinn, Kasseim, God only knows who else before them. At least this time you'll get Lynden Hall and the Jamison jewels in return. A more than generous recompense, madam."

"You bastard! You . . . you . . ." She launched into a tirade of the worst oaths she'd learned on the waterfront, spewing them out in Italian as she advanced on him, ready to claw his eyes out.

"That sluttish little tongue will earn you the cut direct," he said, seizing her upraised hands in a bone-crushing grip and hauling her against his chest as she continued to curse him. "I'll teach you to mend it before we reach England."

Even though their argument was loud enough for the servants to overhear, none would have dared interfere. Sir

233

Percival, however, was under no such constraints. The sound of his mistress's shrieks of distress brought him on the run from her studio, where he'd been asleep in the sun. He bounded down the stairs toward the struggling couple, who were so intent on each other that neither noticed his barking until he sank his teeth into Derrick's ankle and held on with a loud growl.

Now it was Derrick's turn to spew forth a barrage of furious oaths as he released Beth and tried at the same time to kick free of the dog. The King Charles spaniel hung on with the tenacity of a pit bull. Fortunately his "master" was wearing boots and the dog's sharp teeth did not penetrate the leather. Unfortunately the dog's jaws were incredibly strong and the discomfort of the bite considerable.

Derrick tried raising his foot to shake loose Percy's hold, but the dog weighed too much and he nearly overbalanced himself in the attempt. Beth shrieked at him not to harm her rescuer, delivering a stout blow to his shoulder just as he reached down to try to pry the dog's jaws loose. At that same moment Percy jerked his head backward, teeth still firmly embedded in the boot. This time Derrick did lose his balance, pitching headfirst toward the stone stairway.

Percy reached the decision that it might be judicious to relinquish his grip just before Derrick landed . . . face forward . . . against the newel post. As he slid down onto the bottom step, holding one hand to his bloodied nose, the other massaging his aching ankle, the dog trotted over to his mistress, well content with the afternoon's work.

Beth knelt beside Percy, more to inspect from a safe distance the extent of damage to her husband than to pat the dog for his heroism—which she did anyway. Derrick's oaths were now muffled in the handkerchief he held to his battered face. He seemed otherwise unharmed. She deemed it prudent to take the dog and withdraw, allowing her husband to explain what he would to the butler after she instructed him to bring an ice pack to the foyer.

That night Beth paced in her studio, uncertain what to do. Derrick had stormed out of the villa within an hour of their fight and had not as yet returned, although it was well past midnight. There were many divertissements in the city, especially if one had money enough. Now that he was a bloody earl, Derrick certainly need never again worry about possessing enough of the ready, she thought bitterly, imagining him in the arms of one of the beautiful Neapolitan noblewomen who had practically thrown themselves at him.

"I must not sit about and brood all night," she murmured to Percy, who hovered close at her side, knowing all was not well in the household. She could go to Vittoria, but Piero was there and he was Derrick's friend. No, there was no use burdening the contessa with her problems.

To further tangle matters, her father would be concerned about her going to England. If anyone knew how ill she would fit in such a society, it was Quintin Blackthorne. What would she tell him? And Vittoria? They had both urged her to wed Derrick and would feel guilty about this disastrous turn of affairs. Perhaps after he cooled down, Derrick might consider leaving her here. Divorce was possible, especially given the fact that she was a foreigner with a scarlet reputation.

But that course of action was predicated upon her not being pregnant. And for the past several weeks she had grown increasingly sure that she was. She felt different from the way she had before they were married when everyone had been so certain she was breeding. Since her last courses, she'd begun to experience fatigue, irritability and stomach upset. Even her breasts were growing tender. She could feel her body changing and knew the cause.

At least he'll believe the child is his. . . .

That thought gave her little comfort since the child would also bind them together in this bitter union for the rest of their lives. Before this afternoon, she had been turning over in her mind how to tell Derrick that he was going to be a father. There was a good likelihood that he would not have been pleased in any event. Even as plain Mr. and Mistress Jamison, they had unresolved issues, but as members of the peerage, the problems would be a hundred times worse. Any son of hers would one day become the tenth Earl of Lynden. And Derrick believed she was unworthy of mothering his heir.

"This stewing is not good for the babe," she said to Percy, who gave a woof of agreement. "What I need is a good night's sleep. Then I'll consider what to do in the morning."

But she would not sleep in the same bed with Derrick, who—assuming that he did come home before daylight—would reek of some courtesan's perfume. She instructed Donita to prepare the guest bedroom for her. The little maid nodded sorrowfully. She knew that her employers had had a terrible fight and suspected that her lady was breeding. Such a way to treat his wife! Donita would never understand foreigners, especially Englishmen.

Beth took a languorous bath to relax herself, then retired to the small bedroom adjacent to her studio. The fatigue that had been her constant companion for the past weeks soon sent her into blissful oblivion.

Across the city, Derrick had been seeking oblivion of his own. In a bottle. He raised his head and gave the waterfront cantina a bleary-eyed inspection. It was not the worst place on the quay, but neither did it cater to the better sort of clientele. The ceiling was low, its beams blackened by decades of thick smoke that rose from the huge fire pit in the center of the room where the morrow's mutton roasted on a spit, giving off a strong greasy aroma.

"What in the hell are we going to do, puss?" he asked the empty tumbler in his hand. It held no answers.

From their first encounters in Naples she had made it abundantly clear that she valued her unconventional life more than hearth and home. When faced with the possibility of motherhood, she'd still had to be cajoled into marriage, and that only with his assurances that he would do nothing to stand in the way of her painting pictures on commission, attending radical salons and visiting the quay dressed like a virtual prostitute—hardly socially acceptable behavior by the standards of the ton!

She would be ostracized and wretchedly unhappy as his

countess. They had never discussed what they would do about children. She'd told him that she did not want any long before they wed. When her courses came on their wedding night, he had been greatly relieved, not only because the doubt of his paternity had been removed, but also because she would not be happy as a mother. But now he was the last of the direct Jamison line and it was his duty to have a son and heir.

"My duty . . . my bloody duty," he slurred into the glass as he poured himself another drink, emptying the bottle. Duty was what had landed him in every mess since he'd been a callow twenty-year-old whose honor demanded a duel. Duty had sent him to purchase a commission but end up a spy. Then it had led him to Beth . . .

"There, there, *caro,* let Angelina cheer you." The inn-keep's pretty daughter ran her hands over his shoulders and nuzzled his neck so that he was afforded a close-up view of the bounty spilling out of her low-cut blouse. Angelina was young, clean and rather pretty in a coarse sort of way, with long straight black hair and huge breasts. He could do worse. He often had . . . but not tonight.

When he declined her offer she huffed off, stamping her feet and wriggling her hips to show him just what he was missing. He got unsteadily to his feet and paid the bill, then headed for the door. Even half-drunk, he had sufficient experience to know how dangerous it was to drink alone in a bad neighborhood. As he walked, he kept his hand on the pistol at his waist and watched for any sign of movement from the other patrons seated at tables scattered about the large, dimly lit room.

No one in the cantina wanted to tangle with the dangerous-looking armed Englishman. He walked around to the stable where he'd left his mount with the inn's ostler. Several other stablemen stood about as he paid the man, then swung up into the saddle and headed for home. The streets were narrow and dark, silent as the tomb at this hour. Derrick felt a familiar prickling of unease, that sixth sense he'd developed over the years working for his government.

Someone was following him, cutting stealthily through back alleys to head him off. He tried to clear his liquor-addled wits and recall the lay of the land between where he was and the open piazza at the edge of the city. If he could make it that far, he'd be in the clear. Were there more than one of them? He could not tell for certain, but he heard the faint pad of footfalls coming from his left side. Then he saw it two blocks ahead: the best place for an ambush, a low archway over the intersection with a second street.

Whoever wanted to attack him—a robber or someone with a more personal and deadly motive—had probably intended to make his move when Derrick left the inn, then found the stablehands waiting with his horse and had to revise the plan. Derrick slowed his mount ever so slightly, calculating quickly. If one man dropped from the archway as he rode beneath it, others could rush him from around the corners of the buildings on either side of the intersecting street.

Now the only sound he could hear was the steady clop of his horse's hooves. No sign of the watch. He had only one chance. He shoved the reins between his knee and the saddle. Drawing his pistol, he shifted it to his left hand and pulled the dirk from his boot with his right. He kicked the big bay into a full gallop, controlling it with his knees. Just as he was almost clear of the arch the attacker dropped, missing his shoulders but seizing his left arm as he began to slide from the horse's rump.

Derrick slashed wickedly at the man, unable to see his face. The sound of a high-pitched curse echoed down the empty streets as his blade found its mark. The man fell away as two others rushed at him, one from each side of the street. He shot the one on his right and kicked the one on his left.

Derrick realized he'd been very fortunate. Going into the slums and getting drunk was suicidally stupid. He knew why he'd done it: Beth. As he rode he considered how their lives might have turned out if Leighton had not gotten himself senselessly killed. In time they might have been able to make the marriage work. They enjoyed simple pleasures such as riding, sailing and sharing quiet meals while they watched the sun set on the bay. Lord knew they enjoyed bed sport together. She had ruined him for other women, damn her! He felt the hard tight itch of desire just thinking of her and his groin throbbed in spite of the prodigious amount of rum he had consumed in the past hours.

By the time he reached the villa it was very late and the whole household was asleep. The entryway was in utter darkness. When he stepped inside, he nearly broke his neck over a large urn that a servant had rearranged at some point after he'd departed in the afternoon. He groped his way to the stairs, cursing the fact that no one had thought to leave so much as a candle burning for his use. Once he reached the upstairs hall, the moon lit his way to their bedroom. The door was ajar.

He could sense even before he lit a candle that the bed was empty behind the canopy. Damn her! He knew where she'd be. His blood was pounding in his ears as he sat on the chair in the corner and pulled off his boots and stockings, carefully removing the knife and pistol and laying them on a bedside table. Tearing off his shirt, he stalked down the hall.

By now his eyes were growing accustomed to the dark. Barely leashed fury had begun to sober him slightly as he opened the door to the guest bedroom. Just as he'd imagined, Beth lay curled up once more on the small mattress, a sheer layer of mosquito netting covering the bed. He moved soundlessly into the room, then froze at the familiar sound of a low growl.

"Call off your dog or I'll throw him out the window, so help me God," he rasped out as Beth awakened and sat up.

Derrick stood towering over her angrily. As she scooted up against the pillows, she said, "We've played this out before, Derrick. I do *not* choose to sleep with you tonight." *Or ever again!*

"Since you agreed to become my wife, your wishes as to

239

sleeping arrangements no longer signify," he said inso-
lently.

"Seek comfort from your whores. You reek of alcohol
and their cheap perfume," she spat.

"Your concern about my fidelity is touching, madam,"
he said with a mock bow. Anger churned like acid deep in
his gut. He had passed up numerous opportunities to bed
other women since he'd met her and here she was, bidding
him go to them!

Percy stood up on the foot of the bed, legs braced, still
growling. Derrick stared at the dog, feeling furious at what
he perceived as the animal's perfidious switch in loyalty—
even though Percy had never been loyal to begin with. His
eyes moved back to hers as he reluctantly admitted, "I
want no other woman but my wife. 'Tis a fine irony, is it
not—since she wants quit of me and all the odious duties
with which I've now been saddled?"

This time when he took a step closer to her the dog
quieted, sitting down once more. *Traitor,* Beth accused
Percy as she watched Derrick's knee rest on the edge of
the bed. He was too close. She could not think with him
towering over her, practically naked. His scent filled her
nostrils, and in spite of the faint aromas of liquor and perfume, she felt a small involuntary ripple of the old familiar
longing stir her blood.

Still, she could not give up without a fight, for to go
docilely with him was to open herself to more pain than
she could imagine. "The first odious duty you were forced
to perform was marrying me! You've said as much yourself. No need to deny it now." She was breathless, and her
voice caught as she babbled on. "Go to London and find
yourself a suitable wife. Leave me behind. 'Tis what we
both want."

Slowly, implacably, he reached down, ignoring her protests even though every word wounded him to the very
soul. "No," was all he said as he pulled her into his embrace and lifted her from the bed while Percy sat observing
the bizarre mating rituals of humans with keen interest.

Derrick carried her from the room and down the hallway as she lay stiffly in his arms. His gait was none too steady. What would she do if he were thoroughly foxed? She'd heard stories from Vittoria about her second husband. "How much have you had to drink?" she asked, alarm beginning to thread her voice.

"Not nearly enough," he replied grimly. He could feel the rigid resistance in the way she held herself, yet he could also feel the frantic pounding of her heart. Her body wanted him even if her mind rejected him. And he damn well meant to have her, this night of all nights. He needed the comfort of a woman's soothing touch to ease the misery that seemed to be closing in on him from all sides.

I am the earl. The bloody earl! The responsibilities seemed crushing. He'd been ostracized by the ton, saddled with the additional burden of caring for his sister-in-law and her infant daughter, and the near bankruptcy of the family. The solicitor's litany of woes had been lengthy, overwhelming. Then his wife calmly announced to him that she preferred to remain in Naples and he should secure a bloody divorce! He dropped her on the bed unceremoniously, then began unbuttoning his fly.

Beth watched, unable to look away as the lone candle gilded his magnificent body with a soft glow. A glow that certainly did not extend to his cold blue eyes as he sat on the bed beside her. "Derrick, I think we should . . ." Her words died on her lips as he dropped like a stone onto his back, then rolled on his side, flinging one arm possessively across her breasts. And proceeded to pass out cold, snoring softly.

Chapter Nineteen

Beth tried to slip soundlessly from the bed. Bright sunlight spilled through the windows like warm butterscotch, but the comparison only served to make her stomach pitch more furiously. She had to make it to the dressing room. If she could close the door before the morning sickness overtook her . . . no use. She had only to stand up and try to take a step before realizing that she'd never make it. Kneeling quickly by the side of the bed, she seized the chamber pot from beneath the frame and emptied the contents of her stomach into it.

Derrick awakened gradually, sensing that Beth was no longer by his side. Then the sounds of her distress brought him bolt upright in bed, a dreadful mistake. He would have had good use for the chamber pot himself had it not been preempted by his wife.

Beth had always been abstemious, seldom consuming more than a glass or two of wine with meals. Surely she did not suffer from his malady, he thought as he tried to clear his woozy head enough to think straight. Gritting his teeth, he took a deep breath, swung his legs over his side of the bed and stood up. "Here, puss, let me help you," he murmured, rounding the bed to where she sat hunched over the pot, clutching the rim with whitened knuckles.

"Go away, Derrick, please," she whispered raggedly.

"I don't think so," he said, holding her long hair back when another spasm struck her. Finally she collapsed against him, allowing him to gently wipe her mouth, then assist her to sit up on the edge of the bed. "I have good reason for needing the solace of the chamber pot, but from what little I can recall of last night, you should not." He touched her forehead and looked into her eyes, trying to ascertain whether she was falling victim to some dangerous summer malady. "Do you have a fever—dysentery? I've heard there's an outbreak of influenza on the waterfront," he murmured with anxiety.

Beth shook her head. There was no use putting this off. "I don't have influenza, Derrick. I'm with child." She forced herself to look at him, trying to gauge his expression.

Relief that she was not ill combined in Derrick with alarm. Beth had not wanted children. "Are you sorry, puss?" he asked before considering whether or not he wished to hear the answer.

That was not exactly the response she'd expected. *What did I want—for him to be deliriously happy that I'll provide him with his precious heir?* "A better question might be, are *you* sorry."

He sighed, trying to read behind the strained pallor of her face. "It would seem that no matter how I answer I'll be damned. If I'm not happy, you'll be angry that I don't want the child I gave you. If I am happy, you'll accuse me of only wanting an heir for Lynden."

"You'll require an heir, most certainly—but you need someone more worthy than I to be his mother." She waited, daring him to deny it.

"For God's sake, Beth!" He stood up and turned to pace, combing his fingers through his hair, then wincing when his head throbbed even harder. "The whole world's crashed around me . . . but we've made this baby together.

We must share the responsibility to care for it."

Her hands fisted, clenching the coverlet as the pain sliced through her. "Yes, we have—at least you cannot but admit 'tis yours. 'Twould be unthinkable that some corsair's or Algerine princeling's by-blow inherit Lynden Hall."

"That is some consolation, madam," he replied icily. Would she never cease reminding him about the other men in her past? "I will have a physician examine you at once. If he agrees that it is safe for you to travel, we sail for London within the week."

"And what if he says I may not travel? Will you leave me behind?" She did not know which she dreaded most—a yes or a no answer.

Derrick only shook his aching head, too confused to argue further. "First, let us see what the leech says."

The physician assured Beth that the sickness she had been experiencing upon rising in the mornings would quickly pass. He mixed an herbal posset to soothe her stomach, then pronounced that there should be no impediment to her accompanying her husband on the voyage to England.

After the physical examination, Derrick insisted on hearing what the doctor had to say about his wife's health. Beth had always possessed a strong constitution, but women died in childbed and he was worried. It was bad enough that he had impregnated her with a child she did not want; he would do nothing further to endanger her health. If the leech had said she must remain in Naples until she was delivered, he would have waited by her side.

It was with great relief that he greeted the news that they could travel. Another letter had just arrived from his solicitor in London. Since it had taken them the better part of a year to locate him, his distant cousin, Albert Wharton Jamison, had been informed that he was next in line. If Derrick had not been found, then the title and estates would have by law been given to a man whose only connection to the family was a great-great-grandfather on the paternal side.

Derrick dispatched yet another reply to the solicitor, assuring him that he was indeed alive and able to assume his responsibilities, explaining the reasons for his delay in departing for home. As he composed the letter, he considered very carefully how he would introduce his new countess to the ton. It was bad enough that she was untitled and an American to boot, but if word ever got out about her reputation in Naples—or, worse yet, her Algerine captivity—she would be cruelly cut by everyone and banished from polite society.

Even the legitimacy of their child would be called into question if anyone learned about her time in a seraglio. No matter what either of them had done, an innocent must not be made to suffer for their mistakes. It might be wise to invent some story of how they'd met in America and become affianced there. No one of consequence ever visited the new republic, although a great many did tour the Continent. Fortunately, the war had curtailed such visits until quite recently. With luck, Beth could be satisfactorily established in London society and no one would be the wiser.

However, when he broached his idea to her at dinner that evening, Beth did not take the suggestion in quite the spirit he intended.

"Let me get the right of this," she said, plunking her spoon back in the consommé and shoving the soup bowl away. "You wish us to concoct a lie about meeting at my parents' home in Georgia so that no one will learn of my shame."

"I said nothing of shame," he replied tightly. "I'm trying to protect not only your reputation but that of an innocent babe." Why could she never accept anything he told her?

"By all means, we must preserve the reputation of your precious heir! Such a great pity that his mother is a slut!" she cried, jumping up so abruptly that she knocked over her wineglass.

When she turned and tried to leave the room, he caught her in one swift angry stride, seizing her shoulders and forcing her to look at him. "I am trying to be patient because of your condition, but you do tax me, damn it!"

245

"I am with child, Derrick, not chuckle-headed," she said through gritted teeth.

"I never said you were chuckle-headed, but there certainly are times when you act it!"

"Do you think I cannot see what you intend?"

"Oh, and pray what do you think I intend?"

" 'Tis quite apparent that you are beside yourself with fear that I shall disgrace you. Has it not become obvious that it would be best if you did not take me to England?" she asked stubbornly, able to see no other way out of the impasse they had reached.

"So, we are back to that again. 'Twill do you no good, puss. I'm not leaving you behind and there's an end to it." He took her arm and forcefully propelled her to sit at the table once more, than rang for Arcello to clean up the mess. Taking his seat at the head of the table, he said, "Now, you will finish your consommé and eat the meat course. The leech said you need good nourishment for the babe to grow properly."

Not a care for me. His only concern is for his child within me. Swallowing back her tears, Beth picked up the spoon and began methodically sipping the now cold consommé as the butler scurried about, soaking up the spilled wine and refilling her glass.

Derrick made arrangements for them to sail the following week. Quint, overjoyed to learn that he was about to become a grandfather, wrote immediately to his wife, explaining the joyous news. He mentioned the fact that their daughter was now a countess merely as an afterthought. But he was forced to concede that the responsibility of being a member of the peerage would also provide the benefit of preventing her from painting pictures for money or attending salons where the females discussed such insane ideas as free love and women's suffrage.

With both Derrick and Quint leaving, Piero had to arrange for someone else to assume control of the new shipping business. Until that was settled, he and Vittoria would have to remain in Naples.

"Do not look so grim, *caro*. We shall eventually be able to return to your home." Vittoria entered the room where he was poring over correspondence and ledgers. Walking up behind him, she massaged his shoulders gently and bent down to nibble his neck.

Piero sighed, giving up on accounts for the night. Tossing the pen, which had gone dry, back onto the desk, he chuckled, replying, "The farther in the future that eventuality, the happier you will be." He turned and pulled her down onto his lap.

Vittoria returned his kisses voraciously, murmuring between them, "Perhaps so . . . but I will go wherever I must . . . just to be with you, my beloved husband."

"So dutiful a wife. What man could ask more?" he breathed against her neck as he arose and swept her into his arms, carrying her from his office to the big bed in the adjoining room.

After they had made love, Vittoria lay with her head on his chest, taking such comfort in the steady thrum of his heartbeat that she dared broach the subject that she had kept secret for the past several weeks. "You were very happy for Beth and Derrick when you learned that they will have a child. Have you ever wanted one of your own?"

He stroked her back, making lazy circles with his fingertips. "I did not want to burden a child with illegitimacy . . . so I did not have any. Now that I have you, it no longer matters, *cara*. I am content just that we have the rest of our lives together."

"What if you could have a legitimate child, Piero?" she asked, raising her head so she could look into his eyes.

His hand stopped its stroking abruptly. "What do you mean, Vittoria?"

His face looked suddenly strained, haggard. She became afraid to say more, but there was no backing out now. "I am going to have your baby, Piero."

"What! You cannot—you said you'd never conceived in all these years—I assumed that you could not." He sat up and pulled her into his arms.

"Then you are displeased," she whispered, fighting back tears. "I had hoped . . . you were so pleased about Beth—"

"Beth is but one and twenty! You are twice that! 'Tis not safe for you, *cara*," he added, trying desperately to keep the fear from his voice. "I cannot—I *will* not lose you, not now!"

Vittoria's tears evaporated and a beatific smile spread across her face as she took a fistful of his sideburns in each hand and pulled him to her for a hard kiss, then said, "I come from hardy stock. My grandmother had seven children—the last one when she was older than I. The reason I never had a child was not barrenness. 'Twas the same as yours, *caro*. If it was not to be with you, it would be with no one else. I've always taken precautions . . . except with you. After my family separated us, I prayed nightly that your seed had been planted in me . . . but it did not happen . . . until now. Please, Piero, say you are happy, that you want this child as much as I," she implored.

He framed her face with his hands and kissed her again, this time with exquisite tenderness. Smiling, he replied, "When you put it that way, how can I deny you? Of course I would love to have a daughter or son with you. We will be very careful of your health. No riding, no staying up late, definitely no sea voyages on the storm-tossed Atlantic until after you're safely delivered." He searched her beaming face and chuckled indulgently. "If I didn't know better, I'd say you planned this just to keep me in Naples until next spring."

"Dr. Policella assured Beth and Derrick that it would do her no harm to travel. I'm sure he'll say the same for me," she replied, so relieved that he accepted the idea of the baby that she did not even mind leaving her home.

"We will remain here where you shall be under Dr. Policella's constant care until the little one arrives," he said sternly.

"As you wish it, *caro,*" she replied, feeling as if her happiness was complete.

* * *

And it would have been . . . if not for Beth. Vittoria knew Beth and Derrick's relationship had been strained ever since word of his brother's death reached them. No one had dreamed that the young couple would be forced to leave Naples and assume such burdensome responsibilities. She had hoped that the coming babe would mend things, but it seemed only to create more difficulties. Her friend looked wan and pale, was losing weight and had no appetite. Vittoria concluded that the fault lay with Beth's husband.

With only two days left before the young couple sailed, Vittoria decided to go to the shipping office on the quay and confront him face-to-face. She found him discussing a spice cargo with a Genoese captain. Seeing her, Derrick handed the man a copy of the manifest with curt instructions to make certain it was loaded before the morning tide. When he approached her, she could sense his wariness.

"Your Italian has improved markedly since first we met," she said as he offered her a seat in his crowded office.

"You did not come to the quay to discuss my linguistic skills, contessa," he replied, slinging his leg over the corner of his desk. He stared at her, waiting for her to get to the point.

"No. I did not."

The ball had been returned to his court. "Has my wife been complaining of hardship now that she's been forced to become a countess?"

"Quite the contrary. Beth complains about nothing whatsoever. She just grows more pale and tense with every passing day. 'Tis good neither for her nor the babe."

"And, now that you too are with child, you have become an expert on such matters?"

"In spite of Piero's fears, I have never felt better, but we're speaking of Beth, not me."

"And, of course, the fault for Beth's malaise lies with me," he ground out.

"I rather suspect the fault lies with both of you," she

replied, causing him to raise his head in surprise. "See here, Derrick, I did not come to place blame, only to try to help the two of you . . . for you know, if a marriage is to be happy, husband and wife must put forth considerable effort."

He smiled cynically. "And you, of course, speak from a vast reservoir of experience."

Vittoria let the insult pass. "After my first two husbands, I certainly learned what does *not* make a marriage happy, but with Piero"—she was unable to resist a small, private smile—"well, we are very happy. I believe you and Beth could be, too."

"What, pray, is the secret then, contessa?"

Some of his arrogant facade was slipping in spite of his best efforts to conceal his feelings. *Are you so afraid of the truth, Derrick?* "Love," she answered simply.

Now some of the agony did show through. His shoulders slumped as he slid from his seat on the corner of the desk, and paced over to the window to stare intently out at the bay. She could see his face in profile, watched as he swallowed what must be a huge knot of misery.

"I know much of duty, contessa, but little of love."

Those words spoke of a desolate childhood. "What of your family? Was there no love when you were a child?" she prompted.

"My parents despised each other. An advantageous marriage, of which you are more than passing familiar, I'm certain." She nodded, encouraging him to continue. "We were both of us, my elder brother and I, raised by a succession of nurses, tutors and other servants, when we were not away at school. A fine old English tradition," he said with a mirthless laugh. "My mother never showed the slightest interest in us."

"What of your father?"

"My father took some pride in me. You see, I was an exceptional shot and rider, and my marks in school were much better than Leighton's. Poor Lee; he could please neither parent . . . and he did try . . . for a while. What was inculcated into us was our duty to the Jamison name. After all, we were the sons of the seventh earl of Lynden. We owed society a return on its investment."

"Noblesse oblige," Vittoria murmured. "The English take it rather more seriously than is done on the Continent." She was beginning to see another side of Derrick Jamison, perhaps one he'd never revealed to anyone else before. One Beth desperately needed to understand. "That is why you have risked your life in service of your country. And why you wed Beth—'twas your duty—or so Quintin Blackthorne made you believe."

Derrick scoffed. "More like he threatened me with dire retribution."

"Do not try to tell me that you wed Beth because you were afraid of her father. I'll not believe it for an instant."

He shrugged uncomfortably, knowing that she had the right of it. "All right, I did not want to kill him if he challenged me."

"Because of Beth."

"He is her father and she loves him."

"She loves you even more." Vittoria heard his sharp gasp before he could muffle it.

"Perhaps once she did . . . before I betrayed her and left her here," he said bitterly.

" 'Tis a strange thing about love," Vittoria said musingly. "It cannot be willed away, even if the one you love hurts you or leaves you for many years. It lives"—she paused as he turned to look at her, then touched her heart—"in here."

"You are speaking of yourself and Piero. Beth and I . . . we are different," he said uncomfortably, unable to put his feelings into words.

"Why did you wed her?" she asked baldly.

"I desire her in my bed," he replied equally as baldly. Cursing silently, for he had already revealed more of himself than was his wont, he admitted, "I find other women of no interest . . . I want only her, damn it!" *Would that she had shared my single-minded obsession while we were separated!* "Does that satisfy you, contessa?" he snapped. "For if it does not, I can give you no other answer."

Vittoria smiled beatifically. "Yes, I believe it does, Derrick." She turned to leave, then paused and said, "Oh, by the by, since I wed Piero, I am no longer a contessa. In America I shall be plain Mistress Torres and all the happier for it. I will go with Piero to his world. Your wife will go with you to yours . . . only allow her time to accustom herself to it. Beth loves you. Be good to her and all will be well."

The posset the physician had given her finally began to help—or her own body had become accustomed to the changes going on inside it. Either way, Beth felt better than she had in weeks. Even her appetite, alarmingly vanished, started to return and she was able to hold down what she consumed. That was a good thing since she had so much work to do overseeing preparations for the move to England.

England. London. The ton. Beth had read her cousin Alex's amusing letters describing his extended visit, sanitized for family consumption, she was certain. Alex thoroughly loved the Great Wen's myriad enticements, but the sort of life he had enjoyed in London would be far removed from the life of an earl and his countess.

She knew her husband feared the repercussions if anyone learned about her past, but she refused to make up some Banbury tale about their falling in love while he was visiting Savannah. She was who she was, and there was no way to gild the lily. She had struggled to find her identity, to perfect her gifts as an artist, to enjoy the simple pleasures of life. If being American and an artist in the bargain scandalized the Quality, bugger 'em!

"If he must be so stubborn as to drag me to London when neither of us wants me to be there, then he must pay the consequences," she muttered to herself as she selected winter gowns, which would be sent aboard the *Lady Barbara* with them when they sailed. En route, Donita could begin to let out the seams as needed. Since most of her clothes were airy and light for the year-round warmth of the Mediterranean, not to mention scandalously low cut

252

and clinging, Derrick had instructed her to leave them behind. As soon as they arrived in England, she was to have a new wardrobe made up, including a number of gowns in various shades of gray and purple, the colors decreed for the latter stages of mourning for Leighton. She looked abominable in both, but it was the least of her problems.

Beth was busily tossing a rainbow hue of dresses—vibrant blues, greens and yellows—into the pile headed for storage boxes when she heard Derrick's footfalls on the stairs. Odd, but she could always tell when it was he, not one of the many male servants around the household. She turned as he entered the room. "Good afternoon, Derrick," she said in the cool, civil tone they'd adopted. At least they were no longer yelling curses.

"The ship's master wants our trunks aboard by tomorrow." he said, scanning the apparent disarray of the room. "If 'tis not possible, I'll tell him he must wait. I don't want you overtaxing yourself."

"Everything will be ready. This is the last of it. All of those clothes will remain behind," she said, gesturing to the huge pile strewn across the chaise longue in her dressing room. "I am feeling much better, Derrick."

"You still look pale. Vittoria has commented upon it."

"When did you see her?" Beth knew her friend had not visited her while Derrick was home for the past week.

He cursed his errant tongue. "She and I chanced to meet earlier this afternoon."

"Chanced to meet?" What had Vittoria been up to?

"She came to speak with me at the office on the quay," he admitted. "She was concerned that I have been treating you ill. I have not intended that, puss."

"I know, Derrick." Her voice was soft. She looked away lest he see the naked longing in her eyes. How she wanted things to be as they had been. They had many difficulties to work out, but in the early days of their marriage it had seemed possible that they might, in time, be able to do so. At least then they had shared passion, but since he'd become the earl, they had done nothing but fight. And since he had learned about the babe, he had not touched her.

He's afraid he might harm the child. Always the child . . . never me. Her thoughts were selfish, she knew, and she castigated herself for having them, but . . .

She stood there looking so lost and vulnerable that his heart ached. "Beth, I am truly sorry. I will not leave you and I cannot stay," he said in frustration, stepping closer to her without realizing that he had done it.

"Cannot stay—or will not stay?" The instant she asked it, she wished to call back the words. "Now *I'm* sorry. I know you must go."

"And you do not wish to go with me." It was not a question, for he already knew the answer. She stood very close to him now . . . too close. He could smell the faint essence of vanilla, see the way her breasts had grown even fuller, her whole lush body ripening like succulent, forbidden fruit. To taste of her was to invite more pain into a life already overflowing with it. But to live without her, to live without touching her, that was more painful yet.

His hand reached out, and one finger touched her chin, tipping it up so that he could read what lay hidden in her eyes. What he saw robbed him of breath. Her hands clutched his wrist and she swayed toward him involuntarily, desire a hot, dark fire blazing in the hazel green depths of her eyes.

Derrick swept her up into his arms and carried her from the small dressing room directly to their big bed, murmuring, "By God, I will make you glad—nay, eager—to stay with me."

Chapter Twenty

They sailed the day before Quint was scheduled to depart for America. Beth's father, along with Vittoria and Piero, stood waving from the quay as they were rowed out to the *Lady Barbara*. It had been a difficult leave-taking for Beth, maintaining the fiction that all was well between herself and Derrick, that she was looking forward to her new life as a countess in cold, distant England. The only thing she did not have to pretend enthusiasm about was the coming child.

She wanted Derrick's baby more with every passing day, a small part of him that could love her in return. If the child's father could only desire her, never love her, so be it. She must learn to content herself with what was and not waste her life dreaming impossible dreams about what would never happen. She sat in the small boat, holding on to Percy with one arm, waving with her other. When her small circle of family finally became tiny specks on the distant horizon, she turned to face the looming outline of the sleek Baltimore clipper owned by Blackthorne Shipping Ltd., her uncle Dev's company.

" 'Tis a fine ship. Your father guaranteed 'twould make the passage swiftly and smoothly," Derrick said as he prepared to help her climb aboard.

"My uncle named it for his wife."

"Ah, yes, Rushcroft's sister, who scandalized the ton by wedding an American," he said.

"Uncle Dev is part Creek Indian. I can imagine how that must have fanned the flames of gossip."

"Merely being American would have been sufficient," he replied, before realizing that she might take his remark amiss.

She did. "Then I shall deal famously with the Quality, I warrant," she said, stiffening when he took her arm and helped her onto the boarding ladder.

Derrick cursed to himself. "Everything I say, you take amiss."

"If you refrain from saying things that are amiss, I will not be able to take them that way, will I?" she replied oversweetly.

Sighing in defeat, he reminded himself that she was breeding. He vowed to be patient during the voyage . . . and more careful with chance remarks.

The seas were rough with unseasonable storms, but in spite of Derrick's fears for her, Beth proved to be a marvelous sailor. Unless the weather prevented it, she always rose at daybreak and went abovedeck to sketch. He brooded about whether she would take it into her head to resume her "career" once they were settled in London.

They would have to have a discussion about her art, and he dreaded it. Their shipboard routine, removed from all outside sources of friction, had been almost idyllic. There was a great deal of time to spend lying abed, making love, and they found themselves able to do so without the frenetic overtones that had so marred their relationship recently. Finally, as they approached the coast of Brittany, he could put the matter off no longer.

Beth entered their cabin, flushed from a successful morning's work. After the earlier storms, the sea was now smooth as glass and the sunrise spectacular. Derrick stood by a small table where a repast had been laid out.

"That looks marvelous," she said, taking the seat he offered her and digging in. "Did you sleep well?"

"Quite," he replied, recalling the lusty way they'd made love before retiring. Something in his eyes conveyed the memory to her, and he was pleased to see a faint flush stain her cheeks. *No time like now while she's in good humor.* "We'll be landing within two days, channel weather permitting," he said by way of opening.

A pity, she wanted to say, but held her tongue. "I expect you'll have a great many things to attend to," she replied noncommittally.

"Yes, but there is one matter that we need to discuss before we're at sixes and sevens settling into our new life. I know how much you enjoy painting—and I want you to continue it—but there will be other demands on your time as well."

"I've been expecting you to bring up the matter of my work." She pushed her plate away, all appetite fled. "I will do my best to perform whatever social obligations are necessary, but from what I've seen and heard of English noblewomen, much of their time is wasted with mantuamakers, tea-time gossip and dancing masters. I see no reason that I cannot continue to paint instead of holding court from a fainting couch."

The tone of disdain in her voice was unmistakable. "A trifle blunt, puss," he said, trying to cajole her.

" 'Tis an American fault, I fear. We say things as we know them to be."

"You've yet to set foot on English soil. I doubt you know anything about it to be true or false. I'm not trying to forbid you to paint. But you cannot sell your paintings in England. Even among the merchant classes, women do not work for money. It would certainly cause you to be ostracized by the upper ten thousand."

"And the peerage, of course, defines the order of the cosmos," she replied, her disdain quite open now.

"Do you want to be cut, Beth? To spend your life in complete isolation?"

She sighed raggedly. His damnable sense of duty to the Jamison name meant everything to him. "I told you I'd be a hopeless misfit but you refused to listen."

"I listened, all right—to my wife tell me that she would prefer to be rid of me and return to her old life and loves. That will not happen. You *are* my wife!" He bit off each word furiously. So much for cajolery! "Nor will you engage in selling so much as a pencil sketch. Do I make myself clear?"

"Quite, m'lord earl. What will you do? Banish me to the country? There's nothing I should like better!"

"Your time at Lynden Hall shall come quickly enough. But first you must be presented to society. We were wed abroad, and gossip about the legitimacy of our child shall abound if I hide you away before everyone sees that you are not already showing your condition. Would you want that for your son or daughter? Do you care enough about the child for it to matter in the slightest?"

His remark cut her far more than any member of the ton could ever have done. "Very well, I will play your games. I see no need—or even a way—to obtain commissions, but I will paint. If you take that from me, I . . . I do not know what I should do." She hated the desperation that she'd just revealed, but Derrick's thunderous expression immediately softened.

He reached over and took her hands in his, massaging the pulse points in her wrists with his thumbs. "I would not be so cruel. Nor will things be so terrible, puss. I will be at your side when we face my family."

The Jamison city house was located on Pall Mall, just a short distance from Prinney's famous Carlton House, a trying ride from the docks. Beth was in a veritable daze since landing, trying at once to get her "land legs" back and not lurch like a drunken sailor, then to assimilate all the sights, sounds and smells of the greatest city on earth. The smells were by far the most difficult.

Percy found them fascinating and had to be restrained from jumping from the carriage, but Beth found them ghastly. Coal smoke hung thick in the air, which carried on its turgid currents the odors of emptied chamber pots, tannery chemicals and lord knew what else. The waterfront in Naples was a veritable perfumery compared to the seeming miles of warehouses and noisome slums surrounding them. The narrow streets and alleys were overcrowded with the most wretched collection of humanity she had ever seen.

"The *lazzaroni* are better off," she said as their carriage passed several beggar boys who chased after it, shouting for coins. Diseased prostitutes, little more than children themselves, hawked their wares boldly on the busy streets. "There is no excuse for this in the richest nation on earth."

"I quite agree," Derrick replied. "You have no idea of the ghastly conditions of the poor since the industrialization in the north drove so many thousands from the land. Now that the war's over, 'tis well past time members of Parliament turn their attention to mending what's ill in our own nation."

"And you will have a seat in the House of Lords." She had not considered that there might actually be something worthwhile for an earl to do in London. Rather, she had envisioned the wastrel pursuits of the beau monde, fashionable men who spent hours with tailors and dressers, then went out to spend their nights gambling, wenching and drinking. Alex had outlined an expurgated version of that life in his letters to her.

"Yes, but I'll also have to sit down with my solicitors and unravel the mess Leighton made of the family estates and investments."

"Are you in debt?" she asked, knowing that his stiff English pride would forbid him to accept from her any financial assistance if that was the case, no matter that her family was well able to do so.

"Apparently not yet. Lee's been dead for nearly a year now, else 'twould have been worse. The solicitors have curtailed his wife's excessive spending."

She wanted to question him more about her sister-in-law, Annabella, but the driver stopped their carriage and

Derrick climbed down, assisting her out so that she could get her first look at the imposing stone edifice that would be her new home. The dog jumped down, tail wagging with excitement, but Beth grew tense as she viewed the three-story mansion. Everything about it was gray, from the austere granite walls to the cloudy skies above. A chill wind hinting of early autumn blew a loose strand of hair across her face and she shivered.

As they climbed the age-worn steps to the front door, it was flung open and a small, dainty female with blond ringlets and round pale blue eyes swept regally toward them. Annabella. She was young and very pretty in the vapid sort of way Beth had always imagined English beauties, dressed in pale lavender silk trimmed with fine Belgian lace.

"Oh, Derrick, dear brother! 'Tis so good to see you in this time of trial," she said, dabbing at nonexistent tears with a lacy kerchief, careful that her perfect cream and rose complexion not be marred in the slightest. She bussed his cheek with more than sisterly enthusiasm in Beth's opinion.

"How have you been, Bella? And your daughter—Constance, is it not?" he inquired politely, taking her busy little hands from about his neck and holding them discreetly between his.

"Constance is an absolute darling. She'll be walking in no time, or so the nurse tells me," she said dismissively, batting her eyes at Derrick.

Barking loudly, Percy chose that moment to jump from behind a carriage wheel, where he'd been attending to a call of nature. "Ooh!" Annabella shrieked, jumping back as if the tail-wagging greeting were the attack snarl of a Bengal tiger.

"Pay no mind to Sir Percival, he doesn't bite," Beth said, kneeling to give the dog a calming pat.

"This must be your bride," Annabella said, recovering her voice as Beth stood up, towering over the diminutive widow. " 'Twas very wicked of you, dear Derrick, not to let anyone know where you've been these past years—and to marry abroad and not tell us!"

"Bella, may I present my wife Elizabeth? Everyone calls her Beth." Derrick's hand pressed the small of her back, urging her forward. "Beth, this is your new sister-in-law Annabella."

"Beth, how charming. I'm certain we shall become great friends," Annabella said with cloying sweetness that indicated to Beth that she'd best beware of the Englishwoman whose title she'd usurped. "Our solicitors informed me that you're from the colonies."

Beth could imagine being American was slightly more acceptable than being a leper. "Yes, I am American, from Savannah, Georgia."

"But you wed dear Derrick in Naples? That was where they finally ran you to ground, was it not, you naughty fellow?" she said, turning back to him.

Derrick only smiled that calm, noncommittal spy's smile of his and replied, "Naples is a very romantic city, Bella. You must visit it one day," he added as he ushered the women inside.

When the dog followed, Annabella looked askance at him but said nothing until Derrick explained, "Beth is quite fond of the rascal. We shall see that he's confined to our apartments, won't we, m'dear?"

Before she could reply, Annabella had recovered and began prattling. "Of course, propriety demands that I wait until my full year of mourning for poor Leighton is over before I can throw a gala to properly welcome you home, but I have arranged for dear Cousin Bertie and a few old friends to join us for dinner this evening. If that is all right with you?" she said to Derrick.

"My wife might be overtaxed from our long journey," he replied, turning to Beth as they entered a long narrow foyer cluttered with Louis XV furniture and a depressing array of bric-a-brac. "She is expecting the Lynden heir in late spring."

Annabella's tiny mouth made a small O of shock and dismay. "Well, then," she said, recovering quickly, "if she is too taxed, we shall simply have to postpone. I remember how exhausted I felt with dear Constance."

"Nonsense. I have never felt better in my life," Beth interjected, thoroughly aggravated by being spoken of as if she were absent or an incompetent.

"If you're certain, puss," Derrick said, trying to read her expression. He was not the only one adroit at hiding his feelings. Beth was becoming alarmingly skillful at it.

"Splendid! Then I shall tell Cook to begin preparations!" Annabella replied.

The meal was perfectly dreadful. The guests Annabella had invited were a stuffy, foolish lot to Beth's way of thinking and the food was boiled and bland. She decided one of her first tasks when she took over the household would be to have a stern talk with the cook. As she pushed a mushy slab of beef brisket and creamed parsnips about on her plate, she observed the other diners.

The Count d'Artois and his wife were fat, arrogant French émigrés who had fled the revolution one step ahead of the guillotine over two decades ago. Impoverished as most of their kind were, they became parasites on the British peerage, willing to return to their homeland only if Louis XVIII provided sufficient fiscal incentives to do so. Thus far, they had received no such offer. A painfully shy and homely spinster aunt of Annabella's picked primly at her food, offering nothing to the conversation.

The only one livelier than the hostess herself was her "dear Bertie," Albert Wharton Jamison, the distant cousin who would have inherited if not for Derrick. He was balding and jolly, with pale eyes that crinkled when he laughed, which he did a great deal, mostly at his own witticisms, which were anything but amusing. Cow-handed in the extreme, he was none the less a likable enough chap, Beth supposed, giving him the benefit of the doubt since he was the least repugnant of her dinner companions.

"I understand Exmouth's set sail to teach those Barbary corsairs a lesson in manners," he said at length as he and Derrick discussed British military operations around Sicily.

"That's already been attended to," Beth interjected, bored to tears with Annabella and the Countess d'Artois's

discussion of French dressmakers. "Commodore Decatur—
you do recall him from the late . . . ah, misunderstanding
between our countries?—has destroyed the Dey of Algiers's entire fleet and forced him to sign a treaty forswear-
ing any more depredations."

Derrick could see Annabella's eyes light with curiosity
and cursed Beth's impetuosity. Why couldn't she be like
other females? If he could have reached her, he would have
given her a swift kick beneath the table, but since he was
seated at the head as befitted his station and she down
toward the opposite side, all he could do was say, "Decatur took a bite from the old fox, but I imagine Exmouth's fleet will be even more effective in bringing about
the permanent end of piracy in the Mediterranean."

"Now, now, gentlemen, if you must speak of pirates and
politics, I believe 'tis time we ladies took our leave and
allowed you your pipes and port." Annabella stood up,
the signal for the other women to follow her as they retired
to gossip in her sitting room, as was customary. The
Countess d'Artois and Aunt Augusta also rose, but Beth
did not.

"I find politics quite stimulating," she said, refusing to
bow to what seemed to her an idiotic convention. Being
cooped up with those three women for ten minutes, much
less an hour, held only slightly more appeal than a return
to Fatima's seraglio. Besides, she was the countess now,
not her sister-in-law; if she chose to stay, she bloody well
would. Turning to d'Artois and Bertie, she asked, "Since
Napoleon was so popular in France, do you believe King
Louis will be able to hold on to his throne?"

Derrick was furious with her deliberate rudeness. Annabella stood for a moment, too flummoxed to make a
rejoinder. Her aunt and the French countess glared at the
gauche American as if she had just burped. The other
women stiffly filed out of the room, leaving Beth and the
men to continue their conversation.

After spending the end of the evening listening to Annabella torture the pianoforte, Beth and Derrick retired to
their quarters. "I think your cousin is rather nice, if a bit

263

pudding-headed," she said when they were finally alone.

"You should have left with the women. 'Twas rude in the extreme to embarrass Bella that way."

"Really, and was it not rude of her to say that because American women don't cut off their hair as is all the rage in London, 'they've no more fashion sense than chickens'? She also insinuated that our marriage was irregular."

"Our marriage was irregular—and you didn't help the situation by entering the discussion about Algerine corsairs. I saw the look of blatant curiosity in Bella's eyes when you spoke."

"Ah, yes, 'Bella,' your dear sister. Just how dear was she, 'dear Derrick'?" The affectionate nickname had grated on her already raw nerves.

Damnation! Did nothing escape his hoyden's attention? "We were affianced briefly when we were little more than children. Then Lee fell under her spell and her family wisely decided an earl was a better catch than a second son." He'd always had a guilty conscience about Bella, but confessing his guilt to Beth would be a stupid mistake, one he never intended to make.

"A pity she made the wrong choice," Beth replied scathingly. "She wishes to be the countess and I don't."

"You've made that abundantly clear, Beth," he said, stripping off his shirt and tossing it on top of his jacket. He'd grown used to dressing and undressing without the aid of a valet. That would probably have to change, but not tonight . . . with his wife standing before him.

Beth walked nervously around the old earl's cavernous dark room. Percy, who had been sleeping quietly on an overstuffed chair, jumped down with a yawn and padded over to her. Absently she patted his head as she inspected the dreary place. An adjoining door, now closed, led to the countess's chambers. Annabella had not yet vacated them. Beth supposed she would be expected to sleep separately from her husband when the transition was complete. The idea of that did not appeal to her. She would miss the warmth and comfort his big body gave her, just lying beside her. Since their marriage, she had become quite accustomed to that simple intimacy.

She startled herself by asking, "When will Annabella leave?"

He grinned at her jealousy as he continued stripping. "As soon as her dower house is ready. The painters are working there now. When they've finished, you may have them redecorate here if you wish."

Of course she wished, she thought with a shudder of distaste for Annabella's execrable taste. A small smile curved her lips when she saw that Percy had made his statement as well. One corner of the leather chair he'd been sleeping on bore teeth marks, and a bit of stuffing was oozing out. "Good boy," she murmured beneath her breath as Derrick continued speaking of Annabella's new quarters.

" 'Tis a nice enough place just across Grosvenor Square, according to the solicitor's report."

"But not the earl's residence." *Poor vain Annabella.*

"Enough about her," he said, having now stripped down to nothing but his breeches while she examined the room. He walked over to her and pulled her into his arms. "Propriety demands you have a lady's maid to undress you, but not tonight . . ."

His fingers were swift and clever as always. She did not resist.

A high-pitched squeal of dismay echoed from the next room early the following morning as Beth was just stepping from her bath. She'd been given to understand that her sister-in-law was a very late riser. Considering that it was only eight, she wondered what had occasioned Annabella's change in schedule.

"Get that . . . that creature, that brute, that beast out of my sight! Ooh, look at my Dresden vase. The water from the chrysanthemums is soaking into the Turkey carpet! And he's destroying one of my new kid slippers!"

Beth had heard the sound of glass breaking a moment earlier but thought a servant had dropped a breakfast tray.

"Percy, can't you ever stay out of trouble?" she asked rhetorically, unable to suppress a grin. Perhaps this would hasten her sister-in-law's departure. Now the sounds of a chase filtered through the walls, followed by more breaking glass as several maids wielding brooms attempted to drive Sir Percival of Inverness from the former countess's bedroom, all of it punctuated by Annabella's shrieks and cries of fury.

By the time Beth had dried off and donned a robe, Derrick had arrived from downstairs and held the offender firmly in his arms. He gave over the culprit to the butler, who had brought a leash that he attached efficiently to Percy's collar. As Percy walked briskly away from the scene of his crime, Annabella turned to Derrick, all pretty tears once again. Beth stood in the doorway, unnoticed, as the quivering blonde flew into his arms.

"Oh, Derrick, I don't know what I shall do now, all alone in the world . . . and you, wed to that odious American baggage. I should have been your wife." She tightened her arms about his neck and looked up, her big blue eyes glistening with tears. "What a muddle we've made of things."

"We? 'Twas you who cried off, Bella. You wanted to be a countess and that meant Lee, not the lowly second son." Although he had thanked his lucky stars nightly for the past seven years that he'd escaped her web, her rejection had been painful in the extreme for a youth barely out of leading strings.

"And now you're the earl. If you'd not used those nasty old French letters, you'd have gotten me with child and I would have had to wed you instead of Leighton." She hiccuped disconsolately. "If only there weren't those silly old affinity laws."

She was still a child, always would be, petulant and spoiled by her parents. If he did not take a hand with Constance, the girl would turn out the same. Another responsibility to weigh on him, he thought, repelled by the way Annabella clung to him like a limpet.

Beth watched, exceedingly aware of the delicate English

beauty's enticement. The very proper Annabella, daughter of a viscount, had been her husband's lover. And he, the hypocrite, dared to think *she* possessed no morals! Did he still care for the stupid little chit? He did not exactly appear to be shoving her away.

"Being an odious American baggage, I could not help eavesdropping, *Bella*," she said, emphasizing the pet name as she swept into the hall.

Annabella jumped away from Derrick as if a wasp had just stung her. "Ooh! I did not mean—"

"For me to hear you?" Beth supplied in a honeyed tone that her husband had learned meant trouble.

Derrick could see the murderous fury in his wife's eyes. He'd been a fool to allow silly little Bella to manipulate him. Comparing her to Beth was like comparing a glass of flat champagne to a snifter of fine aged brandy. Beth's hair spilled in great masses of russet curls, tumbling over her shoulders and down her back, framing that strong, striking face, her eyes glowing with an unholy fire. Damn, she was stunning!

"Bella was upset over Percy's latest depredations," he soothed, standing between the two women, a position he was not certain was any wiser than being caught between Bonaparte and Wellington.

" 'Tis well then that she'll be leaving for her own house shortly. Percy has begun helping me get rid of the things I find offensive in this one," she said to Derrick, then turned to the red-faced blonde. "Oh, I lied earlier. He does bite."

"That will do, Beth," Derrick cautioned. "As the new countess, the least you can do is be civil."

"Why? 'Tis apparent the former one suffers under no such constraint." Beth turned and stamped back into the master bedroom.

Chapter Twenty-one

After overhearing the emotional little scene between Derrick and Annabella, Beth knew she had to find something to occupy her mind while he went to meet with his solicitors. Whatever had happened when her husband was seventeen scarce meant he would still find a creature such as Bella appealing, she tried to reassure herself. Still, the idea that the two of them had been intimate upset her.

After breaking her fast, she went about the household, determined to meet the members of the staff and win them over, a daunting task since the servants seemed stiff and humorless at best. But she was the new mistress; they knew she would be in charge, even if she was an American nobody. By noon she had learned the names and duties of most.

Two of the upstairs maids and the cook's helper actually smiled at her. The cook did not. She'd tried to tactfully suggest a few menu variations, to which he frostily responded that she might be able to find home-grown delicacies in Italy, but here such things as asparagus tips and fresh fruit were neither available nor desired. She made a mental note to go to the public markets the following morning, as well as to begin a discreet search for a new cook.

When Derrick did not return by noon and Annabella came downstairs, Beth decided to inspect the mews and meet the stablemen in charge of the horses. She was on her way up to change when the sounds of a child's gleeful squeals echoed from the opposite end of the long hallway. The nursery. As was the usual English custom, Constance and her nanny had been banished to the farthest reaches of the house.

Beth decided she wished to meet her new niece and walked toward the sounds of babyish laughter. A young woman with a pleasant smile was sitting in the middle of the floor rolling a ball to a chubby little girl of approximately eight months. Although not adroit enough to catch it, Constance was quick to crawl after it, moving across the carpet on all fours with good coordination.

"Hello. I'm Beth Jamison, the earl's wife," she said to the nanny, still uncomfortable using her new title in spite of raised eyebrows among the servants.

"Oh, how-do, your ladyship. I'm that honored to meet you," the young nursemaid replied, jumping to her feet and bowing as her charge crawled up to Beth with a big grin revealing four perfect tiny white teeth.

"She's an absolute love," Beth said, kneeling down to scoop up the baby in her arms and cuddle her. "So affectionate." In fact, she seemed hungry for attention, and Beth could not help wondering how much loving the little girl received. Certainly none from her own mother.

The nanny, Tilda, was only an upstairs maid temporarily assigned to care for Constance while the special French governess Annabella had hired was ill with an infected tooth. Without saying so directly, Tilda indicated that the woman left much to be desired as caretaker for a child. Beth made a mental note to speak with Derrick about the matter, but feared that once Annabella moved to her own household she would do what she wished. Of course, the earl would be paying the bills. . . .

As she sat on the floor with Tilda, playing ball with Constance, she did not see Derrick in the doorway. He'd heard the sounds of Beth's voice blending with a child's laughter and had come to see what was happening. The sight of her with his niece stunned him. Beth actually seemed to be enjoying herself, to have a natural way with children in spite of what she had said about wanting none of her own.

Of course, he knew well that many women of the upper classes spent a few moments a week cosseting their offspring, then sent them off with servants and promptly forgot them. That sort of motherhood was little inconvenience, the variety his own mother had chosen. What kind of mother would Beth be?

Before he could mull further, the serving girl saw him and began scraping and bowing to the new earl. Unselfconsciously holding Constance, Beth got up and walked over to him. "Meet your new niece. Connie, say hello to your Uncle Derrick."

"We've already met," he surprised her by replying. "Earlier this morning." When he reached out and took the little girl, she came eagerly into his arms. He thoroughly enjoyed the expression on Beth's face.

"I would never have credited that children would like you," she finally managed.

"Odd; I would have said the same of you," he replied as his eyes met over Connie's silky blond head.

He always knew how to wound her, she thought sadly, not realizing she had just done the same thing to him.

The following week, Annabella and her entourage moved. Beth would have been overjoyed to see the last of the hateful woman if not for her daughter. But she was able to see that Tilda was assigned as the little girl's permanent companion. The chilly French governess was dismissed. If Annabella cared at all, she did not indicate it. Beth decided she would have Tilda bring Connie over for frequent visits.

Derrick threw himself into straightening out the affairs of the estate. In the weeks that followed, he was closeted with solicitors, bankers and factors who oversaw the various enterprises the Jamison fortune had been built upon. In addition, Parliament would convene in a fortnight. He made friends with several influential members of Lords and Commons and joined Brooks, an exclusive Whig men's club on St. James Street, so as to keep abreast of political machinations.

Beth spent several weeks with decorators, selecting colors and fabrics for walls, draperies and carpets, to give the dark old house a touch of the light airiness of Naples and Savannah. The place was vastly improved once Annabella departed with her bric-a-brac and baroque furnishings. Beth replaced them with clean-lined Greco-Roman pieces.

The climate was less amenable to change. Leaden skies soon began to pour rain and sleet, promising a long dreary winter. The public market yielded none of the marvelous variety of tropical fruits and vegetables and little of the fresh seafood she had grown used to in Italy. Derrick was gone more than he was present, often missing dinner because of late meetings with political or business associates.

Beth dutifully accompanied her husband to several functions, but until the following month, when their official period of mourning for Leighton was over, a full social calendar was not acceptable. She wore pale gray and purple and felt at times as if she were turning into one of the lengthening shadows that filled every corner of the city house.

Surprisingly enough, the only friend she found among the Quality was Bertie Jamison. The day after Annabella moved out he came calling. Beth was upstairs when he was announced. Derrick was gone as usual; she would have to greet him. Hurriedly she smoothed her hair and removed the apron covering her day gown. Giving one last glance into the mirror, she sighed and headed downstairs to the receiving parlor where Bertie waited.

"So good to see you, Cousin," she said with an uncertain smile. "I'm afraid Derrick is not at home—"

"Tut, m'dear, I did not come to see him but you," he said, bowing over her hand. The buttons on his waistcoat strained across his thickened middle as he straightened up, bestowing on her a twinkling smile. "After the other evening, I felt you were owed an apology. Demned if there's any race as stiff-rumped as the English . . . unless it's the Froggies."

Beth's smile broadened. "Cousin Bertie, I do believe you and I shall deal quite well together. Please have a seat and I'll ring for some tea."

"Wouldn't happen to have some of that perfectly marvelous American coffee about, would you?" he asked with a grin.

"As a matter of fact, 'tis my favorite beverage."

Over coffee and scones, which Bertie consumed in sufficient quantities to place an additional strain upon his waistcoat, they discussed life in London, politics, even art when Beth chanced to mention that she had gone to Naples to study painting.

"I was a great admirer of Angelica Kauffman. Reynolds brought her to London, but of course, the ton couldn't accept a female painter back then," Bertie remarked wryly.

"Women in the arts are still considered dabblers, I'm afraid." Beth sighed.

"Sad but true. Most men are afraid of intelligence in a woman."

She grinned at him. "But you are not."

"I appreciate capability in either gender, perhaps because I'm chitty-faced and a bit cow-handed to boot," he confessed, remarking upon the unfortunate combination of a baby-faced countenance with a prematurely receding hairline, as well as his propensity for clumsiness. He grew a bit red-faced when she tried to remonstrate that he was nothing of the sort. Changing the subject, he asked, "Wouldn't happen to have any of your work I could view, would you?"

Beth was flattered. He seemed both sincere and knowledgeable. "Cranston has just uncrated two boxes in the room that's to be my studio when the redecorating is done."

"Then by Jove, let us have a gander." He rubbed his

plump white hands with enthusiasm as she led him upstairs to where the heavy wooden crates sat in the center of a room stripped bare of furnishings.

He exclaimed over several of the landscapes, making lavish comparisons to her idol, J. M. W. Turner. When he saw the portrait of Derrick, he studied it with fascination for several unnerving moments. Thinking better of her plan to present it as a wedding gift, she had never shown it to another soul since completing it. *It probably reveals too much about me . . . and my feelings for him,* she thought uncomfortably.

Bertie walked around it, almost tripping over Percy, who had entered the room with uncharacteristic silence as they were talking. The dog walked to her side and stood perfectly still when Bertie said, "You could rival Reynolds himself, m'dear." He continued to study the portrait, then murmured sadly, "I can only imagine what it would be like to be loved this much."

"Is it that apparent?"

He flushed again, embarrassed, then shifted the subject. "All of your work has great emotion in it. I've heard it said the greatest artists give a part of their soul to each painting. You've skill enough for admission to the Academy."

"I did work for commissions while we lived in Naples. Of course, that was before Derrick inherited the title," she hastened to add. "I do miss the salons and the friends we had in the art community."

"Although I know we're poor recompense for Italian wit, I would be most happy to introduce you to Lady Holland and her friends. You must understand, she's not received in the best circles. Divorced, you know. But her salons are famous—artists, actors, writers—even Byron favors her with an appearance from time to time, as does George Dance. You would enjoy his portrait sketches."

"That sounds positively exhilarating!" Beth replied with delight, then realized how Derrick would react. But surely if Bertie went, her husband could not object to her attending with his cousin as escort.

"Smashing!" Bertie exclaimed. "I shall send word as soon as our mourning period is over. Then we're for Holland House."

With Derrick being gone so much of the time, Beth came to look forward to Bertie's visits and kept busy as best she could inside the house. Her time spent with her husband was confined largely to the bedroom. At his insistence, for which she was secretly relieved, they continued to share the master bedroom, leaving her adjoining suite unoccupied.

Outside of Bertie's friendship, her only salvation lay in painting. Beth threw herself into it with abandon. The largest room on the third floor had at last been converted into her studio. It was no equal to what she'd had in Naples, but it served.

Their official mourning ended just in time for the galas of the holiday season. They were besieged with invitations, many of them issued because Derrick was a scapegrace and the ton wanted to see how he would conduct himself now that the weight of Lynden rested on his broad shoulders. But even more, they were dying to meet his strange American countess. It was whispered that the earl had wed her in Naples before he knew of his ascension to the title. Did he repent the ill-made bargain? Lady Annabella certainly hinted that it was so. The gossip was positively delicious!

"We have been invited to the Duchess of Westover's ball," Derrick said, sorting through the stacks of engraved white velum piled on the breakfast table, tossing most, choosing a few to which he felt it judicious to respond. " 'Tis Friday next. Here are several more. If any of the others interest you, we shall attend them as well." Knowing his wife's dislike of society, he imagined she would choose to go nowhere. Truthfully, he was not at all fond of the endless rounds of holiday parties, but Beth needed to do more than commandeer scullery maids to pose for her sketching.

"I've already looked through them. I know none of these people so must rely on your judgment. The Westover gala will be fine," she replied without enthusiasm.

"You'll require some new gowns now that you're out of mourning." Any other female of his acquaintance would have leaped at the offer of a trip to the dressmakers. His other mistresses—mentally, he cursed and corrected himself—his mistresses had always been ecstatic. His *wife* was not interested.

"I brought quite a few things from Naples. I'll not require much beyond a warm cloak or two."

"Fashions in London are a bit more . . . decorous than on the continent. It would be wise to consult with someone who understands the nuances."

"Someone such as Bella?"

She was baiting him, damn it! "I was referring to one of the dressmakers on Oxford Street. Since you have no female companion suitable to accompany you, I shall do so myself." He was trying to be conciliatory.

"I can select my own clothing, Derrick," she said very quietly.

He knew the warning in her voice. "You can't go about town alone, Beth. It simply isn't done."

"Tut, you're beginning to sound like Drum," she mocked. Then her expression turned serious. "Derrick, you know well that I'm already the subject of gossip, an impossible American baggage—"

"I regret Annabella's outburst—damn it, I regret Annabella. I'd scarce hold her up as a paragon of virtue to be emulated, but you could make friends and find a place for yourself here if you'd but give it a chance."

He seemed earnest about wanting her to make a life in London. Working up her courage, she said, "If you're concerned with my making friends, Bertie has issued a marvelous invitation—to us both—to attend a salon at Lady Holland's on Wednesday."

"Lady Holland is not received, Beth. You will not be either if you mingle with her crowd."

"Bertie attends her functions and he is received. So do a great many of the upper ten thousand."

"Not the women. This isn't Naples, puss."

Although she'd not experienced a bit of morning sickness in two months, the kippered herring on her plate suddenly smelled like the scullery garbage bin. She shoved it away. "In Naples you weren't an earl," she said angrily. "In Naples we could enjoy life."

He threw down his napkin and stood up. "Yes, but now I am Lynden. If you think I like it one bit more than you do, you're considerably in error."

She watched in silence as he stalked from the room.

Derrick's frustration did not altogether stem from his worries over his wife. His irresponsible brother and sister-in-law had done more than their share to gray his hair with their profligate ways. True to the predilections of the ton, Lee had been scrupulous to pay his gambling debts but let everyone from tailors to chandlers go begging for the sizable sums he owed them.

The mews behind the city house were filled with expensive horseflesh and the very latest in fancy rigs. He'd given Bella a team and one small carriage. After spending the morning inspecting the stables and questioning the men who worked there, he made decisions about which pieces of equipment to sell. He and Beth did not require four phaetons, two barouches and a racing sulky.

But that left the horses, and Derrick confessed to sharing his brother's weakness for fine horseflesh. That was why he decided to test the best of the racers and carriage horses himself before deciding which to sell. He patted the big black stallion's neck, almost certain it would be one he wished to keep.

" 'Ee be a good 'un, m'lord," Spralding, the head stableman, said in his thick Yorkshire accent as his gnarled hands held the reins, steadying the horse while a stable boy threw a lightweight saddle on the black's back and secured it with deft ease.

"I'll take him over to the park for a good run."

"That 'ee'l give ya, m'lord." Spralding's toothless mouth spread wide in a grin as he bowed respectfully to the new earl.

Derrick swung smoothly into the saddle and kneed the stallion into a trot. Since it was considered a savage hour by ton standards, no one was about except for a few tradesmen and household servants. Derrick carefully wended his way toward Hyde Park to give the horse a thorough run. Patting the glossy black neck, he murmured, "Do us both a world of good to work off some tension, eh, boy?"

The feel of a fine horse beneath him and the wind blowing his hair exhilarated him as he let the black have his head. It felt good, an escape from the confinement of city life and the troubles pressing him. He leaned forward, urging the stallion to take a hedge several dozen yards ahead.

Effortlessly, they breezed over it as if the black had wings on his hooves. Derrick grinned, knowing he'd keep Night Dancer. He turned the stallion sharply and headed for another hedge across a slight swale, confident now that the horse was able to make the jump, which was a good bit higher than the first one. Just as he felt Dancer's muscles tense for the leap, the saddle began to slip to the left. He considered for an instant trying to rein the horse in and turn him, but feared injuring his mount. Instead, he kicked free of the stirrups and jumped.

The saddle came sailing off and hit the ground with a loud whump as Derrick landed hard on his right shoulder and rolled up into a ball to avoid Dancer's flying hooves. As the horse cleared the hedge, Derrick sat up and took inventory of his body, thanking his luck for the dreary soaking rain that had fallen earlier in the week, softening the earth considerably. No broken bones, but he'd have one devil of a set of bruises.

Quickly he got to his feet and climbed through an opening in the hedge. Dancer had stopped and turned, tossing his head nervously. Derrick spoke soothingly to the skittish stallion as he approached and took the reins, leading him around the hedge back to where the saddle and blanket were strewn on the grass.

Within the hour he was back at his stable and Spralding

was examining the tack. "Yer that lucky, m'lord. See 'ere." The old man held up the saddle girth that had broken.

"It's been cut halfway through. A wonder it didn't break when I started to race Dancer and made that first jump," Derrick said, realizing how easily he could have broken his neck flying through the air at such a speed.

"I'm that sorry, m'lord. I don't know 'oo cudda done this'n." His rheumy brown eyes met the earl's penetrating blue ones, the question unasked—did Derrick have any enemies?

"Then this was deliberate." He had been pretty certain when he'd checked the saddle in the park.

"Aye, m'lord. I'd stake m'soul on th' lads whot work 'ere . . ."

"But you have someone new?" Derrick prompted.

The boy's name was Jem and he'd been working on tack that very morning. A search of the mews revealed that he was no longer anywhere around. One of the stable hands said he had left without a word just after Derrick rode off on Dancer.

As he soaked in a tub that afternoon, Derrick reviewed a number of potentially dangerous events that had occurred since he'd become Lynden. He'd dismissed nearly being run down by a drayman en route to his solicitor's office and the tiles that had fallen from a rooftop and shattered on the street inches from where he was standing while engaged in conversation with an old acquaintance from Eton. If he added the attack just before he'd left Naples, there might now have been four attempts on his life. Until the tampering with his saddle, all had seemed random bad luck.

Over his years as a spy, he'd made more than his share of enemies. Between leaving Spralding and retiring to this soak, he'd visited Lord Burghley at the Foreign Office and learned some interesting news that might well have a bearing on the attempts to put a period to his life.

Evon Bourdin was in London. Amazingly, Murat's former palace guardsman was descended from one of the oldest and highest-ranking noble houses of France's Ancient

Regime—and he was cousin to Bella's odious friend, the Count d'Artois. Ardent hater of Bonapartists that he was, the count was forced to acknowledge Bourdin because of his cousin's pedigree. Proper lineage was all. That was the way things worked in the ton.

Bourdin certainly has reason enough to want me dead. Placing the Frenchman at the head of his list of potential suspects, Derrick decided to confront him tonight at the Duchess of Westover's soiree.

The orchestra played a waltz, still considered a scandalous innovation in England, although it had been danced on the continent for years. The crowd whirled and dipped, laughed and chattered all around Beth in a kaleidoscope of color and noise. She had never felt so alone in her entire life as she watched Derrick spin a viscountess across the floor. They made a striking couple, he so tall and dark, elegantly handsome in a perfectly tailored black cashmere jacket and trousers. The snowy white linen of his perfectly tied cravat contrasted dramatically with his sun-darkened face as he smiled at the striking brunette in his arms.

He had become the toast of London over the past few days. Apparently, if one was a dashingly handsome earl, the ton found it easy enough to forgive youthful wenching and dueling. His reinstatement in the good graces of the upper ten thousand was complete when some unknown functionary in the Foreign Office let out word that Derrick had been on secret assignment, working directly for Lord Castlereagh the past five years. Derrick went from pariah to hero overnight.

Beth wondered if one of his new friends in the House of Lords had not decided it expedient for their political agenda to have Derrick's popularity enhanced. Her husband had shrugged off her questions, saying only that he disliked being the object of silly adulation in the news sheets but expected it would soon die down. She was not certain about the political implications of his sudden celebrity, but she could clearly see how it affected the ladies.

Across the room the gleam of sexual excitement in his

beautiful dance partner's dark eyes was unmistakable.
Charlotte was everything Beth would never be—dutiful,
obedient and English. The viscountess might share a discreet affair, but she'd always do what society expected of
her in public. Beth felt an acute stab of jealousy as visions
of her husband lying entwined with Charlotte crept into
her mind.

He'd been surrounded by drooling females ever since
their arrival. Oh, everyone had been polite enough to his
American countess—on the surface—but Beth had felt
their hostile glances and overheard the tittering whispers
behind their fans as they discussed the earl's very unortho-
dox marriage. A pity he'd been so precipitous.

"Don't let them see you're hurt by their hen's pecks. The
lot of 'em ain't worth the pinky finger on your left hand,
Beth," Bertie Jamison said as he handed her a glass of
champagne.

The bubbles tickled her nose as she sipped, then replied,
"I'm grateful you've been so kind as to sit with me this
dance. Each time I take the floor I feel like the fish my
friend Vittoria kept in a huge glass bowl . . . on display for
everyone present to comment upon."

"And what could they say? Certainly not that you're
gauche, ill-mannered or anything but exceedingly lovely
and the picture of ladylike decorum. No need to be jealous
of the attention the earl's receiving."

"Am I that transparent?" she asked with a wan smile,
her eyes returning to her husband's beautiful dance partner.

"Ah, Charlotte's no more a blue-blood than are you, if
that's your worry. Her father's a Cit, wanted her to marry
into a title. Flush in the pockets, so he could afford to pay
Viscount Marleigh's asking price—no matter the groom
was the same age as her father."

Bertie was an incorrigible gossip but terribly sweet. "The
poor thing," Beth said, trying to imagine how horrible it
would be to wed an old man.

Bertie laughed as he took a gulp of champagne. "Save
your pity, Beth. The new Viscountess Marleigh wanted to

land her catch every bit as much as her father did. A real proper pair of mushrooms, she and Ben Binghamton."

"Ben Binghamton!" Beth gasped, almost dropping her glass of champagne.

"I say, Beth, do you know the blighter? A real nip-cheese with the employees at his factory, but he has gingerbread enough to mingle with the better sort."

His pale gray eyes studied her worriedly as the very ground seemed to pitch beneath her feet. "Do you mean he's present tonight?" At Bertie's confirmation of her worst nightmare, Beth prayed for the floor to open up and swallow her before Ben Binghamton saw her and recognized that she had been aboard the *Sea Sprite* with him when they'd been captured by Liam Quinn.

Chapter Twenty-two

Derrick had not been attending Charlotte's idle chatter. The chit had half the sense of a sand flea and was twice as irritating. His mind was occupied with the earlier meeting he'd had with d'Artois and Bourdin in the Westover card room. The fat old count had been red-faced, making furious threats, but it was the oily young fortune hunter's smirking menace that worried him.

Bourdin had not denied that Derrick's death would have afforded him pleasure, but he had said that any scandal would bring to light his regrettable past affiliations. Since he did not wish it bandied about London that he'd served under Bonaparte's favorite general, he was content to leave the earl alone . . . if the earl would be content to do likewise for him.

Every instinct honed by his years as a spy convinced Derrick that Bourdin was lying. The safest way to ensure that he would not expose the Frenchman was for Bourdin to kill him . . . or hire someone else to do so. Derrick had dispatched Bow Street Runners in search of the stable boy Jem earlier that afternoon. If they located the youth, he might be convinced to implicate Bourdin to save his own neck. In the meanwhile, all Derrick could do was be very wary.

Right now his life had complications enough, he thought, watching Beth engaged in conversation with his ninny of a cousin Bertie. If not for the fact that he was rich as Croesus, Bertie Wharton Jamison might be a suspect on Derrick's list of enemies. As to coveting the title, Bertie was Baron of Wharton. He'd spent his life much the same way as Vittoria, moving among artistic and literary circles, little concerned with the proprieties of the ton, although he was received by the upper ten thousand, right up to Prinney himself. Annabella doted upon him, although he could not imagine why a woman such as his sister-in-law would find Bertie appealing. Beth seemed exceedingly fond of him as well.

Derrick could understand that Bertie and Beth were kindred spirits. The thought rankled, although Bertie was such a bran-faced clunch that Derrick could not imagine his wife finding the man physically attractive. Still, she was isolated and unhappy. Perhaps it might be best to send her to the Hall now. She could paint and would not have to worry about the social whirl.

She'd be safer away from him in the meanwhile. What if the next "accident" injured her instead of him? The thought was enough to make his gut clench with fear for her and their child, a totally new emotion for him. He'd risked his life without a care over the past half dozen years and never given the danger a moment's worry. Perhaps because he had nothing to lose before he met Beth.

"You've done nothing but nod and smile at me, then stare across the ballroom floor in a brown study since the music started." Charlotte pouted as the dance ended.

Just then the young Duke of Westover approached Beth. Derrick's eyes narrowed. Westover was slender and blond. And he was fair slobbering down the front of Beth's low-cut gown. Damnation, her generous breasts looked about to pop from their moorings right into Westover's all too eager hands! Derrick could not wait to deposit Charlotte back with her circle of tittering friends and go to his wife, but the young matron was having none of it.

She fastened one dainty white hand over his arm and said insistently, "You simply must come and meet Daddy. I just saw him arrive."

Having said that, she launched forth with a suprisingly steely grip on his arm, headed toward a portly bald man with a jowly, self-important face. He studied Charlotte's singularly unattractive father, who looked disturbingly familiar. Then suddenly Ben Binghamton's identity hit him.

Across the room, the same jolt of ghastly recognition had just struck Beth. "Please, I feel unwell," she whispered to Bertie and Westover. "Would you please excuse me, gentlemen?" But before she could turn to fly from Binghamton's presence, the young duke interceded.

"Perhaps a bit of fresh air would help. Allow me?" Without waiting for her agreement, he took her arm and whisked her toward the set of open doors leading out onto the terrace gardens.

It accomplished what she wished, escape. But as they made their way to the exit, Beth could see her husband in thrall to Binghamton's daughter, being led to meet Papa. *Please don't let that pompous old jackanapes recognize me!*

Too late. She could feel the vibrations as whispers began to spread across the crowd after Binghamton stiffened his multiple chins and spoke to the Marchioness of Singleton. He *had* seen her and, in spite of her finery, had recognized her. Beth could well imagine his indignation upon being informed that she was now the Countess of Lynden.

Of all the passengers on the *Sea Sprite*, he had been the most priggishly insufferable, but because he was a Cit, it had never occurred to her that she would encounter him in the rarified atmosphere of an aristocratic ballroom. Derrick's plans to redeem his tarnished family name were ashes now.

Woodenly, she allowed young Westover to lead her down the curving stairs into the formal gardens of his city house. The perfectly manicured topiary and elaborate gazebos befitted the home of a duke, but Beth did not notice the enormous white and gold chrysanthemums waving in the evening breeze. Nor did she smell the lush fragrance of the honeysuckle. All she could think of was that awful Ben Binghamton spreading his venom the length and breadth of London.

"You seem distressed, my lady. Would it help to talk about it?" Westover said with a sincere smile.

"Once I tell you the cause of my distress, you may not wish to spend another moment in my company."

"That would not only be unchivalrous but unkind. I would like to believe that I am neither." His smile was gentle, sincere.

"I have been, as you English like to say, right properly dished up tonight." Beth quickly outlined her voyage and capture by Algerine corsairs, the time spent in the seraglio and her rescue by Decatur, mentioning Derrick only at the last when he had assisted the American commodore in securing her release. When she finished, his expression was troubled but not condemning.

"You have suffered much and come through it quite bravely, I believe. You are to be admired, my lady, not ostracized."

"I fear your mother will not agree," she replied gently.

Westover sighed. "Probably not. She's quite of the old school, very starchy, outspoken to the point of telling Prinney his immoral behavior is a disgrace to England!"

"She did not!" Beth had heard much whispering behind their prince's back, but no one bearded the vain old devil openly since the Beau had done so—and suffered disgrace for it.

"Right to his face. At Brighton three years ago."

"And she's still received at court?"

"She's his first cousin," he replied, as if the fact were a blemish rather than a distinction.

Beth genuinely liked the boy. "Ah, then that would give her a bit of latitude Brummel did not have. Being American to begin with, I have nothing whatsoever to redeem me. And I fear that it would be in your best interests not to spend any further time with me, lest you upset your mother, but I do thank you for being so kind as to listen to my tale of woe."

He took her hands, quite distressed. "Never say so! What sort of person deserts his friend in time of need?" he importuned earnestly.

Derrick had searched for his wife for the better part of the hour since Binghamton's disastrous appearance. The juicy gossip had already spread faster than smallpox on a prison ship. By morning Beth would be a pariah in London. He had to get her out of the city until the worst of the scandal died down. But first he had to locate her.

He feared she had bolted on her own, but their phaeton was still in the drive. It was much too far to walk. He was growing increasingly worried when from the edge of the terrace he saw her standing half hidden beneath the leafy canopy of a tree, her hands in those of Westover. The young pup looked about ready to kiss her, but she turned away and he followed like a lapdog as she made her way back to the stairs.

Derrick stood glowering down at her as she ascended. She was still so engrossed in conversation with Westover that she did not notice him. Damn, the woman had not one shred of propriety—to slip away alone with a man just as a maelstrom of scandal erupted all about her! *She did not come to you for comfort.* The thought rankled.

Beth looked up, suddenly sensing his presence. Derrick loomed above her, looking more formidable than the huge stone lions standing guard at either side of the terrace staircase. Westover, trailing her, practically collided with her when she stopped abruptly on the second step. Moistening her dry lips, she said, "I imagine the gossips inside have fair flayed me to the bone by now."

"So you've chosen to sequester yourself with a sympathetic listener for the past hour," he said with a meaningful glance at Westover, who had the good grace to flush with embarrassment.

"Terribly sorry, Lynden. I was not thinking of the countess's reputation—er, that is—"

"No, you were not, nor was she," Derrick replied.

"Since my reputation is already in the black book, it scarce signifies if his grace was kind enough to offer a bit of sympathy," she retorted. Why just once, in such a nightmare as this evening had turned out to be, could her husband not offer solicitude rather than condemnation? She avoided his outstretched hand and walked stiffly up the stairs, head held high, steeling herself to face the ugliness that awaited her inside.

Derrick made a curt bow to Westover, then turned to catch up with his wife. "Bloody hell, will you wait until I accompany you?" he hissed, seizing her arm and placing her hand on his sleeve just before they reached the doorway into the ballroom.

"You cannot protect me," she replied woodenly.

Although she was right, he could not bear the desolation in her voice, or the thought of his powerlessness to control the whirlwind of scandal that was already enveloping them. "You've never been afraid of breaking social conventions before, puss. Show that bravery now," he said as they walked into the crowded room.

The music continued, but the dancers stopped, parting as had the waters of the Red Sea. Like Moses and the Israelites, the Earl and Countess of Lynden passed through without looking left or right until they came to his cousin Bertie, who smiled and nodded encouragingly. At his side, Annabella stood frozen rigidly, her expression mirroring the shock of the other guests. She did not acknowledge them in any way. The dowager duchess was nowhere to be seen as they took their leave.

On the ride home they sat side by side in the carriage, letting the sounds of the city at night make up for their lack of conversation, each lost in private misery. At first neither could think of anything to say that would not make matters even worse between them.

Beth had been grateful for Derrick's arm by the time they'd reached Bertie. Dear lord, his cousin had been the only human being in the room who had not looked at her with scathing disdain or titillated pity. She could imagine the whispered conversations at Westover's behind women's opened fans and in the men's card room. If the young duke defied his mother and called on her, she would have to refuse to see him for his own sake. Bertie . . . she supposed Bertie could take care of himself if he chose to visit her.

Derrick's mind spun with plans to whisk Beth away from the scene of so much hurt for her. He knew the ton well enough to realize that now the "little season" had begun in earnest, other scandals would displace his shocking American wife's recent history. Then the city would empty of the upper ten thousand as they departed to spend Christmas at their country estates.

By spring, after their child was born, she could return to London . . . if she wished to, knowing that no one of consequence would receive her. Except Bertie, of course. He felt petty because that bothered him in some vague way, even though he knew the feeling was not jealousy. His reaction to young Westover had been foolish enough— a green stripling who would never take Beth's fancy. All she had wanted from the duke was someone to take her away from the odious situation. As her husband, that responsibility now fell to him. He would send her to Lynden Hall, even though he dreaded the idea of spending the long weeks without her. It was for her own good—not to mention her safety, he reminded himself.

Once they were in the library of the city house, he poured a sherry for her, a stiff snifter of brandy for himself and said, "I think it best if you retire to the Hall now. I should be along in time for the holidays."

His back was to her so he could not see her reaction. *He's trying to rid himself of me!* She felt pain lash her, then willed it away, replacing it with cold anger. 'Twould do no good to bare her soul to this hidebound Englishman who could see nothing but duty. "I told you I'd be an embarrassment, Derrick, but you refused to listen. My coming to England in the first place was a terrible mistake."

"Do not prattle to me about Naples," he said, biting off

each word. "You are my wife and you will go to the Hall until the scandal dies down."

"And when, pray, will that be? Within the decade? I daresay you can have your heir enrolled in Eton before I need venture from the country again. How convenient for you."

He threw the glass of sherry that she had refused against the fireplace. The wine caused the flames to flare for an instant as the crystal shattered and lay glittering on the dull gray hearthstones. "There is nothing convenient about any of this, m'dear, but we shall nevertheless have to get through it as best we can."

"Spare me your tiresome English fortitude. I've had enough to last me a lifetime! I have not felt free since we set sail for this wretched, dreary country, filled with the stink of cabbage and coal smoke! I want my life back, Derrick. I created a good one for myself once before—I will do so again. I long for laughter and the simple pleasure of warm sun on my face."

His heart stopped beating for a moment. He could not lose her this way! He blurted out the first thing that came to mind. "I'll not let you sail to Naples. I will not let you leave me. Even if you care nothing for the babe inside you, I do. A sea voyage this late in the year would be dangerous."

"Your heir. Your precious heir for the earldom. I know you don't give a fig for me or this child, so do not use it as an excuse to bend me to your will. It will never work again, Derrick."

He stood by the fireplace, the brandy glass clutched in his whitened fist as she walked past him and went upstairs, leaving him to stare into the flames while he drank deeply. Then he ground the shards of broken crystal beneath his boot and poured another drink.

Beth not only adamantly refused to be packed off to the country but decided that her vainglorious boast to Derrick the night before would not be an idle one. She would make a life for herself in London . . . at least until their child was

born. After that she would have to reevaluate what would
be best to do. Bertie called the following day after Derrick
had departed for his round of political and business appointments.

She was devoutly grateful when he cheerfully announced
that since she was in such bad loaf with the ton, there was
nothing for it but to give the old biddies something to
thicken their broth. Lady Holland had issued a personal
invitation through him to "that fascinating American
painter." He told Beth he had been describing her work to
Lady Holland and her friends and they were eager to welcome her into their circle. Beth had little doubt that her
time as an Algerine captive added a certain titillation as
well.

Derrick had been so busy attending to his affairs, he
would not notice her absence. In her heart of hearts, she
longed for him to say that they need not concern themselves with the ton any longer and that he would spend
the rest of his life in the countryside with her. But, of
course, he would never do that. Duty did not permit it.

She refused to remain melancholy. It was not good for
her child, and in spite of Derrick's cruel accusations, she
did love the baby growing in her womb. But she would
not allow any son or daughter of hers to grow up under
the oppressive regimen its father had endured.

In the meanwhile there was the salon at Lady Holland's
tomorrow night . . .

The room was crowded, filled with all manner of people,
talking and laughing animatedly, arguing good-naturedly.
A faint aroma of hashish floated over the house's rowdy
occupants and wine bottles littered every table, even the
mantel. This was the nearest to a Neapolitan gathering
she'd ever seen in stuffy old England. Several of the guests
had asked her how she'd survived captivity in Algiers, but
they did so in a forthright manner, seeming to be genuinely
concerned.

"Quite a contrast to her grace's soiree the other night,
eh what?" Bertie said to her with a chuckle, pointing out

the lionized and scandalous libertine George Gordon, Lord Byron. "Would you like an introduction, m'dear? He's all the rage in literary circles, even if the diamond squad don't approve of the way he lives."

Beth studied Byron. He was handsome in a flamboyant manner, moving about the room with a dramatic flourish. His curly black hair framed a classically chiseled face with a delicate pouty mouth and deep-set dark eyes that seemed to bore into people and hold them mesmerized as he spoke. "I have heard about his numerous affairs, even rumors about one with his own sister. At the risk of sounding like the very people who shun me, I find the way he treats his unfortunate wife distasteful."

"Anne Milbanke was a dreadful choice for a wife, but the fault does not lie entirely with him," Bertie said.

"In any case, the great poet is busily engaged with his audience now. You promised that there would be other women artists here," she replied.

Across the room a handsome woman whose straight back and vibrant gestures belied her sixty years described in heavily accented French her time painting at the royal courts of Versailles, Vienna and St. Petersburg. At once Beth knew that she must be Elisabeth Vigée-Lebrun, by her own humble admission, "France's greatest woman painter." "Oh, Bertie, that is Madam Vigée-Lebrun, is it not?" she whispered in awe.

"I shall allow Lady Holland the privilege of introducing you to her," he said as their hostess glided toward them. The scandalous divorcee was a plump, almost matronly looking woman of middle years, not at all what Beth had been led to expect. Well, what did she imagine most people thought of *her?* Probably that she danced naked through the sitting rooms of her house!

Lady Holland was gracious and charming. Although Madame Vigée-Lebrun was neither, she was fascinating and incredibly talented, with a wealth of information to impart. After hearing Bertie's opinion of Beth's gifts, she agreed to look at the younger woman's work and offer a critique.

The two women engaged in a detailed discussion of portrait techniques, joined by a number of other well-known male painters, including several members of the Royal Academy. Eventually she drifted into a group of political reformers, including the young cartoonist George Cruikshank, who argued vociferously with several members of Commons regarding protective tariffs against imported wheat.

Beth almost forgot her unhappiness for a few hours, joyously embracing a return to her old, carefree life. *This is where I belong.* She felt fortified to return to the forbidding Lynden city house and resume her painting. Already that night she'd been offered two commissions, one for a portrait of a tabloid writer's young daughter, the other for a landscape from the younger son of Baron Rutherford. Should she accept?

As she was mulling this over, Byron sauntered over to her, a glass of claret in his hand. He moved very carefully so as not to draw attention to his crippled foot, about which she knew he was extremely sensitive. He raised his glass to her and smiled.

"A diamond of the first water, and a new countess to boot. With your beauty, 'twere best you'd wed a royal duke instead of a mere earl," he said, saluting her fingertips with a kiss that was not quite proper, but not unpleasant either.

" 'Twere better I wed neither, m'lord," she replied.

Byron chuckled wickedly. "We have much in common, m'lady. Not only are we highly talented and scandal-prone, we're also baldly outspoken."

"What do you know about my talents?" Beth could not believe she was engaging in such blatantly suggestive banter.

His deep, dark eyes studied her from beneath heavy lids. He was the perfect picture of sensuous debauchery . . . and utter charm. "I have heard on good authority that you were one of the finest young painters in Italy. Never forget, I have spent a deal of time there and have numerous friends who keep me informed. Why are you not painting in London?"

Beth was taken aback by the abrupt switch from what had been sexual teasing to such a forthright question—and praise for her art. "I have begun to paint again," she replied almost defensively.

"But you've not displayed anything. Does your earl forbid it?" he asked with the gleam of a dare in his eyes.

"You should well know that what is permissible in Naples is not acceptable in London."

"That depends upon whether one gives a fig what the public thinks. After outwitting the Algerines, I would think you'd be less fearful of the good opinion of the ton."

"I care little for the good opinion of the ton but much for the legislation my husband sponsors in Parliament," she replied.

"You're in love with your earl then? A pity." He shrugged. "I've heard Turner praise the way you handle light, and Pignatelli, that old rascal, says you're portraiture skills are considerable. The public is fascinated with Orientalia. Have you ever considered painting scenes from the seraglio? You have unique qualifications to do so."

Beth was stunned by the idea . . . and highly intrigued. Before she could reply, Byron continued, purring, "You're already in the suds because you had the misfortune to be captured by corsairs. Why not capitalize upon it?"

"Why not indeed . . ." she murmured as several other guests approached and the conversation shifted to Byron's favorite subject—himself.

When she broached the question to Bertie, he encouraged her. "Byron has the truth of it, m'dear. You're dished anyway. A demned good way to put the diamond squad at sixes and sevens—show 'em you don't give a fig for the done thing. Recall earlier when you were telling Madame Vigée-Lebrun about the seraglio?"

"Everyone certainly hung on my every word," Beth admitted. Even the much traveled and worldly wise Frenchwoman had been openly intrigued by Beth's descriptions of harem life.

"A series on the daily lives of the odalisques would raise quite a breeze—and I'd bet a score of the Quality, not to mention those priggish merchants, would stand in line to purchase your work."

The idea certainly held a strong appeal. Everyone was fascinated with the forbidden, the mysterious, the exotic . . . even if the oh-so-proper English would never confess it. Byron and Bertie were right.

"Derrick would be horrified." She shook her head, recalling the earlier discussion of reform measures pending in Parliament. "What if this further undermined his position in the House of Lords?"

Bertie disagreed. "Stuff. Might even help his cause, having a famous wife. The Quality are incredible hypocrites. Caro Lamb's antics haven't put a flea bite on Lord Melborne's career."

"I shall think about it," was all she replied. What would Derrick do? Would it get his attention? Certainly her attending this salon with Bertie had not. She had left a note on his desk earlier in the afternoon explaining that their cousin was escorting her to Lady Holland's. She had hoped it might bring him to her quarters—if for no other reason than to forbid her to go. Since their last fight he had not spoken to her. And this time when she'd moved to the adjoining bedroom, he had not come to drag her back to his bed.

Just then the late supper was announced, a very informal buffet with guests balancing plates and glasses as they scattered about the lower floor of the house. Bertie insisted that they should eat although her appetite had fled. He directed her to find a seat over in a secluded alcove half hidden by potted palms, mentioning that one of Turner's early landscapes hung there. While he went to fetch the food, she lost herself in admiring the painting.

"His use of light is quite remarkable . . . even if he is a bloody Englishman," a voice behind her said in a lilting and familiar Irish brogue.

Stunned, Beth turned and looked up into the bright green eyes of Liam Quinn. The floor seemed to evaporate beneath her feet. For an instant she was once more on the deck of the *Sea Sprite,* surrounded by his savage crew of corsairs. But Quinn no longer wore the heathenish garb or gaudy jewelry of a corsair, although the faint marks on his earlobes still revealed where they'd been pierced. His flaming hair was meticulously barbered, his beard shaved clean away, revealing a genuinely handsome face. He was dressed in a well-tailored cutaway coat of dark green cashmere and tan kerseymere pants. The white cravat at his throat was tied perfectly enough to meet even Drum's exacting standards. Yet there was still an aura of wildness about him that made her wary.

Regaining her composure, she said, "By all rights you should have fed the fishes months ago. How did Decatur miss killing you?"

He threw back his head in that same booming laugh. "Ah, colleen, bloodthirsty as ever! Haven't you heard of the luck of the Irish? Your redoubtable American commodore gave us chase, taking out two of my schooners, but my brig escaped . . . loaded with a prize taken from a Maltese galleon. 'Twas no longer safe to ply my trade in the Mediterranean. I sold my cargo in Lisbon and sailed to London."

"Reconverting to Christianity en route, no doubt," she said scornfully.

"By the Holy Rood, so I did. I could not believe my good fortune when I heard about this hoyden of an American who dared to wed an earl. The gossips described you, but the English lack the poetry to do your beauty justice." He deftly took her hand and raised it to his lips before she realized his intent.

Beth jerked her hand away. "Don't try your flummery on me after selling me to the day of Algiers!" she hissed furiously.

He looked crestfallen. " 'Twas poor recompense for the way you nursed me, I do confess, colleen," he said, sounding not the least bit contrite. "But I stand before you a reformed man."

"Blarney," she scoffed. "I thought there was a price on your head set by the English. By all rights they should hang you at Tyburn."

He shrugged, as if it was of no concern whatever. "That was in Ireland, many years ago. Long forgotten now . . . unlike your own scandalous past. You should welcome my company, sweet kitten. After all, we're both strangers in this most inhospitable land."

"The difference being, you went there willingly and I did not," she snapped, turning to walk away from the dangerous rascal before she clawed his eyes out. *Derrick believes that you gave yourself to him!*

Before she could negotiate her way around the palm, he seized her wrist and turned her back into his arms, saying, "Not so fast, colleen. We've unfinished business, you and I."

"Release me or I'll see you in Newgate before sunrise," she gritted out, wishing desperately for the stiletto she had always carried in Naples.

"I see my kitten no longer has her sharp claws, else I'd lie bleeding by now—did your earl take your knives away from you?" he murmured.

Derrick had insisted she did not need them. How wrong he'd been, she thought as she felt the pressure of Quinn's arms squeezing the breath from her. He was a giant of a man, and an utter savage! His eyes glowed like strange greenish coals dredged from the pits of hell. Beth raised her foot and stamped down as hard as she could on his instep with the pointed heel of her slipper.

He grimaced but did not relinquish his grip. She raised her foot a second time, and he moved his foot to avoid another blow. This time she aimed higher. Her knee came up between his legs—very hard. At last he relinquished his grip, collapsing against the wall. Unfortunately Beth was caught between it and the Irishman, who pinned her for a moment as he cursed and gasped for breath.

She ducked down and pulled away. Suddenly Quinn's weight was gone and he seemed to fly into the potted palms beside them, breaking several canes. She turned with chagrin to thank her rescuer.

And stared into Derrick's icy blue eyes.

Chapter Twenty-three

Beth was left breathless by the force of his glare, but the gasping sounds emitted by Quinn quickly reminded her that it would be wise to get away from the corsair . . . and probably her husband as well. "Please don't create a scene, Derrick," she said as he grabbed her hand and pulled her behind him, facing Quinn, who now had managed to stand upright once more.

"I will deal with you later," he told Beth, advancing on the big red-haired man as several of the guests, hearing the altercation, approached the alcove to watch.

"Ah," Quinn coughed, then continued, "you are the colleen's earl, I presume?"

"And you are the walking dead man who dared to put his hands on my wife."

"Not nearly so effectively as where she placed her knee on me, alas," Quinn said with an insolent grin. "I am Liam Quinn, but whether or not you shall be able to kill me remains to be seen."

Derrick stiffened, stunned to see his wife's abductor in

the flesh. "I've often dreamed of killing you, but I never imagined you'd make it so easy."

Beth watched the deadly adversaries circling each other like two great jungle cats. Blood lust was thick in the air and the audience stood back, fascinated. No one would dare to interfere. She knew Derrick was skilled with knife and pistol, but Quinn was a renegade who would stoop to any depravity to survive. "There's no need for this," she said to her husband. "I have already dealt Mr. Quinn's pride a severe enough blow—not to mention certain sensitive portions of his anatomy," she added sotto voce.

Without ever taking his eyes off the Irishman, Derrick replied furiously. "No need? You've amply illustrated how little value you place on your honor, but you are the Countess of Lynden and, as such, my responsibility." To Quinn he said, "We will settle this matter between us on the morrow."

"Lady Holland has my direction. You will have no difficulty finding me . . . only killing me," the Irishman added with silky menace.

Derrick had a steel grip on Beth's arm as he strode past the guests. A distraught-looking Bertie tried to remonstrate with him, but Derrick only snarled, "Stay out of this, Coz, or it will go ill with you."

Beth nodded to him. "I shall be all right," she said, even though she had considerable doubt.

Derrick escorted her to the carriage waiting in the street, practically throwing her onto the cushioned seat, then taking the reins and driving as if he were a madman escaped from Bedlam. By the time they reached the residence on Pall Mall, the matched bays were winded and sweating in the cool night air. Beth was freezing, having been dragged from the soiree before she could retrieve her cloak. She sat stiffly, her back pressed against the squabs, her fingers embedded in the cushion edges to keep her seat during the wild ride. Her husband leaped from the carriage as a groom approached, then reached up and lifted her to the ground.

As the rig was led toward the stables, they walked silently into the house. He headed straight for the library, closing the heavy walnut doors behind them with an ominous whoosh. Beth moved to the center of the room and turned to face him. "I had no idea Quinn was in London. You must not challenge him, Derrick. He's—"

" 'Tis a bit late for that," he interrupted curtly, "since I found him pawing you as if you were his slave." The instant he said the words he regretted them, but the fury churning in his gut gnawed at him.

" 'Tis quite a bit too late to undo what is past, Derrick. I was his slave . . . and you can never forget it—or forgive me for it."

"You give me little help in that endeavor when you persist in behaving as if you were still in Naples. I specifically forbade you to attend Lady Holland's salons, yet you went."

"Why should I not? What further disgrace can come to me after Binghamton's denunciation?"

She looked defiant yet so vulnerable that it hurt him. His anger began to lessen as he struggled to regain some semblance of control over his temper. "When you refused to retire to the countryside, you laid yourself open for just this sort of pain, Beth. At the Hall you could paint and enjoy a measure of freedom—dress as you like, take Percy with you. It may not be Naples, but 'tis better than London." *And safer.* "You would have none of the social duties you find so onerous."

"And you would be free to pursue your social duties unencumbered by your wanton American countess—even if it meant dying senselessly in a duel with Quinn."

"Your concern for my life is touching," he replied with a tight smile. "Leave the corsair to me."

"You can't undo what happened to me by killing him—if you *can* kill him."

"Whom are you more concerned for—me or him?" he snapped.

She snarled a ripe Neapolitan oath, then said, "He sold me into that hellish place where you found me and you dare ask that!"

Shirl Henke

Derrick's shoulders slumped and he combed his fingers through his hair, exhausted and dispirited. He'd spent half the preceding night hashing out a compromise bill in Parliament to prevent the worst abuses in the workhouses, then met in the afternoon with the overseer from Lynden Hall, who had come to the city to explain discrepancies in the bookkeeping.

By the time he'd returned home and found her message it had been near midnight. He'd been furious with her for acting with such reckless irresponsibility, then insanely jealous when he found her tussling with that big red-haired oaf. Leave it to Beth to come out the victor, even against a cur like Quinn. Her gown had been torn, her hair disheveled . . . and she'd never looked more alluring to him, damn her!

"All we do is tear at each other, puss. We cannot go on this way."

"Then let me go, Derrick," she said quietly. "Divorce can create no greater scandal than what has already transpired. You will be vindicated if you—"

"No!" he roared, past all patience. The idea of losing her tore at his soul. Why was this her constant refrain? "You are my wife and I will not relinquish you. There is but one way to prove it . . . the same way I made you mine that very first time . . ." He advanced on her.

Beth stepped back. "No, Derrick. This will settle nothing."

"It will settle the fire in my blood . . . in yours. I remember when you first came to me, so bold yet virgin." He reached out and grazed her cheek with his fingertips, tracing the furiously beating pulse from below her ear to the base of her throat.

"I am no longer that virgin, Derrick," she reminded him, knowing full well what he believed of her, powerless to convince him otherwise. Just seeing his reaction to Quinn had proven the futility of that.

"How well I know," he whispered as he wrapped one arm about her waist and pulled her to him, "and how little I care . . ."

300

As his mouth lowered to hers, all she could think of was that Quinn might kill him; this might be the last time he held her in his arms. Nothing mattered at that moment but that he live. She would do anything to save him . . . even sell her own soul.

They sank to the floor gradually as the kiss deepened, running their hands over each other, pulling at clothes fastenings, eager for hot naked flesh on flesh. In the fireplace across the big room a cheerful blaze danced counterpoint to the autumn chill, casting shadows around them. He leaned over her as she lay stretched out on the thick Kirman carpet, his tongue tracing a moist trail over her collarbone to her bared shoulder where Quinn had torn the sleeve of her gown. Derrick brushed a delicate kiss on the already forming bruise.

Beth worked the studs from his shirt and slid her hand inside to feel the solid wall of his chest, reassured by the strong beat of his heart. How she loved him! Her hands moved up to his shoulders, urging him closer as she arched into his fierce, sweet kiss. When she felt the cool air on her thigh as he pulled her gown up, she spread her legs, reaching down to unbutton his fly, her fingers clumsy with haste and need.

She guided his hard staff toward her, but at the last moment he shoved her hand away and plunged deep inside her with a feral cry of possession. They rode hard and fast, slick, hot and gliding in the joining, their bodies desperate as they rolled across the wide floor, alternating with him on top, then her. He cradled her hips in his hands, her gown ruched up around her waist, her hair falling like a russet curtain that shielded her face and danced with the reflected light from the fire.

The end came swiftly. They both gasped at the suddenness and intensity of it. She sat straddling him, her arms braced on his chest, looking down into his face. He stared back at her; their eyes locked and held for a moment. "Is this all there is for us, Derrick?" she asked raggedly.

His hands glided up her arms, tenderly pulling her down to lie upon his chest, holding her in this most intimate of embraces, as if unwilling to let the world and all its problems come between them. He caressed her back as she laid her head against his throat. He could feel the silky wetness of her tears dropping on his bare skin. "We will survive this, Beth, somehow, some way, but it would be better if you were out of harm's way."

Out of Quinn's way, his mind taunted, but he brushed that aside, knowing that she despised the corsair for selling her to the dey. Whatever had been between his wife and the Irishman was well and truly over. As her husband, it was his duty to protect her and keep her safe. "I will see you safely to Lynden Hall. Please."

"But you will not stay with me," she murmured against his throat. It was not a question.

"I cannot. There are very important issues to be settled here in London, but I shall be along in time for the holidays. My word 'pon it, puss."

Beth sighed in defeat. If she remained in London to enjoy the exciting new people she had met at Lady Holland's salon, Derrick would never forgive her, and in his mind he already had much to forgive. But there was one trump card she must play. "I shall go if you agree not to duel with Quinn."

He lifted her off him and sat up. "You once said I did not lack for nerve. Neither do you, m'dear, asking such a thing of me. I have challenged him. There is no way I can renege without being disgraced."

And that, of course, settles that, she thought disconsolately. "Derrick, he is not a man who abides by your code of honor. He'll kill you."

He gave her a lopsided smile, daring to believe for a moment at least that she actually might still love him. "Do you think I survived being a spy all those years abiding by the rules? I know his kind and I've dealt with them. I can handle Liam Quinn."

He stood up and reached down to help her to her feet, then winced involuntarily as he pulled his injured shoulder. Beth saw him flinch and then looked at the huge dark bruise visible now that his shirt hung open. "Derrick! What have you done?"

" 'Tis nothing. I was jumping Lee's black and he unseated me," he said, removing her hand and trying to button his shirt before she saw the extent of the injury.

Beth shoved aside his hands and pulled it open. "You're lucky you didn't dislocate your shoulder at the least—what were you thinking of? Jumping a horse was what killed your brother," she said as she inspected the purpling flesh. "This will require a poultice to take down the blood. Come with me," she instructed in her sternest nurselike tone.

As he followed her upstairs, he considered it fortunate that she'd been distracted enough by his injury not to defy his wishes. He would see her safely ensconced at the Hall after dealing with Quinn on the morrow. When he returned he would have to face the rest of the damnable tangles in his life. Being a spy had been considerably easier than being an earl.

The next morning when Derrick made inquiries at Liam Quinn's lodgings, he was informed that the Irishman had mysteriously vacated them the preceding night. By midafternoon, it was apparent that Quinn, for all his braggadocio, had thought better of fighting a duel with a member of the peerage.

Upon learning there would be no danger from Quinn, Beth felt a slight bit of reassurance regarding her move to the Scottish border, where Lynden Hall was situated. She spent the following day immersed in packing, hoping that this exile would not be the end of her life with Derrick. Would he take mistresses and leave her to raise their child alone? She would just have to wait and see what happened when Derrick joined her at Christmas.

By the time all Beth's trunks were loaded into the coach, it was half past ten. She went to her studio for a final check to see that none of her art supplies had been overlooked. If she was to be banished, at least she could paint. Byron's idea of doing the seraglio paintings hovered in the back of her mind. If she painted harem scenes, Derrick would be furious. Better she sketch nice, safe English subjects.

When all was completed, she sent Donita with the last of the boxes, then started down the stairs. Midway, she heard Bertie's voice and hastened to the door to greet him. Of course the dear man would have called to see if she was all right after the way her husband had dragged her from Lady Holland's home.

"Bertie, how good to see you before we leave," she said as he turned, smiling up at her.

"I was surprised to learn from my cousin that you're retiring to the country so early." His watery pale eyes held a question.

Beth smiled, trying to reassure him, as they strolled out the front entry toward the waiting coach. "Yes, 'twill be restful to be away from the gossipmongers. I shall paint and rusticate until the arrival of Lynden's heir."

"That sounds a good plan. I intend to spend an early holiday this year. Should be at Wharton by December. 'Tis a modest place, not far from Lynden. We shall practically be neighbors." He hesitated, then added uncertainly, "I . . . er, that is, Annabella and Constance will be spending Christmas with me. It would be good to have the family together for the occasion—that is, if you wish," he ended on an uncertain note.

Although Beth would have preferred old Fatima's company to Annabella's, she nevertheless replied, "Of course I would welcome Annabella and Constance . . . if you think my sister-in-law will wish to associate with me after the scandal. I would love to play with Constance again."

Bertie's eyebrows rose and he puffed out his portly chest. "I will see to it that she agrees. After all, we're all the Jamisons left alive. No sense in letting such nonsense keep family apart. I will see that she introduces you to the neighbors around the Hall."

Walking up to the coach, Derrick said, "I would appreciate it if you'd look in on Beth after your arrival, Coz. I shall not be able to get away from London until Christmas."

Bertie's brow crinkled in confusion as he looked at the

black stallion Spralding was tying to the rear of the coach. "I understood that you were staying with Beth at Lynden Hall."

"I am accompanying her, but I'll have to return as soon as she's settled," was all Derrick volunteered. Let his cousin draw what conclusions he wished.

"In that case, perhaps I will move up my schedule and leave London sooner," he said with forced joviality. "Can't have you rattling about all alone in the countryside with naught but a few old chawbacons for company."

The Count d'Artois frowned, his already florid face growing redder from the exertion of lowering himself into a Rococo chair. Once comfortably seated, he looked up into his young cousin's insolent face, and the frown grew deeper. The stupid young pup was going to ruin everything for them if he did not put a period to it. "My wife has given me to understand that you sent Burleigh's daughter a most expensive trinket Friday last. A sapphire pendant, was it not?"

Bourdin nodded brusquely. "The lady was suitably impressed. These silly English misses are as enthralled by baubles as their counterparts in France. I shall offer for her within the month."

"And you will be refused," the count said flatly. "We live in England on sufferance of its peers. They may admire our bloodlines, but they do not admire blatant fortune hunters. When Burleigh catches wind that you're spending beyond your means just to impress the chit, the parsimonious old goat will never agree to the match."

A feral smile spread across Bourdin's wide mouth but did not reach his cold gray eyes. "I am not living beyond my means," he asserted.

D'Artois snorted indelicately. "Pah. Do not try my credulity by saying you have won at the gaming tables. I know better."

Bourdin shrugged and strolled over to the window of the Duke of Kent's small but elegant town house, which he graciously allowed the elderly émigrés to occupy while he was out of the city. "Let us just say I have been offered a substantial reward for performing a task."

"What sort of task?" the count asked suspiciously.

"One of a professional nature."

A prickle of unease ran up the old man's spine. "Your only profession was killing for that Corsican horse thief!"

Bourdin only shrugged and smiled again. "I am very good at it, cousin. You would do well to remember that."

This is the prison where I shall spend my exile. Lynden Hall was everything Beth had expected . . . and dreaded. An immense limestone monolith, it sprawled across a ridge overlooking a small river that flowed out to Solway Firth on the English side of the borderlands. The earliest portion, a medieval castle, had been constructed in the fourteenth century. Over the years, additions had been made. The building's two vast wings gave it the appearance of a huge griffin ready to pounce upon its prey.

Beth felt weary to the bone, a fact that she did not wish her husband to note. In spite of her assurances that she was strong and healthy, he had worried about the child ever since they'd started out two weeks earlier, arranging for frequent stops during the day. The nights were spent in uncomfortable inns with dreadful food. To ensure that she received enough rest, he had abstained from making love to her on the trip. Although she tried to deny it, his aloofness increased her feeling that her husband valued her less for herself than for the child in her womb.

Lynden Hall's grounds, which would have appeared bleak in late October anyway, were made even more dreary because of neglect. Hedges jutted out unevenly and withered grapevine twined throughout the shrubbery. She noted several dead trees that stood like skeletal sentinels as their coach approached the main drive.

Beth could see how the poor appearance of his childhood home affected Derrick. "Your solicitor warned you the estate manager had not been very diligent."

"If Leighton had ever bothered to leave the gaming hells long enough to check up on it, he could have dealt with

Farley as I did." Derrick had fired the overseer after one interview in London. He'd engaged another man who came highly recommended. "Mr. Harris has been here for several days," he continued. "I informed him that putting the household to rights was his first assignment. At least your quarters and some of the downstairs sitting rooms should be cleaned. I'll leave the rest to you." He paused, looking at her bleak expression. "That is, if you feel up to the task of hiring more servants and overseeing the refurbishing."

She had noted that he said "your quarters." It was obvious that he did not intend to stay long. This would be her home . . . for as long as she could bear to live in such isolation. When they had first arrived in London, she had envisioned retiring to paint in the picturesque countryside. The utter isolation of this bleak open river valley and the cold gray pile of stone facing her were not the stuff of her dreams.

"Can we afford refurbishing all this?" she asked, knowing what the upkeep on her parents' Georgia plantation house cost. This great monstrosity dwarfed Blackthorne Hall. Just keeping the fireplaces burning to ward off the bitter northern winter would be a huge expense.

"Lee and Bella did not bankrupt the estate entirely. Wool profits were quite substantial last year. I expect to put business matters to rights in a few months."

"Have you spoken with Mr. Therlow at Uncle Dev's London office?" Her father had suggested that Blackthorne Shipping would be interested in a business arrangement that might be lucrative for Derrick. Her husband had not indicated how he felt about engaging in trade now that he was an earl, but she knew his prickly English pride would probably reject the idea.

"My family lands are profitable enough. We will not require any charity, Beth," he replied stiffly, then realized how harsh that sounded. "I did not intend to appear ungrateful. You may redecorate the Hall any way you wish, puss."

She softened at the wistfully sweet sound of the old endearment. "I have no idea how to manage a vast household such as this, but I will try."

"You'll have Donita to help you—and Percy for companionship," he said placatingly. "Perhaps my wardrobe can last out the year with him removed from the vicinity of my closet."

That brought a ghost of a smile to her lips. "The day we left London your valet was shrieking just like Drum."

"You'd have been shrieking too if you picked up a riding boot and found a dog had made water inside it—and that water was now dripping down the front of your trousers." Derrick saw little amusement in the dog's antics. "The bloody beast gives me ill payment for saving his miserable hide from those *lazzaroni.*"

"I am sorry about your boots and the cravats . . . and the new riding breeches," she added, knowing full well that the tally of Percy's war on Derrick's belongings was far higher. The spaniel had become her protector and seemed to intuit whenever her husband made her unhappy. Percy retaliated in the only ways he knew how. After a moment's hesitation, she dared to ask, "Derrick . . . how long will you stay at the Hall?"

Before he could reply the coach jerked to a sudden stop and a footman opened the door. Derrick jumped lithely to the ground and reached up to assist her down. This was a replay of their wedding afternoon, only this time the servants assembled in front of the house to welcome the master and his new wife were not jovial Neapolitans but dour Cumbrians, as grim and gray as the rainclouds overhead. Beth felt it an ill omen as she smiled at the household staff.

No one smiled back. Derrick presented the chief housekeeper, Mistress Campbell, a tall reed-thin woman with a lantern-jawed narrow face. Her iron-gray hair was knotted so tightly that her facial muscles seemed permanently frozen. She spoke without moving her lips, making a perfunctory curtsy as she murmured, "Welcome to Lynden Hall, your ladyship."

Her eyes reminded Beth of a copperhead snake's just before it struck—cold, dark and pitiless. Repressing a shiver, the new countess moved on to greet the butler, three maids and two footmen, wondering how she would survive once Derrick left her alone here. She was immensely grateful for Donita, who had climbed from the second coach and was supervising the unloading of the trunks in her unique mixture of Italian and English while Percy barked and wagged his tail, following the little maid about.

The interior of the Hall was even more forbidding than had been the city house. It, at least, had been filled with Annabella's tasteless clutter and felt lived in. The old manor was practically empty, stripped of rugs, paintings and many of the best pieces of furniture. Several heavy leaded-glass windows stood bare, denuded of draperies. When Derrick questioned what had become of the family's possessions, the housekeeper replied that the previous earl had them taken to London over the years. Derrick concluded that they'd been sold to pay gambling debts and the high cost of living in the city.

Dinner that evening was a miserable collation of mushy vegetables and gray stringy mutton boiled until it was fit only for slopping hogs. Beth reconsidered. No, the hogs at Blackthorne Hall were fed better than this. By comparison Annabella's dreadful chef at the city house had been a culinary master. After spending weeks arranging household matters in London to her satisfaction, Beth would have to begin an even more daunting task here in the wilderness.

Derrick could see how disheartened his wife was by the Hall. He, too, was shocked by the way it had been treated, but it was the home of his childhood and he loved the wild isolated beauty of the Cumbrian countryside. " 'Tis not Naples, Beth, I know, but you will come to appreciate some things," he said, taking a sip from his glass of bitter claret. Leighton had ravished the wine cellars.

Beth shoved a lump of turnip about on her plate, ignoring his comment as her stomach lurched. "Do you suppose Mistress Campbell thinks to run us off by serving such swill?"

"She has been in service to the family all her life. I shall speak to her about the cook if you wish."

"I will handle it myself. 'Tis best if I begin asserting my role as the countess."

He studied her over the rim of his glass. "You say that as if you are an actress, playing a part that will one day end."

Beth was not sure how to take his remark. *Are you changing your mind about divorce, my love?* "There are times when I feel as if everything since we arrived in England has been but a dream."

"More like a nightmare, I'd warrant," he murmured beneath his breath, finishing off the last swallow of the claret. It was still bitter.

They slept in the old earl's suite. It was cold and drafty, since the chimneys had not been cleaned properly in a decade and the fire went out during the night. Beth had burrowed against Derrick in her sleep for comfort as well as warmth. She awakened alone, chilled to the bone without the heat of his body beside her. The skies outside were still dark owing either to the early hour or the weather, she could not tell which.

It was both. She learned from Mistress Campbell that his lordship had ridden out with his new estate manager at dawn and was not expected back until the dinner hour. There was no time like the present to begin the daunting task of reorganizing the household. "I would like to speak to you regarding the cook, Mistress Campbell," she said, eyeing the breakfast sideboard, which was filled with dishes of lumpy oatmeal, vile-smelling herring and a pot of the blackest, most bitter tea she had ever tasted.

"What of her? She does her job. Never a meal late in this household," the old woman said defensively. Beth could see the hackles rising on the housekeeper's back.

" 'Tis not punctuality I'm concerned with but edibility," she replied sternly. "Please ask her to brew me a small pot of coffee and warm some fresh bread. Then I would like to discuss a new menu plan with you after I've broken my fast."

"We've no coffee on the premises, your ladyship. There's bread already on the sideboard. Cook bakes but once a week."

The remarks more than bordered on insolence. "Then Cook shall learn to bake daily or seek new employment. And I want coffee placed on the next market order," Beth said peremptorily.

The housekeeper straightened her already ramrod stiff spine and replied with venomously narrowed eyes, "As you wish, your ladyship."

This did not augur well, but the shrieks and curses that suddenly erupted from the kitchen were an omen of more immediate disaster. Beth could hear Donita's rapid Italian interspersed with someone—probably the cook—cursing in a rough country accent, followed by Percy's loud bark.

What now? She flew down the long hallway toward the kitchens following the housekeeper, whose long strides were more than a match for her own. The sight that greeted them when they opened the door required immediate action—or else Sir Percival of Inverness would lose his head. The cook stood with a huge cleaver raised in one meaty red fist, ready to deliver the killing blow.

Chapter Twenty-four

"Stop!" Beth commanded in her loudest, most authoritative voice as she pushed past the housekeeper and swept Percy up in her arms. A squab leg dangled from his mouth.

The cook, an old woman as fat as Mistress Campbell was thin, lowered her cleaver grudgingly, her round red face scrunched with fury. " 'Ee stole one 'o me bleedin' birds, 'ee did! 'Anging fer over a fortnight, it were! Just gettin' good 'n ripe fer roastin'."

"Hester, you will cease such vulgar outbursts," the housekeeper said in an icy voice that immediately changed the enraged cook's expression to fawning docility.

"That sorry I am, Mistress Campbell," the cook replied, bowing to the housekeeper before acknowledging the countess.

As the housekeeper upbraided the cook for her cursing, Beth took Percy's prize from him and set him down, then made a swift visual inspection of the kitchen. She was appalled. Several braces of pigeons hung molting from a line stretched across the counter. She could see where the dog had jumped up and snatched one of the decomposing birds, whose noisome stench filled her nostrils. Unwashed pots and pans were stacked everywhere. The hearth was black with soot, and pools of congealed grease lay splashed across the floor.

"I want this kitchen scrubbed from the rafters to the floor by nightfall," she said, getting both women's attention at once. She watched the cook's piggy little eyes narrow in outrage, but it was the housekeeper's silent basilisk glare that worried her as both women nodded in resentful obedience.

The maids and footmen took instruction more politely and set to cleaning cobwebs and grime from ceilings and windows. Making the manor habitable would be a far more daunting task than setting the city house to rights had been. By the time Derrick returned that evening, mud-covered and exhausted, it had become apparent to Beth that both the housekeeper and the cook had to be replaced as soon as possible. However, when she suggested this to him over a supper of fatty roasted pork and stewed rutabaga, he was not completely amenable, to say the least.

"I know the food's abominable. If you must, fire the cook—once you make certain you can hire another one, else we'll be out grazing with the sheep—but I don't want Mistress Campbell dismissed yet. She's been with the family too long and, in truth, she's had no one in residence to serve since my father died."

Beth forbore saying that the old earl had probably died from eating the food in Lynden Hall. Then, seeing the fatigue etched in his face, she asked, "How did your inventory of the land go?"

He sighed wearily. "The crofters' houses are falling down, the sheep scattered from here to Hadrian's Wall, the fields choked with weeds and the stables as denuded of good horses as the manor is of furnishings. But Harris seems quite able. He assures me by spring he can have things up and running properly again. The tenants certainly appeared happy to see the last of Farley. They'll work for the new overseer once I'm forced to return to London."

"I fear that's more than I can say regarding Mistress Campbell," she could not resist adding, angry and frightened at his mention of departure.

Derrick did not leave that week. But he might as well have, Beth saw so little of him. When not out riding about the countryside, he was cloistered in the great cavernous library with Lloyd Harris. Much to Mistress Campbell's dismay, Beth found a new cook, a sweet young widow from an adjoining estate where the elderly baron had just died. Together they planned new menus, and Beth went with Martha to the village to shop for fresh produce, milk and cheese. By spring, they would have their own dairy operating once more and a garden planted.

The meals improved dramatically. Unfortunately, Derrick's company at table did not. When they entered the dining room each evening, he was so weary they did not even argue. Although they continued sleeping in the same bed, he did not make love to her. Her body had started thickening now and she began to fear that he found her physically unappealing.

But perhaps it was only the crushing workload, she tried to convince herself as she stood naked before a cheval glass mirror after climbing out of her bath. She lifted her breasts, now heavy with milk, no longer pert and erect, then slid her palms over her belly, feeling the life growing inside her. It was both her comfort and her sorrow. She dearly wanted Derrick's child, a part of him that she could declare her love to—something she would never be able to do with her husband.

Yet, if his obsessive passion for her was all that held them together, then she would soon lose him. What would happen when he left her, slow and shapeless, and returned to London, the greatest city on earth, filled with slim beautiful women . . . Englishwomen with bloodlines impeccable enough to match his own? Beth seized a towel and began to dry herself off, unable to think of it a moment longer.

She did not see her husband standing in the shadows, watching her. He'd just returned from a grueling day mucking about in ruined oat fields and intended to bathe. He studied the way she ran her hands over her rapidly changing body and his mouth went dry with desire.

He had never found her so beautiful as he did now while she ripened with his child in her womb. But how did Beth feel about it? He could see the small frown marring her brow as she examined the changes in her breasts, the swell of her belly. She had not wanted to carry a babe any more than she wanted to be a wife responsible for a household, he bitterly reminded himself.

'Tis done now and we must make the best of it, he thought as the ache seeped through every pore in his body. An ache that went far beyond physical desire . . . straight to his heart.

By the end of the following week, Beth had organized the household as much as could be done for the present and had begun ordering new furnishings. Until they arrived, there was nothing to stand in the way of her painting.

"It promises to be a good clear day tomorrow," she said that evening over dinner. "I think I shall take a drive to the firth on the morrow and see how different the sea is in the north from the Mediterranean."

At first Derrick seemed not to hear her. He had been thinking about the solicitor's letter that had arrived that morning. He needed to return to London as quickly as possible. He was well pleased with Harris's work and felt he could trust the man to care for matters while he was absent, but he dreaded leaving his wife. Then her words sank in. "Drive to the firth?" he echoed.

"You said 'tis only a couple of miles. I shall take the small gig and that gentle mare, Bessie."

"You shall do nothing of the kind," he said abruptly—and immediately regretted it when he saw the warning flash in her eyes. "What I mean is—"

"You said I could paint if I did not take commissions. Is this how much your vaunted English word is worth?"

315

she said scathingly, throwing her napkin over the pink slice of meat still lying on her plate.

He could not tell her that he feared for her safety even here in the wilds of the north. That morning someone had taken a shot at him, narrowly missing. If Harris's mount had not shied and bumped into his, the bullet would have slammed into his back. The overseer had exclaimed angrily, saying the local gentry were avid hunters and often poached. Derrick explained the situation to Harris, instructing him to see the countess was always guarded. But the fear that Beth might somehow become injured because of him haunted his thoughts.

" 'Tis not safe for you to be out riding about unescorted," he tried to hedge.

"This is not London. You promised that once I retired to the country I could dress and act as I wished—and that I could paint."

"You can paint," he replied, striving to leash his temper. "Paint the Hall, the servants—"

"What appropriate subjects—if I wish to terrify the babe in my womb!"

Always it turned on the fact of her pregnancy . . . and her unhappiness about it, he thought disconsolately. "You should think of the child's safety even if you have a reckless disregard for your own."

"I would never endanger my child!" She felt the bile rise in her throat. He believed her so worthless that she would risk her child's life. "How dare you accuse me of such a thing!"

"Riding could cause a miscarriage. What if the mare was spooked and the gig overturned?" he argued.

"That is beyond absurd. You act as if I was proposing to jump a racer on a foxhunt like your brother—or take a careless fall as you did in London."

"My brother died for his foolishness and I could have broken my neck—an eventuality you might welcome, but until then I am your husband and I say it is too risky."

"Slowly driving a sturdy vehicle such as that gig a few miles over a flat road is no risk at all," she replied stubbornly, desperate to escape the suffocating imprisonment of Lynden Hall. "Nevertheless, I will be willing to take the calash with one of the grooms to drive. What could be safer than that?"

"You will not ride to the ocean or anywhere else. Do I make myself clear, Beth?"

"When are you returning to London?" she asked abruptly.

His cold blue eyes settled on her flushed face with chilling intensity as he smiled at her. It was not a nice smile. "On the morrow, madam, I will rid you of my odious company—but do not think that you may then disobey my expressed wishes. I will instruct Mr. Harris to see that you do not leave. Not a man in the stable will outfit a rig or allow you to touch any of the tack. That, I believe, settles that," he finished icily, pushing his chair away from the table.

Beth sat, stunned by the enormity of his cruelty as he stormed from the room. He was leaving her alone in this big hideous dungeon, isolated from every friend and amenity. Even her art was being taken away from her. What could she do to remain sane?

They lay in the large master bed, side by side that night, each feigning sleep. Hot tears scalded her eyelids, but Beth choked them back, willing herself to hide the terror she felt at the thought of losing him. Would he ever return to Lynden Hall—even to see his heir?

Of course, if the babe was a girl, he'd need to do his duty once more. The very idea of that made her blood run cold . . . *cold as an Englishman's heart.* Were those not Liam Quinn's words? They rang true. As she lay in the silence and darkness, trying not to feel Derrick's heat or listen for the steady thrum of his heartbeat, she thought back to that last London outing when she'd encountered the Irishman. She had also met Lord Byron, who had made a very interesting suggestion. . . .

Derrick could sleep no better than Beth. Every impulse in his body cried out for him to roll over to her and take her in his arms. They could lose themselves in the magic and the torment of their shared passion one last time. But his will overrode the demands of his body . . . or perhaps it was some deeper impulse he could not comprehend. He only knew that it did not seem right.

No. Such passion had proven their undoing. They held different values and viewed life in such opposite terms that there never would be an accommodation between them. After the child was born he would have to set her free. The thought of it was unbearable now. But in time he would grow used to the idea of living without her. While she pursued her art in Italy he would have a part of her with him always . . . her babe . . .

With the dawn, he slipped silently from the bed, relieved to see that she, at least, had finally succeeded in falling asleep. She needed the rest for the burden she carried. He could see purple smudges beneath her eyes and wanted to caress her face, but that might awaken her—to what end? She would remain safe here, guarded by Lloyd Harris while he went to London and untangled the dangerous web that threatened not only his own but her life as well.

He dressed hurriedly, then went downstairs to his library and composed a note for her, promising to return by Christmas. That should give him time enough to learn what Bourdin was up to and deal with him . . . not to mention Liam Quinn. In the meanwhile, Beth would be out of the line of fire and, if all went well, after Christmas he could spend those last bittersweet months with his wife before she left him forever.

For several days after Derrick left Beth moped about, unable to muster enough energy to do anything. True to his word, he had instructed Lloyd Harris to see to it that she was not permitted to ride anywhere. Since she had learned how to handle tack as a girl on her parents' plantation, she considered slipping into the stables while everyone was asleep and rigging up the gig herself. But where could she go in the middle of the night? That would indeed be reckless, and she would do nothing that might endanger her child, no matter what its father believed.

There was one matter to which she could attend: She fired Mistress Campbell. The vile old crone reminded her of Fatima as she stared implacably at Beth with fathomless glowing dark eyes, saying stiffly that once his lordship returned, he'd soon enough deal with his foreign wife and restore his faithful employee to her rightful place in Lynden Hall.

Beth breathed a sigh of relief when the old harridan was gone and found that many members of the household staff immediately became friendlier to her, actually daring to smile and perform tasks cheerfully. She sent inquiries to the vicar in the nearby village and soon located a new housekeeper with excellent references. Mistress Widlow was plump, with a lusty laugh, but she knew how to run the manor with no nonsense.

All of this freed Beth's time to consider what she would do for the six weeks until Christmas. She'd read Derrick's note and prayed that he would indeed return to spend the holiday with her. Perhaps she would give him the portrait as a Christmas gift. He had never seen it. Would he like it? It recalled a far happier time in their lives. Perhaps remembering it would bring him closer to her.

In the meanwhile she busied herself doing sketches of the servants and, on the rare sunny days, drawing the bleak hills and river valley, even the old stone monstrosity in which the Jamison clan had lived for centuries. As she worked at such mundane endeavors, thoughts about doing the seraglio paintings teased the edge of her mind, but she refused to consider them. That would drive a wedge between Beth and her husband that could never be breached. No, she would wait for the holidays and see if they could make some sort of peace for the sake of their child.

She received a post from Bertie saying he would be arriving at his estate within a week. Mercifully, Annabella would not be coming until a few days before Christmas. Beth hoped her sister-in-law and husband did not decide to travel together, then dismissed the idea as silly jealousy. Derrick did not suffer fools gladly.

Biting off her pride, Beth sat down to compose a letter to her husband, assuring him that she was staying close to the Hall. She gave a glowing report of Mistress Widlow and the changed demeanor of the staff, asking him to forgive her for dismissing the former housekeeper. She told him she was looking forward to their spending a quiet Christmas away from London.

As soon as he arrived in London, Derrick set out to locate Evon Bourdin. The Frenchman was living in rather elegant quarters on Chapel Street. How the devil did an unemployed professional soldier afford such luxury when his cousin the Count d'Artois could not? Derrick intended to find Bourdin's source of income. He hired a Bow Street Runner to watch the Frenchman's movements and report to him. Sooner or later, Murat's old comrade in arms would make a mistake.

Liam Quinn was nowhere to be found, although the Runner continued to search. Derrick was dismayed to learn that many of the city's literati had actually found the corsair dashingly romantic. Beth had been given the cut direct because she had been Quinn's victim while the bastard was feted for despoiling innocent women. He itched to deal with the Irishman just as he'd dealt with enemy agents.

Did he miss the excitement of his former life as a spy? No, the rush of danger no longer lured him. Ironically, he, too, was feted by the ton, a sought-after celebrity who cut a dashing figure of mystery and romance. A patriot. A spy. What would his father think about it? he wondered sadly. He was not at all certain the old earl would find his method of serving their country totally acceptable.

The Earl of Lynden immersed himself in business affairs and politics. He attended social engagements only if they were essential for political purposes. At one such event, a scant two weeks after returning to the city, he chanced to encounter his cousin Bertie, who informed him that he was leaving for the country shortly.

Since the day he'd ridden away from the Hall, leaving Beth sleeping with so much left unsaid between them, he had tried not to think of her. And, of course, failed. She was in his dreams nightly. He ached for his wife and knew no way to express his feelings for her. She was doubtless still furious with his high-handed methods of keeping her safe, although she could not know his motives. Perhaps he would oil the waters a bit in preparation for his return at Christmas. He even dared to hope some reconciliation might be possible as he composed the letter.

The fog was thick as molasses, swirling in eddies so dense with foul-smelling smoke that it brought home to Derrick again the necessity for appropriate legislation to improve conditions in the city. He had just left a soiree at Lord Buckingham's house, where he had made several converts to his agenda. Immersed in thought, he took the reins from the groom outside the stable and swung up on Dancer. Kicking the big stallion into a brisk trot, he headed for home.

Home. Where was that? Certainly not in the empty city house where every room bore Beth's imprint. It was tasteful and lovely and utterly empty without her presence to light it. What would he find when he returned to Lynden Hall? He mulled over the situation, his preoccupation dulling long-honed instincts. He did not see the two men materialize from the fog behind him. A third leaped from the top of a carriage, tumbling him from his horse as the other two ran up. One seized the reins of the black and the other joined the melee on the ground.

Derrick had the knife from his boot drawn before they hit the hard cobblestones. The thug who had jumped him felt it bite deep, striking his heart before he could cry out. But the dying man's weight pinned Derrick. Through the noisome swirl of the London fog a stiletto gleamed as it descended. He felt the icy slice of the blade, then the impact of a pistol ball tearing into his gut.

They were professional and quick. Someone spoke in a familiar accent, instructing the two assassins to strip his body. Then he heard the swift pad of their feet and the clop of Dancer's hooves vanishing into the darkness. He lay in the street as the shrill sound of a charley's whistle rent the cold night air.

Then the fog closed in and he felt nothing at all . . .

Chapter Twenty-five

Keening moans and wracking coughs were interspersed with muttered curses and frantic pleas, but the stench of excrement blending with that vilest of human offal, putrefying flesh, wrenched Derrick gagging to consciousness. He tried to move, but his body screamed in protest. With a gasp, he inventoried the origins of the agony. Both his chest and lower abdomen were afire, while his right arm merely throbbed.

When he managed to pry open his eyes and look about, he ascertained he was in a huge room with small, high windows ringing three walls. They were so grimy from the accumulation of city air, almost no light penetrated. Row after row of small, lumpy pallets lined the floors, leaving only narrow aisles between for walking. On these rude beds lay the patients.

At first the scene from hell surrounding him made no sense, but then the fog-drenched street, the three thieves attacking and robbing him, stripping his clothing and valuables, all came back to him. He was in a charity hospital.

Strip him of anything of value.

Bourdin! Telling his minions to be certain the death looked like a robbery. His thoughts swirled as he reached up to touch his itchy face . . . and found a heavy growth of beard. How long had he been lying here?

Then a husky female voice said, "So, ye've finally come 'round, 'ave ye? Me nursin' ain't been wasted."

A tall robust brunette with the pale complexion and apple cheeks of an English schoolgirl stood at the foot of his pallet, looking down at him with a smile that revealed several missing teeth. Other than that defect, she was pretty in a wholesome countrified way. Heavy eyebrows arched over deep brown eyes that had seen more of human misery than most people three times her age. "Me name's Peggie, 'n' I be given yer charge," she continued, still smiling.

"How long have I been here?"

"It be three weeks yesterday, sor. The very devil's luck yer alive after them cutpurses tried to finish ye." She knelt by his side and added in a whisper, "The leech, ole Kitchner, 'e weren't goin' ta bother stitchin' ya after 'e dug the ball out'n yer gut, seein' as 'ow ye were cut so bad. Said it weren't no use, but I told 'em ye were Quality. Even if 'e laughed at me, the ole fool did 'is sewin'. After that I kept yer wounds clean like I were showed, 'n' give ye plenty o' water whilst the fever took ye."

Derrick realized he owed the young woman his life. Even in decent hospitals many patients died from lack of proper attention, and in a dumping ground for the impoverished such as this, his chances of survival without this woman's diligence would have been nil. "I'm profoundly grateful, Peggie . . . but what made you think that I was Quality?"

"Aw, cor, ye talked up a storm in yer fever, ye did, talked like an apothecary . . ." She flushed brightly and looked down. " 'Sides, ye 'ave that look about ye, refined 'n' 'andsome. I knowed ye 'ad to be a gentleman, sor."

"I'm Derrick Jamison, Earl of Lynden." At that announcement her eyes grew enormous and her jaw dropped in awe.

Peggie bathed his face with cool water and gave him a drink, assuring him that she'd been taught to boil the dirty

324

water by the physician who had trained her, a nobleman who had given his life in service to the poor of London. The last thing he remembered was asking her to send word to his house on Pall Mall.

Liam Quinn replaced the glass in his saddlebag and cursed in frustration, then turned his mount and rode carefully from the elm hedgerow where he had hidden as he watched Beth sketching. He had pursued his quarry back to Naples only to find that she had wed Jamison and sailed for England. Kasseim would not be pleased. But abducting an American female wandering the streets of an Italian city was far easier than kidnapping a countess. When he was told that she would be a guest at Lady Holland's soiree, he had been certain he could accomplish his assignment. The new Dey of Algiers had become obsessed with recapturing her and offered the last of his dead father's corsairs an exorbitant reward for bringing her back.

Either she had been utterly remarkable in bed . . . or else Kasseim had not yet had her. Although the arrogant young prince would never admit such a thing, the Irishman knew it was the latter. He'd heard rumors from the palace that the night she'd been presented to Kasseim a large amount of opium was found missing from a secret hiding place in the women's quarters. He grinned, thinking of the haughty prince waking up with a brain clouded by opium-spun cobwebs.

"Ah, colleen, what a pair we'd make . . . if I could but afford to keep you," he murmured to himself. Of course he could not. It was ironic that he and Kasseim wanted a woman who had bested them both.

But he would have her first.

Bertie arrived early just as he'd promised, and Beth considered his visit a gift to save her sanity. The boredom of her confinement in the manor had been intensified by the worst winter in memory. Snow piled up until the dead shrubs in the gardens were white shapeless humps and the roads were all but impassable. Derrick's cousin managed to get through between storms and bring a ray of cheer into what had been the gloomiest December of her life. At her entreaty, he remained at Lynden Hall instead of proceeding on to Wharton to open up his manor. It made sense for all the Jamisons to spend Christmas here.

"Never fear. He'll be along," Bertie assured Beth as she sat disconsolately staring out into the gathering darkness.

"Christmas is only three days away, Coz." She had explained about the numerous letters she'd sent Derrick. The first had been conciliatory. The last beseeching. He had not deigned to reply to any of them. "I do not believe he will come."

"Don't do no good to be all Friday-faced, m'dear," Bertie replied with false heartiness. "Why, my cousin is a man of such unbending principle, he'd never give his word, then break it."

Unable to think of what she would do if Bertie proved wrong, she changed the subject to another almost as unpleasant. "When will Annabella arrive with Constance? I am so looking forward to seeing how much my niece has grown."

"On the morrow, I expect. She and her maid are taking the Carlisle coach, with the nurse for Constance, of course," he added dismissively.

Beth would never get used to the way the English upper classes distanced themselves from their children practically at birth. What would she do if Derrick insisted upon separating her from her babe? Hiring a wet nurse? The practice was not unknown in America, but Beth's mother and Aunt Barbara had never considered it. Nor had she or her siblings and cousins been raised by servants. She would fight Derrick bitterly if he insisted upon English tradition.

"You needn't fear that Bella will spoil the holiday, m'dear," Bertie said, breaking into her brown study. "I read her a peal before I left London. Family and all that. She understands how things are to be," he said, red-faced.

"You are very sweet to think of me after all the trouble I've caused this family."

"Stuff! Our puritanical old Scots roots needed some

pruning, if you ask me. Derrick will learn to appreciate that. Probably has already. I imagine he's riding pell-mell for the Hall even as we speak."

Mid-afternoon of the following day Annabella and her entourage pulled up in a hired coach. As Bertie had assured Beth, her sister-in-law treated her courteously. If it was flummery, Beth did not care as long as they could maintain the veneer of civility sufficiently to get through the holidays. She spent more time with Constance than she did with the child's mother, which suited both women—as well as the little tot—just fine.

Christmas day arrived; Derrick did not. For a change, the weather was bright and sunny, as if mocking her misery. Beth had cursed the rain and snow for weeks but now would have welcomed it—any excuse to explain her husband's untimely delay. There was nothing to be done but put a good face on it, pretending that she was not wounded to her very soul by his absence. She walked down the stairs to the tantalizing aroma of roasting Christmas goose and plum pudding.

Everyone was gathered in the great hall before a roaring fire, even little Connie with her nurse. The mantel and windows were hung with festive greenery trimmed with red velvet bows. And brightly wrapped gifts were scattered about the hearth. Beth looked at the largest one—her portrait of Derrick, which she'd had framed by the village cabinetmaker and lovingly wrapped herself.

Swallowing a lump of utter misery, she managed a smile as she entered the cavernous room. "Merry Christmas, everyone," Beth said brightly.

Annabella smiled tightly and nodded, saying, "The same to you, dear sister." Then, as Beth proceeded to pick up Connie, she added, "I do not see how you can remain so . . . limber in your delicate condition. I was quite unable to lift so much as my jewel case when I was as far along as are you."

"We Americans are a hearty lot," Beth said, winking at Bertie, whom she knew to be embarrassed by any mention of "female matters."

They unwrapped gifts, oohing and aahing over scarves

and hair clips and all manner of extraneous things that no one needed but everyone felt obliged to give. If not for the joy of watching little Connie tear into the toys and then cuddle her new doll, Beth would not have been able to make it through the afternoon. As they withdrew to the dining hall for the traditional feast, she cast one last bitter glance at the largest of Derrick's unopened gifts.

Perhaps she would burn the painting in the Yule fire that night.

"I say, Coz, are you there?"

The gentle tapping at her studio door caused Beth to put down her brush and rise, bidding Bertie to enter. "I've been so busy that I quite forgot the time." She had begun work at dawn that morning after spending Christmas night tossing and turning in the big empty bed. By the time the first hint of light gilded the eastern horizon, the idea had become fixed firmly in her head. She had painted through the day, and dusk was descending. Now she wondered if she dared let her friend in on what she was doing.

"You have been busy. Mind if I take a peek?" he inquired as he walked over to her easel.

"You may be shocked," she cautioned. She watched as he studied the work. Although only just begun, the sketched-in outlines made the subject matter quite apparent.

His eyebrows rose and then he doubled over as a hoarse guffaw of laughter burst forth. Slapping his thigh, he said, "Ain't you the dry boots, Coz! I love it! 'Tis positively smashing!"

"I won't sign them, but 'tis possible my identity will be discovered. Are you sure you don't mind that I might bring further disgrace on the family?"

" 'Twas Byron who gave you the idea. Demned good one, if you ask me."

"Since he's been in the suds, all he may wish is that my scandal will distract from his peccadilloes," Beth replied dubiously.

"Painting nudes in a seraglio bath hardly compares with carrying on with one's own half-sister," Bertie said dryly.

"How many paintings do you think to do? I know an art dealer on Berkeley Square who will be all cock-a-whoop to handle the sales."

Bertie and Annabella departed for London, leaving Beth to her paints. By the end of January she had completed six, four of which were already with Bertie's dealer. She nervously awaited word about how they were received in London. If nothing else would bring Derrick back to Lynden Hall, this just might. Of course he'd be livid and most probably take away her art supplies. As a precaution, she hid in dusty trunks another dozen freshly stretched canvases, pigments, oil and solvents, along with a complete assortment of brushes.

Let him come and try to stop me. Her bitterness had grown with each passing day since the heartbreak of the holidays. She vowed to leave him after the birth of their child. If it was a girl and not his precious heir, she would take her infant daughter with her to America. Not even the bloody Earl of Lynden could take her child from the power of the Blackthorne family.

But what if it was a boy? How could she deprive her son of his birthright? How could she leave her own child behind? The idea tormented her nights as she grew heavy and neared the time for her delivery. The idea of spending her life in this gray wilderness was mind-numbing. The idea of spending her life without Derrick was even worse, but it was his choice to remain in London and banish his scandal-ridden wife to the country.

"I've become a vacillating coward," she murmured to herself as she stood in front of her easel and rubbed her aching back one sunny day in mid-March. In the past she had always worked standing, but that was no longer possible owing to her condition. To keep to the rigorous schedule she'd set herself, she had resorted to using a high kitchen stool, a suggestion of Martha, who was most sympathetic, having carried six children while working in the scullery at Barton Manor.

The cook and housekeeper had become her friends—

outside of Donita, the only companions she had. The forbidding Lloyd Harris refused to allow his master's recalcitrant wife to leave the grounds. He kept the entire outside staff away from her with the exception of old Miller, the gardener, who, with the approach of spring, was mucking about in the rain, preparing the rose beds. Harris had hired Miller from the village to begin restoring the neglected grounds to their former glory. Beth worked with the gardener, who loved to tell stories about the exploits of "those wild Jamison boys."

How sad that her best insights of Derrick were gleaned from an elderly gardener. But Beth quickly shook off her self-pity, pacing across the studio floor to look out the window. Faint hints of green dusted the rolling hillsides and the short, straggly trees were starting to fatten with buds. The sky itself grew brighter. Spring was indeed coming, and with it, her baby.

About to return to a dark and brooding portrait of old Fatima instructing odalisques, Beth paused and squinted down the lane. A coach was approaching! Her first visitor since the holidays. Could it be Derrick? *Do not be foolish,* she chided herself. He had been informed explicitly by the physician in London that the child would not be born for several weeks yet. Of course, he could be here because of the seraglio paintings. She walked slowly downstairs with her heart in her throat. When Bertie climbed clumsily from the carriage and assisted Annabella down, Beth did not know whether to feel relief at the appearance of company or disappointment that it was not Derrick.

"Heigh ho, we've come to celebrate your success," Bertie called out cheerfully.

"My success?" she echoed.

"My, yes, the mysterious artist who signs her work with a black thorn has become the toast of London," Annabella practically gushed.

For a woman who had given her the cut direct when her fate as an Algerine captive became known at Lady Westover's ball, Annabella was behaving oddly. Doubtless she was titillated by her sister-in-law's sudden fame. Smiling,

Beth simply said, "I hoped by using only a symbol taken from my maiden name, I might save the Jamisons embarrassment."

"Even if the truth comes out, 'twill be but a flea bite compared to Byron's latest," Bertie said with a dismissive shrug.

As they walked into the hall Annabella proceeded to detail for Beth the latest scandals involving the lost and brooding George Gordon. Beth identified with his isolation and felt a stab of pity in spite of his sins. Or perhaps because of them. When she could get in a word, she inquired about Connie and was told the child had been left in London with her nurse.

Her sister-in-law felt not the slightest concern over being separated from her daughter. *How can she do it?*

It took him a month after he was brought to the house from hospital to be able to walk across his room. After the long confinement in bed, his muscles were weak, and the doctors clucked about his taking a fall and breaking open the stitches in his chest, abdomen and arm. He ignored them, walking supported by his good arm around Peggie's sturdy shoulders.

The plucky nurse had saved his life, and in return he intended to fulfill her life's dream—installing her in her own infirmary in the East End, among the poorest of the poor. He'd arranged to purchase a building and sufficient medical supplies for the staff she would hire. In the meanwhile, Peggie nursed him with love-struck devotion. Her infatuation was a bit discomfiting, but she possessed great common sense and experience when it came to convalescence.

"There now, 'ow—er, how does that feel?" she said, carefully correcting her speech as she inspected the long pink scar running down his right arm while he flexed the muscles, clenching and unclenching his fist.

"Better, much better," he replied. " 'Twill be good to be able to write legibly again. The solicitors have been most unhappy about deciphering my scribbling."

He stood up and strode across the library to his desk,

where a mountain of papers had been deposited during his disappearance and then the long convalescence after his rescue. He came downstairs now each morning after exercising. Even though busy setting up her infirmary, Peggie had popped in to check on his progress, something she did every day at noon, when he was brought his luncheon tray.

"Be certain ye eats—you eat the beef and barley soup. I made it me—myself. 'Tis good for building strength," she finished, pleased with the turn of phrase.

"I shall do so, Peggie," he replied with a smile as he rolled down his shirtsleeve.

She'd been listening to the servants who worked at the earl's elegant house and wanted to fit in with them. All her life she had striven to rise above the dreadful circumstances of her birth, and now she'd been given an opportunity to learn proper English.

Peggie Halloran looked forward to her new project with decidedly mixed emotions. When that wonderful day arrived she would have to bid farewell to the earl. If only he were not so lonely. What must his American wife be like that she never replied to any of his lordship's letters? Peggie had seen how he searched the mail brought into his library each morning, hoping for word from her. Letters from his overseer at the great manor house arrived regularly, but not a single line from the cruel countess.

Although he never spoke of his wife, Peggie had listened to servants' gossip since she came to work for the earl. The woman was apparently a libertine, used to the debauchery of the Italians and, even more scandalous, she had actually lived in some heathen seraglio! Whyever had a fine honorable man such as the earl wed such a wanton?

She knew that the main reason the earl was so desperate to recover his strength was so that he could ride to Lynden Hall in time for the birth of his heir. Although he never said so, she could tell that he was still in love with his wife. A man as well-favored as he could have his pick of paramours—from the highest ladies of the peerage to the fanciest of the Covent Garden bits-o-muslin.

Yet he remained faithful to his Beth.

Wanton Angel

*   *   *

The scandal spread from one end of London to the other. That mysterious painter of harem life was none other than the Earl of Lynden's American wife, who had actually been one of those decadently lounging nudes. No one dared to mention this in front of the earl, of course. He learned about the debacle from his highly embarrassed solicitors, who informed him of the astronomical sums the Quality as well as the Cits were paying for his wife's work. It was rumored that even the Regent himself had one of the paintings hanging in his bedroom.

The name of Elizabeth Blackthorne Jamison, the Countess of Lynden, was on everyone's lips. Even though Derrick's finances were certainly on the mend, he could not afford to buy up all the paintings to get them out of circulation. What he could do was ride at once to the Hall, destroy what she was currently working on and take away her paints.

It would be tantamount to taking the breath from her body.

"Ah, puss, what a fine tangle we have made," he murmured sadly, staring at the erotic and lovely work of art, the last of the new arrivals on display at a gallery on Berkeley Square.

"Her use of light is quite extraordinary," Ralph Hightower, the gallery owner, said hesitantly as he approached the earl. "She is almost the equal of Mr. Turner."

"She studied with him in Naples last year," Derrick replied, still staring intently at the haunted expression in the eyes of the woman being perfumed and powdered in the painting. She bore no physical resemblance to Beth, but he knew his wife had put a part of her soul into the work.

He bought the painting and extracted an oath from the dealer to bring any more of the countess's work to him. After arriving home with the canvas, he locked himself in the study with orders not to disturb him until further notice. Sitting before the picture, he then proceeded to empty a bottle of brandy as he stared into the fathomless eyes of the odalisque.

333

Chapter Twenty-six

Evon Bourdin had waited for the perfect opportunity since his disastrously failed attempt on Derrick's life the past December. No more hiring cheap, ineffective thugs to waylay Derrick on public streets. The Frenchman composed a note very carefully and had it delivered to Derrick's house late in the afternoon, just as a light spring rain began to fall.

Derrick read the message. The Count d'Artois requested the pleasure of his company this evening to discuss a matter of some delicacy. He had come into possession of a most shocking painting done by the earl's wife. The note suggested that the work far surpassed the others in the nature of erotic detail.

Derrick's first impulse had been to throw the sly missive into the fire and watch the Frenchman's spidery script turn to ashes. But something stayed his hand. Could she have painted something so lascivious that a jaded old roué such as the count would be titillated sufficiently to attempt blackmail? Her other works were exquisitely rendered, haunting and far more sad than titillating. He had spent hours studying the one he'd purchased and felt as if he had looked into Beth's tortured soul. It was an expression of genuine art, not the sort of erotica about which the count hinted.

Does she hate me so much that she'd paint such a thing as d'Artois describes?

The question haunted him as he rode Dancer through the gathering darkness to the count's current lodgings. The stallion had been returned to him when the thief attempted to sell him at Tattersalls. Derrick had one of the Bow Street Runners riding with him, posing as a groom. Both men were alert for assassins. Either Bourdin or Quinn could be lurking around the next corner.

Derrick was ushered into the narrow foyer by a grimfaced servant who merely pointed toward the sitting room door, which stood ajar. The old itch was back. Something did not feel right. The moment he stepped into the room and saw the count lying on the floor, he knew his instincts were still good. D'Artois had been shot through his heart. An ugly red stain stood out starkly on the gold satin waistcoat stretched across his fat belly. He was stone cold dead.

"I'll simply place the count's weapon in his hand after I shoot you with it. You, sadly, will already have shot poor d'Artois," Evon Bourdin purred as he stepped from behind the heavy velvet draperies at the window with a fancy new LePage percussion lock pistol leveled at Derrick.

Beth had worked all day in her studio to escape from Annabella's cloying presence. Frankly, she preferred her sister-in-law's snide hostility to false solicitude. "Listening to her go on at the dinner table makes my head ache almost as much as my back," she groused to Percy who barked agreement. He had been banished from the dining room for the duration of the family visit as he terrified Annabella into fits of the vapors.

Beth rubbed the persistent pain low in her back that had been plaguing her for the past several days. Small wonder; she was large as a sow about to birth a dozen piglets. There was no help for it but to dress for dinner. Perhaps she could prevail upon Annabella to torture the pianoforte. Even though she was a wretched musician, it was better than listening to her prattle. After ringing for Donita and ordering a bath, she sank into the big tub.

The little maid startled her, saying in Italian, "The master will be here soon."

Beth stiffened. Donita had never spoken of the tense situation between her and Derrick before. "What would make you think that?" she asked guardedly. If this had been any other of the servants but her longtime maid, Beth would never have tolerated the comment.

"The babe has dropped. Your time is coming soon, and I know he will wish to be here to see his child born."

"The physician Derrick engaged from Carlisle insists I have several weeks to go yet. What makes you think it will be sooner?" Beth wondered why the girl seemed so certain that the earl cared enough to come for the birth, but she did not ask.

"My mother was a midwife. I assisted her at many births. If you would like . . . I would be with you during your time," she said shyly. "I do not believe that fancy doctor knows as much as he thinks he does. Women know how to care for women—men do not," Donita sniffed.

"I would like that very much, Donita. Thank you," Beth replied.

As she walked down the hall toward the stairs, Beth mulled over Donita's remarks. Was her time nearer than she had been told? And would Derrick come in any event? Money had been pouring in from the sale of her seraglio paintings and she could not believe he had taken no measures to stop her work. He must be making arrangements for a divorce that would disinherit her child. That was the only reason he would ignore her transgressions this way, she decided bleakly.

Her troubled thoughts were broken when she heard Bertie's voice coming from Annabella's quarters at the head of the stairs. Even if they were cousins by marriage, it was hardly proper for him to be there. A draft from the open window at the end of the hall must have pushed the heavy door ajar just a tiny crack. She could hear their angry exchange quite clearly as she approached the room.

"We must wait until the child is born, my love. If 'tis a boy, then we will let that Irishman take her, but if 'tis naught but a girl, she can pose no threat."

"No!" Annabella responded to Bertie's wheedling tone. "I want that loathsome American baggage gone. I can endure not another day of feigning civility to a . . . a seraglio harlot. Why, look at those paintings she's doing! How will we ever live it down if she remains in England? I simply won't have it, Bertie, do you hear me, I won't have it! I want her sent back to that dreadful dey."

"Now, now, Bella, don't work yourself into a pet. I shall have to send word to Quinn in any event, and that will take time. . . ."

As he continued on, Beth backed away from the door, robbed of breath by the horror of what she'd overheard. Quinn! Here in the north, ready to abduct her and return her to Algiers! Her head reeled with the terror of it—and the treachery. Was there no one in this accursed place whom she could trust?

Harris! She would go to Lloyd Harris and tell him what she had overheard. Derrick had utter faith in the man. She turned to flee down the stairs when a sudden stabbing pain ripped through her abdomen, wrenching a sharp gasp from her as she doubled over, holding her belly.

The baby was coming! Donita had been right. She forced herself to straighten up and head for the stairs, but Bertie had heard the sound and noted the crack in the door. With a muttered curse he flung it open. Moving with amazing speed and grace, he seized her by one wrist and yanked her to his side. Had his cow-handedness also been an act?

As Beth looked into the cold, implacable depths of his gray eyes, she knew that the fumbling, kindly personality certainly had been. She opened her mouth to scream, but another contraction tore through her, once again robbing her of breath as he dragged her into the sitting room and closed the door.

"We need something to bind her with," he said to Annabella. "The drapery cords will do," he instructed as he extracted a white linen handkerchief from his waistcoat, preparing to stuff it in Beth's mouth.

"Why, Bertie? Why are you doing this?" Beth asked.

He looked at her with what appeared to be a touch of genuine regret. "Why, to be the next Earl of Lynden, m'dear. My darling Bella quite enjoyed being the countess and will be again after we're wed."

The expression on his face reminded her of Liam Quinn's that night at Lady Holland's salon and she felt chilled to the bone. "You plan to kill Derrick," she said with dread choking her.

"Your precious husband will soon be dead," Annabella said with all the venom of a woman scorned. "He made far too many enemies while he ran about Europe as a spy, I fear. Evon Bourdin salivates to kill him." A sly smile curved her tiny bow mouth.

"No!" Beth cried out, wrenching away from Bertie's grip when he reached for the bindings. Using strength born of utter desperation, she shoved Annabella against Bertie and lunged for the door. He was after her in a flash, capturing her just as she pulled it open—and felt the terrible agony of another contraction. She screamed through it as Bertie cursed and tried to haul her back into the room before any servants chanced to hear her cries.

But Beth held on to the doorknob with a white-knuckled grip while Bertie hissed to Annabella, "My pistol's in your bedroom. Get it!"

"You can't hold the entire staff of the manor at bay, Bertie. Release me and I'll let you go," Beth said as Annabella dashed into the adjoining room. They had been sleeping together here in the manor! "Can't you see, she's just using you to regain her title."

"Perhaps," he said in that oddly regretful voice. "But I adore her; have ever since we were children. Sad to say, I'm only a baron, and my gel has her heart set on wedding an earl."

Annabella dashed back into the room, holding the pistol in front of her awkwardly. It was apparent that she had never shot a gun in her life. Beth released her hold on the doorframe suddenly, throwing Bertie off balance as she lunged awkwardly against him. Her hand shot out toward Annabella as she tried to seize the double-barreled Manton pistol.

"Ah, no you don't," Bertie said, grabbing the gun dexterously and swinging it around to her breast.

Just then a loud bark sounded as Percy burst into the room. Bertie's eyes shifted for an instant to the dog, and Beth seized his gun hand in hers, raising the pistol overhead as they struggled with it. He started to slap her with his left hand, but the dog sank his teeth into his leg before he could connect. The searing pain in his hamstring brought forth a torrent of curses as he kicked at the dog and yelled at Annabella, "Demme, give some help here!"

Beth wanted to scream, but she needed every ounce of her strength just to hold on to Bertie's deadly weapon. Annabella stood frozen in horror as they struggled over the pistol. The dog, who terrified her, would not relinquish his hold on Bertie's leg. He and Beth overbalanced and fell against the doorframe, smashing her arm into the wall, but still the American would not relinquish her hold on the pistol, gripping it with maniacal strength as she fought her way through another contraction. She and Bertie both had their hands wrapped around the weapon, waving it wildly back and forth between them, neither quite able to point it at the other.

Trembling and sobbing, Annabella picked up a poker from the fireplace and tried to get near enough to strike Beth, but the struggling combatants kept twisting and turning so that the dog was between her and them. Feeling another contraction beginning to tear at her, Beth made a desperate lunge forward. This would be her last chance. She succeeded in slipping her thumb inside the trigger guard on the pistol and pressed against Bertie's finger as they stumbled on the edge of the carpet. Their hands moved in a downward arc from above their heads while Beth tried to turn the barrel toward Bertie, squeezing with all her strength.

The gun discharged with a deafening roar. Annabella fell backwards, the poker dropping from her hand as she stared dumbly down at the blossoming red stain on the front of her pink silk gown. She teetered for a moment, then crumpled to the floor as Bertie cried, "Bella! My darling Bella!" and shoved Beth away. Percy released his hold and stood protectively in front of Beth, snarling.

She doubled over in a contraction as Bertie knelt and cradled Annabella in his arms, frantically trying to staunch the bleeding and sobbing uncontrollably. "Don't die, Bell, my Bell, please don't die, my beloved, my only."

Beth felt the stream of wetness flowing down her legs as the agony of the contraction began to fade. Her water had broken. She could hear the pounding of footsteps from down the stairs and the cries of servants. She stumbled out into the hall with Percy.

A young footman approached, white-faced and breathless, followed by the butler and Mistress Widlow, both puffing to keep up. "Whatever has happened?" the housekeeper asked, taking charge when the other servants made way for her. They all stood back and gawked at the countess, who was doubled over, panting and disheveled, with her gown torn and her hair hanging in ratty clumps.

"Inside . . . they . . . tried to . . . tried to . . ." Beth got no further as the breath was squeezed from her lungs by searing pain. With the end of the fight for her life, the frantic strength deserted her, and she crumpled onto the floor. Donita came running past Mistress Widlow and knelt beside her mistress. Percy moved back, whimpering frantically now as he watched Beth.

"The babe comes," Donita said in her broken English, seeing the puddle of water around Beth. "Take her to room." She pointed toward the master bedroom down the hall.

Just as two of the footmen came forward to do her bidding, a second shot reverberated through the open door of Annabella Jamison's sitting room.

*　　*　　*

"Would you please be so kind as to open your greatcoat and remove the pistols I know you have concealed within—very carefully." Evon Bourdin glided across the carpet, stepping over the fat old count's body as negligently as if he were a stray dog dead in the gutter.

Derrick slowly opened his dampened raincoat. "I did not come here alone," he said. "Before you can arrange the little scene to your satisfaction, my man will hear the shot and come rushing in."

Bourdin laughed nastily. "Ah, I believe my man Valeri can take a mere groom. You see, I had this old capon"— he nudged d'Artois's body—"dismiss his household servants for the day, then arranged for Val to admit you to the house."

"Why kill your cousin? He was your entrée to English society," Derrick said as he slowly slipped the coat from his shoulders. *Come closer, Bourdin . . . come closer.*

Bourdin sneered. "The pompous fool was displeased with my enterprise. The pistols, Jamison, the pistols," he purred, pointing to the brace of stubby Clark pistols in Derrick's sash.

"You seem to have made a life's work out of unsuccessful attempts to kill me. I'd scarce call such enterprise," Derrick said as he dropped one pistol onto the carpet.

"Ah, but there is more, so much more . . . involving your bitch of a wife." When Derrick's eyes flared with anger, the Frenchman could not resist taunting him. "She and your heir will be disposed of quite neatly. In fact, if your sweet sister-in-law has her way, I imagine the American whore will be in Quinn's clutches shortly. Tut," he scolded, gesturing to the second pistol. "Drop it."

Quinn at Lynden Hall! Derrick struggled to remain calm as thoughts of Beth and their child in danger set his heart pounding. With the greatcoat still hanging from his left hand, the Englishman tossed the second pistol on the floor as he said, "Bella could scarce mastermind a scheme to rid herself of Beth, no matter how much she may hate my wife."

"Ah, but your dear cousin Bertie could. He is really quite

clever, you know, a veritable chameleon. When he becomes the earl—"

"His dear Bella will become a countess once again." It was all coming horribly clear.

" 'Twas very cooperative of you to banish your wife and return to London." Bourdin stepped closer to stage the exchange Derrick would appear to have had with d'Artois. "Now I have the pleasure of killing—"

When Bourdin's hand tensed on the pistol, Derrick flung his greatcoat at the Frenchman's arm. The heavy garment threw off his aim and the shot grazed Derrick's jacket sleeve as he sprang forward, knocking Bourdin back. He tripped over d'Artois's body and tumbled to the floor. Derrick was on him, the knife from his boot now in his hand. The Frenchman had dropped his weapon when he hit the floor, but as they rolled across the carpet, struggling over the dagger in the Englishman's hand, Bourdin groped frantically to recover one of Derrick's pistols.

Derrick was still weakened by his long ordeal, but sheer terror for Beth lent him superhuman strength as they fought. From the corner of his eye he saw the pistol in Bourdin's hand. He lowered his head, butting it hard into his foe's face. Derrick's grip on the dagger never wavered as he slashed the blade directly across the Frenchman's throat.

Bourdin made a horrible gurgling noise, then dropped the pistol to the carpet. The sound of the shot and ensuing struggle had brought the Frenchman's thug on the run, but it also brought Derrick's man pounding up the front steps. Seizing the pistol from the carpet, Derrick rolled onto his back and aimed at the figure in the doorway, firing a split second before the false butler was able to shoot him.

A second shot hit the man from the other side of the door an instant later. Then the Bow Street Runner came rushing into the room. "Are you all right, yer lordship?"

"He didn't hurt me," Derrick replied tersely as he scrambled to his feet and quickly retrieved his pistols and coat. "Summon the authorities and then remain here to explain what happened. Bourdin killed the count. He planned to kill me and make it appear as if we'd shot each other. That fellow dressed in butler's clothes is one of his hired ruffians," he explained as he headed for the door. "I'm going after my cousin—Albert Wharton Jamison is behind this whole thing!"

When he reached Bertie's house no one answered his frantic pounding on the door. If Bertie had seen him racing up the steps, he would try to flee after instructing the servants not to answer the door, Derrick reasoned. He would take great delight in choking the life from his dear deadly cousin—once he learned from the bastard just what Quinn's plans were for Beth. Perhaps it was not too late to call off the corsair before harm came to her.

"She is such a love," Martha Rumsford said, smiling down at the infant nursing at Beth's breast. The cook placed a tray beside the chair where the new mother and child sat, instructing Beth sternly, "Now you eat every bite. I've made all yer favorites. You got to keep up yer strength to feed the little dumpling."

The "little dumpling" made a cooing noise and fell fast asleep. Beth smiled down at her child, feeling a wave of love well up so strongly that it brought tears to her eyes. Now she understood what her mother had tried to explain to her about having children. If only she and Derrick could have a relationship like her parents'.

But that was not to be. She prayed he was safe. Mr. Harris had ridden pell-mell for London to warn Derrick about Bertie and Annabella's perfidy and to explain the tragedy that had occurred here. She stroked the child's soft cap of dark hair, thinking of all the additional scandal and disgrace her involvement in a murder suicide would bring.

Poor Bertie had been so deranged when he saw that his beloved Annabella was dead, he'd fired the second shot from his Manton and ended his life. They had been buried together quietly in the family plot.

When Beth had explained to the local sheriff what had transpired, she knew he did not believe her. Who would take the word of a notorious American adventuress, even

343

if she was a countess? The village officials only waited for the return of the earl before they dared to charge her with her sister-in-law's murder. If not for her child, Beth would not have given a fig for her own life. It stretched so bleakly before her . . . without Derrick.

Suddenly, she heard the sound of footfalls and excited voices raised outside the door of the master bedroom. Then the door swung open and he strode into the room, a fierce, unreadable expression on his face.

"Hello, Derrick," she said softly, clutching the babe close to her breast.

Chapter Twenty-seven

"Hello, Beth," he replied, struggling to stay on his feet. On the punishing ride to the Hall, he had used up every ounce of his strength. He felt light-headed as he studied her. She looked positively radiant. That wretched spaniel sat on the bed beside her, as proud as if he were the new father. "I understand I have a daughter," he said, looking down at the infant in her arms, ignoring the dog.

" 'Tis not the heir you sought. I know how much you wanted a son." Her voice sounded unnaturally tight and high to her ears.

"We could always have a son, puss." *We could . . . if I did not have to let you go.* "The important thing is that you are unharmed and our daughter is safely delivered after all that's happened. Have you named her?"

He did not even care enough about a daughter to select a name. "If you wish, we can name her for your own mother," she said stiffly.

"No," he replied more sharply than he intended. "That is, I believe you have the right to choose her name. Have you?"

She looked down at the sleeping infant. "Vittoria Madelyne . . . if that is agreeable to you?" she said uncertainly.

Derrick smiled a bit sadly, nodding. "Vittoria Madelyne it is, puss."

She could have been killed because of him and his bloody title. He stepped closer to the bed, fighting the urge to take her in his arms, knowing that it would only make what he had to do more difficult. Beth was loyal. She had pledged her troth to him and she had struggled in a hostile and alien world to make the best of her bargain—in spite of his neglect. He'd gone out to save the world and his family's honor and almost cost his wife and child their lives. But as usual, his resourceful American had managed to save herself.

"Beth, there is much we have to discuss—"

"Have the servants explained about Bertie and Annabella—that the sheriff wishes to speak to you? He believes I was responsible for what happened," she said, struggling to keep her voice steady. He looked oddly pale, and perspiration dampened his brow in spite of the coolness of the day.

"The sheriff is a fool. I'll deal with him," he said dismissively, trying to focus on what he had to say, but the room kept spinning as he attempted to gather his thoughts. How many days had it been since he'd slept? "Beth . . ."

"Derrick!" she cried as his eyelids fluttered down and he started to fall. Still holding the baby in one arm, she reached out to him with the other, pulling him onto the bed before he crashed to the floor.

In a moment, she had half a dozen servants racing into the room. Ever since her brush with death at the hands of Bertie and the former countess, Beth found everyone hovering about her protectively. "Put him in this bed," she said, sliding from the opposite side as two burly footmen did her bidding. She could sleep in the adjoining room . . . for the short amount of time she would be here.

Handing Donita the sleeping baby, Beth began undressing Derrick, horrified to see how thin he'd become since

346

last fall. Then she saw the shiny pink of newly healed scar tissue on his chest, abdomen and arm. Dear God, he could have died of infection from injuries such as these! Bertie must have hired other assassins besides Bourdin.

Looking down at Derrick's haggard face and newly healing injuries, she could not be sorry she had accidentally killed Annabella, nor that Bertie had decided to kill himself. With them both dead, her husband and child were safe.

Beth caressed his brow, brushing back that lock of black hair that always fell over it. He was pale and sweating, utterly exhausted from the long ride. Had he learned about Bertie and Annabella before she did? Was that why he had exhausted himself, riding from London?

"Always duty, my love," she murmured sadly as she finished stripping him with the aid of one of the footmen. Then she called for lots of warm water and soap. He was filthy, as if he'd not taken time to bathe in a week. Perhaps it was foolish not to have one of the male servants do it. She was letting herself in for even more pain. One last time, Beth would touch his body, caress it as she ministered to him.

You're not the only one who's a slave to duty, she thought ironically as the soapy cloth glided across his chest.

Beth sat at the credenza in the small suite of rooms adjoining the master bedroom. With Derrick tossing and turning next door, she'd gotten little rest. The family physician who was supposed to deliver Vittoria had been summoned from Carlisle to examine Derrick. Her husband was more in need of his services than she had been.

Placing the pen aside, she allowed herself a bit of a smile, remembering how Donita had guided her through the birth. By the time Dr. Fielding had arrived, she had been sitting up in a chair feeding her newborn daughter. The pompous old man had almost scolded her for daring to bring the child into the world before he was present.

This time he clucked over Derrick's injuries but assured

Beth that they were healing nicely. Derrick only required several days of rest and nourishing food to restore him to health. The physician insisted on putting a sleeping potion into the herbal tea Martha had prepared and stood sternly over Derrick as he, unaware, drank it down.

The impetuous young earl should not have risked his health on such an arduous ride, Dr. Fielding sternly told Beth. He had heard all the gossip about her and the deaths at Lynden Hall and seemed to imply that everything was her fault, even if he did not say so directly. She knew everyone from Carlisle to London blamed her. Derrick would have no difficulty at all securing a divorce.

Beth returned her attention to the letter she was composing for Derrick. By the time he awakened and read it, she would be gone, taking Vittoria with her. He would have more children. She would not give up her daughter.

As if understanding her struggle, Percy sat at her side, his brown eyes sorrowful as he looked up at her. She finished the letter and signed her name, then laid her head down on the desk for a moment.

By twilight everything was ready for their departure. The only one who knew her plans was Donita, who had pleaded to go with her. But the little maid was desperately homesick and Beth knew it would be far kinder to send her back to her family in Naples. With only Percy for company, she and her daughter would sail for America.

All the stable men had gone to the kitchens for their evening meal when she slipped into the musty barn where the rigs were kept, leading two of the steadiest of the carriage horses. Seated in a pile of straw nearby, Percy guarded the sleeping baby, watching Beth as she hitched up the team.

Derrick was awakened from his drugged slumber by a very hesitant valet, who informed him that the sheriff had just arrived from Carlisle and was waiting downstairs. "He says it is a matter of great importance, m'lord," Conway said apologetically as Derrick struggled to sit up on the edge of the bed, trying to clear his fogged brain.

"I feel as if I've been drugged," he muttered half to himself. "How long have I slept?"

"Since you arrived, m'lord. A bit over four and twenty hours," Conway replied as he assisted his master in dressing.

Derrick stopped midway in sliding his good arm into a shirtsleeve and narrowed his eyes at the valet. "Damn, I *was* drugged! 'Twas that idiot Fielding and his accursed possets."

"I'm sure I wouldn't know, m'lord. Her ladyship did say you needed your rest . . . but the sheriff—"

"Another damned idiot," Derrick snarled as he fastened his shirt while Conway brought him a pair of breeches.

His mouth felt as if he'd chewed through the stable floorboards and an itchy growth of beard gave his face a piratical cast when he walked into the library to greet Sheriff Bosley. Although he was not in the mood to deal with the officious ass, the sooner he set the fellow straight, the sooner the fool would cease harassing Beth. "I understand you have something urgent to tell me, Sheriff," Derrick said brusquely as the man struggled out of the side chair in which he had made himself comfortable.

The sheriff was a short, squat man of sixty years with a pale doughy face that tended to redden whenever he exerted himself. Since he weighed over fifteen stone, just standing up required significant exertion. "Yes, m'lord, I do." Bosley harrumphed as he produced two thick bundles of envelopes.

"These are for you and her ladyship, m'lord . . ." Bosley handed the papers to Derrick. His voice trailed off in nervous silence before he cleared his throat and continued, "One of the village lads who worked at Wharton Hall brought the whole of them to me after learning of the baron's death . . . and that of Lady Annabella. It seemed the baron had bribed the post rider to turn over all correspondence coming into and going out of Lynden Hall so that he could inspect it before it was forwarded. These were held back."

Derrick had torn open the ties holding the packets and

could see that one was his letters to Beth, but the other packet was letters sent by her to him in London. "Why did he not want us to communicate?" he said more to himself than to the sheriff as he tore open the first of her letters.

"It was not the baron, m'lord." Now Bosley's face grew quite red. "After I received these, I felt duty bound to go to Wharton Hall and question the staff. It seems the baron only wanted to read them, then pass them on after he learned the contents. . . . Several of the servants accused the former countess of holding back the letters."

Bella's jealousy. Yes, it made tragic sense, he supposed. If he and Beth were gone, she could wed Bertie and once more resume what she believed to be her rightful place. He thanked the sheriff for performing his duty so well and dismissed him after making it clear that the baron and former countess had attacked his wife, who was an innocent victim in their conspiracy. Apologizing profusely for ever suspecting Lady Lynden of wrongdoing, Bosley departed.

Derrick sat down to read her letters. How lonely she had been. He'd exiled her, then seemed to desert her with callous disregard for her feelings. Her appeals had begun earnestly, much as his had—and much as his had, her letters took on sharper tones each time there was no response. But was he reading too much between the lines when he dared to hope that she wanted to be his wife and looked forward to the birth of their child? The only way to find out was to speak with her, to offer her the freedom to leave him and their daughter if she wished to do so . . . and then pray she would stay.

Slowly he approached her quarters, his heart hammering in his chest so loudly that he feared she would hear it over his knock on her door. When she did not answer, he turned the knob and pushed the heavy oak panel open. She was not in the small sitting room. Years of instinct told him that she was not in the bedroom either. But a small envelope with his name on it sat propped against the candlestick on the table in plain sight.

A feeling of intense foreboding swept over him as he tore it open and extracted the letter, reading:

My Dearest Derrick,
Please forgive my taking the coward's way out, but it seemed easier. I possess the courage to write what I could never say directly to your face, for I know your stubborn sense of duty would force you to bid me stay when we both know it is best that I leave. I have become even more of an embarrassment to you than I was in London. Bertie and Annabella's deaths will fuel the gossip mills across the nation and I shall be at the heart of it. Please believe that I intended no harm to either of them. The servants will verify what went on just prior to Vittoria's birth. I am taking her with me since I cannot bear to be parted from her. She will only grow up to be a wanton hoyden like her mother. If I had borne your heir, I do not know if I would have possessed the courage to leave him behind. Perhaps 'tis an omen, that I did not have to make such a painful decision, for I surely would have stayed rather than lose my child. Now you may have a dutiful English wife from a noble family, a woman who will make you happy as I could not. There is nothing to stand in the way of that happiness now.
Beth

She had added a postscript, explaining that she had sent for Constance and her nursemaid and begged Derrick to allow Tilda to continue to care for his niece now that the little girl would be his ward.
As always, puss, I have completely misunderstood and underestimated you.
How long could she have been gone? Frantically, he tore down the stairs, yelling for Mistress Widlow to assemble the entire staff. In moments, he knew that she had not been seen since the preceding evening, having instructed Donita to bring a tray to her quarters at half past six. The maid tearfully confessed under his daunting interrogation that

Shirl Henke

her mistress had set out for Bowness, the nearest small port, so that she could arrange passage to Liverpool, where Blackthorne Shipping had offices.

The small seaport was just beginning to show signs of life when she reached the waterfront. She'd driven by the light of a full moon until it set, then fed Vittoria and dozed in the carriage until sunrise. Feeling unutterably weary and sad, she surveyed the small coastal trawlers bobbing in the tiny harbor. The smells of ocean brine, fish and early morning fog were familiar, reminding her fleetingly of Naples.

But she must not think of that, for to do so would bring memories of Derrick and she could not bear it. She had taken only the jewelry she owned, leaving behind all the Jamison heirlooms for his new bride, including her wedding ring. If the money she had brought along was not sufficient, she hoped the glitter of an opal brooch would be impressive enough to convince a simple fisherman to make the long passage south.

As a safety precaution, she carried not only her old stiletto from Naples but also the small Parker pocket pistol that had been a gift from her brother Rob when she'd left Savannah. A woman alone with an infant would be at best a curiosity and a scandal, but at worst she might attract thieves or rapists. Because this was a small, hardworking community, she doubted there would be trouble. Percy remained close by her side after she climbed from the carriage. The village shacks were rundown and dirty, reeking of fresh fish and old poverty.

She did not see the tall shadow of the figure following at a discreet distance. He observed as she approached the lone fisherman sitting at the bow of an old craft that looked not at all seaworthy. Blessing the good fortune that had sent her his way, he waited until the man told her what he had been paid to say. Beth turned and headed for a large deserted-looking shack standing some distance from the rest.

Having been informed not to knock but simply to enter

and call upstairs, she cautiously opened the creaking door and stepped inside. He did the same from the rear, blinking his bright green eyes until they became accustomed to the dim light.

"Hello," Beth called up the rickety stairs. The place was filthy, with thick dust and cobwebs everywhere. If not for the candle on the desk, she'd think the fisherman had misinformed her. The pistol hidden in her cloak pocket gave her a measure of confidence, but she knew that she could do little to defend herself while holding Vittoria. Just as she took a step toward the table to place her daughter on it and instruct Percy to guard her, the dog began to growl.

"Tie the beast to that post, else I'll be forced to kill him," Liam Quinn said conversationally as he stepped out from a hallway of the old warehouse. He sighted in on Percy with one of the ornately engraved Neapolitan Miquelet-lock pistols he had carried as a corsair. Another of the deadly weapons was in his left hand, pointed at Vittoria.

"The baron is dead, Quinn," she managed in a far calmer voice than she felt. "He cannot pay you, nor can Annabella. She's dead, too."

He shrugged, drawing slowly closer, then stopping far enough back so the dog could not get a running jump at him. "Alas, a pity, that. I would have been paid double. Now I shall just have to settle for the price Kasseim promised me. Perhaps I'll get a bonus for bringing him your girl child. He can have her trained to be a much more proper odalisque than you."

Beth fought the surge of nausea that swamped her at the mention of such a fate for her innocent daughter. *Think! You have a pistol and a dagger. Get Vittoria out of the line of fire.*

She commanded Percy to sit and stay, then laid her baby on the floor by his side. "I have nothing with which to tie him," she said in what she hoped was the dull voice of defeat, starting to move away from them.

"Not so fast, sweeting. Stay close by your little one's side just as a good mother should always do . . . you are a good mother, are you not?" he asked as he tossed a length of rope at her feet.

"My husband will pay you more than Kasseim," she bargained. Quinn was without principles, but not without sense.

He laughed aloud. "The earl would hoist me by my balls if given the chance. He does have the devil's own luck. Have you any idea how many attempts on his life have failed since his dear cousin finally learned he was in Naples?"

"You're afraid of him." Perhaps anger would cause him to become careless. But Quinn only watched her closely, seeing that the knots fastened to the dog's collar were secure. She was three steps from Vittoria. This might be her best opportunity for a shot without endangering her daughter.

"I would have liked nothing better than to kill another Englishman, most particularly an earl, but a duel in London would not have been . . . expedient. This is the better revenge—taking his woman from him. I have been waiting and watching you since winter's chill. Imagine my delight when you rode off with your babe and no man to protect you. Your earl's servants kept a close leash on you until now.

"He was the lover you pined for when first we met, was he not?" Quinn studied her for a moment, then said, "I thought so. If I had killed him, a swift version of English justice would have been meted out to an Irishman."

"If you had succeeded in killing my husband, I would have been the one to mete out justice," she said through gritted teeth, reaching into the pocket of her cloak.

He suddenly shifted his attention from the dog to her. "Remove whatever weapons you have hidden on your person and toss them on the floor. I know better than to repeat the mistake of my hapless crew members." His left hand leveled a pistol directly on the baby.

"This is all I have," she said, throwing the pistol on the floor. "Take me, but leave my daughter here. Kasseim won't want her." She was certain he would refuse, but she needed to get close enough to him to pull the dagger from her garter. "I'll do anything you wish," she said in a low husky voice as she took a step nearer.

"I do believe you will at that," he replied with a leer. "And the tiny colleen will insure your good behavior. Pick her up and walk quietly with me. My ship is waiting just the other side of the harbor."

Derrick arrived in Bowness by early morning. *Please, God, let me be in time,* he prayed as he had never before prayed until his desperate ride from London. The village people were not forthcoming to a stranger. At first he was met with only sullen stares and bare deference for his rank.

"Please, I beg you, if you've seen anything at all, tell me. All I wish is to see my family safe," he urged one small woman, frailly thin with shoulders stooped by a harsh life and four small ones borne before she'd reached the age of twenty and widowhood.

"Ye might speak t' Pike. 'E's an old un, too old t' fish, but he gets up 'fore t' sun 'n' mends nets fer t' others."

Pike was a gnarled old salt whose body bore testimony to the harshness of wind, sun and cruel winter's chill. His rheumy eyes measured the earl as Derrick described his wife and explained that she had their infant daughter and a King Charles spaniel with her. He did not like the crafty glint in the old man's eyes. To save time he pulled a sack of coins from his belt and shook it, then tossed it at Pike.

The fisherman hefted the sack and opened it, then grunted in satisfaction. "I thought a bleedin' earl'd 'ave more blunt 'n' a damn paddy," he said with a cackle.

Derrick could not restrain himself. He seized the old sailor by his frayed shirt collar, choking him. "There was an Irishman after her?" he roared.

"Aye, big un 'e was, w' 'air red as sunset," Pike answered.

Quinn! "What did he do with her? Tell me everything or I'll kill you, and you won't die quickly."

The threat was all the more fearsome for the sudden softness of the earl's voice. Pike explained what Quinn had paid him to do and directed him to the deserted warehouse, pleading that he knew nothing more.

It had been but half an hour since she'd vanished into the old building. Derrick's mount skidded on the rocky ground as he leaped from the saddle and pushed to the door. He could hear furious barking coming from inside. He jerked the Ferguson breech-loader from his saddle, holding the rifle ready as he entered. Percy strained against the heavy rope securing him to a support post in the center of the room.

After checking to be certain no one was about, he approached the dog, whose neck was bleeding from his futile attempt to break free of the restraint. Patting Percy's head, he spoke soothingly to calm the frantic animal as he cut the rope. "Percival, you leather-loving flea bag, if you can lead me to her, I will gladly allow you to chew every pair of boots I own, even buy you Hoby's cobbler shop on Piccadilly!"

The spaniel took off in a dead run after his mistress. Derrick followed on horseback, searching the horizon for signs of Beth, his heart hammering with sheer terror. What if Percy made a mistake? What could be over the rise . . . except Quinn's ship! He kicked the gelding into a hard gallop and bypassed the dog. If the Irishman called for help from his crew . . . it did not bear thinking of.

Quinn heard the sounds of hoofbeats clattering up the opposite side of the hill, then the barking of that infernal dog. He should have shot it back in the village but feared the noise might have brought attention to them. Shoving Beth to the ground, he commanded, "Stay down and hold the colleen or I'll be forced to harm her."

Beth did as he bid, hunching over Vittoria while at the same time reaching beneath her skirt to the dagger concealed in her garter. She recognized Percy's loud barking echoing over the barren landscape yet dared not hope as her eyes scanned the horizon, but there he was—Derrick! She watched her husband rein in his horse and raise his rifle to fire at Quinn's tall figure, but the Irishman was quick for a man of his size. As Derrick's shot whizzed by him, he dived to the ground, seizing the baby and knocking Beth down beside him.

"Drop the rifle and the pistols in your sash, Englishman!" he yelled as Beth crawled toward him with the dagger hidden in her hand.

Derrick could see his daughter's small body in Quinn's big hands and tossed aside the breech-loader as Percy came racing past him. Quinn's attention was diverted to the approaching dog, and he fired one of his Miguelet-lock pistols but missed. Cursing, he withdrew another pistol from his sash and fired again. Percy went down as Beth leaped upon Quinn, grabbing for Vittoria, who was wailing loudly now as they struggled.

Unable to get a clear shot, Derrick rode toward them, one of his powerful stubby-barreled Clark pistols ready to fire at the first opening. He jumped from the horse, but Quinn maintained his hold on the screaming baby. "Shoot me and I'll throw her against the rocks 'ere I go down," he said.

Beth stilled at once, the dagger in her hand clutched tightly, knowing she could not inflict sufficient damage quickly enough to keep Quinn from doing as he said. Derrick tossed both of his pistols to the ground. "You ran like a coward in London. Surely one mere Englishman does not frighten you . . . or do I?" he taunted, steeling himself to focus past the baby's cries and Beth's chalk-white face.

Quinn appeared to consider for a moment. They were near enough to the inlet for the shots to have carried. Selim would come to investigate. "I always welcome the opportunity to kill an Englishman," he said with a roar of laughter, slipping an ugly curved blade with a serrated edge from his belt.

"Derrick, no!" Beth had seen how weakened his condition was when he'd collapsed at the Hall. Quinn would kill him with merciless glee and it was all her fault.

"Take Vittoria and stay back," Derrick instructed Beth as he slipped his dagger from his boot, ready to face the Irishman.

"Come, take your colleen," Quinn purred to Beth, his eyes never leaving Derrick.

She walked around Quinn from the back to reach out for her daughter. If she could only place the baby on the ground, then she could attack him from behind with one of her husband's pistols. But as she felt the precious weight in her hands, the Irishman spun away from her, closing with Derrick. The men began circling each other, taut as big cats ready to pounce. Beth hurried to find a safe hiding place for the baby behind a rocky outcrop a dozen yards away. Then she returned, watching for an opening in which to seize one of the discarded pistols and use it.

"Fate cheated me out of my pleasure when I captured her, but I intend to enjoy your lady on the long voyage back to Algiers, your lordship. Then 'twill be Kasseim's turn. She should have let him take her, not made a fool of him, drugging him. That way, perhaps he would have forgotten her," Quinn taunted as Derrick's blade nicked his long arm, and he glided backward as if stalling for time.

"You're a privy-mouthed bastard, even for an Irish mercenary," Derrick gritted out, stunned by Quinn's unwitting revelation. Why had Beth not told him the truth about them? The bitter answer to his question came instantly: *You would not have believed her if she had.*

Beth was startled by the corsair's confession, wondering if Derrick believed him but far more concerned that the shock of Quinn's announcement would give him another advantage over her husband, who was gradually weakening. Could the Irishman see it? As she edged very carefully around the men to where her husband's discarded pistols lay, Beth watched the contest, her breath catching each time Quinn's blade came close to Derrick.

Derrick was tiring and he knew it. He sensed more than saw Beth moving to get his pistols and thanked God that she was a sensible American, taught to handle weapons, not an English drawing-room miss who would not have the faintest notion of how to kill a man.

Quinn's reach gave him several inches' advantage over Derrick, but the Englishman had survived by speed and cunning for many years. He knew a trick or two himself. He waited until Beth reached his pistols and scooped them up, checking the primer pans to see that they would still fire after being dropped on the rocky ground. When Quinn shifted his blade for an instant, repositioning himself, Derrick glanced at Beth. The Irishman took the bait and pivoted away on the ball of one foot, certain Beth was coming at his back.

His mistake would have left the way clear for her to fire, but just then a shout erupted from down the hill as two of the corsair's crewmen came running toward them. Vittoria, whose cries had quieted to breathy sobs, lay directly in their path. Beth did not hesitate as one of them nocked a quarrel in his crossbow and took aim. Slipping one of the Clarks into her pocket, she knelt on her right knee, clutching the other pistol with both hands. She rested her left elbow on her left thigh, sighted in and squeezed the trigger. The crossbowman was dead before he hit the ground. His companion dove behind a shale outcropping.

Derrick did not hesitate either. As Quinn divided his attention between the menace of the woman and the arrival of his men, Derrick used the opening to lunge against him, toppling the bigger man to the ground. Derrick landed on top, his blade a scant inch from Quinn's heart, Quinn's blade held just as close to Derrick's throat. Each man held the other's weapon hand immobilized as they strained back and forth, but Derrick's right arm was still weakened from the attack in London. He could not quite sink the blade into the Irishman's flesh.

Beth wanted desperately to use her last shot on the Irishman, but Selim—she recognized the corsair's second in command now—was moving closer, using rocks and low shrubs for cover. She turned away from their struggle and sighted in very carefully on the Musselman. *Come on, come on!* her mind screamed at Selim as she gauged her shot. When he moved out from behind the cluster of rocks, she was ready. He went down with a bullet in his chest.

The sweat on Quinn's brow ran into his eyes as he struggled to hold the Englishman at bay, but gravity was on

Albion's side. Then the sound of Beth's shot fueled Derrick's flagging strength. All the firearms were empty. Nothing stood between his family and the corsairs but him. His right arm moved a fraction of an inch, closer, closer . . . then the blade bit flesh.

" 'Tis amazing . . . how fragile the human body . . . how swiftly the blood flows . . . when 'tis breached," Derrick panted as Quinn's knife dropped. Then the corsair's bright green eyes glazed over and blood bubbled on his lips.

He died cursing the English.

Chapter Twenty-eight

When Derrick looked up, still winded from the ordeal, Beth stood only a yard away, the small stiletto he remembered so fondly from Murat's gardens clutched in her hand. Seeing no menace on the horizon, he asked, "Quinn's men?"

"I shot them both," she replied with no more ado than if she'd just swatted a fly.

"You are an incredible woman, puss," he gasped out, shoving the corsair's body away so he could climb to his feet.

Vittoria chose that moment to begin crying lustily again. Beth turned and raced to her, picking up the infant and holding her protectively. "Shhh," she said softly, rocking back and forth. When she felt Derrick's hand gently touch her shoulder, she turned and looked up into his eyes. "You saved us from my folly, m'lord."

"When it comes to folly, puss, you can claim no monopoly 'pon it," he replied gently, aching to gather her and their daughter into his arms but hesitating, uncertain how to say what was in his heart.

This was a different Derrick Jamison from the indolent, charming rogue or the arrogant, angry aristocrat of the past. His eyes spoke of things she had only dreamed of before. "Derrick, I—"

The sound of a dog's hoarse cry interrupted her. "Percy! Quinn shot him," she said as Derrick turned and loped shakily up the hill toward the blood-soaked dog, who was struggling to crawl to them. He knelt and examined the long furrow the Irishman's bullet had cut across the dog's head.

"His thick skull may have saved his life," he called out to Beth.

"He found us, didn't he?" she said, dropping onto the ground beside Derrick, who was calming the dog with his hands much as he had when they'd rescued him from the *lazzaroni*.

"I would've had no idea where to search if not for him," Derrick admitted. "I'm afraid I made him some rather extravagant promises as a reward for finding you."

"Oh, and what might they have been?" she asked, smiling. This was the way things had been between them when they'd first met.

"The little matter of all the boots in my closet plus all those in Mr. Hoby's shop on Piccadilly."

"My, you do value us highly, m'lord," she said, striving for a light tone but knowing that her voice gave away that she was saying much more.

As he picked up the whimpering dog, he replied, "I have done an ill job of showing you just how much, puss."

Jenna, the cooper's wife, was the village healer. Beth was able to secure yarrow from her to stop the bleeding from Percy's head wound, which upon closer examination proved not to be serious, although it had stunned him into unconsciousness when he was hit. Derrick watched his wife work her healing magic as he held his infant daughter in the rude cabin. Her fit of crying having exhausted her, Vittoria slept peacefully in his arms. He studied the child's tiny perfect features.

"She's your very image," he murmured, stroking the cap of russet hair covering the baby's head.

"Look at her eyes once she awakens. They are yours. As for the red hair, it often changes color."

Percy gave a small bark of agreement as Beth applied the yarrow paste to his battle wound. "You must tell me what happened in London. You're wraith thin, and those scars . . ." She shuddered just thinking about how near death he must have been. "If only you'd sent word—"

"I did. Just before Christmas, as soon as I was able to put pen to paper, even though I'd received not a word from you since I left the Hall," he replied.

"But I wrote you four letters before the holidays," she said, mystified.

Noting Jenna's avid curiosity at the doings of the Quality, he replied, "I will show you the purloined letters when we return to the Hall. Then we will have a greatly overdue conversation, puss."

On the long ride back they spoke of many things, mostly catching up on what had transpired while they were separated. He explained about Bourdin and the nearly fatal attempt on his life, Bella's vicious theft of their letters to each other, and his desperate ride from London when he feared Bertie was going to kill her. She told him about the lonely winter months awaiting the birth of the baby, her disappointment when he failed to come for the holidays and the horrifying way in which she'd learned about his cousin's plotting.

Neither said how they felt about the problems in their marriage.

They arrived at Lynden Hall after darkness had fallen. Every light in the huge manor was burning, the windows glowing with welcome. The landscape, so bleak and forbidding when she'd first seen it last fall, was now gently caressed by early spring. A warm breeze stirred the clear air and not a trace of fog hovered as the stars began to pop out one by one in the night sky.

Derrick helped her from the carriage, and a groom led

the team and Derrick's horse to the stables while they made their way toward the front entry. "It seems so different now . . ." Beth said quietly. "Almost . . . welcoming. I could never have imagined that the first time I saw the place."

As he carried the dog in his arms, he replied gravely, "I grew up here. Since 'twas the only home I ever knew, I always thought it welcoming, especially when I returned from school. I did not see it with your eyes, Beth. Or perhaps I simply wished to punish you because I was hurting—too blind to see that you were, too."

Whatever else he would have said was interrupted when Donita came running out, followed by Mistress Widlow and the rest of the staff. Vittoria awakened and began to cry with hunger as everyone clucked over mother and child. Derrick issued instructions for Percy's care and handed him to Martha, who had a special fondness for the dog. Beth agreed to bathe and rest after she took care of Vittoria only if he would do the same. He promised they would share a meal and talk that night.

In spite of lost sleep and exertion, they were both too tense to linger over their baths. Nor were they hungry as they picked desultorily at the sumptuous cold collation Martha Rumsford laid out in his lordship's quarters. Vittoria slept blissfully in her cradle as her parents gathered their thoughts.

At length, Derrick put down his fork and took a swallow of claret, then said, "When I read the note you left, it . . . gave me cause to hope that . . ."

This was not the glib spy who charmed or the haughty earl who commanded. He seemed to be struggling for words. "Hope, Derrick?" she prompted.

His eyes were haunted as he said, "I'd decided to set you free, Beth. You see, after I studied the painting of the odalisque I purchased—"

"You purchased one of those awful paintings! I am so sorry I did them—I was furious when you left me alone at Christmas, so I painted them to get back at you and defy the ton."

"They are not awful. . . . They're haunting, sad, profound. I looked into that woman's eyes and felt your suffering. You are a very gifted artist and I tried to take that away from you—the most important thing in your life."

"No! Painting is not the most important thing at all!" She surprised herself by admitting it but would say no more until he explained his feelings more clearly. "What did you mean, you were going to set me free? I left you so that you could find a suitable English lady to wed."

"So your letter said." *What is the most important thing if not your art?* he wanted to ask but dared not . . . yet.

She nodded uncertainly. "After all that I've done to ruin your reputation as well as my own, 'twas the least I could do to make amends. I painted seraglio nudes, became embroiled in a murder suicide—I was an Algerine captive who had the bad grace not only to survive but the audacity to wed an earl. I know your sense of honor, Derrick—'tis ingrained in you. You wed me because of it and you would insist that I remain your wife because 'twas your duty—"

"Bugger my duty!" he shouted, then forced himself to calm down. "On that ride to the Hall, I started to realize that I no longer gave a damn about duty or honor or scandal or anything else but you, Beth. Then, when you left me, I finally saw what I'd been too blind to see before— that I'd killed the most precious thing any man can be given . . . the love of a brave and brilliant woman."

"You did not kill my love, Derrick. I tried, and I could not," she confessed haltingly.

A blaze of joy lit his eyes, then dimmed as he said, "I do not deserve your love, puss. I blamed you for sleeping with Quinn and Kasseim and learned you had not—"

"I should have told you the truth."

"But you did not because I would not have believed it— is that not so?" He did not wait for her reply because he knew that he was right. "What is more important is that whether you were forced to lie with them—or any others— has nothing to do with us. I did not come to you a virgin."

"Men judge women by different standards," she said with a sad little smile.

"Only if they're fools. And besides, women like you are above conventional rules. Have you not said so many times in the past, puss?" Now there was the hint of a smile on his lips. "I wanted to set you free because you did not want to be a countess—which is true—but also because I thought you did not want the burden of a child—which is most certainly not true. I've watched you with Vittoria and realize that you could not have left her with me as I expected you would."

Her eyes widened. "You wanted to keep her? I . . . I did not think you'd mind so much since she was not your heir . . . If she had been, I would have stayed . . . for I could not have borne leaving."

" 'Twas good that you did leave, for it made me realize how very much I needed you and how very little all else matters. When I read that you were setting me free, I realized what a foolish mistake it was ever to consider doing likewise to you."

He had been willing to make the same sacrifice as she—for the same reason. The revelation dawned on her, sweet as sunrise. Her smile lit up the room more brilliantly than all the candles in Canterbury Cathedral.

"What fools we've both been, puss," he said softly as he reached across the table and took her hand in his, raising it to his lips. "I love you, Beth, a poor thing though that may be. I never thought myself capable of that tender emotion . . . until now."

Her heart felt as if it would burst with joy. "I have always loved you and always will. We made a bad start of it, Derrick, wedding for all the wrong reasons, two people who believed the only thing they could share was passion . . . but with love, with love all things are possible."

He held her hands in his, looking deep into her eyes, seeing the radiance of that love. "I believe I have something that belongs to you," he murmured, reaching into his pocket and extracting the small emerald ring she'd removed when she'd left yesterday. He slid it reverently on the third finger of her left hand, saying, "This time I will not give you another chance to fly free . . . and I will never break my word again either. I promised you that I wouldn't stop you from painting and I tried to do just that."

She kissed his hand, murmuring, "Once I believed that art was the most important thing in my life. Now I know that it is a secondary passion. You and our children are the most important things there can ever be."

He raised one eyebrow. "Children?"

"I want many children. Lynden requires an heir. Need I remind you that I have four brothers, m'lord?" she asked with a saucy grin.

"By all means, m'lady, we shall have to apply ourselves with all due diligence." Then he could not resist teasing, " 'Tis my duty."

"Bugger your duty," she replied with a cheeky grin.

Epilogue

Derrick reclined on the carpet in front of the roaring fire in their bedroom as Beth fed him dried figs. They lay naked, arms and legs entwined with her atop him. From the mantel above them, the portrait of him that she had painted in Naples looked down, the mysterious blue eyes seeming to study them with self-satisfied amusement. It had been her gift to him on the first Christmas they had shared three years earlier.

"Merry Christmas, my angel," he murmured as he fed her a bit of sweet dried fig.

"I'm no angel, as I have just amply demonstrated, m'lord," she said, wriggling her buttocks provocatively over a strategic portion of his anatomy.

"A wanton one, but an angel nonetheless, all dressed in that filmy white silk you wore at dinner," he replied. "I'm glad that French modiste on Bond Street talked me into having it made for you, puss."

With that he pulled her into his arms, rolling them across the thick rug until he was on top. Her arms tugged at his neck, pulling his mouth to hers for a deep, slow kiss.

Their loving now had a playfulness about it reminiscent of the first times they'd coupled in Naples, with none of the desperation that had driven them during the early months of their marriage.

"Mmm," she said, rimming his lips with the tip of her tongue, "you taste of figs . . . and other delightful things . . ."

They rolled to their sides, hands caressing and examining each other's bodies in a discovery of delights that were somehow new each time they made love. She pressed her lips to the many scars he bore, remembering how close she had come to losing him. He trailed soft kisses to the frantic pulse beating at the base of her throat, the insides of her wrists, loving the way her skin flushed pink in the soft candlelight.

"I love what your telltale fair complexion shows, puss," he whispered, plunging his tongue deep inside her mouth. Then he raised himself up on his elbows and took a fistful of her hair in one hand, using it to tickle and tease her breasts, which had begun to swell slightly once more in pregnancy.

She gasped as the nipples puckered and frissons of pleasure shot all the way to her toes. "Ah, you know how sensitive they get when I'm breeding," she whispered.

"Really, I should never have guessed it," he murmured, using his fingertips now, tracing the fullness of one heavy globe. "They're so beautiful this way . . . you're so beautiful."

"Soon I'll be fat as a cow again," she said, not sounding the least bothered by the prospect.

"You're most beautiful when you're heavy with child," he replied. Then a lascivious grin split his face. "Of course, I cannot ride on top when your belly grows too big, so I suppose I shall have to take advantage while I still can."

As his knee spread her legs and he slid into the welcoming heat of her body, she whispered, "Take advantage of me. I am at your service." Her hips arched up and she locked her long legs around his hips, holding him tightly to her.

"This time . . . we shall . . . make it . . . last," he gasped out, stroking very slowly as he gazed into her eyes.

When he lowered his head and took one nipple in his mouth to suckle her, she cried out and buried her fingers in his hair. "If you . . . keep doing . . . that . . . I shall not . . . last." When he felt her begin to crest, he held absolutely still inside her. "Beast," she murmured softly.

"Wanton," he murmured when she wriggled her hips, and he was unable to stop himself from moving again.

" 'Tis the way I am," she whispered as the contractions blissfully swept over her in slow undulating waves.

" 'Tis the way I want you," he rasped out, his entire body stiffening as he poured his seed deep within her.

They lay on their sides after that, holding each other gently. She brushed the lock of hair from his sweat-dampened forehead and he caressed her jawline as they gazed into each other's eyes. There was no hiding the unconditional love that shone forth in those gazes.

She smiled, recalling their holiday feast downstairs. Vittoria had spilled her milk and her sister Connie, whom they had adopted, had drunk her soup directly from the bowl. Baby brother Quintin, the future tenth Earl of Lynden, named for his doting grandpa, had expressed his delight by rubbing mashed potatoes in his hair. And Percy had stolen a beef bone from Derrick's plate. All in all, not unusual events in the Jamison household. The revelry had been especially wonderful that season because her parents, as well as Piero and Vittoria and their son Aaron, had come to spend the holidays at the Hall.

For a man who had never been given love by his parents, Derrick had learned exceedingly well how to be a loving father. Perhaps part of that was because of the letter the servants had found stuffed in the back of a drawer in Annabella's city house while packing up her effects. It was written to his son by the old earl just before he died.

When word of Lynden's imminent death reached Lord Castlereagh, the Foreign Secretary had told the earl the truth about his son's gallant sacrifice. The old man had begged Derrick's forgiveness and told him how very proud he was of his second son, how much he wished that he, not Leighton, would inherit the title. And, most important of all, the old earl told his son that he loved him. His only mistake had been entrusting the poignant letter to his daughter-in-law, asking Bella to give it to Derrick when he returned.

As Beth looked down into his eyes, he studied her expression, reaching up and touching her cheek softly. "You seem suddenly subdued, puss. Sad thoughts on such a joyous day?"

She smiled. "No brown study at all, my love. I was remembering when you read your father's letter for the first time, how overjoyed you were. I believe it made you the wonderful father you are."

"Not so, m'lady. You made me the wonderful father I am—if indeed I am so wonderful. If not for you, puss, I would have made one of those horrible dynastic matches such as my father did, with equally disastrous results."

"All because of your sense of duty?"

"As a very wise woman once told me, 'Bugger my duty!'"

They burst into laughter as the fire crackled its merry defiance at the icy wind howling outside Lynden Hall. In two weeks' time they would be off to Naples to spend the rest of the winter while Derrick looked after their children and Beth painted.

AUTHOR'S NOTE

After completing *Wicked Angel,* my associate Carol Reynard and I couldn't wait to begin another Regency romp. The Blackthorne clan was so much fun to write about! Although most of *Wanton Angel* takes place in England, the plot moves through some pretty exotic climes en route. Carol busied herself surfing the Net for flora and fauna of Southern Italy and the Barbary Coast as well as searching out furnishing and fashions in early nineteenth-century Naples.

Since our heroine was an artist, Carol located reams of information on the Net about famous female painters, and my husband Jim found the perfect book on our heroine's idol, J. M. W. Turner. He also made countless scouting trips to the library, digging out books on everything from Barbary pirates to harem life. Not only did Jim choreograph the fight scenes as usual, but sadly, with the passing of our dear friend Carmine DelliQuadri, he took over the job of weapons researcher.

Although our dashing spy Derrick Jamison, his countess Beth, and the other main players are fictional, we did use many actual historical figures, such as the famous naval hero Commodore Stephen Decatur, the celebrated British landscape painter J. M. W. Turner, Madame Vigée-Lebrun, Lord Castlereagh, and the tragic figures of Joaquim Murat and his wife Caroline. All readers of Regencies have already met Prinney and Lord Byron.

For readers interested in our research, the following are a few of the works we used. *Naples Through the Centuries* by Lacy Collison-Morley captures the sights, sounds, and smells of that enchanting city. *Turner in the South* by Cecilia Powell not only gives a detailed itinerary of the artist's travels through the Kingdom of Naples, but also includes breathtaking color plates of his work. *Escape from Elba* by Norman MacKenzie is a fascinating account that gave us the "Oil Merchant," a real spy who did indeed uncover Napoleon's plan for landing in France. *The Betrayers* by Hubert Cole chronicles the brief reign of the Murats in intimate detail. For information on the Barbary pirates we used *Tripoli and the United States at War* by Michael L. S. Kitzen; *White Slaves, African Masters,* edited by Paul Baepler; and *Pirates* by David Mitchell. Alev Lytle Croutier's *Harem: The World Behind the Veil* is an utterly spellbinding account of life in a seraglio. The lush yet sad illustrations in it inspired the idea for Beth's paintings. For information on the Regency era in England, we refer our readers to the works described in *Wicked Angel*.

Carol and I hope you have enjoyed our tale of a duty-bound earl and his adventurous American countess. We enjoy hearing from our readers. Please send a stamped self-addressed envelope and we will reply to your letters.

Shirl Henke
PO Box 72
Adrian, MI 49921

You can also visit our website at www.shirlhenke.com.

WICKED ANGEL — SHIRL HENKE

A gawky preacher's daughter, Jocelyn Angelica Woodbridge is hardly the type to incite street brawls, much less two in one day. "Holy Hannah," as those of the *ton* call her, would much rather nurse the sick or reform the fallen. Yet ever since a dashing American saved her from an angry mob, Joss's thoughts have turned most impure.

The son of an American Indian and an English aristocrat, Alexander Blackthorne has been sent to England for some "civilizing." But the only lessons he cares to learn are those offered by taverns and trollops. When a marriage of convenience forces Jocelyn and Alex together, Joss knows she will need more than prayer to make a loving husband of her . . . wicked angel.

___4854-X $5.99 US/$6.99CAN

Dorchester Publishing Co., Inc.
P.O. Box 6640
Wayne, PA 19087-8640

Please add $2.50 for shipping and handling for the first book and $.75 for each book thereafter. NY, NYC, and PA residents, please add appropriate sales tax. No cash, stamps, or C.O.D.s. All orders shipped within 6 weeks via postal service book rate. Canadian orders require $2.50 extra postage and must be paid in U.S. dollars through a U.S. banking facility.

Name_____
Address_____
City_____ State_____ Zip_____
I have enclosed $_____ in payment for the checked book(s).
Payment <u>must</u> accompany all orders. ❏ Please send a free catalog.
    CHECK OUT OUR WEBSITE! www.dorchesterpub.com

LOVE A REBEL... LOVE A ROGUE

SHIRL HENKE

"A fascinating slice of history and equally fascinating characters! Enjoy!"
—Catherine Coulter

Quintin Blackthorne will bow before no man. He dares to despise his father and defy his king, but a mutinous beauty overwhelms the American patriot with a rapturous desire he cannot deny.

Part Indian, part white, and all trouble, Devon Blackthorne will belong to no woman—until a silky seductress tempts him with a passion both reckless and irresistible.

The Blackthorne men—one highborn, one half-caste—are bound by blood, but torn apart by choice. Caught between them, two sensuous women long for more than stolen moments of wondrous splendor. But as the lovers are swept from Savannah's ballrooms to Revolutionary War battlefields, they learn that the faithful heart can overcome even the fortunes of war.

___4406-4 $5.99 US/$6.99 CAN

Dorchester Publishing Co., Inc.
P.O. Box 6640
Wayne, PA 19087-8640

Please add $1.75 for shipping and handling for the first book and $.50 for each book thereafter. NY, NYC, and PA residents, please add appropriate sales tax. No cash, stamps, or C.O.D.s. All orders shipped within 6 weeks via postal service book rate. Canadian orders require $2.00 extra postage and must be paid in U.S. dollars through a U.S. banking facility.

Name_____
Address_____
City_____State_____Zip_____
I have enclosed $_____ in payment for the checked book(s).
Payment <u>must</u> accompany all orders. ❑ Please send a free catalog.
   CHECK OUT OUR WEBSITE! www.dorchesterpub.com

ATTENTION
BOOK LOVERS!

Can't get enough of your favorite **ROMANCE**?

Call **1-800-481-9191** to:

✳ order books,

✳ receive a **FREE** catalog,

✳ join our book clubs to **SAVE 20%!**

Open Mon.-Fri. 10 AM-9 PM EST

Visit **www.dorchesterpub.com**
for special offers and inside
information on the authors you love.

We accept Visa, MasterCard or Discover®.
LEISURE BOOKS ♥ **LOVE SPELL**